Singing Boy

Also by Dennis McFarland in Large Print:

A Face at the Window

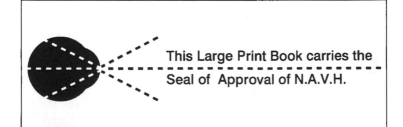

This Large Print Book carries the Seal of Approval of N.A.V.H.

SINGING BOY

Dennis McFarland

Thorndike Press • Waterville, Maine

Grateful acknowledgment is made to Houghton Mifflin
Company for permission to print material from *And This Is Cape
Cod*, by Eleanor Early, copyright 1936, The Riverside Press.
"Fire and Ice" from *The Poetry of Robert Frost*, edited by Edward
Connery Lathem, © 1923, 1969 by Henry Holt and Company,
© 1951 by Robert Frost. Reprinted by permission of Henry
Holt and Company, LLC.
Excerpt from "Dream-Catching," from *The BFG*, by Roald
Dahl. Copyright © 1982 by Roald Dahl. Reprinted by
permission of Farrar, Straus and Giroux, LLC.

Published in 2001 by arrangement with
Henry Holt and Company, LLC.

Thorndike Press Large Print Basic Series.

The tree indicium is a trademark of Thorndike Press.

The text of this Large Print edition is unabridged.
Other aspects of the book may vary from the original edition.

Set in 16 pt. Plantin by Rick Gundberg.

Printed in the United States on permanent paper.

Library of Congress Cataloging-in-Publication Data

McFarland, Dennis.
    Singing boy : a novel / Dennis McFarland.
      p.   cm.
    ISBN 0-7862-3517-9 (lg. print : hc : alk. paper)
    1. Children as witnesses — Fiction. 2. Mothers and sons
— Fiction. 3. Boston (Mass.) — Fiction. 4. Bereavement —
Fiction. 5. Widows — Fiction. 6. Large type books. I. Title.
PS3563.C3629 S56 2001b
    813′.54—dc21   2001034743

For my parents,
Evelyne and Herschel,
and for Schmooey, Kaati, Meesh,
and Tellis,
with all my love

For their invaluable help and inspiration, I thank Steve Alexander, John Traficonte, Angela Damazio, Randall Ferrell, Jane Butler, Hans Stumm, Becky Kennedy, Ted Lewis, Helen McElroy, David Savitz, Gilda Barabino, Eileen Finnegan, Darryl Sutton, Gail Hochman, Katharine McFarland, John Sterling, Jennifer Barth, Linda Mizell, and Frances Kiernan.

Many thanks to Sam McFarland for suggesting the title; to Mike Lew for suggesting the place; to Tellis Lawson, without whose many generous contributions I couldn't have written this story; and to Michelle Blake, for everything.

One saturday afternoon in August, after they'd been in the house for about three months, she lay on a quilt in the grass near the great old rose of Sharon, whose branches, as they climbed toward the roofline, brushed the sagging porch screens. It had been another fine day in a string of fine days, warm and breezy, the occasional cloud a comfort, tempering the vastness of the sky. Earlier, she'd tried arguing Harry into a nap, then bribed him with the promise of an Italian ice from the stand in town. In the unfinished end of the attic — where they'd put down a sisal mat, whitewashed the gables, and painted a flowering vine on the stair railing; the only part of the house in which Harry would sleep — she'd read to him for five minutes from *The Jungle Books*, an edgy little passage about the python Kaa's turning his hypnotic circles in the sand, enticing monkeys to walk into his mouth. She thought she understood Harry's fondness for the attic, with its low sturdy beams — enormous, like whole squared-off trees — and impossibly broad planks, some

7

two and a half feet broad, dark brown, furry with age; it was something like camping under the inverted hold of an ancient schooner, cavelike, defensible. Before falling asleep, he'd complained that the tip of his penis hurt; he wouldn't allow her to see for herself, so she asked him some detailed questions, and though he assured her that there was no redness of any kind, she suggested applying a dab of calendula.

"That would sting," he'd responded, without too much expression but with a look from under his brow that said, Are you crazy?

"Oh," she'd said, and almost added "sorry," but stopped herself and then fetched him a cool cloth from the upstairs bathroom, which he accepted.

"Thanks," he said, and in it she heard both a whisper of apology and a remnant of his former "sanks." His *th* had been thoroughly in place for some time, except in "thanks," and now, to her regret, even that was going.

Leaving him, she'd descended the back stairs, steep and narrow (like those of a ship), and before reaching the turn near the base, she'd begun to cry — not the runaway stagecoach crying with its ever-loosening wheel, but the quiet hopeless variety, blundering around the canyon floor. She'd found the quilt, found her book, and gone outside. Soon she too had fallen asleep, and a short time later she'd awakened into an odd increasing silence. She'd fallen asleep with her sunglasses on, which had dug into the bridge of her nose.

She sat up and looked at the glaring white sky, uniform overhead, through the locust trees, and all around. Then a sudden utter stillness hit, a strange conspiracy of wind and surf that nearly took her breath away. It lasted for only several seconds in real time, and seemingly from its core came a low approaching buzz, the crescendo of a small machine: a hummingbird visited the rose of Sharon, a blossom under the eaves of the porch and then another blossom not more than a foot from her right ear. She didn't dare turn her head — whatever lull had come over things, she'd joined it — though she had a clear up-close view of the bird in the margin of her vision past the rim of her sunglasses. It was a male — iridescent ruby at the throat, tail downturned as if for balance — and tiny, the blurred triangles of its wings nearly menacing at this range. The bird backed out of the flower, hovered an instant, then cut an angle straight down to her face. It tapped three times on the left lens of her sunglasses with its needlelike beak and flew away, gone.

A breeze stirred the wind chime in the distant locust tree . . . one resonant clang of the vertical pipe, two . . . a red pickup truck gunned its engine high on Tom's Hill. She'd been holding her breath, willing herself inert, a garden statue with living eyes. She thought of her grandfather, who'd planted the rose of Sharon decades ago as a gift to her grandmother, whose name was the same as this cultivar (white flowers with a reddish-purple base), Helene; she thought of the Doppler effect, recalling both the whir of wings and the receding truck engine; and she thought she'd glimpsed something — mysterious, for sure, and passing, surely — the faintest hint that she and Harry would be all right.

That hadn't happened before, not even an inkling of a bearable future. This was a first, and she resolved to try to remember it.

PART I

The Hospital
in the Dream

As they came to a stop at Walden and Huron, Malcolm said, "That's my car," referring to the old cream-colored Corvair in front of them. A moment later, he said, "Poor old Dad." He drummed out some kind of transitional rhythm on the steering wheel, looked at her, smiled, reached for her hand, and said, "How are you feeling, Sarah Vaughn?"

"Whatever it was," she said, "it went away. I think I just needed to eat something."

He released her hand, lowered his head a bit, squinting through the windshield, and then absentmindedly began to sing the opening bars to an old song Sarah recognized as Gershwin but couldn't quite name.

Harry, up way past his bedtime, bored with a long night of adult business, groaned, almost inaudibly, in the backseat, his plight now enlarged by his father's singing. The traffic light changed from red to green, but the Corvair in front of them didn't move, and that interrupted Malcolm's song.

Sarah said, "I think he's fallen asleep," meaning the driver of the Corvair.

Harry, misinterpreting her, said, "I'm not asleep," then sat forward, put his face between the two front seats, and said, "Why aren't we going?"

Malcolm tapped the horn once, politely, but still the Corvair didn't move. Sarah thought the driver was a teenage boy, though she couldn't have said why she thought that; all she could actually see was the back of his head, in silhouette. They were in her Jeep wagon, as Malcolm's car was in for a tune-up, and briefly, sitting high above the low-slung Corvair, Sarah wondered if they mightn't just lurch over it, tanklike.

"Or dead drunk," she added, and then, for no apparent reason, the Corvair slowly moved forward. Without signaling, the driver made a right turn, onto Huron.

"Oh, great," said Harry, "he's going the same way we're going," and Malcolm asked Harry to please sit back.

They crept along behind the Corvair at about fifteen miles an hour. It was a quarter to ten, and in this quiet residential district the Corvair and the Jeep were the only cars on the road. "Pass him," said Harry. "We're going too slow."

Malcolm glanced in his rearview mirror and said, "Remember what we talked about, Harry . . . earlier this evening."

14

As they came to another stop, Harry let out a dramatic sigh. This was the long traffic light at the parkway. When at last the signal changed to green, the Corvair did not move. Malcolm tapped the horn, to no response. "Here we go again," he said and raised the parking brake.

"What are you doing?" Sarah asked.

"I'm going to see what's up with this guy," said Malcolm, opening the car door.

"Don't, Malcolm," she said. "Just pull around him. He's probably stoned out of his mind."

Malcolm, already out the door, leaned in and said, "Well, if he's that stoned he's liable to get somebody killed. Besides, he might be sick or something."

"Can I come?" shouted Harry, but Malcolm had shut the door against the cold, and Sarah told Harry to stay put.

For a moment, she noticed how eerie Malcolm looked, lit by the Jeep's headlights. Suddenly, for no apparent reason, she recalled the name of the Gershwin song, "Things Are Looking Up." She watched as Malcolm rapped with his knuckles on the driver's window.

Then Harry, who'd again slid forward between the seats for a better view, said, "Wouldn't it be funny if that guy was going to

15

our house . . . if we just followed him the whole way and he stopped in front of our house?"

Sarah turned and looked at him. His skin caught some of the green glow from the traffic light, and while she was looking at him the glow changed from green to yellow to red. Briefly, she worried about how tired he would be at school the next morning. She said, "That would be funny," and started to lean toward him, intending to kiss his cheek, but something changed suddenly in his eyes. He said, "Mommy —"

Ever afterward, she would recall that she'd seen nothing like terror in Harry's face. His expression was alarming only because it had gone so absolutely neutral, as if some vital force inside him had abruptly shut down — that and his using "Mommy" rather than the more usual "Mom." He said it again, "Mommy —" and she thought she heard at the same instant another sound, from outside, a kind of popping noise, perhaps from under the hood of the car. When she turned to see what Harry was seeing, Malcolm was already moving slowly back toward them.

She thought Malcolm had been wearing his plaid cap with the earflaps, but now he was hatless, and there was something odd about his hair; it looked spiky, and some of it hung down over his forehead the way it did when he was just out of the shower. As he moved closer, into the direct blaze of the Jeep's headlights, he caught her eye, through the windshield, and looked at her with a disappointment so enormous she thought her heart would break. For reasons she would never entirely understand, her second-grade teacher passed through her mind, a black-haired grumpy old woman named Mrs. Cole who'd fancied herself an artist. Sarah actually did feel something odd in her heart, a kind of rough single quake, and then a great scalding sensation in her ears. A druggy hum had started up inside her head; she whispered Malcolm's name . . . or maybe his name was whispered by some other voice, deep inside the hum. And then she watched as Malcolm leaned against the front fender of the Jeep and slid down to the street out of sight.

Somewhere off in the vast wasteland of the future, Harry would ask her why she had shoved him so hard against the seat when he'd tried getting out of the Jeep, but she would not recall doing that; nor would she recall getting out of the Jeep herself, or telling Harry to climb up front and to keep blowing the horn until she told him to stop. She would recall Malcolm on the cold pavement, slumped against the front wheel of the car, one leg folded under the other. She would recall the surprising moment when the Corvair began to move idly away across the parkway, leaving Malcolm's plaid hat lying precisely in the middle of the street's double yellow line.

Then there was a woman in a motorcycle jacket, a tough-looking woman with a diamond stud in her nose and very short platinum hair, leaning over her and Malcolm. She told Sarah that somebody would be there in a minute — Sarah thought the woman said something about "empties," which made her think, bewilderingly, of soda bottles — and then the woman opened the door to the Jeep and told Harry to stop blowing the horn. Oddly, she called Harry "honey" and "sweetie" and took him in her arms, not lifting him out of the car but only holding him there in the seat, and Sarah thought they must know the woman, though she couldn't think how. Meanwhile, Sarah was now the one slumped against the front wheel of the Jeep. She held Malcolm's head in her lap. There was a smudge on his white shirt, near the collar, put there earlier, before they'd left for the dinner, when he and Harry had done some roughhousing in the window seat at home. Sarah wanted to keep Malcolm warm and reached forward over him and struggled with the buttons of his coat. While she did this, she tried to prepare a statement in her mind, an explanation that began, My husband has been shot, but somehow *shot* had too many meanings, and she felt she needed to add, with a gun, which then seemed utterly foolish. She thought she could get the coat buttoned and keep Malcolm warm, and she could get her explanation right if she could only stop herself from shaking. A comprehensive sense of failure was overtaking her — she recalled a heat lamp she'd stupidly left burning in the lab at school two years earlier — and though she couldn't stop herself from shaking, couldn't control the horrible disjointed spasms in her arms and shoulders, and wasn't able to manage the backward buttons on Malcolm's coat, she was comforted by the thought that Malcolm wouldn't mind, that he would forgive her, which was like him.

This occurred on the second day of March, a Sunday. Harry had recently returned to his second-grade year at school, following a ten-day February vacation. That night, they'd all attended an awards dinner at the Historical Commission, where Malcolm was honored for his restoration of the Planck Building. No one at the Historical Commission had expected Harry to come, and an extra chair and a place setting had to be squeezed in at their table. It was like Malcolm not to check with anyone about whether or not children were invited to the dinner, and it was like Sarah to be overly embarrassed. Harry wouldn't eat anything that was served — Sarah thought the menu was meant to be historical: roasted squab, wild rice, spiced apples, bread pudding. Fortunately, he had managed to fill up on buttered rolls, and somewhere near the midpoint of the evening, it seemed to Sarah that spreading iced butter on spongy dinner rolls was what she'd come for, wife of the honoree, mother of his offspring. The thing had gone on longer than it should have, and it was nine-thirty by the time they got out.

All winter the weather had been warmer than usual, with little snow. While they'd been inside the Historical Commission, a brief rain shower had left a clear sheen outside on the streets. There were isolated, perfectly round dots of water, like tiny magnifying lenses, dotting the Jeep's windshield. The night world had a hard edge to it somehow, and the air felt colder than it actually was.

When, at the intersection of Walden and Huron, Malcolm had said, "That's my car," he referred to the 1965 Corvair his father had given him on his sixteenth birthday — automatic transmission, new tires, six-cylinder engine, black interior, and only 38,000 miles on the odometer. In this car, Malcolm had taken Patti Bolling, vice president of the student council, to see *Psycho* at a drive-in theater. He'd put his arm around her, and after about ten seconds his whole life had become focused in his arm, what his arm was feeling, what it was causing Patti to feel, and he left it there, paralyzed, until it went numb. When he started smoking Pall Malls, he carried a bottle of Lavoris in the glove compartment of the car. He'd got his first speeding ticket doing thirty in a twenty-five-mile-an-hour zone in front of the junior high school. When Malcolm had become involved, as a high school senior, in some civil rights work in Baltimore, the car had been trashed by anonymous eggers. All this Sarah knew, all this was contained in "That's my car." Afterward, whenever she would recall the night of the shooting, she would sometimes think of young earnest Malcolm putting his arm around Patti Bolling's shoulders, and it would make her cry.

Malcolm's father, a career man in the navy, had been retired early from the service on account of some mysterious mental episodes that were eventually diagnosed as petit mal. Three years into his retirement, his wife, Malcolm's mother, had died of a stroke, and he'd become increasingly fond of raking pine needles into small round piles in the backyard of their Maryland home; he would set them ablaze and then stand leaning on the rake handle, watching them smolder and smoke. In the Jeep, when Malcolm said, "Poor old Dad," he meant too bad about how lost the man had become in his last years, too bad about how his life had gone off course and had never found a new footing, too bad about how he'd seemed to welter into his own grave at the age of sixty-three.

When they'd been stuck behind the Corvair the first time, at Walden and Huron, and Malcolm asked Sarah how she was feeling, it was because she'd complained during the dinner that she had a headache. And "Sarah Vaughn" was a kind of joke name for her. At the time of their marriage, eighteen years ago, she'd not taken his surname for the obvious reason — it would have made her Sarah Vaughn, and though she liked Sarah Vaughan, the singer, she didn't want to spend the rest of her life being teased and asked to sing a few bars of Cole Porter. She'd re-mained Sarah Williams, and when Harry had come along he was christened Harry Vaughn-Williams — a name with a similar problem but involving a much smaller audience. As they waited for that first traffic light to change, Malcolm's choice of song, his beginning the intro to "Things Are Looking Up," most likely reflected his mood; though he'd pretended not to care about the Historical Commission's award, Sarah knew it actually meant a lot to him.

When Malcolm said to Harry, "Remember what we talked about . . ." he referred to an exchange they'd had earlier that evening as they were getting dressed for the Historical Commission dinner. Harry had come into their bedroom for the third time in ten minutes to say in a whiny voice, "When are we leaving?"

Sarah, the only one of the three who wasn't ready, had snapped at him, and Malcolm had taken him out of the bedroom, into the hallway, and sat him down in the window seat. "Harry," he said. "Why are you always in a rush to get on to the next thing?"

This question was followed by a long silence, which meant that Harry was pondering it; Harry tended to view questions of this sort as puzzles to be solved, as something to be made into a game. "I don't know," he said at last. "I guess I was born that way . . . it's in my genes."

In the bedroom, Sarah could hear this exchange. She thought, He's understood the implied criticism in Malcolm's question, turned it around, and made Malcolm responsible for it. Fourteen hours she'd been in labor with Harry, and it occurred to her to call out to them from the bedroom and remind them that Harry hadn't been in any big rush in the delivery room.

But Malcolm said, "Well, Harry, I doubt that's true, because you sure weren't in a hurry to get born."

That was funny, Sarah thought, the way Malcolm had spoken a version of what had just passed through her mind, but he'd phrased it so that it included not only the long hours of labor but also the six years of their trying to get pregnant.

"Do you remember when we were at the county fair last summer?" Malcolm said to Harry in the window seat. "Remember how, when we were on one ride, you'd be talking about what we were going to ride next? You see, you can't enjoy where you are now if you're always thinking about what's next. I want you to try practicing a little patience and not always be thinking about what's next. Okay? Also, when you rush other people, they tend to make mistakes."

Another long silence. Then Sarah heard Harry say, "Can we go back to that same fair next summer?"

This made Malcolm laugh, and they'd done some roughhousing in the window seat

24

that left a brown smudge from Harry's shoe on Malcolm's white dress shirt. Sarah had urged Malcolm to change the shirt before they left, but he pulled on his jacket and said it wouldn't show. He'd returned to the bedroom and, briefly admiring himself in the wardrobe mirror, said something about not looking too bad for a forty-three-year-old man. She came and stood behind him, gazing over his shoulder, and with the impeccable timing he now and then managed, he turned and kissed her. He said that for a forty-three-year-old woman she didn't look too bad herself. I'm forty-five, she told him, and he pretended, as he always did, to be surprised.

The afternoon of Malcolm's funeral, Sarah will recall that she was irritated at Malcolm when he got out of the Jeep, deeply irritated by his decision to confront the driver of the Corvair. It will seem to her that Malcolm was always on some princely mission, always taking the high road. After the cemetery, back at the house, she'll say to Malcolm's best friend, Deckard, as Deckard sits in a chair in the corner of the living room, weeping, "Of course, we lesser beings would just blow our horns and drive around the fucking car, but not Malcolm. . . . Malcolm was always looking for the nobler thing." Harry, undetected at a nearby doorjamb, will overhear her say this, and then, despite all her penitential efforts, he'll refuse to look at her or speak to her for hours. When finally he relents, he'll speak only to tell her that she has bad breath.

And late at night, night after night, as she lies sleepless in bed, Harry's face will float up out of the darkness, glowing green, then yellow, then red, and then go neutral, and she'll hear his startling "Mommy —" first when he saw an arm extend from the Corvair's window, an arm with a hand, a hand with a pistol; and again, "Mommy —" when he saw what looked like sparks fly out of the short barrel, when he saw his father turn and look back at the Jeep and put his hand first to his stomach — the way he did sometimes when he had indigestion — and then to his head, knocking his good cap off onto the street but not stopping to pick it up, as if, inexplicably, he no longer cared about it.

Most dreadfully, Sarah will hear again and again the popping noise — dreadfully because, when she hears it, she fears she'll dream of it again: sometimes the sound is the branch of a tree, snapping in a storm. In this dream, she's asleep in her bedroom, the howling of wind wakes her, and, surprised to find that Malcolm has left the bed, she walks to the window and looks out just in time to see the great tree limb crack in a sudden gust. Some-times, in another dream, the sound is electri-cal. She and Harry are having dinner at home — alone, because Malcolm has mysteriously failed to show up — when suddenly all the lights go out; she finds a flashlight and goes down the stairs to the basement, where she opens the circuit box; when she flips a switch, there's an electric pop, and sparks in the dark. And sometimes — this by far the worst one — she will dream of the murderer himself. She and Harry and Malcolm are walking on the beach near the summer house; Malcolm trots ahead of them and disappears over a dune be-tween the beach and an immense parking lot; when she and Harry reach the parking lot, it's empty except for a white Corvair, and there's no sign of Malcolm; a man sits behind the wheel of the Corvair, apparently sleeping; they walk to the car, and when she asks the man whether he has seen her husband, he turns his face to her, a neon-white oval with a mouth, no eyes and no nose; he opens his mouth and makes a horrible clucking noise with his glossy pink tongue, the sound of the gunshot.

With each of these nightmares, Sarah will wake at the moment of the pop, and always with a burning in her ears. She'll often think of Mrs. Cole, her second-grade teacher, a frightening witch of a woman who, whenever Sarah drew pictures of green trees, would come around with a yellow crayon and add sunlight to the topmost leaves, explaining that the topmost leaves always catch the sun. (The yellow looked stupid to Sarah, as if someone had broken a giant egg over her trees, and she hated Mrs. Cole.) Why the woman should have visited her that night when she turned and saw Malcolm's face through the Jeep's windshield, she will never entirely understand.

Malcolm's face through the windshield, lit by the headlights: it said, Sorry, my love. Sorry about how long it took for Harry to come along, and sorry for everything. . . . Sorry that, in a way, we were just getting started. . . . I guess we won't be . . .

Harry behind the steering wheel, blowing the horn to arouse the people in the houses, trying to stir up some help: another sound that will visit Sarah in her dreams, disguised as the air-raid alert in old British movies about the Second World War. She'll recall the short-haired woman in the motorcycle jacket who was the first to reach them in the street, and she'll regret not having got the woman's name. Unexpectedly, forgotten details will ambush her. Pouring apple juice into a jelly glass for Harry, she'll suddenly recall a uniformed policeman poking around the Jeep, a young man who looked like a movie star . . . but what movie star? And what had he been doing writing down the license plate numbers of all the cars that were parked on both sides of the avenue? Surely he could see that none of these was the white Corvair. Sorting through junk mail, she'll suddenly think, for the first time, of a red-and-blue bumper sticker on the back of the Corvair . . . an ad for something, but an ad for what? Boarding the bus, she'll drop quarters into the change post and think of a young Latino intern at the hospital — a kid, really, with gold hoop earrings in each ear — whom she'd seen holding Harry's hand in a hallway somewhere, squatting down to Harry's level and talking with him quietly; as she approached them, the intern glanced up at her before moving away down the hall, and she saw that he had been crying.

For a long time, Sarah will not button a coat without thinking of Malcolm, and though details of this sort will prompt her grief again and again, in a wider deeper way, the world itself, life itself, life's plain refusal to brake, its idiotic scheme to proceed, will fan her sorrow. As she leaves Harry at school and descends a flight of stairs, something about the echo of her own footsteps in the stairwell fills her with remorse; outside, witchy Mrs. Cole's sunshine swoops down, causing her to shield her eyes and dig into her pockets for sunglasses; on the lawn, she spots a Japanese magnolia, about to blossom, and thinks irrationally of Malcolm's red-and-black plaid hat, chosen for him by Harry out of a mail-order catalog. Her grief will be too large somehow, larger than it ought to be, and she'll feel indicted by others as inhumane for keeping such a large animal indoors. At every turn, everyone will encourage her to set it free, let it go, and to allow her feelings to change. She will, of course, also feel misunderstood — a kind of moist subterranean labyrinth beneath her loneliness. For what will seem an eternity, no one will quite see that she isn't interested in having her feelings changed: not the head of her department, who'll try urging her back to work before she is ready; not Malcolm's friend Deckard, who'll endlessly offer advice, telling her what's best for her and best for Harry; not her own mother, Enid, the actress who can't leave her play in New York to attend Malcolm's funeral and who'll try coercing Sarah into the offices of grief counselors she has found. No one will seem to understand that for nearly two decades Sarah envisioned her life only with Malcolm. No one will seem to grasp that

Malcolm is actually dead, that he was shot, apparently freakishly, apparently at random, by a total stranger, and that he didn't survive, that he truly died, that he was dying already as she sat in the cold street and held his head and struggled with the buttons to his overcoat. No one will understand that her grief is what she has left of him, and if she were to lose that, she would have nothing at all.

Sometime shortly after New Year's, Deckard Jones had noticed something he wanted so strongly not to be true that he hadn't mentioned it to anyone, a modest change in his life that, once recognized, really began to get its legs: women no longer looked at him.

His birthday was coming up soon, a prime number breathing down the neck of fifty (forty-seven), and, six months separated from his girlfriend Lucy, he couldn't remember the last good night's sleep he'd had. After a single, childless marriage — ancient history — he'd had several girlfriends and, on the side and in between, enjoyed his share of recreational no-strings sex; "bopped a lot of babes" was how he put it not too long ago, a swaggering diction that embarrassed him to recall. (He'd been taking down some middle-aged guy's data at the hospital when a white girl in a miniskirt walked by — possibly a college girl, for Christ's sake — the guy said something about wishing he was twenty years younger, and somehow "bopped a lot of babes" worked its way in; as soon as these words were out of Deckard's mouth, he experienced a terrible bird's-eye view of himself and the other man as two old droolers talking shit at the VA because shit was all they had left to talk.) His observation that women no longer looked at him was at the heart of his raging insomnia, and it had a corollary, too: throughout his connections with women, long-term and short, he'd kept in the back of his mind the thought that there were several others waiting in the wings, and these ladies-in-waiting (as he'd thought of them) accounted in large part for his one-foot-out-the-door approach to coupling. The women, the ladies-in-waiting, were real, not illusion. They knitted their brows and chewed on pencil erasers in the Periodicals Room at the public library; careful not to chip a nail, they operated the registers at Tower Records; riding the T, they let one shoe dangle free from the toes of one foot. All over town, hesitant at the perfume counter in Lord & Taylor, restless in line at the P.O., bored on the Esplanade, bored to death in the Public Gardens and passing by in swan boats, they cast Deckard honest-to-goodness unimagined glances. The women were real.

Or *had* been real. Trouble was, Deckard had failed to note their departure, an insanely stupid oversight.

In the hour of deepest darkness, usually somewhere between 3 and 4 A.M., he would remind himself that he was lucky to be alive at all. He reminded himself of all he'd survived: a father whose idea of how to build a kid's character was to send Deckard to an all-white school in the burbs, where he was routinely beaten to a pulp, and then, at home, to beat Deckard again for letting himself get beaten at school; a mother whose idea of how to make bad things go away was to ignore them absolutely; two years in reform school for chronic truancy and possession of marijuana; a month of solitary in a six-by-six box cell for trying to escape from reform school; forty-two months, one week, and three days of drug abuse and cosmic dementia in Vietnam; addiction to the buckets of diazepam and chloral hydrate regularly dispensed by the VA on his return, leading fairly quickly to bona fide junkiehood; two consecutive six-month prison sentences for drunk-and-disorderly and breaking parole; two attempts on his life by white supremacists, one in a parking lot in Scranton, P.A., one in prison; ironically, afterward, a suicide attempt; eight detoxes; and thirteen years, finally, of staying clean. Sometimes, when Deckard reviewed these difficulties, it had the intended effect — he was lucky to be alive. Sometimes, it had an unintended effect

— he'd led a cursed, reckless life that had rendered him incompatible with women, and consumed by an abiding love-hate entanglement with his own solitude.

His one-bedroom apartment, on the fourth floor of a brick building in Jamaica Plain, had a small window behind the toilet in the bathroom, and from this window you could see the tops of the trees lining the Jamaicaway and, above the trees, the hospital. Deckard kept the shade pulled over this window at all times, not for reasons of privacy — it was too high up to matter — but because of the undesirable hospital view. Lucy, every morning when she'd slept over, would raise the shade, and he thought maybe it was a white thing; maybe white women liked a lot of light. He would feel her leave the bed, and then he would lie half awake in the dark, eyes closed, and listen — the squeaky floorboards in the hall, the lowered toilet seat, the pinched hose of her peeing, the flush, water in the sink, the fuzzy static of her toothbrushing. And then, just before leaving the bathroom, solely to drive him nuts, the snap of the window shade. Why? Because it was "too close" in there with the shade pulled all the time. And besides, why did he insist on having it down?

"You know why," he would say for the hundredth time. "I don't like to bring my work home with me."

It was, they both knew, a ritual exchange serving the sweet cause of territory, and she would laugh, poke him or goose him, and sometimes they would make love.

Then there was the morning — how long ago, he couldn't begin to say — when she'd returned to his side, placing her head next to his on the pillow; he'd said, There you go again, raising that goddamn shade, and she'd flounced back out of bed, whipping the sheet down behind her, and said, Oh, fuck you, Deckard.

Could that have been a direct expression of her unhappiness? A sign of things to come? Could she have meant, Fuck you, Deckard, and your set-in-your-ways bullshit, my place, my things, no I don't want to get married, been there, done that, I like things the way they are, you've got your place, I've got mine, why rock the boat, we're both a little old to start playing house anyway, Mama . . . and while we're at it, Fuck your fire extinguishers in every room, fanny-pack pepper spray, retractable nightstick, be-prepared go-everywhere first-aid kit, and all your other big-bad-white-world, doom-around-every-corner, post-traumatic-stress idiosyncrasies?

Probably that was just what she meant. Or something like it.

And now where in the world was he supposed to find another good-looking woman who didn't smoke, drink, or snort coke but loved to go fishing?

Spring was approaching, the start of the third season without her, and secretly he'd hoped the joy and complication of Christmas would have brought them back together. He'd thought the arrival of colored lights on the bare trees of the Common, memories of Christmases past, and the smell of wood smoke in the midnight clear would somehow reunite them. But it hadn't. Apparently, it hadn't. The particulars of the reunion were the problem. Somebody would have to call the other one, somebody would have to confess need and risk a turndown.

Except for a modest canister of pepper spray, he'd stopped carrying any kind of weapon in his waist pouch, and he'd had fantasies about calling Lucy and telling her about this change, but in his heart he knew it was too late now to make any difference. Long ago, he'd concluded about women that at any given moment, they usually had something very specific in mind, that they sat around crafting very specific expectations of men, right down to the word, the gesture, the breath. He imagined Lucy brushing her teeth at the bathroom sink, thinking of some very specific thing she wanted him to say or do when she returned to the bed and put her head next to his on the pillow. And whatever it was, it wasn't There you go again. . . .

The second day of March had been a magnificent, bright, heart-wrenching Sunday, the kind of day that inspired people to get off their duffs and do a good deed for humankind. Deckard had bundled up, biked down to the shelter, and put in a couple of hours in the soup kitchen. He knew that putting in a couple of hours at the shelter wasn't really a good deed in the traditional sense, not unless you expanded good deeds to include doing something good for yourself. It was, for him, a there-but-for-the-grace-of-God thing. There were quite a few vets at the shelter (even, like himself, one ex-marine), and Deckard had discovered that whenever he took the time to observe the hangdog desperation behind the vets' every small urgency — choosing a hook for their ratty coats, negotiating the silverware, bumming a cigarette, striking a match — it helped him, later, with counting his blessings.

After the shelter, during the warmest part of the afternoon, he'd biked forever, everywhere, way past reason and fatigue, with the goal of perhaps sleeping that night. Toward evening, he'd paused somewhere in Allston near the Charles River. Couples strolled along the bordering walkways, arm in arm, enjoying the weather's intimations of spring, and mothers and fathers had brought their kids down to try out the bikes or blades they'd got two months earlier at Christmas. Upriver, there was a lovely bend where the water was busy changing colors, and Deckard let himself dwell on these brown-to-green, green-to-gold, gold-to-lilac adjustments of the light just long enough to get a clue about what kind of sunset it was going to be. Then he decided to head for the movies before the sun went down. Pouring sweat beneath his parka, unhappily alone, he figured a resplendent sunset was the last thing he needed.

That night, when he returned home — back to the apartment building after a disappointing Clint Eastwood double feature — it was a little after ten o'clock, and though he was plenty tired he'd already begun to worry about not sleeping. The weather had changed while he'd been at the movies; a rain shower had wet down the streets and left a cold bite in the air that made him feel, as he'd biked home, wide awake. He climbed the four flights of marble stairs to his floor, hauling the bike over his shoulder, and as he reached his landing he heard the telephone ringing inside the apartment. A weird surge of panic caused him to fumble with the door key. By the time he got to the phone, the answering machine was running, he had trouble finding the button that shut it off, and when he finally got the line clear, the caller was gone.

A knock came at the door, which, in his rush, he'd failed to close. It was shaggy old Mrs. Rothschild, his neighbor on the same landing, and she couldn't have materialized at a worse moment. Easily two hundred years old, she was only about four feet tall and always appeared to Deckard to be needing someone to pick her up bodily and carry her from wherever she was to some other place. It was a mystifying temptation. Right now she stood trembling at the door like some kind of scandalized cat who'd fallen into a water ditch. Deckard — winded from the stairs, frustrated and disappointed about the telephone, and still a bit panic-surged — was more brusque than usual, when even at his kindest he surely scared her. "What can I do for you?" he said, lumbering to the door.

Visibly startled by the sound of his voice, she said, "Oh, Deckard, honey" — pleading way up at him with soggy eyes — "I hate to bother you, but do you think you could turn that music down just a bit? Mr. Rothschild is trying to sleep."

There was, of course, no music playing, not that Deckard could hear, and there hadn't been any Mr. Rothschild for at least a dozen years, but Deckard said, "Sure, I'll turn it down. I'll go do it right now."

"Oh," she said, startled again. "Well."

Deckard walked into his living room, out of the old woman's view, twisted an invisible knob in the air, and returned to the door.

"There," he said. "Is that better?"

Mrs. Rothschild cocked her head. "Thank you so much," she said. "That's *worlds* better."

Deckard's telephone began to ring again. "That's my phone," he said quickly and told her to watch her step on the landing. (He knew it was only a matter of time before she pitched down the stairs or simply died climbing them.) But she didn't move from her spot, and somehow Deckard couldn't bring himself to shut the door in her face, so he simply said good-bye and moved away, leaving the door open about six inches.

When he'd answered the phone, he recognized Sarah's voice immediately. "Deckard, is that you?" she said.

"Sarah," said Deckard. "What's up?"

"Is that you?" she said again.

"Of course it's me. What do you think?"

He was breathing hard, and something

41

about the silence at the other end of the line, something about the sound of his own breath returning to him amplified by the receiver, frightened him. He noticed that the hand holding the telephone was trembling a little. As calmly as he could, he said, "What's wrong, Sarah?"

"Oh, Deck," she said, and then he noticed the jumble of background noises that meant she was calling from a public place.

He stretched the phone cord far enough down the hall so that he could whisper to the unwavered Mrs. Rothschild, "I've got to close this door now."

"Deckard, honey, I can see you're on the telephone," she said, "busy as a bee, busy as a bee," and began slowly to turn away.

As soon as Deckard saw the old woman pass into her own apartment, across the landing, he kicked the door shut, harder than he'd meant to, and left a scuff mark on the white paint. Then he pulled the cord around the doorjamb to the kitchen so he could reach one of the dinette chairs. His ear was away from the phone for a couple of seconds, and when he got situated back in the hall, he said Sarah's name, but all she seemed able to say was, "I can't . . . I can't . . ."

"Come on, Sarah," Deckard said, "talk to me. Tell me where you are. Tell me what's happened. Is it Harry?"

"No, no," she said. "I'm sorry. I'm having some trouble with my voice. We're at the hospital, Harry and me, and we need you to come over here, if that's okay. Malcolm's been hurt really badly. There's a lot to do and a lot of people and —"

"What happened?" he asked, but she started that "I can't . . . I can't . . ." business again, so he said, "What hospital, Sarah? Where are you?"

He heard her asking someone, away from the phone, the name of the hospital, and then she said, "We're at Mount Auburn. . . . I couldn't remember . . . I've been here dozens of times but I couldn't remember —"

"I'll get a cab," he said. "It'll probably take twenty minutes. You must be in the emergency room, right?"

"I'm here where the phones are," she said. "Where the ambulances park. The automatic doors, and there's a rest room here and, oh — some folded-up wheelchairs. The floor is dirty."

"I'll find you," Deckard said. "You go find Harry now, okay?"

"Yes," she said.

He told her he'd be right there, and he was about to hang up when she said, "I'm sorry, Deck . . . I'm sorry . . . but could you please bring Harry something to eat?"

He told her he would.

After he phoned for a taxi, he went to the kitchen and found a box of granola bars. He wasn't sure which flavor to bring, so he stuffed the entire contents of the box into his coat pockets. When he returned to the hallway, he paused for a moment before a color photograph that hung on the wall — his best buddy, Malcolm, burned dark brown for a white guy — no shirt, khaki shorts, work boots, straw hat, riding a red tractor over a mound of tall beach grass, Harry wedged up between his legs, both of them grinning ear to ear and waving. Deckard moved closer to the picture. It was very dim in the hallway, and he thought he'd seen something in the picture he'd never noticed before: Malcolm and Harry each had a piece of straw stuck between their front teeth.

As he descended the stairs, he recalled the little surge of panic he'd felt as he'd fumbled with the door key a few minutes before on the landing. He wondered if it had been a premonition or if it was only some kind of special panic that lonely people often feel. He'd been around victims of psychogenic shock before. Sarah's conduct on the telephone didn't necessarily mean that Malcolm was dead. Smaller events, much less serious blows, could cause that kind of shock.

In the vestibule, zipping his coat and pulling his sock cap down over his ears, he feared he'd forgotten something important — a nearly physical sensation that had begun to hound him more and more frequently, sometimes for a reason, sometimes for no reason at all. As he opened the outside door and felt the cold night air on his face, a kind of weary grunt escaped his throat, a blip, he thought, of . . . what? Not despair, exactly. More like self-doubt, a deep, deep sense of unpreparedness.

On the steps, shivering for cold, sat ten-year-old Angela Abruzzi — half Italian, half Puerto Rican — from the second floor.

"What are you doing out here in the cold this time of night?" Deckard asked her. Beneath her, as protection from the rain-wet stoop, was the sports section of the Sunday paper. "Don't you have school tomorrow?"

She looked up at him for a second, then back out at the street. "I'm waiting for my mama," she said.

"Where is your mama?" he asked.

"She's over there," the girl said, not removing her hands from her coat pockets, pointing with her chin. "In that van."

Deckard could see, across the avenue, a white Ford Econoline. "What's she doing?" he asked.

"Talking to my daddy," said the girl. "She said I was to sit and wait, and if she wasn't back over here in ten minutes I was to go inside and call the police."

"The police?" Deckard said. "What in the world is she talking to him about?"

The girl looked up at him again, as if she would ask him why he was so nosy, but then decided, instead, to confide. Her face, normally hard, went soft with shame, and she said, "She's talking to him about my shoes."

"Your shoes?" said Deckard.

"Yeah," Angela said. "I need new shoes for gym. Coach said I couldn't come to P.E. anymore in these."

Deckard looked down at the black leather boots the girl wore, one with a busted zipper.

"How long's Rosa been talking to him?" he asked her.

Angela shrugged her shoulders. "I don't have a watch," she said. "I was counting before you came along and messed me up. One-mississippi, two-mississippi —"

"How far had you got?"

Now Angela took her hands from her pockets and looked at her fingers, where, Deckard surmised, she'd been keeping track. "About eight minutes," she said.

Deckard reached for the girl's hand, tugged her up, and told her to go back inside where it

46

was warm, that he would check on her mother and be sure she was safe. Just as the girl went reluctantly back into the building, Deckard's taxi pulled to the curb. He told the driver to wait a minute and was about to cross the avenue when he saw Rosa step down out of the van and slam the door. The van sped away, peeling a modicum of rubber.

She met him behind the taxi, looking worried. "Deckard," she said, "where's Angela?"

"I sent her inside," he said.

He figured Rosa to be about half his own age — and already with a ten-year-old. She was wearing a big bulky sweater, no coat, some kind of heavy tights on her legs, and a pair of green suede boots that looked like they might have formerly belonged to an elf. Her eyes were dry but her nose was bright red, and he could see the clear delineation of finger marks on her right cheek. She noticed he'd seen this and put her hand to her face. He took out his wallet and gave her three twenty-dollar bills. "Don't ask him for anything else, Rosa," he said. "Just don't ask the man. There are people who can help you in a situation like this. There are people whose job it is to help people in situations like this. It's the only job they have. It's what they get paid to do."

She folded the money into her palm, utterly

miserable, gave Deckard a quick hug, and started for the steps. At the door, she turned and pointed her finger at him. "I'm going to pay you back, I mean it," she said, making it sound so much more like a threat than a promise that the cabbie greeted Deckard with a raised eyebrow.

In the warmth of the cab, in the dark, waiting for a light to change on the Jamaicaway, it suddenly came to Deckard what it was he'd forgotten. He'd closed his apartment door, failing in his rush to turn the dead bolt. Why had he not turned the dead bolt? Because, once again, he'd shut his keys inside the apartment, locking himself out, perhaps for the third time in a single month. Now, at God knows what hour, he would have to go down on his knees in the scrap of dirt behind his building and dig around in the dark for the spare key he kept buried back there beneath a brick.

Moments later, crossing the bridge over the river, he again confronted the specter of Lucy's absence, this time in a particularly loathsome form: maybe whatever had happened to Malcolm would bring her back. Ashamed, he kept his eyes closed most of the rest of the trip and tried to pray.

The man named Sanders had pulled some strings and found a room for Harry and Sarah to wait in, a sort of antechamber to a shut-down lab, and then asked Sarah if there was somebody she might call. She supposed she must have laughed, which clearly struck Sanders as odd, and, feeling really crazy, she said, "It's just that the first person I thought to call was my husband."

Sanders did again what he'd done from the start: He knitted his brow, shook his head, looked over at Harry, and said, "This is tough . . . very very tough."

Sarah didn't mind this about Sanders, the "tough . . . tough" and the head-shaking. She could tell he was sincere, and it felt especially helpful that he was near her own age and wore a jacket and tie. Before his arrival, every single person in authority — the cops, the EMTs, the doctors, the nurses, everyone — had been very young and wearing some kind of uniform. Sarah could make no real sense of this, but it seemed to suggest that an alien occupation was afoot whose bright young agents had not yet mastered the variousness of civilian clothes; that she, old and sad, should be set down into a lower caste and Harry taken from her and molded into an enemy leader; that life as she'd previously known it, along with a host of smug assumptions about rational progress and harmony, was over. At one point, she was so desperate for something familiar, some lifeline back to reality, that she found herself sitting in the waiting room just inside the hospital's ambulance entrance, holding Harry in her lap and watching a late show on the TV. Even here she couldn't help noticing how the grand-faced monitor, suspended from the wall on its strong iron arm, seemed aimed at them reciprocally.

She also noticed the uneventful, dreamlike quality of the emergency room, a misnomer in a ghost town. People came and went idly, clutching their mild complaints, their mysterious chest pains and low-grade fevers, ailments brought here only because their personal physicians were home sleeping. Now and then the nearby automatic doors would sigh and slide apart, the cold night would tumble in. Sarah, chilled and chilled again, thought in a kind of dreamy stupor that the room itself was a great lung, its breathing through the automatic doors erratic because it, like the whole wide world, was dying into the same strange dream.

Harry, though he was still angry at her for fainting in the car on the way to the hospital, had allowed himself to be taken onto her lap. He watched the TV — not so much what was on the TV, but the TV itself — and every few seconds he would put his lips to her ear and whisper his metaphorical question: "Can we please change the channel?"

That was where Sanders had found them. He introduced himself as Detective Sergeant Forrest Sanders but said, directly to Harry, that everyone usually just called him Sanders. Immediately Harry whispered into Sarah's ear, "Can we ask him to change the channel?"

Sarah explained to Harry that she thought Sanders wanted to talk to them, and Sanders nodded and asked Harry if he thought his mom would let him have a Hawaiian Punch. It seemed to Sarah that she hadn't heard the term Hawaiian Punch since her childhood, and she didn't think Harry even knew what it was.

"What . . . you never had one?" Sanders said to Harry. He reached for Harry's hand and said, "You really better try this. There's a vending machine right around that corner over there. Come on."

Harry declined Sanders's hand, but stood and walked away toward the indicated corner.

Sanders, watching Harry go, knitted his brow, shook his head, and said to Sarah, "This is tough . . . very tough."

She told Sanders she wanted to use the washroom, and while he took Harry to the vending machine she found one of those toilets for the disabled, accommodating one person at a time, with steel support bars anchored to the walls all around. It was a perfect tiled box with a drain hole at the center of the floor and a gleaming fire sprinkler at the center of the ceiling. A fluorescent light hummed overhead, a gizmo mounted to the wall dripped a powerfully sweet disinfectant through an IV tube into the thigh-high john. Briefly, she caught sight of herself — from the neck down, headless — in the down-angled mirror, a woman dressed for a formal occasion that had occurred ages and ages ago, almost in a former life. She locked the door, turned off the light, then groped her way to the john, closed the lid, wrapped her coat tightly around herself, and sat. It was the nearest she'd come to anything like a feeling of control — isolation booth, locked door, darkness — and, ironically, it harbored a permission to let go. She worried about the whereabouts of Malcolm's plaque, his award from the Historical Commission; she envisioned Harry, on tiptoe, dropping coins into a vending machine; she recalled the face of a man they'd seen in a training-school commercial on the TV, minutes before, who'd reminded her of a neighbor from years back when she and Malcolm had rented their first apartment together, a man exceedingly warm and friendly by day, but who beat his wife late at night; she recalled the police cars summoned by Malcolm that would arrive at the man's house and Malcolm's grim vigils at the bedroom window overlooking the neighbor's front lawn; and something about this chain of thought — Harry's upstretched arm, Malcolm's sadness at the window, the neighbor's daytime geniality, the paradox, the split, the man's unthinkable other side — caused her to weep.

Seconds into the weeping, a theme (unrelated, apparently, to the chain of thought that had brought on the tears) emerged: the exact nature of her incompetence. While she'd been struggling with the buttons of his overcoat, his overcoat was soaking up quarts of his blood underneath him; while she was busy trying to keep him warm, he was quietly, invisibly, bleeding to death; and in the backseat of the police car, on the way to the hospital, when Harry could have used a sure sign of *her* permanence, what did she do? She fainted. "Wake up! Wake up! Wake up! Wake up!"

he'd shouted, pounding her with his fists, and from within her misty cloud she could hear him, feel his small fists, was even aware of the squad car stopping in the street, the young officer opening her door, guiding her head toward her knees, reassuring Harry — "She's just fainted . . . she'll be all right" — details she observed with detachment. That's what fainting was, wasn't it, an aggressive detachment, medically considered to be "self-correcting," but wasn't the fainting itself a kind of sorry attempt at self-correction? Inside this limbo, this fading refuge, she'd been, for a few final seconds, with Malcolm. She'd felt the moment of his actual dying — was he still in the ambulance? was he being wheeled on a gurney to the operating room? — and her blood disclosed its sad desire to go with him. When she'd come around, Harry was furious at her.

A band of light glowed beneath the door of the washroom. She moved to the sink and splashed some water on her face, trying to recall the name of the detective she'd just met outside, the kind well-dressed stranger claiming to be a policeman whom she'd allowed on the pretext of buying a soft drink to take her child. Layers and layers of incompetence . . . and all she could think of was "cinders."

She went looking for Harry, and immediately the man hailed her from down a hallway, beckoning her to the little room outside the closed lab. Harry sat in a chair in a corner of the room, looking at a *Sports Illustrated* and sipping Hawaiian Punch from a red-and-blue can. Sanders was his name, Sanders, who now scrutinized her face, undoubtedly able to see what she'd been up to in the toilet. He told her he'd found this more private place for them to wait, this little room, and it was then he asked her if there was somebody she could call, and she had laughed, thinking first of Malcolm.

As Sarah left the washroom, she'd resolved to be responsible and intelligent, to focus on Harry's needs, not to let Harry down again. And here she was, less than a minute later, being stupid.

That was why, in the next moment, she thought of Deckard Jones. Deckard would be the best person for Harry. She was about to say so when a sanitary-looking young blond man, wearing green hospital scrubs, appeared at the door. "Excuse me," he said, his voice shot through with scolding, "but who are you?"

Without missing a beat, Sanders said, "I'm Tom Cruise. You're the first person in my whole life who didn't recognize me. It's kind of refreshing."

"That's funny," said the young man. "You

people are not supposed to be in here."

"We people —" Sanders began, but stopped himself short. He went to the door and took the young man by the elbow, escorting him into the hallway.

Sarah heard their voices taper off as they moved away, and when she looked over at Harry he was staring at the empty doorway through which Sanders had disappeared. She spoke Harry's name, with no specific remark in mind — she wanted to bring him back from wherever he'd retreated, from his halfhearted quarantine of her — but he only continued staring at the doorway. For the last two or three years he'd often seemed hard to read, sometimes nearly impenetrable. Once, she'd thought of him as, like Malcolm at times, hard to *see,* and she wondered if this was part of a boy's nature, a protective device in the personality, as indelibly coded as the concentric bands on snakes that camouflage their forward motion in the reeds. In bed one night, she'd put this theory to Malcolm, who listened carefully, considered it for a minute, then said, "Maybe . . . I don't know," proving, she thought, her point.

"Harry," she said again, but at that moment Sanders reappeared in the doorway, the event, apparently, that Harry had been anticipating.

"This is very tough," Sanders said. "I'm really sorry about that. The guy just came on duty. Sorry about the joke, too. It's no time for —"

Sanders noticed Harry staring at him, and when he returned Harry's intense gaze, Harry said, "You're not Tom Cruise."

"That's right," said Sanders. "I'm afraid I lied."

Harry returned his eyes to the magazine, as if some important matter had been settled.

"There *is* somebody I would call," Sarah told Sanders. "A close friend of ours."

"Good," said Sanders and, apologizing for not having a cell phone with him, offered to show her where the hospital's public telephones were located.

"I'm sure I can find them," she said, feeling ridiculously, falsely prideful; she hadn't a clue where any telephones wcre.

Sanders pointed her in the right direction, back toward the waiting room, and she began, immediately, her struggle to recall Deckard's number, knowing, also immediately, that it was a hopeless cause.

"What?" Sanders asked from behind her, for she'd stopped a few steps down the hallway.

She returned to the door and asked Harry for Deckard's number. Harry recited it without hesitation, without looking up from the magazine.

Sanders, quick to pull out a pen and pad, wrote the number down, tore off the page, and gave it to her. Back in the hallway, he placed a quarter and a dime into her palm. "Are you okay?" he asked. "You want me to get somebody to do this for you?"

"No, I'm all right," she said, noticing a gold wedding band on his finger and feeling she would cry again. "I'm fine."

"Come right back, okay?" said Sanders.

"I will," she heard herself say, and suddenly the whole prospect of promises and expectations struck her as absurd and utterly wretched. For a few minutes, in the washroom and inside the little room by the lab, she'd thought she possessed herself again, but now these words — *come right back . . . I will* — caused her to reenter the dream of the occupied world, from which she'd been forcibly estranged. She was able to move down the bright white hallway — it was a learned thing, like recognizing the bank of pay phones near the automatic doors, like lifting the receiver, dropping in the coins, and pushing the buttons that corresponded to the numbers written on the slip of paper in her hand — but she hadn't prepared herself for an answering machine, and it frightened her when she heard it.

She quickly hung up. At that moment the automatic doors opened, triggered, she guessed, by someone passing by on the walkway outside, and she took this as an invitation. From the corner of her eye, she could see that a man with an entirely bald head (which gleamed as if it had been polished) was seated behind a nearby reception desk and was watching her as she moved toward the doors, but she decided not to explain herself.

An empty police car and two ambulances were parked in the drive under a concrete canopy, one ambulance dark, the other lit up and warm-looking inside like an ice-cream truck on a summer night. It sported a bold red stripe and glossy gold lettering on its exterior, medport, which she took at first as the name of a town but then realized it was a blending of *medical* and *transport*. An alien youth in a paramilitary uniform sat behind the wheel, dangling his whole arm out the open window, a muscular arm braceleted at the bicep with a dark blue tattoo; he was smoking a cigarette, breaking the rules, trying to keep the odor out of the ambulance. She noticed that he was also chewing gum, and suddenly a young woman wearing an identical uniform appeared from the cabin behind him; the woman twisted awkwardly forward and leaned over the man, kissing him passionately on the mouth. When the woman came up for air, she caught sight of Sarah through the open window and gazed back at her sharply, wide-eyed, admonishing her to mind her own business. Sarah thought, They're here to take Malcolm away, they're waiting to take Malcolm, and she felt the dizziness she'd felt in the squad car right before she'd fainted. The smell of the cigarette smoke reached her, and she spun around toward the sliding doors.

Back inside, she searched the pockets of her coat for more coins, panic setting in now, a wide, purposeful panic having to do with things lost. Where was the clutch purse she'd taken with her to the dinner at the Historical Commission? Had she locked the Jeep and, if so, where were the keys? Where were the eyeglasses she would need in order to drive the car? What had happened to Malcolm's good hat? Gratefully, she found another quarter and dime; gratefully, she still had the slip of paper on which Sanders had written Deckard's number, and for the first time that night, as she began placing the call again, she prayed. She had no idea whom she might be praying to: everybody else's God, she supposed, a borrowed deity, for drastic occasions. She prayed that Deckard would answer, though it seemed very unlikely, and when he did answer, miraculously, against all odds, she was so surprised that she had to ask him twice if he was really Deckard. Hearing his voice, detecting the immediate fear in it, she began to feel herself coming apart. "I can't . . . I can't . . ." she heard herself saying repeatedly, the object of her phoning, the logic of speech, its impossible linear organization, slipping in and out of her grasp. But Deckard was resourceful enough to ask questions, to keep her on track. Though some of her answers seemed ridiculous — she told him, for example, that Malcolm had been hurt really badly — and though she'd had to turn to the man at the nearby reception desk and ask him for the name of the place, Deckard was, in the end, on his way to the hospital in the dream. At the last minute, she thought to ask him to bring some food for Harry.

As she moved back through the waiting room, she heard the echo of *hurt really badly*, and suddenly it occurred to her that no one — no doctor and no policeman, including Sanders — had ever actually told her that Malcolm was dead. She herself had not said it to Harry. The fact of Malcolm's dying, as far as she could recall, had never been spoken by anyone, and yet somehow it was generally known. She thought this very odd, perhaps the oddest thing in the whole dream, and she decided to ask Sanders about it.

When she rounded the corner into the hallway that led back to Harry, she saw him, from a great white distance, standing outside the door to the little room where she'd left him. Kneeling before him, holding his hand and talking to him, was a young intern, and it seemed to her she'd seen this young Latino man before — somehow she already knew he was an intern — and the gold earrings in each ear were familiar too. As she neared them, the man glanced up at her briefly, she saw that he'd been crying, and, as if this embarrassed him, he stood and walked away down the hall.

"Who was that?" she asked Harry, but Harry, without answering, turned and went back to his chair in the corner of the room.

"Who was that?" she repeated, as he once again took up the *Sports Illustrated.*

He looked at her, met her eyes. Quietly, he said, "Ernesto."

"Ernesto who?" she said.

He continued looking at her, almost as if he were frightened. "I don't know," he said.

"And where is Sanders?"

"He had to go somewhere, and he asked Ernesto to stay with me."

"Well, where did he go? Is he coming back? What did he say?"

Harry stood, the magazine sliding from his hands, hitting the floor. He shrugged his shoulders, looking directly up at her, mystified, and she saw a dark stain enlarging down the left leg of his pants. "I don't know, Mommy," he said. "I can't remember."

She went to him and took him in her arms, whispering, "Sorry . . . sorry . . . sorry. . . ." She sat in the chair and pulled him onto her lap, holding him tight, rocking him. She heard him tell her that he was wet, and she said it didn't matter, it was okay, Deckard was coming, they would take him home; she said again that she was sorry. He'd grown so big now that when he sat on her lap like this, his head reached the soft part of her shoulder, just above her breast. She recalled how, as an infant, he'd so quickly given up the breast, rejecting it in favor of the much faster bottle; he still wanted everything fast, so he could move on to what was next. And the prospect of what was next, its brutal entry into her thoughts, seemed to begin in her a kind of slow waking, a dim return from the dream.

"Where is my . . ." Harry murmured.

"Where is your what?" she said softly, but he didn't answer.

She pressed her hand against the side of his head, covering his ear, and felt his body going limp against her, growing heavier, as if he would hold her down in that one spot forever, and by the time Sanders showed up at the door less than a minute later, he was asleep.

Standing in the doorway, Sanders knitted his brow and shook his head.

"Asleep?" he whispered.

She nodded.

"Did you get somebody on the phone?"

She nodded again.

After another moment, Sanders moved inside the room, looking especially troubled, and shoved his hands into his trouser pockets. "I'm really sorry to have to ask you this," he whispered, "but I'm afraid you're going to have to identify . . . you know . . . your husband," and went on to explain in hushed tones that she could do it there, now, or later at the morgue. His personal recommendation would be to do it now; it would only take a second, and he would be happy to hold Harry while she went in. She told him that Harry was wet, but Sanders smiled apologetically, as if, somehow, Harry's being wet was his fault, and said he didn't mind, not to worry.

"Well then," Sanders said, fists still shoved deep in his pants pockets, and Sarah noted — while observing also a certain waywardness of her mind — how this made the sleeves of his jacket corrugate like the bellows of an accordion, like the rubber spring casings on the Jeep's shock absorbers. She further noted that it was a nice jacket, a wool-silk blend, not heavy, not fuzzy, but not shiny, a brown and gray herringbone, like some of the brick sidewalks in the oldest parts of town. Khaki pants, short-cropped hair, salt-and-pepper, a cop's cut, good-looking — Malcolm would have liked him — Malcolm who was always favorably inclined to cops, arriving home from work ("I met a really nice cop today"), telling her about a conversation he'd struck up with a cop at a construction site; it was an alliance he apparently wanted in his life, this odd, friendly connection to the official enforcers of law, to the official protectors of the community — Malcolm would have liked Sanders.

Sanders said, "Can I get you anything first,

before you go in, soda, coffee?"

She thought she might throw up, pinned there in the chair by Harry, but all she said was, "No, thank you," and then began the ordeal of passing Harry out of her arms to Sanders. She felt very weak, nearly paralyzed, and Sanders essentially undertook to lift Harry from her without assistance. She thought, He's not an alcoholic — the quiet stirring of a prejudice she hadn't known she held; she wouldn't have been passing Harry into his arms if he'd smelled of whiskey. As Sanders lifted Harry from her, Harry opened his eyes wide and said, "No no no no no no no," then closed his eyes and repeated, "No no no no no no no," but the second time, each "no" quieter than the one before, until finally, his head resting on Sanders's shoulder, he was only moving his lips, forming the shape of the word, slowly, twice more.

She was about to cry again — Harry's wet leg dangling over Sanders's hip, Harry's no no no, Sanders's kindness.

Sanders, misunderstanding, said, "Sorry about this. It's a technicality . . . something that has to be done."

She shook her head, stood up, and stroked Harry's cheek. "I'm ready," she said, and Sanders led the way into the hall. It seemed, right now, too complicated for her to explain, but what Sanders obviously didn't understand was that she *wanted* to see Malcolm. It was the first thing in this weird jumble that she had wanted.

In the hallway, Sanders turned to the right, the opposite direction from the waiting room and emergency entrance. Sarah, behind him, could see the top of Harry's head over his shoulder. She was no longer about to cry, but her ribs seemed to be clamping down around her lungs, and she could feel little spasms in her back, in the lower trapezius muscles between her shoulder blades. With a kind of morbid fascination, she noticed that her mouth, though her lips were pressed together, was moving in an unusual way, and she didn't seem able to control it.

Two female nurses — teenagers in sneakers and chalk-blue pajamas — who looked mysteriously like identical twins, met them in the hallway. As they passed, Sarah heard one say to the other, "Just watch your back — all of a sudden he's Mr. Clean." Then Sanders stopped. He knocked on a door that was mounted with a clear Plexiglas box; in the box, a green file folder. The door opened inward, and it was a moment before Sarah could see the person inside, a tall dark-skinned black woman who smiled and offered Sarah her hand, which was very warm. She asked Sarah to please come in, and told her her name, but Sarah didn't understand it — it sounded to her like "Dot your i's."

Already Sarah could see, in a corner of the bright-white room, a young uniformed policeman and, in the middle of the room, a table, a white sheet, the shape of Malcolm's body beneath it.

Sanders said, "We'll wait for you back where we were before," and of course he referred only to the little room outside the lab, but there was something confusing about his words, *back where we were before,* suggesting a possible reversal of events, a kind of temporal Möbius ring returning her to what-had-been, if only she continued moving forward.

Once Sarah was inside the room, the woman closed the door. She did this very carefully, using two hands, so that it made no sound. The policeman in the corner of the room nodded to Sarah, turning the corners of his mouth down, and made a move to pass the woman a clipboard he was holding. The woman whispered, "Just a minute," and stepped around the table so that she and Sarah were on opposite sides of it; in this way, she placed between them the tricky chore at hand, as if, getting at it from both sides, they could be more effective. Behind the woman was a stainless-steel sink in a built-in counter cluttered with boxes of latex gloves, a stack of brown paper towels, an unlit desk lamp, a large red plastic can labeled SHARPS. A metal straight-backed chair with an orange vinyl cushion had been pushed against the wall, where it had left a series of marks and dings. The woman said to Sarah, nodding as she spoke, "I'm going to pull the sheet down and simply ask you to tell me if this is your husband, Malcolm Vaughn. Do you feel all right?"

Sarah's eyes were fixed on the sheet, the top hem of it, where she could see the shape of Malcolm's face, and she was only dimly aware of the policeman's moving alongside her. She heard the woman ask her again if she felt all right. When Sarah looked up, she actually *saw* the other woman for the first time: she wore a pair of horn-rimmed reading glasses, and her hair, cut very short, was speckled with gray — she was older than Sarah had first taken her to be, probably in her fifties; Sarah was now struck by the woman's obvious physical elegance, a kind of understated self-confident beauty she'd sometimes noticed in stage actresses. At last Sarah understood the meaning of the woman's question. The policeman was there to catch her should she fall; they had heard of her fainting in the squad car. She began to speak but couldn't find her voice, so she cleared her throat and said, "I'm all right," first to the woman; then, lowering her eyes to the sheet, she said again, to Malcolm, "I'm all right. Please . . . may I see him?"

She had wanted to see him. In the squad car, in the waiting room, in the dark washroom, and all the rest, throughout the strange brief eternity, she'd thought the sight of him might move her toward some comprehension maybe, some comfort maybe, she wasn't sure; but now, seeing his handsome face under the chalky glare of the fluorescent tubes sunken into the room's ceiling, she felt only vastly robbed. It appeared that someone had combed Malcolm's hair, with a part on the side, not the way he wore it, a sad emblem of his having been claimed by invisible strangers. Razor burn lingered on either side of his windpipe — he'd shaved too hurriedly that evening before the dinner. His razor would be resting on the basin upstairs where he'd left it, would still be there when she and Harry got home. The towel he'd used would be thrown over the shower rod; it might still be damp, deep within its fibers the cast-off cells of his skin. Sarah knew somehow that indeed she was not fainting again, and yet there was something about the moment that felt like falling, a kind of plunge through something dark and close on all sides. She heard the question asked her by Dr. Ives — she saw the nameplate on the woman's white smock, Clarissa Ives, M.D. — and she heard her own answer, yes, yes, that's my husband, and then Malcolm's face disappeared, covered again by the white sheet. The doctor thanked her, her hand trembling a bit as she glanced at her wristwatch and wrote something on the forms fastened to the clipboard. Then she looked at Sarah from across the table and said, "I'll walk you back if you like."

Sarah said, "I wonder if I could have a couple of minutes alone. With my husband, I mean."

"Of course," the doctor said, but caught the eye of the young policeman, who had already opened the door to the hallway. The two of them, the doctor and the policeman, stepped outside, leaving open the door; after about twenty seconds of murmuring, the doctor returned alone to Sarah and said, "I'm sorry. The policeman asked me to tell you that you mustn't touch — it would be better if you didn't touch. . . ."

The woman pulled her eyeglasses from her face, letting them fall to her chest on their black woven cord. For a moment Sarah seemed to see herself through the older woman's eyes: a limp-haired chalky-white widow in a blue cloth raincoat, forlorn, standing by her husband's body. And then Dr. Ives did a surprising, undoctorly thing. She closed the door and stepped forward toward Sarah, holding out her arms, and said, "Come here, dear, come here."

Without hesitation, Sarah allowed herself to be taken into the woman's arms, where she began to weep in high contractional arches, separated by narrow columns of breath. This went on for an indefinite period of time, and when at last Sarah spoke, she heard herself spluttering into the woman's shoulder, "I did everything wrong."

"What do you mean, you did everything wrong?" the doctor said.

"I should have tried to stop the bleeding. I sat there in the street like an idiot fumbling with the buttons of his coat. I should have applied pressure to the wound. I *know* that. I should have tried to stop the bleeding."

Dr. Ives maneuvered her into the chair with the orange seat and then knelt on the floor beside her, taking both her hands in her own. "Have the police not told you anything at all?"

Sarah could think only of how Sanders had asked her if there was someone she might call, which was why she'd phoned Deckard. But it was clear that Dr. Ives had asked the question with a combination of sympathy and outrage against some broad injustice, and Sarah latched on to this and answered in the same tone, "No . . . nobody's told me anything."

"Listen to me," said Dr. Ives. "This gunshot — I don't know what kind it was, but it was a bad one, a terrible weapon — this gunshot tore your husband's spleen. Listen to me; it's important for you to know this. He didn't die of external bleeding. It would have been virtually impossible for him to die as quickly as he did from external bleeding. The spleen is a very vascular organ, dear. Your husband died from the internal hemorrhaging, because of the lacerated spleen. There was absolutely nothing you could have done. I'm not telling you this to comfort you, it's the truth. You couldn't have stopped the bleeding."

The woman waited long enough for Sarah to absorb this information, continuing to hold her hands. Sarah envisioned Malcolm's spleen, fist-sized in the abdominal cavity, filtering his blood, and she felt grateful for the doctor's gift, this fragment of cause-and-effect: Malcolm was dead because his spleen had been ruptured, not because of anything she had done or failed to do, and not for no reason at all. At last Sarah nodded, and after another interval of silence Dr. Ives released her hands and said, "Now I'm afraid I'm going to have to ask you to give me a little help here. I've got a trick knee that slips out on me sometimes. I know just what to do, I only have to guide it back in carefully as I stand up, but I need some support. A hand here just under my elbow, if you don't mind."

As Sarah stood and helped her to her feet, the doctor said, "You'd think I would learn not to do foolish things like kneeling on the floor." Once she was satisfied with her bearings, she moved to the counter and switched on the desk lamp, then moved to the door and switched off the glaring overhead lights.

"Thank you," Sarah said.

The doctor glanced again at her wristwatch. "You better get started with that time alone."

When the heavy door had whispered shut, Sarah moved to Malcolm's side. She reached for the hem of the sheet, saying softly, My love . . . my love . . . and lowering it to just below the gray-ringed wound at the base of Malcolm's rib cage, a small, brown, circular impression, awful in its candor, in its clean, quiet modesty.

The cabbie had a card dangling from his rearview mirror, a religious icon of some sort — the Virgin maybe, with her three-dimensional heart showing, glowing like E.T.'s. When Deckard was finished with his praying and opened his eyes, he noticed that every once in a while the card would twist enough for him to see words printed on the flip side, possibly a prayer, and each time the taxi came to a stop the cabbie would gently pinch the card between his thumb and fore-finger to stop it from swinging. This habit of the cabbie's, of touching the card again and again, made Deckard think of touchstones, and he thought for a moment that a touchstone was a good-luck piece, some-thing a believer touched in order to ward off misfortune, but then he suspected he'd con-fused the word with some other *t* word, and that a touchstone was actually something else altogether. As the taxi turned into the hospi-tal's emergency entrance, Deckard thought of the Blarney stone, which he knew for sure to be a good-luck thing, located in a castle somewhere in Ireland, and that if you kissed it it gave you skills of some kind, but he couldn't recall what kind of skills specifically.

He'd learned about touchstones and the Blarney stone and Irish castles at some point in his travels, a word he used for referring to his life in general, since, outside of Parris Island and the northern border of South Vietnam, he'd actually traveled very little. He imagined these bits of knowledge must have seemed at one time important, *memorable*, and he imagined they were still recorded somewhere in the folds of his brain, pickled and fried, perhaps, but still recorded. The chief trouble was that his retrieval system had deteriorated over the years, rivaled only by the poor state of his retention system. What got retained, what didn't, what was retrievable, what wasn't — it all seemed entirely random now. He'd locked the keys to his apartment inside his apartment, thus locking himself out of his own home. Was this a symbol or a symptom? Either way, it indicated a late stage of some serious human disorder, a decline toward a condition in which the subconscious, miffed and bratty and middle-aged, finally runs the show.

As he reached for his wallet, he thought of a day in early boot camp, nearly thirty years ago, when the base commander, a white man

— all the generals in those days were white — hoping to defuse any racial strife that might have spilled over into the corps from the society at large, had addressed the whole regiment on a Sunday, just after church services. "Now listen up, all you men," said the commander, a major general with a gravelly voice. (You could see from fifty feet away the bright dispatch stoking his eyes.) "I'm only gonna say this once. As far as I'm concerned, which is exactly as far as you need to be concerned, there is one color in the Marine Corps and one color only. The only color in the Marine Corps is green."

And from way at the back of the throng of men, this little black runt of a recruit yelled out, "Yeah — light green and dark green!"

For no clear reason, this memory came to Deckard, and came to him whole-cloth, ran like a clip on the inside of his forehead, started and ended in the two seconds it took for him to pull his wallet from his hip pocket. The taxi driver stopped outside the hospital's emergency entrance and steadied the dangling icon on the rearview mirror.

Deckard paid the fare, got out, and stood for a moment under a concrete canopy that sheltered the hospital doors. He noted the one police car and two ambulances parked there and noted also that his mind felt sharpened by the precision of the little memory he'd just had — he thought of the thirty-second tape he played through his Walkman now and then to clean the heads. It was a mystery, this memory thing, the way he could recall, vividly, moments from thirty years ago, and further back even than that, events from childhood, smells and tastes and sounds and sights and feelings — could stand under this concrete canopy and recite for you right now, "Some say the world will end in fire, / Some say in ice. / From what I've tasted of desire / I hold with those who favor fire," memorized in eighth-grade English class for skinny Miss Monica Riley — but if you were to ask him where his reading glasses were, for example, or who the guests were on Letterman last night, or what was Rosa Abruzzi's husband's first name, for example . . .

Two weeks ago he'd searched the stacks of the public library for books on memory and memory loss and memory-loss reversal. He'd checked out the smallest one he could find, a softcover that would fit easily into his back-pack and not weigh him down. He'd begun reading it, a few pages each night before try-ing to sleep, but he was having trouble the next day remembering what he'd read. Also, though he'd made a concerted effort to keep the book on his bedside table, he'd somehow managed to misplace it three or four times in the apartment. The chapter on depression had been depressing — he definitely remembered that — as was the chapter on the irreversible damage done to the brain and the brain's vital memory by excessive use of alcohol.

He shivered in the cold and took three steps toward the hospital doors. The doors slid open with a quiet, menacing hiss. He looked back with vague longing toward the retreating taxi, watched its single working taillight tremble away and disappear. That marine, that runt of a schoolboy who'd yelled out "light green and dark green," making even the base commander laugh, that mother's son from Johnson City, Tennessee — fucked six ways from Sunday on opiated pot, Jim Beam, and pure unadulterated fear — had squatted under his hooch one night about a half mile south of Con Thien, armed one of his green pop-ups (M125 Handheld Illumination, a flare), stuck the open end into his mouth, and smacked the cap with his free hand, lodging a sizzling star cluster inside his skull. And whatever had happened tonight exactly, this night, whatever particular form it had taken — there was, after all, an infinite variety to choose from — Deckard's best friend Malcolm had been snatched into some similar void. He knew it. He'd heard it clearly in Sarah's voice on the telephone, heard it most clearly in her failure to say specifically what had happened. Sarah and Malcolm's was the marriage Deckard most admired and secretly coveted — it baffled him, actually, how it had seemed to come so easily for Malcolm, this thing that eluded Deckard with such persistence — and now Sarah, who deeply loved her husband, was in some stinking room inside this stinking hospital starting her life as a widow. And if Deckard knew Sarah, she wasn't going to handle it very well. Circumstances of one kind or another equipped some women for this sort of thing, but Sarah was definitely not one of them. As for Harry, Harry would now be fatherless, stripped of a *good* father while all the countless rum-soaked shit-for-brains fathers survived to brighten the daily lives of their countless children. Deckard had heard Malcolm's permanent, indisputable exit in Sarah's voice — never mind her actual words — but he hadn't let himself really think it till now, in this mild occasion of hissing automatic doors. He'd known it somehow in the memory of the marine from Johnson City, in the murky trivia about stones that could ward off misfortune, known it especially when he'd shamed himself into a stint of formal prayer by speculating that this still unnamed, unfaced heartache might bring the errant Lucy back. The mind was tricky, all right. A regular little circus dog.

The ER was nothing like those on TV. Right away he noticed the silent, abandoned feel of the place, which was dismal — much worse than a patronless bar or café — a place so deeply unpopular that people didn't use it even in an emergency.

He estimated the distance from the sliding doors to the waiting area to be only about twenty feet — there were a bank of public phones, three collapsed wheelchairs, and a reception desk to get past — but he could already see that Sarah and Harry were not around. For a moment he feared he'd come to the wrong hospital, that Sarah, in shock, had given him the wrong name.

A bald-headed guy manning the reception desk was busy checking somebody in, an ancient Asian woman who gripped her throat as she leaned over the counter and whispered answers to his questions. Most people could simply stroll into the waiting area, poke around a bit, and explore the explorable domains until they found what they were looking for. A busy bald-headed guy behind a reception desk wouldn't even take notice of most people coming through the doors. He would stay busy and wait until somebody asked him a direct question. But this didn't apply to Deckard. When Deckard entered a place of business, be it office, hospital, store, church, or school, some friendly joker would pounce on him within the first ten or twenty seconds, offering assistance. "Can I help you?" Translation: "What are you doing here, you big black caveman in combat boots?" He was almost used to it. Maybe he would get completely used to it in the next forty-seven years. One thing he knew: It did no good to play it inconspicuous. That only made you all the more suspect.

Deckard counted his footsteps, a game he sometimes played. He'd taken exactly seven beyond the sliding doors when the old Asian woman turned around and the bald-headed guy stood up and called out, "Can I help you, sir?" (Deckard loved the cloaking device, "sir." For some reason he thought of the canister of pepper spray, illegal, inside his waist pouch, and wished he'd left it at home.) He stepped to the counter and spoke to the man very quietly. He explained that he'd had a call from a friend, a woman with an eight-year-old boy. The man seemed to know who Deckard meant and asked him to have a seat for a few minutes in the waiting area. Deckard observed that there was no sadness in the man's eyes, no indication that the woman in question had just been widowed. But Deckard knew there was nothing concrete to draw from this observation, except maybe that the reason hope springs eternal is that it'll spring from practically anything, from practically nothing at all.

The tweedy-looking office furniture in the waiting area was arranged around a television mounted high on one wall. Deckard was about to sit when he spotted, far down a gleaming white corridor, a uniformed policeman standing sentinel outside a doorway. Without so much as a glance in the direction of the reception desk, Deckard started into the corridor, for his instinct told him he would find Sarah inside the room the policeman was guarding.

The corridor was lined on both sides with doors, most of them shut, and as Deckard neared the policeman, the policeman appeared to grow younger, until at last Deckard judged him to be about fourteen. The young officer stood up straighter when he saw Deckard's approach.

Still a few feet away, Deckard passed the open door to a room in which a man in a sport coat was talking quietly with a tall, skinny black woman, a doctor according to her nameplate; the man's back was to the door, and what stopped Deckard in his tracks was the sight of Harry, slumped lifeless against the man's shoulder. It was a jagged, disorienting moment in which Deckard thought he was seeing Malcolm's back — Malcolm wasn't dead after all, but something terrible had happened to Harry.

The doctor's eyes, lighting first on Deckard, then on Deckard's stricken face, caused the man in the sport coat to turn around. He didn't speak right away, but appeared to run a quick inspection of Deckard from head to toe, a ritual scrutinizing Deckard was accustomed to in strangers. When the man said, "Can I help you?" absent the "sir," there was something about his expression that suggested he was by nature interested in developments, any kind of development, almost as if he was glad to see Deckard.

Deckard, dazed, answered, "That's Harry . . . I'm looking for Sarah . . ."

The man holding Harry now seemed confused — or maybe unconvinced of something — but before he could respond there was a small commotion farther down the corridor, and when Deckard turned toward it he saw Sarah. Apparently the belt to her raincoat had snagged on the door handle as she was leaving the room, and the young policeman was now trying to unsnag it; Sarah, standing too far from the door, pulling the belt tight, was making the policeman's work impossible; she was in a state of panic — she might break out running if she weren't tethered to the door — and then, in a large half-shrinking, half-spinning gesture, she threw the coat to the floor, free at last. Unsurprised, she looked at Deckard and motioned three times with her hand for him to come to where she stood, as if she needed urgently to tell him or to show him something.

Much later, toward daybreak, as he looked out Harry's bedroom window, Deckard would imagine what Sanders had seen back at the hospital — a black man in a black parka, black sock cap, and black combat boots taking a bereaved white woman into his arms, where she sobs briefly, and then, continuing to murmur to her quietly, escorting her slowly away down the hall; the woman is apparently oblivious to the welfare or even to the whereabouts of her child; the young police officer, who has retrieved the woman's raincoat from the floor, stands staring at it in his hands, looks to Sanders for instructions. Perhaps both men shrug their shoulders.

In the corridor, Deckard heard Sanders call out to them. He felt Sarah quake at the sound of Sanders's voice, and he sensed that she wouldn't have stopped, would simply have kept moving forward, away from what she seemed to be fleeing, had he not held her back. Deckard had been saying to Sarah, "I know, I know, I know, I know," over and over again, which didn't entirely make sense, but at the time it was all that had come to him to say.

In another moment, Sanders stood beside them, and Harry, who'd been awakened by Sanders's calling out, was looking at Deckard with glazed eyes and reaching for him. Harry's face was red and creased where it had been pressed against Sanders's jacket, and it seemed to Deckard even a bit flattened on that side, misshapen like a newborn's. He took Harry from Sanders, and the boy nuzzled his face into the fake-fur collar of Deckard's parka. Right away, Deckard thought Harry felt wet, and then he noticed a corroborating dark stain down the front of Sanders's sport coat. In the few seconds it took for Sarah to introduce Deckard to Sanders and to explain that Deckard was a close friend of the family, Harry fell asleep again, his breath warm near Deckard's left ear.

When the young policeman brought Sarah's coat to her, she said, "Thank you" and "I'm sorry" in a weird monotone. The young officer returned to the doorway where he'd previously been standing and was met there by the woman doctor. Both went inside and closed the door behind them.

Sanders said to Sarah that he was wondering where she was headed, that he was really sorry, he knew this was a tough time, but that he was going to need to talk to her. Then he said to Deckard, "I'm going to need to talk to you too."

Sarah said, "I'm afraid I don't know what I'm doing. I guess I need someone to tell me what to do." She looked at Deckard and said, "He's in there, in that room." She reached out her hand and laid it on Harry's back. "I guess it's over. I need somebody to tell me what to do. You see, I remember everything. I guess it's over now."

Deckard found himself nodding, as if he understood this gibberish, but he couldn't for the life of him think of what to say in response.

Sanders said, "Mr. Jones is here to help you, and so am I. You don't have to do it alone."

This remark was a relief to Deckard — it struck him as just the right thing to say — but it appeared only to puzzle Sarah. She looked at Sanders with something like pity and said, "But I think . . . I think I do. I think I do have to do it alone."

Sanders shook his head, knitted his brow.

"This is very tough," he said, "I know, very tough . . . but my problem is that time's passing, you see."

Sarah suddenly changed, seemed to become very sure of herself. "Oh, I wouldn't worry about that," she said bitterly, and Deckard began to have a feeling that he was listening to a conversation spoken in code.

"Some stupid kid fucked-up on drugs," Sarah added. "He probably went somewhere and overdosed ten minutes after he shot Malcolm."

"How do you know that?" asked Sanders.

"How do I know what?"

"What you just said."

"Because I just know it," said Sarah. "I don't know how I know it. Just find the car, and he'll probably be lying in the front seat with a dirty needle sticking out of his arm."

"Actually, we already found it," said Sanders, apparently stunning Sarah; her eyes brimmed with tears. "About a half mile from the scene," Sanders continued. "In the parking lot of the golf course. We're searching that area now. If he was on drugs, like you say, he might've wandered out into the woods around the reservoir, and there's a good chance we'll still find him."

"But who does it belong to . . . the car?" Sarah asked.

"A seventy-four-year-old retired nursery-man in Winchester," said Sanders. "Worked for O'Grady's for thirty-five years. He keeps the car in his garage, drives it maybe once a week. Original owner. Right now he's in Lawrence Memorial recovering from a stroke. Nobody knew the car was missing until tonight."

Deckard felt Harry twitch in his sleep — he hated to think about what the kid was probably dreaming — and then one foot, dangling at groin level, pulled back and let go a kick that, even through the goosedown of the parka, caused Deckard to start doubling over. He thought he might drop Harry, and in an effort not to, he reared back instead, aimed his face at the ceiling, turned away, and began to move gingerly down the corridor, struggling for breath. Little gray and silver roses bloomed in the corners of his vision. By the time he could see straight, Sanders had left Sarah alone with her crumpled raincoat and was busy a few feet away scolding a sleepy ambulance driver, yanking the young guy's headphones off his ears and asking him if he couldn't maybe wait until he had the *wife* out of the hallway. The driver, who wore a uniform something like a naval ensign's dress whites, parked his gurney against the wall and looked hopelessly at his wristwatch. He said something to Sanders that Deckard couldn't understand but it ended with the word "crew," and this made Deckard think of the long spearlike sculls stacked on trailers outside the university boathouses on the Charles, and the bend in the river where, a few hours earlier, those thrilling shifts in light on the water had filled him with dread.

Sanders had led them back to the small room outside the lab and closed the door. Sarah understood perfectly that Dr. Ives and the ambulance driver and the young policeman in the patrolman's uniform had duties to perform, that Malcolm's body would be wheeled down the long bright hallway, through the emergency entrance, out the automatic doors, into the night. She understood that Sanders meant to spare her the sight of this spectacle, and she was vaguely grateful to him. But when she thought of the silent wheels on the gurney that would bear Malcolm's body away, her head began to swim, modest ripples of nausea tightened the muscles of her neck. *Wheels, turning,* she would think, and while Sanders went on talking, asking his questions, she would feel herself slipping away. Every now and then, Deckard, sitting next to her, holding Harry, would speak her name, and this was helpful. He seemed to know what he was doing, speaking her name, calling her back, and she wanted to take comfort from it, but she wasn't entirely sure that she wanted to be called back. What she wanted and what she didn't want, the whole frayed catechism of desire, wasn't to be trusted, and she thought she should defer, whenever possible, to Deckard. When he spoke her name, it was like a stone laid in water, a place for her to take the next step, and she thought he must know this, which was why he spoke her name so regularly. Only a moment ago, he'd spoken it with such significance that Sanders had actually thanked him.

She would have felt more pure gratitude, to both Sanders and Deckard, if she weren't so distracted by everything. Earlier in the day, she'd taken for granted an ability to sift and sort through events and impulses, the durable fanfare of each minute; now the curious hiccuping progress of the second hand on the wall clock behind Sanders's head demanded as much attention as Harry's well-being, whether or not he was warm enough or had eaten anything. She had no choice but to rely on Sanders and Deckard, and she was trying to will herself to believe that neither of them would misguide her. She'd signed some papers a while ago, for example, but since she couldn't recall now what she'd signed, she had to believe they wouldn't allow her to put her name to anything she shouldn't.

Still, believing wasn't easy. Sanders, for all his varied appeal, seemed to have taken his police training from the movies. All his questions had the flavor of melodrama, and there was something very odd in what he *didn't* ask. He inquired about Malcolm's work, about his friends and colleagues, about how he spent his weekends. He asked whether or not Malcolm traveled in his work and, if so, where. He asked what "clubs" Malcolm belonged to, which made Sarah laugh. He asked whether Malcolm had any enemies, which made her laugh again. But he hadn't asked anything about what had happened to Malcolm that night.

Deckard spoke her name again, and there was a sustained silence in the room, during which she remembered telling another policeman, while they'd still been in the street, everything that had happened: the dinner at the Historical Commission, the dots of rain on the Jeep's windshield, the Corvair's stopping and starting, Malcolm in the headlights, his hat in the street. The policeman obviously wrote it all down and passed it on to Sanders. Grasping this at last, she let out a long, "Oh-h-h-h," and after another moment Deckard spoke her name yet again.

"What is it?" Sanders asked, uncrossing his legs, leaning in close. He'd removed his sport coat and thrown it over the back of a chair. He'd slid another chair up near hers and loosened his tie. She thought he looked something like a therapist with a short haircut.

"What is what?" she said.

"Where are you? What were you thinking?"

She misunderstood, heard the question as well-deserved criticism — What *could* you have been thinking?

"When?" she asked.

"Just now."

"Sorry," she said. "I'm afraid I've forgotten what you asked me."

Deckard lifted himself out of his chair, straining under Harry's weight. "That's it," he said to Sanders. "She's in shock, you can see that. Enough's enough. I've got to get her and Harry home. Sarah, did the doctor give you any pills to take?"

Sanders was about to say something when a knock came at the door. He indicated *one minute* with his index finger and said, "Excuse me."

In the hallway stood another young policeman, someone new. Sanders stepped outside the room but left the door open enough for Sarah to see his elbow beyond the edge of the jamb. Deckard was saying, "Come on, Sarah, let me take you and Harry home," and then, from the corridor, they heard, "Jones does have a record, B and E, possession —" Sarah watched the elbow disappear from view, and two seconds later someone's hand pulled the door shut.

Deckard rolled his eyes. "Deckard with a Record," he said. "I'm out of here. Let's go home."

She rose from her chair, grateful to Deckard for supplying this simple, attainable goal. Her husband had been murdered, mysteriously. There was a mystery to solve. People had to do their jobs. People would run checks on friends, to see who had a police record. People had to do their jobs. Hers, right now at least, was to go home.

She said to Deckard, "No, Deck, the doctor didn't give me any pills, and I don't want any." She went up on tiptoe and kissed Deckard's cheek, and as she did this she could smell Harry, could smell Harry's sleep smell, which always seemed to dwell most in his hair. She whispered "thank you" in Deckard's ear and then slipped her hand inside the crook of his arm.

As she reached for the door handle, she heard the muffled electronic signal of a cell phone coming from Sanders's jacket thrown over a chair. While the sound continued, eight or nine rings in all, she released Deckard's arm, walked carefully over to the jacket, and delicately lifted the lapel with her fingers, opening the coat just enough to see the small black telephone inside the breast pocket.

The phone stopped ringing. When she turned back toward Deckard, she saw that he'd been watching her and was now giving her an inquisitive look. Before she could say anything — before she could explain that Sanders had lied to her earlier about not having a cell phone, putting money in her hand and sending her in search of the public telephone — the door opened, and Deckard had to step quickly out of the way.

Sanders looked first at Deckard, then at her, and seemed perhaps surprised to find them both standing in the room, Deckard by the door, as if to leave, her over by his sport coat. If he'd had a question about whether or not they'd heard the policeman mention Deckard's police record, something about the way they looked must have removed any doubt. He put both his hands up in a halting gesture and said, "Okay, I'm sorry. I'm really —"

"We're going now," Deckard interrupted. "We've got to get this boy —"

"Okay, okay," Sanders said. "Go home, try to get some sleep. You're right. But please let me say one thing before you go. You see, the thing about police work is that it isn't anything like what you probably think. There's very little variety in it. Something happens, something really bad happens, like tonight, and no matter how nice the people involved may be — no matter how much you might like them personally — there's a limited number of things you can actually do. You have a limited number of options. There's a routine you're expected to follow. You always do these same things, you see. No matter what. You understand what I'm trying to say?"

As if on cue, Harry raised his head from Deckard's shoulder and looked straight at Sanders. He looked at Sarah, then, pulling back an inch, at Deckard. He perused the available population, perused it again, found it wanting. Disappointed, resigned, he laid his head back down and closed his eyes.

PART II

Broken Column, Female Figure, Orb

No matter how much Deckard sometimes annoyed her with his rampant advice, or with tales of his past relevant to her present, or with the several maxims of right living these tales begot, she would always be in his debt for the wonders he worked that first night. He'd seen to the particulars of getting her and Harry home and into bed — managed their scattered belongings, keys, cars, hot toddies, baths, pajamas, and sleeping arrangements. Above all, he'd put things into an order, deferring what could be deferred, when everything to her seemed dumbfoundingly equal.

"First things first," she remembered his saying, more than once.

"There'll be time enough for that tomorrow," he said, when the fugitive notion *tomorrow* eluded her absolutely.

She thought Deckard had even said things to her like, "Just pull up on that chrome handle," instructions for opening the car door.

In her memory, most of what followed the hospital was a thick curtain, though from time to time a random moment would pierce through it with the purity of an ice pick: she'd seen the NO PARKING sign at the curb in front of their house and recalled a crow perched there earlier that afternoon, recalled Malcolm's passing a football with Harry in the front yard and yelling at the crow, "What's your problem, can't you read? No *parking!*"

Days later, she imagined that first night as an enormous suitcase, which she packed and unpacked and packed again and again, trying to cull what was unimportant, trying to get it sensible — so it could actually be held, carried — but new details seemed always to be turning up, and even the old ones seemed to mutate and reshape themselves. She'd seen a policeman writing down the license plate numbers of cars in the area of the shooting, a thing that had baffled her at the time; later she learned that the owners of the cars were contacted and questioned as potential witnesses. At the hospital, when Sanders had asked her if there was someone she might call, it wasn't just so she would have someone there to help; Sanders was curious to see who she would call (and, intriguingly enough, she'd called someone with a police record). And why had Sanders lied to her about not having a cell phone? Because he'd wanted to get Harry alone for a few minutes, so he could ask Harry some questions without the mother present in the room. When at last Deckard had insisted on leaving the hospital, why had Sanders led them through a dim passageway in the basement and out through an even dimmer parking garage? Because some reporters had arrived and were waiting to waylay them at the emergency entrance.

None of these details really mattered, of course. They were interesting only because they belonged to something that evolved, like a lab reaction she might have going at school. The event, Malcolm's death, viewed as a crime, was a recognizable organism, with, paradoxically, a kind of life cycle. It changed in both predictable and surprising ways. It could be managed, monitored, even controlled to a certain degree, and there were people, like Forrest Sanders, whose job it was to do just that. Limited to the realm of crime were a reasonable imagined outcome (to make sense of something senseless), a set of reliable procedures to apply, an established protocol for analysis and interpretation. The investigation into the crime, the interviews, searches, and interrogations, the hideous bungling and speculation of the press, the funeral directors, insurance agents, and endless ringing of the telephone all formed a diversion from the opaque single-celled cube of

Malcolm's death viewed as plain loss; she had lost her husband, Harry had lost his father, Deck had lost his best friend. Viewed this way, it didn't evolve — it began and ended in precisely the same moment, like something not quite seen before in the universe.

Her training as a scientist was what kept returning her to the first night, as if her "trouble" lay in something overlooked at the conceit. She faintly recalled standing in the shower, having some difficulty with a faucet, the foreign, useless feel of the water, her good black dress crumpled on the tile like something deflated. She recalled Harry, zombielike in the bathtub, eating a granola bar, shedding crumbs into the water, and Deckard kneeling beside the tub, waving her away, out of the bathroom, as if he understood something about Harry that she never would.

She'd wanted Harry to sleep with her that night, but he preferred sleeping in his own room. "Okay," she'd said, "I'll sleep in there with you, on the other bunk."

Harry looked at Deckard, pleading.

"I think he wants me to sleep with him," Deckard said.

She had thought that she and Harry should be together. After all, she would have to sit down with Harry and explain things. Nobody had really explained anything to him.

Deckard spoke to her alone in the hallway. "He *saw* it," he said to her, as if he meant to shake some sense into her. Then he added, more gently, "First things first, Sarah. There'll be plenty of time to explain everything tomorrow."

She said, "Tomorrow . . ." tentative, like a person exploring the sound of a new word.

Did she think, then, outside the bathroom door, that Harry was angry at her for something other than fainting on the way to the hospital, that he blamed her for what had happened? Maybe. But what became clear, eventually, was that something about her, something about her presence in the room, frightened Harry, made things worse for him. It must have been apparent enough — an irregularity in her speech? a look in her eyes? — because Deckard seemed aware of it too.

Later, Deckard had come to her door and told her that Harry was almost asleep and she should go kiss him. "Don't try to say anything," he said.

She recalled asking Deckard, with utter sincerity, if it was okay to say good night.

But when she got to his bed, Harry was already asleep. She knew she'd begun to cry then — it felt as if Harry had left on a long journey away from home, and she'd been too late to see him off — and she could remember

Deckard's hand on her elbow, his guiding her out of the room. And afterward, a long blank period set in.

The next thing she remembered was waking in the night, alone in bed in her and Malcolm's room. She'd been dreaming about something that had really happened when she was a young girl and staying with her grandparents at the family's summer house; she was peeking through the keyhole in the door to the kitchen, where her grandfather, a doctor, was administering first aid to a neighbor who'd mangled his hand in the gears of a windmill. When her grandmother discovered Sarah spying and scolded her, Sarah protested, "But what happened? Is he bleeding badly? Is he going to lose his hand?" The grandmother said, "For heaven's sake, child, why do you ask so many questions?" and Sarah, incredulous, answered, "Because I want to *know*." Now, fully awake, there was no startling moment of recognition. She hadn't forgotten, in sleep, what had happened to Malcolm; she knew, deeply, throughout the sleeping, that he was dead, and she returned immediately to his side, to the small room in the hospital where she'd been left alone with him briefly, where she'd folded down the white sheet and been flooded by memories — of their courtship, the early days of marriage, Harry's infancy. There, at the hospital, the memories had quickly grown too strong and over-whelming; now they revisited her in a watered-down form, and in the familiar setting of home they comforted her as she thought they were intended to comfort her all along.

The house was very quiet, and the quiet, the dark, the memories, perhaps a few hours of sleep, all strengthened her in a specific way — some element of the strangeness of things had gone. No alien invasion was afoot. The world was still the world, only Malcolm, as he'd previously been known to her, was no longer in it.

She had an urge to look in on Harry and to explore the house, to feel Malcolm's absence as the material thing she imagined it to be. When she went to the desk in a corner of the bedroom, she was astonished to find there the small plaque from the Historical Commission, Malcolm's award for his brilliant resto-ration of the Planck Building; she had absolutely no idea how the plaque had found its way home and supposed it must have been another miracle managed by Deckard. She could see well enough in the dark to find a pen and write on a note pad, "Call school," a re-minder to phone Harry's school in the morn-ing and tell them Harry wouldn't be coming in.

Oddly, as she moved toward the hallway, she thought of one of Deckard's maxims for right living: Always live as if you're being videotaped, because the chances are fifty-fifty that you *are* being videotaped. It was odd that she thought it because in the next moment she found Deckard standing in the dark at the dormer windows in the upstairs hall, one knee resting on the window seat where, a few hours before, Malcolm and Harry had roughhoused and smudged Malcolm's white dress shirt. Deckard was looking down into the street, and Sarah had the distinct impression that he'd positioned himself far enough back from the windows so as not to be seen by someone outside. He was wearing only his boxer shorts and a T-shirt. He put his finger to his lips and motioned her to come around behind him and stand at his left.

Looking through the bottommost pane of the window, Sarah could see a dark green car double-parked directly across the street. A man sat behind the wheel, and it was evident from the man's gesturing that he was speaking to another person, not visible, on the passenger side.

Deckard gave Sarah his knowingest nod.

"We're being watched," he whispered, but this mild surprise and Deckard's distress couldn't draw her significantly away from the memories that in their diluted form had just returned and brought her strength.

. . . naked, as is his wont, he's lying on his stomach, the sheet a couple of inches below the line — marked by a little crop of sun-bleached hairs, like gold fibers — created by his swimming trunks, deep tan turning pale ivory. The windows are wide open, as these days it can hit ninety before 10 A.M., and the only hope for survival is to capture as much of the cooler night air as possible. The sun is already beating its sharp arrows through the great slumping limbs of the live oaks, and from within the bedroom they can hear the silly baby talk of a neighbor lady to her Siamese cat in the yard, the buzz and thump on the window screen of a fat kamikaze housefly, the rubbery percolation of an early morning tennis match at the public courts in the park across the street. She briefly examines the perfect line, just above the hem of the sheet, where his skin changes color, a line she has at other times traced with her finger, marveling at its geometrical precision, the unflawed, shortest distance from point A to point B. She looks at the clock on the table next to the bed and sighs at the prospect of moving an inch from the bed: unimaginable, from this vantage, so bogged in love, so thrown and locked up by it, that she should go anywhere for any reason. Let the summer school teach itself, without her, chemical engineering be damned — what could there possibly be, after all, about fluid flow or heat transfer that couldn't be known right here in this pale-blue-pinstriped tangle of white sheets? Let the summer school teach itself, and, for that matter, release the classes and tumble them down the campus hills, flinging off their clothes, to the lower fields' brown snaky ponds and the woods' sweet-chattering streams.

Malcolm pulls a pillow over his head, then reaches blindly for her hand, as if he meant to close out only the world, but not her with it. She allows him to flounder a bit — when, she wonders, did she acquire this sophomoric impulse to tease? — then rewards him with her hand and hears his pillow-muted moan of pleasure. They are high up on Cumberland Avenue, high up on the third floor of an old brick mansion, converted long ago into a beehive of many small apartments. She has taken an instructor's position at a private college in Virginia, enlisted for a summer session and the subsequent fall term. Fresh out of graduate school, he's slated in September, more than five hundred miles away in New England, to start his first job, and has come down here to spend the last half of the summer with her, to live with her. Immediately after he arrived, they painted the plaster walls and horseshoe arches between the rooms white, blue in the bedroom, and Malcolm pulled up the dirty wall-to-wall carpet, revealing, amazingly, beautiful wine and forest-green clay tiles; he installed a ceiling fan in the living room, fashioning for them a little Casablanca. There are four rooms only, four variations, these summer weeks, on a single theme: they've made love on the cool linoleum of the kitchen floor; awkwardly, with their hands, in the big claw-foot bathtub; standing, against a plaster wall, beneath the discreet lulling whir of the fan; and sweating, at night, in the bed. Everything is new, the particulars of toothbrushes and diaphragms and razors and underwear, food shopping, cooking and laundry, sexual research and response, the craggy, breathless adventure of emotional intimacy, and yet everything seems to have a fresh history, imposing itself over what must have been actual history. What was that vast waste of time before this time? Surely this was how life has always been, or, if not, how it was meant to be — torpor, mistaken as sloth, meant to be embraced; language, once thought trite, meant to swell with meaning; music, mistaken as schmaltz, meant to move to tears.

111

Still, for all that, knowing him and all this for three months or so, she's visited occasionally by a little creature who crouches inside the cracks of the baseboards, hums softly beneath the sawmill screech of cicadas in the oaks, vaguely rises even in the sweet smell of him after they've made love: she stands at the bedroom window, watching him, admiring his impossibly graceful gait and the easy swing of his beautiful arms as he trots away to the post office, and she thinks, What if something should happen to him? What if I never see him alive again? What if, running in the park at night, he suffers a freak heart attack? What if, swimming out to the far splintery pontoon in the lake, he should get a cramp and sink and drown? What if, having walked to the corner for milk, he should emerge from the Quik-Stop, step into the sunlight, and be gunned down by a maniac passing by in a crazy Cadillac convertible?

. . . naked and stumbling out of the cold water, prodded by a stealthy breaker, he shakes water from his hair and squeegees it with his hands from his arms and thighs; he runs up the low rise of seaweed-strewn beach to their spot near a grove of cedars, some of whose gnarled branches nearly touch the sand. He shivers and dries himself first with a towel she offers him, then hurriedly wraps himself in a white sheet borrowed from the hotel. Big Sur, California: Yesterday, just over twenty-six hours ago, in the Monterey courthouse, witnessed by another young couple who were waiting their turn, they exchanged marriage vows. As she watched him stumble out of the ocean — she's wearing jeans and a sweater; how can he tolerate those frigid waters? — she imagined his arriving at the blanket, sitting next to her, taking her in his arms, kissing her, and saying, "Happy?" A moment from a romantic movie. Instead, he holds himself fast within the white sheet, stares straight ahead at the Pacific, and mutters, "Freezing, ab . . . so . . . lute . . . ly freezing."

A fog bank hovers about a quarter mile offshore, a stubborn reminder that this sunny day is, after all, assailable. She observes her small letdown, then realizes that all she wants, really, is to tell him that she *is* happy. She kisses his cold temple, tastes salt, and says, "I'm so happy."

"I will be too," he says, teeth chattering, "if I ever get warm again."

She thinks he hasn't absorbed the substance of what she's told him. He reclines on the blanket and pulls her next to him, wedging one arm beneath her and clamping the two of them together hard from head to toe, whispering into her ear, "Make me warm . . . make me warm."

Her eyes are closed. A word takes shape in her thoughts: *years.*

Years and years of this, she thinks; I want years, she thinks, and trembles suddenly — a little from cold, a little from fear — moving him to tighten his grip even more.

. . . alarmed, she wonders how long she has slept — it's dark outside — and where are they, Malcolm and the baby? She feels drugged, and out of fear of falling back to sleep, she forces herself upright. She sits on the edge of the couch in the living room, where apparently she has conked out, and stares into the partial darkness. The house is utterly silent — the way it used to be, she thinks, before Harry's invasion five days ago, and at the instant she thinks this, her milk comes crashing down, bloating her sore nipples. She recalls a Guy de Maupassant story she read in college, about a wetnurse traveling to her job by train, miserably overdue, sharing a compartment with a poor man in need of a meal, and how, in the end, they reached a happy symbiosis. And then the afternoon begins to return to her: Harry was having trouble nursing, biting and gnawing and bawling and wailing and biting and gnawing until she thought she would just put him on the floor, walk out of the room and out of the house, get in the car, drive to an undetermined destination far far away, and then, after about three days of uninterrupted sleep, send a letter in which she would attempt to explain the abundance of her failures. She and Harry were sitting right here, on the living room couch, and among other things she worried about the noise Harry was making, worried about its disturbing Malcolm, who was upstairs in his study trying to get some work done. So far, Harry hadn't slept for longer than two hours at a time, and she knew it was her fault, because she hadn't been able to nurse him properly — he was hungry, unhappy, probably going to get sick, all because of her. She herself had begun to cry, silently, and when Malcolm appeared in the doorway, all she could do was look at him and say, "I'm sorry."

"What's wrong?" he asked, an appalling, man's question, as if anything under the sun were right. He actually seemed surprised to find her crying. Clueless and naive, he'd probably imagined that bringing the baby home would make her happy — after all, wasn't this what they'd wanted for so long, wasn't this what they'd tried for, for six long years, having finally given up and begun looking into adoption; then, without especially trying, she'd become pregnant, a healthy pregnancy, an uncomplicated birth — why wasn't she happy?

She didn't answer him — she thought she might have managed to convey with silence that the question didn't deserve an answer — and he repeated it, this time sandwiching it between her name: "Sarah, what's wrong, Sarah?"

She was thinking something like, Nothing is right, you fool, nothing I can say is acceptable, nothing I feel is acceptable, nothing I ever tried to do has come out right — but all she actually said was "Nothing."

Pathetically, she lifted a corner of Harry's cotton blanket and wiped her cheeks. In these few seconds, since Malcolm had appeared at the living room door, and during which she'd been assessing his stunningly narrow grasp of things and her own poor character and unsuitability to motherhood, the baby had begun quietly to nurse.

Malcolm stepped forward and watched for a moment, then placed a throw pillow behind her so she could settle back without disturbing Harry's angle. It seemed to her that she could actually feel herself emptying out and Harry filling up. As she moved him gingerly to the other breast, he opened his eyes and

looked up at her, as if to ask — with some ves-
tigial wisdom he'd bagged in heaven — what
all the fuss was about. Malcolm sat in the
chair nearby, smiling until Harry was finished. Then he stood and reached for the
baby, saying, "You're exhausted . . . let me
take him."

"Where are you taking him?" she said, as he
moved away out of the room.

From the entryway, he called, "I'm going to
take him for a ride."

"A ride?" she said. "Do you think that's a
good idea?"

"It's a perfectly good idea," he said. "You
try to catch a nap."

"A nap?"

"You know," said Malcolm. "Brief period
of sleep? Often occurring during the day?"

She meant to get up and go to the door and
see them off at least, but somehow the gulf
between thinking it and doing it widened and
widened exponentially, as she remained on
the couch.

Now, having wakened on the couch in the
dark, she recalls telling Malcolm not to forget
to burp the baby, or had she only thought to
tell him that? With a hint of panic, she wonders if it's possible that they haven't yet returned. Where could they have gone for such
a long time? Harry would be hungry. Still

feeling slightly drugged, she moves into the dark entryway, switches on the light in the upper hall, and climbs the stairs. Harry's not in his crib, nowhere in the nursery. The house, the whole place, is silent as a tomb, but as she passes the study and continues down the hall, she begins to hear the steady rasp of Malcolm's snoring.

He lies face up in the middle of the bed, shirtless, covered only by a white sheet that crosses him just below the neck. She leans over him and studies his face in the dim light from the hallway. With a curiosity idle in direct proportion to how much sleep she has just got, she pulls the sheet slowly down to find Harry, in diaper and white T-shirt, nestled next to Malcolm's ribs. Malcolm stirs, shifting onto his side so that the baby's face is now pressed against his father's breast, as if the father will now take over this troublesome business. She even sees Harry's lips move in and out a few times. Briefly, she worries about Malcolm's rolling over in his sleep and crushing the baby, but as she crawls in and rests her head on the pillow next to them, it seems that all good things are possible again, and that the future, if she can keep her busy hands off it, is a skimpy companion to the present, right now, here.

The news media — aggravated, Deckard believed, by Sarah's colossally bad attitude — took its usual find-the-sleaze-angle-even-if-you-have-to-make-it-up approach. Since there was nothing real or substantial, nothing "hard" to report about Malcolm's murder, everybody got to practice their fiction-writing skills, and for a while a good time was had by all.

Deckard Jones, an African-American employee of the Veterans Administration and a convicted felon, slept over at the murder victim's home the night of the crime. Neighbors of Malcolm Vaughn's widow reported having seen Jones visiting the house on a regular basis, both when Vaughn was at home and when he was not, and it was not unusual to see Jones embracing Sarah Williams when he departed the house. A search of Jones's apartment revealed numerous photographs of the Vaughn-Williams family, including several of the widow, in addition to more than a dozen firearms, one of which was believed to be like the weapon that killed Malcolm Vaughn. Jones's colleagues at work described

Jones as a likable but moody fellow who had seemed despondent lately over a breakup with his girlfriend. A veteran of the Vietnam War, Jones had undergone treatment for depressions believed to have been brought on by mental flashbacks of combat and post-traumatic stress syndrome. An elderly neighbor in Jones's Jamaica Plain apartment building said that Jones had always been kind to her but that he was prone to play very loud music at "odd hours," often waking her and her husband. Though police repeatedly denied that either Deckard Jones or Sarah Williams was a suspect in the investigation, it had come to light through unnamed sources that Jones was the recipient, through Malcolm Vaughn's will, of a vintage automobile, a Jaguar valued at around $45,000, and that Williams was the beneficiary of a life insurance policy whose death benefit was in the "quarter-million-dollar range." Meanwhile, residents of the well-to-do neighborhood where Malcolm Vaughn had been shot, stunned by the violent crime more usually associated with other parts of the city, were holding community meetings and demanding more police and brighter streetlamps.

More streetlamps and brighter police, thought Deckard, when he read that last bit in the paper.

Unlike Sarah, who read none of the local newspapers, watched no television, and listened to no radio news, Deckard kept up with the case as it developed in the public eye. From the beginning, he'd taken a less belligerent version of Sarah's approach to reporters, which was not really approach but avoidance. When there was a gauntlet to run — at the police station, at his apartment building, at the hospital — he ran it silently, careful not to hurt anyone. But one morning as he was leaving for work, he encountered what appeared to be a happy variation of the usual gaggle of newspersons on the stoop of his apartment building: with one exception, they were all women, young women, and something about their shouted entreaties moved him in a new way. He suddenly felt what he'd known all along to be true — that he was stronger than Sarah, less uncompromising, and capable of setting some things straight with a few right words. He agreed to take a few questions — which turned out to be an exercise in humiliation. All the reporters' questions came at him not singly but as a single barrage, began with "Is it true that . . . ," and sought to explore some tasty personal item from his past. Was it true that he had a history of drug and alcohol abuse (yes), was it true that he'd once tried to commit suicide

121

(yes), was it true that he'd gone out with Sarah Williams a number of times before she was married to Malcolm Vaughn (no). One reporter, a white woman wielding an especially phallic-looking microphone, even asked him if it was true that he dated only white women. All Deckard did was to avert his gaze, which unfortunately fell on a pretty, young black woman in the crowd who was arching her eyebrows and nodding, as if she already knew the answer to *that* question.

He quickly saw the terrible mistake he'd made and held up his hands in a halting gesture. "I only have one thing to say," he said, "a question for all of you: If Sarah and I were having an affair, which we aren't, and if we somehow arranged or participated in the death of her husband and my best friend Malcolm, would she have phoned me from the hospital that night? Would we have been so obvious about being seen together? Would I have slept over at her house?"

He descended the stoop. The reporters pursued him a few yards along the sidewalk, but he further acknowledged their efforts with a dismissive wave of his hand. He didn't look back, and once he was sure he'd left them in the dust, he felt proud of his performance, felt he'd pulled himself out of a bad situation with confidence and dignity. He wouldn't subject himself to it again, but all in all he'd managed to make his point.

That night, he watched and listened to himself on *The News at Ten*. Again he felt slightly humiliated — this time in a different, less direct way; he noted how old and fat he looked — but he also felt assured that he'd been persuasive, that his central point had come through clearly.

Following the clip, however, a grim anchorman described Deckard's remarks as "Deckard Jones's cool logic." He then introduced a clean, blue-eyed "law enforcement expert" who might have been an organizer for the Religious Right and who told the *News at Ten* audience that a well-known "reverse strategy" might be at work here, in which perpetrators of crimes will deliberately make themselves look guilty in order to convince people of their innocence.

It had been a mistake to talk to the reporters, but in spite of how it had turned out, Deckard continued thinking that Sarah herself might improve their situation if she would grant a well-chosen interview. After all, she was white, she was college-educated, she was a grieving widow. He phoned her the next day from the hospital and asked her how things were going.

"How do you think things are going, Deck?" she said.

Her sarcasm was beginning to get to him, but he let it pass.

"How's Harry?" he asked.

"Happy as a lark," she said.

"Sarah," he said. "I'm the friend, remember? Not the enemy."

"Sorry," she said. "You caught me at a bad moment. Sanders just left here with two of his gorillas."

"What did he want?"

"Hard to tell," she said. "Reassurance, I think. Moral support."

"Moral support?"

"He's not producing any results and he's under a lot of pressure," she said. "Some higher-ups down at the station want to see him escorting me out of my house in handcuffs, but Sanders's heart's not in it. He thinks you and I are innocent."

"He told you that?" asked Deckard.

"More or less," she said. "I think he wants my approval. A pat on the head."

"Well, he's got mine," said Deckard.

"Apparently, it's not yours he especially wants," she said.

"It couldn't hurt anything to be nice to him," Deckard said. "Considering."

"Considering what?"

"Considering that he's on your side."

"Oh," she said, with the cool indifference of

a privileged white woman who'd never been in any trouble with the law. "I think I hurt his feelings by suggesting that he put more people to work trying to match the fingerprints from the Corvair."

Deckard was reminded that she saw the police as public servants and saw herself as the Public with a capital P. From the beginning, she'd done practically everything she could think of to tee Sanders off. She'd gone out and bought a book on criminal investigation and proceeded to criticize him every inch of the way. She'd entered some of her criticisms into her written statement and, worse, fired off a letter to Sanders's captain, listing what she considered to be the detective's shortcomings. (Deckard had not seen the letter, but whatever it said, Sanders had not taken kindly to it; the police had turned Deckard's apartment upside down, rooting through his most personal belongings and leaving behind a mess that took hours to rectify, and two days after Sarah's letter to the captain, they came back to repeat the search; when Deckard complained, one of the cops said, "We're just trying to be *thorough*, Mr. Jones.") Sarah accused Sanders of interviewing Harry when a parent or guardian wasn't present. (Sanders had in fact asked Harry some questions at the hospital when Sarah went to use the telephone, but, being no slouch, he had asked Dr. Ives to come into the room while he did so.) Sarah's general refrain was that the police weren't "doing enough," but in Deckard's opinion most of her criticisms were unwarranted: apparently, the lowlife who'd shot Malcolm had shot him without any particular motive — Malcolm had simply been in the wrong place at the wrong time; they'd found the Corvair right away and taken out some fingerprints, but so far no match had turned up; the ongoing investigation thus consisted primarily of conducting hundreds of interviews — in the neighborhood of the shooting and in the neighborhood where the car had been stolen — hoping somebody, somewhere, might have seen something. What else could anyone do?

Sarah lay at Sanders's feet the field day the press was having as well, accusing him of failing to control the investigation and his officers. Deckard suspected that if the police were leaking suspicious-looking tidbits to the press, it was because Sarah was continually pissing them off with her criticisms. And while Sarah refused to answer a single question from reporters, she wasn't beneath yelling at them from the windows of her house or car. How could Deckard have imagined that he might persuade her to give a well-chosen interview when he hadn't even been able to persuade her to stop screaming at the reporters to get the hell off her property?

After work, he went over to Sarah's and tried to explain to her that all her unfriendly behavior was only backfiring — *he'd* been reading the papers — but she wouldn't listen. "You can catch more bees with honey than with vinegar," he'd told her, but she looked at him as if he'd lost his mind.

"That's flies, not bees," she said, "and what the hell do flies have to do with anything?"

She'd asked him to stay for dinner, and she was making one of his favorites, a cheese omelet with hash browns. He was sitting at the table, keeping her company in the kitchen, while she peeled some potatoes at the sink, so he was having to talk to her back. He tried to keep his voice low, because he was concerned about Harry, who was, as usual, upstairs "playing" in his room.

"You're not helping the situation by antagonizing everybody," Deckard said. "Down the line, you're going to have to take some responsibility for whatever jam you find yourself in."

She turned on the hot water in the sink and switched on the garbage disposal, which sounded like the roar of a metallic monster and made Deckard's teeth go dry. Over the noise, she yelled, "Don't end your sentence with a preposition."

This, Deckard decided, was her most dangerous flaw — she didn't listen, not to him, not to anyone.

The people at her university were worried about how long it would be before she returned to work, but she refused to discuss the matter with them. Apparently her absence might jeopardize some grant money she was overseeing, but Sarah was insulted that they should even approach her with their concerns. Most seriously, Deckard had a feeling that Sarah wasn't listening to Harry either (even though Harry didn't seem to have much to say to her). Two weeks after the funeral, she was still keeping him out of school, despite the fact that Harry himself wanted to go back, despite the fact that Harry's teachers and the principal of the school thought Harry should come back as soon as possible. He'd tried to be patient whenever she talked to him about any of her struggles, but he couldn't conceal his true feelings — that she was going about things the wrong way. On the one hand she wasn't listening to anybody and on the other hand she was being too outspoken, not pausing to think before she expressed herself.

The day of Malcolm's funeral, when everybody had gone back to the house afterward,

Deckard had finally broken down and cried. When Sarah found him in this condition, her way of showing sympathy was to berate Malcolm; she said something like, "Of course anybody else would have just driven around the goddamn car, but Malcolm always had to be the hero," and stupidly, recklessly, she'd allowed Harry to overhear this remark. She was so wrapped up in her own grief, so wrapped up in anger, she wasn't paying enough attention to what was going on with Harry. When Deckard had suggested one day that Harry might need some kind of therapy, Sarah, who had a low opinion of therapists — all therapists — had said to him with a chilling irony, "I'll be sure to keep that in mind, Deck."

Now, when she'd switched off the disposal, Deckard asked her when she thought Harry would go back to school, wishing instantly that he could retract the question. She turned toward him and leaned against the sink, holding an Idaho in one hand and a black-handled peeler in the other, as if she might somehow use one or both of these on him.

"I haven't decided," she said, with a kind of dare in her voice.

"Look, Sarah," he said. "All I'm saying is, I just think this might be a get-back-up-on-the-horse situation, that's all."

"Is that what you think happened here?" she asked him, cold and sharp as an icicle. "Somebody fell off a *horse?*"

She'd shouted the word *horse* so loud that Deckard got up and closed the kitchen door.

"You know what I mean," he said quietly, as he returned to the table.

She was shaking her head, and there were already tears of rage in her eyes. "I can't believe you would compare Malcolm's death to somebody falling off a horse."

"Okay, okay," Deckard said, "I'm sorry. You know I didn't mean it that way. I just mean life goes on. Life has to go on. It's not healthy to —"

"So what you're telling me is that life goes on and if you fall off a horse you have to get right back up there and ride again." Suddenly she was dry-eyed and affecting a cowboy accent.

"I'm not stupid, Sarah," he said, "even though I may not have —"

"I know you're not stupid," she said quickly. "It's just not helpful, Deckard. It's just not helpful, that kind of platitude."

"Look," he said. "When I saw my buddies get blown away in Nam —"

Her face glazed over, a visible thing; he'd lost her, and she was maybe even forcing herself not to roll her eyes at the advent of another of his war stories.

He said, "I'd like to be helpful, Sarah."

"You've been very helpful, Deck," she said, looking sad and relieved. "I've just got too many people telling me what to do, and the message is always the same. Let go, move on, get on with it, get over it, put it behind you. Pull yourself up by your fucking bootstraps, for Christ's sake."

"It's not such a bad message," he said. "People mean well by it."

She said, "I don't even think that's true," and turned back to the sink and stood there motionless for a few seconds, staring out the window.

Later, when Deckard played this scene over in his mind, he thought about what she could see from that window: the weathered stockade fence he'd helped Malcolm put in last summer, Harry's swing set with its cold chains hanging stock-still, an empty yard starting to bud and green up, defiantly, in spite of everything.

She said, "I think people see me and it makes them uneasy. They don't like the way it makes them feel. Their so-called concern isn't really about me, it's about them. They want me to get over it so they don't have to feel uneasy around me anymore."

Deckard looked at his wristwatch, as if he'd

suddenly remembered that he had to be somewhere else. Since he couldn't actually retreat, not physically, he retreated the best way he could.

"Look, I'm sorry," he said. "I don't know about all that. I just thought it might be a good idea for Harry to get back to school and for you to get back to work. I thought it might help, but you're the best judge of that."

She turned to face him again, visibly softened. "Help who?" she said. "That's the question."

"Isn't that a case where you'd use 'whom'?" he said. "'Help whom?'"

She smiled. They'd reached a truce (mainly through his concession), and dinner went peacefully enough, but Deckard didn't feel very good about that conversation in the kitchen. He didn't feel very good about the whole visit. All through the meal, Harry was like some kind of Stepford child, pleasant if a little quiet, agreeable, and apparently unperturbed by his father's recent death. He returned to his room soon after eating, saying he was working on a "drawing."

After a while, when Deckard ran upstairs to say so long to Harry, he found him sitting on the rug in his room putting together some kind of submarine contraption with his Legos.

"Where's your drawing?" Deckard asked him. "Are you designing a house or something?"

As an artist, Harry was way beyond his years. Obviously he'd inherited some of Malcolm's gifts, but he seemed to have quite a few of his own. He did two kinds of drawings: beautiful, colorful pictures of people and animals and boats and landscapes, all done in crayon; and pencil drawings of houses and buildings he designed. Nobody would believe that any of Harry's work, of either type, was the work of an eight-year-old.

He told Deckard that he'd thrown away what he'd been working on. "It wasn't very good," he said.

"I seriously doubt that, Harry," said Deckard. "You could doodle with your eyes closed and it would be better than anything most people could do."

"It didn't come out right," Harry said sincerely, as if he meant to convince Deckard.

Deckard gazed down at the Legos scattered around Harry's feet on the rug. All the little Lego men (and women?) were wearing bubble helmets on their yellow heads, ready to plumb the imaginary depths.

"Well," Deckard said, "see you later, chief," and Harry stretched out his arms.

When Deckard bent down to give him a

hug, Harry kissed him under his jaw twice and said, "Okay, Deckard." There was something too smooth about it, too business-as-usual, too no-problem.

On the way back to J.P., as the train rattled in its dark tunnel, Deckard thought about the Jaguar that Malcolm had left him in his will, a 1954 XK120 Roadster, a dream car that so far had not materialized. Apparently, it was still at the garage where Malcolm had left it to have some work done. Sarah, treading the wild waters of grief and anger, seemed to have forgotten about it — understandable, since she didn't have the news media to remind her — and Deckard somehow hadn't been able to ask. He felt embarrassed about asking, but he also felt embarrassed about feeling embarrassed. Officially, it was his car now, but it was Sarah's job to find the title among Malcolm's papers, and *that*, he decided, was what he was having trouble asking her to do.

The train had come aboveground to cross the river. Deckard gazed — lamely, as if it were an obligation — out at the dark, dark water, slow-moving like a blue-black oil slick under the stars. He was tired at the end of another day and, at the moment, steeped in confusion: A couple of hours ago, at Sarah's kitchen table, he'd been more or less trying to push her in a back-to-normal direction, and then later, up in Harry's room, when Harry had seemed so extremely normal, Deckard was the opposite of pleased. Also, he worried that while he'd been so dedicated to showing Sarah how she needed to listen better to others, he himself had failed to listen carefully enough to her. He hated times like this, when his thoughts went gray and blurry, when nothing would hold still and be plainly one way or another.

Straight out of Park Street station, after he'd changed trains, two white college girls got on and stood right in front of him, looking world-weary under the burden of their book bags and delightfully in need of some kind of deep change. The girls were, of course, oblivious to him — an old man, a little overweight, bald, a heart-shaped food stain on his necktie — and he endeavored to do his observing without being too obvious, but across the aisle he caught the eye of a nicely dressed black woman about his own age who'd clearly been studying him studying them. In a detached sort of way, Deckard noted that she was a looker herself, not *his* type, but the kind of woman who turned some men's heads. She appeared to have taken a break from correcting the poor grammar in a stack of term papers on her lap, and she glared at Deckard over the top of her horn-rimmed reading glasses as if to say, Uh-huh, right, as if . . .

This caused Deckard to think of his ex-girlfriend Lucy — how he'd shamed himself the Monday after Malcolm was killed by calling Lucy and giving her the bad news, only to learn that she'd already read about it in the newspaper and hadn't bothered trying to call *him* yet, and how she said she would see him at the funeral but then didn't show up, didn't so much as send a card saying, Sorry to hear about your loss, I still love you, I miss you, or kiss my foot — and by the time Deckard was mounting the train station stairs, out of the ground and into the night, he felt he bore on his shoulders the dead weight of Sarah's tragic frustration, Harry's I'm-okay-you're-okay sweetness, Lucy's careless neglect, and the scholarly disapproval of an African-American woman he'd never even laid eyes on — that is, on whom he'd never even laid eyes.

You can't change people, you can't change people, you can't change people.

Around 5 A.M., the steam came back on, spooking him awake, and these words — you can't change people — seemed to repeat in the clangs and brays of the radiator, punctuated like a message from hell by the hiss of the air vent. He'd fallen asleep on the living room couch, slept for a while, dreamed something horrible, which now he couldn't remember. You can't change people was all he was left with — that and the dull pain in his neck from having slept poorly. His book on memory loss lay spread-eagled on the coffee table, and he tried to think what he'd been reading about before falling asleep. Some gobbledygook theory about all memories being attached to all other memories — about how new experiences have to hook up with old ones in order to become memories in the first place — he couldn't remember exactly how it was supposed to work, but he did remember being a little worried by it, the way thinking about the edges of the universe used to worry him as a kid. He supposed that the cold cold Lucy was at the heart of You can't change people, but, freshly awake, his mind leapt immediately over her and on to Sarah, to what Sarah had said about people being uneasy around her.

She was right, of course. It was just that he felt a tad indicted by her, so he couldn't come out and admit that she was right. And besides, her being right about that didn't change his legitimate concerns about Harry. In contrast to Sarah's night-of-the-living-dead, sad-as-I-wanna-be firecracker inclination, Harry looked clean and well-groomed, cool as a cucumber, and there was something truly disturbing about it.

In times of truth, like now, in the dark, Deckard, groggy and dream-bogged, had to admit that every time he saw Harry, he himself felt like crying. He'd speculated that this was because — despite Harry's being fishbone thin, despite the dark gaps of his missing canines on either side of his half-descended front teeth — it was Malcolm's good looks that burned through, Malcolm's features and coloring that he saw in Harry's perfect little face. Deckard had felt it that evening, after supper, when he'd run upstairs to say goodbye. Harry kissed him, and Deckard felt like crying. And as he went back down the stairs, he'd had the distinct feeling that Harry had been sitting on the rug in the middle of his room doing absolutely nothing, that the boy had pretended to look busy when he'd heard Deckard at his door. The fact was, Harry, who'd always watched a fair amount of TV, had entirely stopped. He no longer watched anything, not the movies on the Disney channel, not the toons on Nick, not the animal features on the public station, not game shows, not basketball, hockey, or stock-car racing.

Sarah had said "Thank God" about the TV-watching, but it bothered Deckard.

"Bothered, that's me," said Deckard aloud, in the direction of the clanging radiator. He threw both socks at it and sat up on the edge of the couch. He stood and moved in the dark toward the hallway. In the hallway, he said, "Bothered." In the bathroom, at the toilet, he said, "Bothered, bothered, bothered." In the bedroom, in his underwear, standing at the foot of his bed, alone, staring into space like a dumb ox and tugged by some stringy goo back toward what had surely been a very troubled sleep, he said, "That's me all right."

Around ten o'clock at night, Deckard, naked except for a bath towel, stood before the medicine chest mirror, brushing his teeth and staring at himself really hard. It was something he did occasionally, a little trick he played on himself now and then. If he stood there long enough, intensely staring, intensely brushing, he could make the man in the mirror become somebody completely separate from himself, a grinning foaming-at-the-mouth maniac, animated by atoms bumping around in the glass, no past, no future, no human sensibilities of any kind. It was a tiny bit scary — especially in terms of how available it was — but what the hell? He had so few thrills left anymore.

The bathroom door was open, and out the corner of his left eye he thought he saw something move, down near the floor in the hall-way. When he turned to look, he saw a scuff mark on the bottom panel of the apartment door — the spot where he'd kicked the door shut the night Sarah had called from the hospital to say that Malcolm had been "hurt really badly." The scuff mark was shaped something like a crescent moon, a black crescent moon in a white high-gloss sky. He stopped brushing his teeth, stepped into the hallway, and continued looking at the scuff mark — as if it were alive, as if it had spoken to him — and just then the telephone rang, startling him so much he thought his feet might have left the floor for a second.

"What's wrong, Deck?" Sarah said, in a reversal of the exchange they'd had that other night.

"Nothing's wrong," Deckard said, spluttering toothpaste bubbles onto the receiver. "Hold on."

He returned to the bathroom sink, rinsed, and took a washcloth back to the phone. After wiping the receiver, he said, "I was just spooking myself, that's all. What's up?"

"Spooking yourself?" she said.

"Yeah," he said. "At the bathroom mirror. When you're home alone — I mean, when you're *always* home alone — you can develop a kind of complicated relationship with your own reflection."

"Oh," she said, but he could tell he'd lost her.

"What's up?" he repeated.

"Isn't tomorrow the day you go in late for work?" she asked.

"It is," he said.

"The stone's been put in at Malcolm's grave," she said. "I wondered if you might like to go with me and Harry to the cemetery."

"The cemetery?"

"The place where they keep dead people?"

"Well, okay," he said. "Sure. But are you sure that's something Harry wants to do?"

"That's why we're doing it, Deckard," she said.

"You mean he actually asked to go?"

"No, Deck," she said, "I'm forcing him against his will. I think it'll build his character."

It took him a moment to understand that she was being sarcastic again — chiefly because, he realized later, her forcing Harry didn't seem out of the question.

"Fine," he said at last. "You want me to meet you there?"

She suggested he come over to the house early, have some breakfast, and they would drive together to the cemetery.

He didn't much like going over to the house early — if the reporters were out, it meant he would have to walk two gauntlets, one at his building and another at Sarah's — but he agreed to the plan.

Right before he was about to hang up, she told him there was also something she wanted to talk to him about.

"What?" he asked.

"I'd rather wait till tomorrow," she said. "When I see you."

He said okay — not wanting to make waves — but this mysterious ploy really irritated him. Lucy had done it to him off and on, told him over the phone that she wanted to talk to him about something and then said "later," leaving him to wonder what it might be. Was it some kind of game women liked to play? Would it be too simple, too direct — was there some hormonal reason they couldn't just say they wanted to talk about something and then simply *talk* about it?

He recognized it immediately as the kind of thing that would keep him awake — admittedly it didn't take much — and sure enough, an hour later, he lay in his bed in the dark, spinning out a few possibilities, all of them, for no logical reason, having to do with Malcolm's Jaguar. Sarah had decided that she didn't want him to have the car — she wanted to keep it herself or keep it for Harry's sixteenth birthday — and she was looking to negotiate some kind of settlement; or Sarah had searched and searched among Malcolm's papers for the title to the car but couldn't find it, and now they were going to have to undertake some elaborate legal process that would cost

Deckard a thousand dollars; or a thousand dollars' worth of repairs had been done at Malcolm's garage, and since Deckard was now the official owner of the car, Sarah thought he should be the one to foot the bill; or because the car had been left at the garage for so long, the mechanic had parked it on the street and it had been stolen. Come to think of it, even if by some miracle Deckard did actually take possession of the Jaguar, he was going to have to find a place to garage it in J.P., and that was definitely going to set him back a few dollars every month. And why was he thinking about the stupid Jaguar anyway? Chances were one in a million that the Jaguar was what Sarah wanted to talk to him about. And what was the insurance on a car like that going to be? It had to be astronomical. He would never be able to afford a garage *and* the insurance.

Around midnight, he came very close to phoning and telling her he couldn't sleep, thanks to her, but instead he switched on the lamp and tried to read his book. He struggled through a few indecipherable pages about hysterical amnesias, a kind of forgetting that appeared to be caused by "emotional significance" and to which alcoholics and survivors of war were prone. Deckard, who qualified in both these areas, thought if he forgot everything that had emotional significance, he wouldn't have much to remember. In any case, he didn't think emotional significance was the reason he occasionally locked himself out of his apartment or couldn't recall why he'd walked into the living room.

He fell asleep to an image of himself down on his hands and knees, digging around in the patch of dirt behind his building, trying to find the brick under which he'd hidden his spare set of keys. This soon blended with anticipation of the impending field trip to the boneyard, and while he was digging in the dirt his fingernails scraped the mahogany lid of Malcolm's coffin. He gazed up from his doglike crouch to see a desiccated drug addict perched on the gravestone, grinning and foaming at the mouth, tying off his arm with a piece of rubber tubing. The junkie's long stringy hair prevented Deckard from seeing much of his face — only the horrible foamy grin — so he crawled over closer to get a better look, but just as he gained a good position, he opened his eyes and found himself staring at the turban-shaped light fixture on the bedroom ceiling. He glanced at the clock on the bedside table: ten past one. He'd slept about half an hour.

Next morning, as he got dressed, he peered

out the window to see how many vultures were lurking around the front stoop. There were eight, a considerably reduced flock, and he wondered if some of the smarter ones had figured out his work schedule. He intended to walk in the direction of the hospital and then head for the train only after he'd lost anybody who might be bird-dogging him. As he was leaving the apartment, he encountered Mrs. Rothschild on the landing with a young white guy he'd never seen before.

"Oh, Deckard," Mrs. Rothschild said, pushing open her own door. "Good morning, dear."

The guy with her was holding a bag of groceries, which he quickly placed on the landing the second he saw Deckard, then unzipped his gray parka, swung around, and, like magic, produced a camera. A flashbulb went off, blinding Deckard and causing Mrs. Rothschild to let out a little monkey squeak. The next thing Deckard knew, he had the guy pinned against the wall between the two apartment doors, and Mrs. Rothschild was saying quite calmly, "Deckard, honey, this young man is helping me with my groceries."

"Right," said Deckard, in the guy's face, too close to focus. "I bet he volunteered too, didn't he?"

"Well, yes," Mrs. Rothschild said. "He

works for the newspaper."

"No kidding," Deckard said.

Little bright silver suns were still bursting around the walls of the landing as Deckard spun the guy around, shoved him through the doorway to his apartment, and began escorting him around; holding one arm behind him, he dug his fingers into the guy's black hair and pushed his head forward at the door to every room, saying things like, "Thought you might get a more interesting shot upstairs? Something a little more intimate? You want to see my bathroom, you want a picture of that? And here's the kitchen, what about a nice one of me scrambling some eggs in my boxer shorts?" At the door to the living room, the guy somehow managed to fall to his knees, causing Deckard to bend over him, and Deckard suddenly noticed that his own vision had blurred and that it wasn't the aftermath of the flashbulb. He relaxed his grip on the guy's hair enough for him to turn his head and look up at him.

There was real terror in his eyes, but that wasn't exactly what sent a chill down Deckard's spine — it was the combination of the terror in his eyes and the fact that the guy was Asian, not white, spare and light as a feather, trembling like a kid pulled by the hair out of a flaming village hut. Deckard began to cough, as if he'd breathed in a lungful of smoke, released the guy, then helped him to his feet. Ridiculously, Deckard adjusted the guy's camera strap, so that the camera hung properly in the middle of his chest.

"Jesus," the guy whispered, and sidled slowly away down the hall to where Mrs. Rothschild was standing dumbfounded, her hand resting on Deckard's telephone. Deckard heard himself say, "It's okay, it's okay, just get the hell out," and in a matter of seconds, he'd closed them outside his apartment, locked both the locks, and could see through the peephole a distorted Mrs. Rothschild gazing at a small gray figure retreating down the stairwell. She turned and looked straight at the peephole, her nose foremost, beaklike, eyes big as saucers.

Deckard rested his head against the door and noticed that a button had popped off his shirt and that the corresponding buttonhole was ruptured. Now he would have to change. As he moved down the hall toward the bedroom, he stuck his finger through the torn buttonhole, thinking he was glad to have this small piece of evidence; otherwise, he wouldn't have been sure that what just happened really happened, that he hadn't dreamed it.

Of course it was a fine day, sunny, not too

cold — there'd been nothing but beautiful weather since Malcolm was killed — and there were no reporters at Sarah's when Deckard arrived. He figured they'd given up hope, since she so rarely left the house. She greeted him in whispers (Harry was still asleep), and they went out to the kitchen. She was wearing the jeans and sweatshirt she always wore, the only thing he'd seen her in since the funeral, but he thought she looked better than usual, not quite so tightly wrapped, as if she'd had a good cry recently and it had brought some blood into her face. She gave him coffee — nice of her, since she didn't drink it herself — and said she'd had a card from his ex-girlfriend.

"A card?" he said.

She sat down across from him at the table. "Condolences," she said. "From Lucy."

"That's nice," he said.

"You haven't heard from her?"

"Not a word," he said. "Not a word."

She poured herself a cup of tea from an old-ladyish teapot with blue flowers on it, then utterly surprised him by asking why he thought things hadn't worked out with Lucy. It was the first time she'd ever asked him anything on the subject, and for a second he wondered — even though it made no sense — if this could be what she wanted to talk to him about.

"You want to know the truth?" he said. "She just plain got tired of me."

"Tired in what way?"

"In every way," he said. "In all the ways you can be tired of a person. The usual story. She wanted a baby, and I'm too old, but more than that, she wanted stuff from me I couldn't give."

"Like what?"

"You know," he said. "The thing you and Malcolm had."

Why, oh, why did he have to say that? If he'd been *trying* to make her cry, he couldn't have done better. But, again surprising him, she just looked at him sympathetically, completely dry-eyed, and he felt an urge to tell her about what had happened earlier at the apartment building, how he'd snapped and gone berserko with that Asian kid and his camera.

"Are you talking about love?" she asked.

"No, not love," he said. "That other thing."

"Give me a clue," she said. "You mean intimacy? Trust?"

"I don't know what you call it," he said. "It was just that whenever the two of you, you and Malcolm, were in a room together, there was always this part — you could feel it — this small area where you overlapped. Lucy and I didn't overlap. Don't ask me why."

She stared at him, warming her fingers on her teacup.

"Okay," he said at last. "Did you ever notice how I wear my waist pouch with the pouch at the back and the strap at the front? You want to know the reason? Because if you're walking down the street with the strap in the back, somebody can come up behind you with a razor and pop that thing off in about two seconds. This was the kind of thing she got tired of. Me always thinking about what might happen. Me wanting to be prepared for what might happen. But I don't need to tell you — things really *do* happen. . . . This isn't what you wanted to talk to me about, is it?"

Now it was Sarah's turn to be surprised. She obviously had to backtrack for a moment to figure out what he meant. When women said they wanted to talk to you about something and then didn't, they could completely forget about the whole thing while you went spinning your wheels.

"Oh," she said at last, a lightbulb going on over her head. "No, no. I wanted to talk to you —"

Just then Harry pushed open the swinging door from the dining room. He'd wet his hair and combed it flat against his scalp, with a zigzagging part, and he was wearing the dark

151

blue suit and tie he'd worn at the funeral, bought for him especially for the service. He stood still, straight in the doorway, like a little soldier awaiting his orders. Sarah said, "Harry . . . don't you look nice! Say good morning to Deckard," and Harry said, "Good morning, Deckard," but tentatively, as if he were looking for somebody to confirm this perspective.

Deckard said, "Good morning, my man," but then quickly made an excuse to leave the room because he thought his heart might actually physically break. He went to the little half-bath under the stairs in the hallway, closed the door and locked it, turned on the water in the sink, lowered the lid to the toilet, sat down, and wept for about a full minute, thinking, I am not myself, I am definitely not myself.

On the way to the cemetery, Sarah told Deckard that she'd read a couple of days ago in *The New York Times* that in situations where a child goes missing, the parents of the child are always the first suspects, and that an awful lot of time could be saved if the parents just right away asked to be given a polygraph test. She said she'd thought their situation — hers and Deckard's — was very similar, and so yesterday she phoned Forrest Sanders and requested to be given a polygraph and volunteered Deckard for one too. She hoped he didn't mind. That's what she'd wanted to talk to him about.

Deckard was sitting up front with her in the Jeep, and he was very aware of Harry strapped in the backseat; he didn't think this was necessarily the kind of thing to be discussed in front of the boy. He turned around and said to him, "How you doing back there?"

Harry looked at him and said, "I have a question."

"What?"

"If a person gets cremated, do the bones burn too?"

Deckard tried to look meaningfully at Sarah, but she was negotiating the left turn into the cemetery entrance. He told Harry that, yes, they make the fire hot enough to burn the bones and everything.

Now they were going only five miles an hour along one of the winding lanes of the cemetery, climbing a little hill, passing a massive statue of a grieving angel that must have marked the grave of a tycoon. The place was full of monuments and symbols with specific meanings — Deckard had read an article on gravestones somewhere in his travels — but he remembered only that a broken column meant early death, an orb meant faith, and a female figure symbolized sorrow.

Everything else he'd forgotten, though there were hundreds of others.

"I have another question," said Harry, from the backseat.

Deckard turned around again.

"If a person gets cremated," said Harry, "does he still have to get a casket?"

"No," Deckard said. "He gets an urn."

"What's an urn?" asked Harry.

"It's like a little vase with a lid on it," said Deckard.

"I don't understand," said Harry, looking worried.

"You see, they burn everything," said Deckard, "but just like burning a log in the fireplace, there are ashes left over. So they grind those up into powder and put it into an urn."

A look of awe overtook Harry's face, and Deckard saw him swallow a couple of times, as if this were the most outrageous science fiction the boy had ever heard. Deckard nodded, certifying that what he'd just said was the truth.

In a few more weeks, the cemetery would be overrun with visitors, but right now — though the giant weeping willow next to the pond had turned yellow the way willows do right before starting to put out new leaves; some of the sunnier grassy patches were already green; and here and there you could spot a lone crocus or two — the place was still pretty bleak.

They were rounding the pond where the pavement grew even narrower when Sarah, looking straight out the windshield, said, "Well, what do you think?"

"Think about what?" Deckard said.

"About the polygraph?" she said.

He honestly didn't know what he thought, except that she should have asked him first, before she volunteered for the test, and certainly before she volunteered him for it.

"I think you should've asked me," he said.

"I know *that*," she said. "You can back out if you want. I mean, what do you think about the idea."

"And how would it look if I were to back out?" he said, and she was silent.

They'd reached a low stone wall on the side of the lane opposite the pond. Beyond the wall, a path led up a hill, at the top of which was a stand of hemlock trees. Sarah parked the Jeep along the shoulder of the narrow road. It was as close to Malcolm's gravesite as they could get in the car. You had to walk the rest of the way, about a hundred yards uphill.

Sarah turned to Harry and said, "Do you remember where?"

Harry looked out the window, squinted up

the hill at the hemlocks, looked back at her, and nodded. He unbuckled his seat belt, slid across the seat, and opened the door.

"What, you're not coming?" Deckard asked Sarah.

She shook her head. "I'm not ready," she said. "You and Harry take as long as you want. I'll just wait here. You don't mind, do you?"

Harry had already stepped down out of the Jeep and closed the door.

Sarah lowered her voice to a whisper and said, "Please say you don't mind, Deck."

"I don't mind," he said, reaching for the door handle.

"Deck," she said. "I'm sorry about the lie detector thing. I didn't think about what it would look like if I asked to take it and you didn't. I just didn't think."

He shrugged and said, "It's probably a good idea," only to comfort her — he could see that she was having a hard time — but once he heard himself say the words, it actually did seem like a good idea.

He stepped down onto a strip of gravel and one foot rolled out from under him. He caught himself on the Jeep's door — he didn't fall — but as he began to walk up the hill toward Harry, he felt as if he'd stepped off a boat and didn't yet have his land legs. Harry

156

had stopped to wait for Deckard. His necktie was hanging outside the buttoned jacket to his suit, and when Deckard reached him he tucked it back inside and said, "Okay. Let's go."

Harry fell into step alongside Deckard on the path and, after some distance, took hold of Deckard's hand. He said, "I think I want to be cremated when I die."

"That's fine," said Deckard. "I'll make a note of that."

They went on in silence. When they were about ten yards from the hemlocks and Malcolm's grave, Harry pulled back on Deckard's hand, stopping them.

Deckard looked at him. Harry appeared to be thinking very hard, as if he were trying to solve an arithmetic problem in his head.

"What is it, Harry?"

Harry blinked his eyes once and said, "Is it okay if I change my mind?"

At first Deckard thought he meant change his mind about being cremated, but only at first. He knelt down on the grass and took Harry in his arms, holding him tight. "Yeah," he said. "You bet it is."

He stood up, lifting him off the ground, and started back down the hill toward the Jeep.

Harry, his voice notched by the bumpy ride, said into Deckard's ear, "She won't be mad?"

"No," said Deckard, "no," and quickened his pace, noticing in the distance, on the other side of the pond, two white men, grounds-keepers who'd paused to watch, as if they'd never seen a black man come down a hill with a white child in his arms. By the time Deckard reached the bottom of the path and the low stone wall, he was nearly running, and he had to dig in his heels to stop.

Though he couldn't help noticing that in the sad and peculiar aftermath of Malcolm's death, most of Sarah's instincts were different from his own, and though he thought she exercised poor judgment much of the time, in at least one aspect she did eventually save the day. She arranged for them to take their lie detector tests on the Monday following the aborted visit to Malcolm's grave. They told their stories again — while their blood pressure, breathing, pulse rate, and galvanic skin responses told *theirs* — and the intended effect was achieved. Sanders happened to be some-body who put a lot of faith in polygraphs, and when Deckard and Sarah both came through with flying colors, Sanders, irrespective of any leftover grudges, seemed genuinely pleased. The newspapers tried fanning the flames with the perennial debate over the unreliability of lie detectors, but there was something distinctly last-ditch about it. They rehashed everything once or twice more — the widow's unusual "relationship" with Deckard Jones, Deckard Jones's guns, Malcolm Vaughn's life insurance, and so forth — but they couldn't get the pot boiling again. Yes, Deckard had guns (he collected guns), and yes, one of the guns used the same caliber bullets as the one that killed Malcolm, but a simple test had proved that Deckard's gun hadn't been fired in probably several years. Yes, Malcolm had long ago taken out a life insurance policy naming his wife as beneficiary, but there was nothing abnormal about that. Yes, the murder victim left his Jaguar to Deckard Jones in his will, but after all, Deckard had been Malcolm's best friend.

Lacking any further nourishment from the police, the shady interracial murder story involving the Vietnam vet and the silk-stocking college professor soon faded from the front pages. Though Malcolm was still dead, though the freak who drove the white Corvair was sitting on some ratty mattress somewhere eating Ding Dongs and watching his MTV, though all the grieving parties still grieved, from the viewpoint of the press there was no longer any story to tell.

PART III

Horse on Fire

A Saturday morning in April. Deckard has come to take Harry for the day so that Sarah can go, for the first time in nearly six weeks, into her office. She has deliberately chosen to return to the school on a Saturday morning because she has imagined that the quiet of the place on a Saturday, a familiar sense of abandonment in the hallways, will feel like a kind of ally; what would be, on a weekday, a river of sympathy, well-wishing, and advice will today be more like a dripping faucet. She's grateful to Deckard for taking Harry — it simplifies her day — though she wishes Deckard's help didn't have quite so frank a texture to it of a rescue mission. Through Deck's good graces, Harry will have, for the next several hours, a normal boy's life: fresh air (fishing at the river), sports (a college soccer game), and a movie (probably a guy flick) — the great escape, a breather, out from under the heavy black wings of her ever-lasting grief.

Dressed in baggy jeans and a red jersey that nearly reaches his knees, Harry stands at the kitchen counter pouring milk over his cereal, negotiating the container with two hands; and with the force of the milk, the lightweight plastic cereal bowl inches toward the counter's edge. At the nearby table, Sarah suppresses an urge to assist, but Deckard, seated across from her, has seen the alarm in her eyes. As Harry brings the bowl to the table, unspilt, Deckard sips his coffee and smiles over the mug at Sarah; evidently he means to encourage her letting Harry pour his own milk.

"Do you want me to make some sandwiches for you guys?" Sarah asks, and something about the cheeriness of her own voice seems to cause her mouth to go dry. Or maybe it was the idleness of the offer itself, since sandwich-making at this moment feels about as abstract as climbing Everest.

"Nah," says Deckard, "we'll grab a cheeseburger."

"What about some snacks for the river?"

"We'll be fine, Sarah," he says. "Don't worry."

"I'm not worried," she says. "What time do you think you'll get back?"

"What time do you need us back?"

"No special time," she says. "I should be home by around two, so any time after that would —"

"If you say 'snacks for the river,' " Harry interrupts, "it sounds like you're going to *feed* the river."

"That's right," says Sarah. "But Deck knew what I meant."

"Look, Sarah," Deckard says. "No news is good news, okay?"

"What do you mean?"

"I mean if you don't hear from us, it means we're having a good time."

She absorbs this odd device — he's telling her, again, not to worry.

"Oh," she says, after a moment. "Okay." Then: "But what time do you think you'll be back?"

Deckard smiles and sighs, tolerant.

Out of the corner of her eye, Sarah sees that Harry is holding his spoon in midair, halfway between thc bowl and his mouth, and is following their exchange like a cat watching a tennis match.

"Let's see," Deckard says, crossing his arms, gazing at the ceiling, calculating. "The game doesn't start till noon, so we'll probably shoot for a three o'clock movie, which would put us back here between five and five-thirty. Is that all right?"

Sarah glances at Harry, who briefly meets her eye — which tells her all she needs to know. Harry, too, registered Deckard's use of the word *shoot*. It's like a secret society she and Harry belong to, with special watchwords and coded signals, not to mention a grizzly initiation.

"What?" Deckard says.

"Nothing," Sarah says. "Between five and five-thirty is fine."

An interval of about fifteen seconds passes in which Harry slurps his cereal, and a dream cloud of confusion seems to descend over the table; then just as quickly evaporates. Harry looks up from his bowl to observe that both his mother and Deckard are watching him. He returns Deckard's gaze so penetratingly that it makes Deckard say, again, "What?"

Harry says, "We throw the fishes back, right?"

"Sure we do," says Deckard. "If we're lucky enough to catch anything in the first place."

"Do you have to take the fish's picture?" Harry says.

"No," says Deckard, laughing. "Not if you don't want me to."

Harry stirs his cereal with the spoon and concentrates. At last he says, "I don't want you to."

"That's fine," says Deckard, "but how come?"

Harry tilts his head to one side, the way he

sometimes does when he's afraid of being misunderstood. "I just think it must not be very pleasant."

Deckard laughs again and says, "What, you mean not pleasant for the fish?"

When Sarah looks at Harry, he seems to have grown smaller at the table — she's struck by how high the table's edge meets his chest, and then she's struck by how the world, moment to moment, reminds him of his lower status. She imagines the tabletop from his perspective, the heavy mugs, close to eye level, filled with the coffee he's not allowed to drink, and suddenly Harry's concern for the ordeal of the fish, so carefully understated in the hope of being accepted, feels to her very painful.

"And can we not get a cheeseburger?" Harry asks, peering into the cereal bowl.

"What do you mean," Deckard says, *"not get?"*

"I'm a vegetarian," he says, eyes still on the cereal.

"Since when?" Deckard says.

"I just started today," he says, and looks directly at Sarah.

At the door, as they are leaving, Deckard turns and gives her such a bear hug she thinks he'll crush her, and though it takes her breath away, it also awakens her somehow, lifts her out of a grogginess she has felt all morning.

Harry's already halfway to the curb, and she has to call him back for a kiss.

"Love you," he whispers neutrally, the way he says nearly everything these days.

As she returns to the kitchen, she makes an effort to correct her posture; recently, whenever she catches herself in a mirror, she sees a slump-shouldered woman whose head protrudes forward like a turtle's out of its shell. *Ugly* is the word that comes to mind on these occasions, but she's able to let it die the trivial death it deserves — such an ugly word, with such an ugly effect — only to be resurrected another day, before a different mirror.

In the kitchen, as she clears the table, the pressure of Deck's hug lingers in her body. In the first second of his embrace, she thought, with a speck of irritation, that he was giving a stamp of approval to her returning to work; but then, immediately, she felt him trying to say what he couldn't say with words, that he was sorry he didn't do everything perfectly, the way she wanted. She's reminded of Deckard's invaluable kindness, his bumbling goodwill, and she resolves to be more patient, more outwardly appreciative. What she cannot quite escape is the feeling that he's judging all her actions, all her decisions, and it has

168

made her keep things from him lately.

Today, for example, she hasn't told him that, before she goes to her office, she has an appointment with a chiropractor in the square. She hasn't mentioned the chronic pain like a knife between her shoulder blades, and she knows the reason she has kept this detail a secret is that she fears Deckard will somehow blame her for the pain; he'll suggest that she has brought it on herself with her failure to move through her grief quickly enough, her failure to do a thousand things differently. The knifelike pain in her back does in fact seem a kind of catchall for the countless failures of a lifetime, the physical indication of a bedrock truth that Everything Is Her Fault.

She's shrewd enough to see this for what it is, the flip side of a deep narcissism, and knows she must resist it, and yet she's amazed at how ready the world is to confirm the illusion. Last week her mother telephoned from her dressing room at the theater where Sheridan's *The Rivals* (in which she plays Mrs. Malaprop) is having an improbable, successful run in New York. Enid's conversation boiled down to one bare-bones accusation: She, Sarah, was *much too alone.* Well, whose fault was that? Sarah supposed she was also to blame for Enid's not being able to leave *The Rivals* and come to Malcolm's funeral; she should have realized that Enid's ego wouldn't allow an understudy to take over the role at the peak of the play's success, even for one night; she should have scheduled the funeral on a Monday, when Enid's theater was dark, then Enid would have been able to attend. For that matter, why couldn't she have arranged for Malcolm to die on a more convenient day?

There was no end to her lack of foresight. If, over the years, she hadn't so thoroughly alienated Enid's affections, then now, when she needed it most, she would have a mother to turn to. Malcolm himself had often expressed impatience with how unforgiving Sarah was toward Enid, how little effort she made to heal their estrangement. The reason she found herself "much too alone" was because, in her self-absorption, she had alienated the affections of everyone around her. Now, when she could use a close friend, everyone she knew seemed at best a colleague. Deckard was the closest thing to a close friend, and he'd really been Malcolm's. Had she been so mistaken in how she'd lived? Had she only foolishly imagined herself to have a full life, devoted as she was to her work, her husband, and her child?

"Well, Mother, I'm alone, you see, because

my husband was killed a few weeks ago," she'd said into the telephone, and at that very moment, some extravagant theater person in the dressing room with her mother had let out a horselaugh.

Three days later, a greeting card arrived in the mail — a picture of lilacs in a vase, in a sunny window — and, folded inside, a sheet of Enid's lilac-colored stationery with the names and telephone numbers of three "grief counselors" in the area that Enid's secretary had "tracked down." Any day, thought Sarah, the honey-cured Virginia ham would arrive. (Malcolm had once said of Enid, "She thinks there's no human trial or tribulation that can't be solved by throwing a Virginia ham at it.") And yesterday, one day before Harry announced his vegetarianism, a brown-suited UPS man indeed had arrived at their door with a honey-cured Virginia ham.

Sarah opens the refrigerator and looks at the ham, a whole ham, with its recognizable animal body-part shape; the sight of it calls to mind a meat locker, and a wave of nausea pitches through her. According to the bathroom scales, she has lost eleven pounds — astonishingly, the exact weight of the ham — the result of not eating properly, and she hasn't dared to weigh Harry because she knows he has lost weight too. Undoubtedly,

Harry's declaring himself a vegetarian was his way of saying that the thought of a cheeseburger made him queasy. It was a sign of his resourcefulness that he'd come up with a new approach, an approach, she now thinks, that might even work. He has given her a method to use against the problem of their weight loss (the weight loss another secret she has been keeping, another private needle of shame). She and Harry will relearn food, the way they will relearn every other aspect of life. They'll find new ways of doing everything, since so many of the old ones, abandoned by logic, no longer work. On Monday, Harry will return to school, and she'll pack for him a vegetarian lunch. They'll leave early and walk. Today, in the square, she'll buy something new for him to wear.

She opens a drawer in search of a pencil and paper. She means to make a list — things to buy, things to do — but when she sits at the table and writes the word *cookbooks*, her hand trembles so much that the word is nearly illegible; it looks like spooky writing on a Halloween poster.

Too much tea, she thinks. Then, Nothing on the stomach. Then, Go bathe.

At the foot of the stairs, she sees how the morning sun strikes the balusters, how the balusters' precise shadows zigzag over the

gleaming wood of the treads and risers. She
has developed a habit of issuing these silent
orders to herself. Go bathe, Get dressed,
Look in on Harry. Businesslike prompts from
a practical voice she has come to think of as
another woman's, not hers but belonging to
some latent incarnation of herself, a task-
master in khaki jodhpurs and pith helmet,
unslumped, unpale, unmarried, unambivalent,
perched on the bow of a small boat headed up
the Zambesi or some such river. An apt,
comical image, her friendliest idea of survival:
a ridiculous, endearing charade. Now the
voice says, Wear something nice — and as she
climbs the stairs, feeling both drawn and repelled by the sunlight on the stairs, suffering
only a hint of how these uniform bars of
shadow once pleased her, it adds, And for
Christ's sake don't cry.

All successful fishing expeditions with young
children flow from the observation of one
essential rule, Deckard Jones's Adventures-
with-Kids Rule Number One: Leave your
own gear at home.

You have not come to fish. You are taking
him fishing. Your job is to organize the tackle,
carry all equipment to the site, manage all
tasks involving hooks and lures, demonstrate
(in moderation) good casting technique, un-

tangle any tangled line, praise the kid no matter what, maintain an interesting level of chat (sprinkled with facts about river currents and fish behavior), and — unless the kid happens to be Harry — photograph the catch for posterity.

Caveat to Rule Number One: All *unsuccessful* fishing expeditions with children aren't necessarily unsuccessful because of failing to observe Rule Number One.

Sometimes, despite all your best efforts, a child simply will not take to fishing. People have tried to explain this phenomenon with everything from astrology to genetics. Generally, it's easy to tell if a kid isn't taking to fishing, because he complains about everything under the sun — the fish aren't hungry, the water's not deep enough, the sun's too hot, the wind's too cold, you're "making him" use a "stupid" lure, and where is he supposed to go to the bathroom?

If the kid happens to be Harry, however, you'll have to follow your instincts in this matter, because Harry will most likely pay close attention to what you say, learn things quickly, never complain, and soon be fishing perfectly without the slightest trace of joy.

"Harry," Deckard says at last, "let me ask you a question."

Harry stands on a soggy bed of pebbles, the

toes of his sneakers just touching the water, and casts effortlessly, with a skill most kids would have taken hours to achieve. In about forty-five minutes, he's landed a largemouth bass, a pickerel, and a yellow perch, each one laid on the bank more gently than the one before for Deckard to unhook and toss back, each one wowed over by Deckard with more and more futile enthusiasm.

Deckard sits on the grass a few feet behind, hanging his legs over a shelf sculpted there weeks ago by the high strong currents of the spring thaw. He has been studying Harry's red jersey, which hangs a good ten inches below his jacket, and the way the elastic in the jacket's hem makes the shirt flare out like a skirt. He's also been studying the extreme slenderness of Harry's neck — he thinks maybe the boy isn't eating enough — and the shaggy hairline at the nape of his neck. It has occurred to Deckard that Harry hasn't been to the barber since Malcolm's death.

"Are you enjoying yourself?" Deckard says to Harry's back.

"Uh-huh," Harry answers, with what appears to be an involuntary shrug of one shoulder, a kind of lie-detecting tic.

"Because I'm starting to get a little hungry," Deckard adds, providing him a way out.

"Okay, we can stop," Harry says quickly.

As he reels in the line, he adds, in an overly re-assuring tone, "I caught enough anyway."

Two or three times this morning, Deckard has felt that unsettling threat of tears that sometimes comes whenever he looks at Harry. Now, as the boy turns toward him, it occurs to Deckard that the feeling has nothing to do with Harry, nothing to do with Harry's budding resemblance to Malcolm, nothing to do with Malcolm's death. It's something inexplicable, something Deckard's glands are managing without the help or permission of his mind.

As he and Harry are walking across a field of grass, back toward the road, they pause to watch a dozen boys playing touch football. Harry stands with one hand at his brow, shielding his eyes from the sun and peering out so intently that he looks as if he might be surveying the land. The boys playing football are older than Harry, but only by a couple of years, eleven white boys and one black. After a cockeyed play that seems to involve more flailing of arms and screaming than anything else, the boys erupt into a free-for-all barrage of insults that spares no one. Three boys berate their own quarterback — "I was *open!* I was *open!*" — at the top of their lungs; another boy is yelling, "Give me the ball, give me the ball, give me the ball, give me the ball!"; and a hot debate ensues about the correct line of scrimmage. The zeal with which the boys are engaged, and the apparent life-or-death misery that has engulfed them all, strikes Deckard as funny.

"They're serious," he says to Harry.

"No kidding," says Harry, and when Deckard looks down at him, he sees on Harry's face not a polite meant-to-please smile, not a don't-worry-about-me-I'm-fine smile, but a real, unstudied, snaggle-toothed grin.

"We've got some time," says Deckard, as they move on across the field. "You interested in getting a haircut?"

"Really?" says Harry.

Deckard draws his hand over his own shaved head and says, "Sure, I'll take you to my barber."

"Very funny," says Harry.

Sarah's back pain, true to form in all such matters, feels much better today than before, but not better enough to cancel the appointment with the chiropractor. This morning it has felt less knifelike and mostly like dull pressure, distinctly the kind of pressure, she thinks, that could be relieved by an adjustment of the spine.

Since leaving the house twenty minutes

ago, she has been second-guessing the most trivial of all her actions and decisions. She decided to phone Antonia, the woman who cleans the house, and ask her to come on Wednesday — a step that felt in the moment like progress, no longer hiding, a return to order and routine — but now she vaguely regrets the call. She likes Antonia, a Brazilian woman of about forty, a high school teacher of history in her own country, but there's something distressing about the thought of Antonia's scrutiny of things, the required looking into corners that is part of the job. Likewise, Sarah has questioned two or three times her decision to take the bus this morning rather than to drive, a decision based soundly on the fact that she could spend half the morning trying to find parking in the square. She has begun to grow accustomed to this relentless second-guessing — it began, in the days following Malcolm's death, as a small torment at the edges of the larger torment, like the itching at the rim of a wound, but now she pays it little mind, thinking sometimes that she has very little mind to pay.

Everything about being out of the house today has seemed experimental, complicated, and vaguely risky. On her walk to the bus stop, she found herself looking down at her own feet, purposely avoiding the eyes of strangers. As she boarded the bus, she suddenly thought of the young teary-eyed Latino intern at the hospital who'd held Harry's hand in the corridor, a memory that made her feel oddly unsafe. And, of course, as she wavered down the aisle to a seat, the already-seated passengers stared at her. People on buses do that — people on buses *always* stare at new arrivals, it signifies nothing — and yet she felt panicky, as if she'd put on her sweater backwards or forgotten to zip her pants.

Her hardy inner voice said, Completely normal anxiety, Sarah. To be expected. One foot in front of the other.

Then, during the short ride, it seemed to her that the deep vibration of the bus — the shuddering of the floor beneath her feet, of the seat she sat in, even of the cool window where it touched her shoulder — would lull her to sleep; she recalled some historical parental warning about not falling asleep on buses or trains, and she got off two or three stops early.

Now as she moves down a narrow alley alongside a sandwich shop toward the building that houses the chiropractor's office, she thinks she's making a terrible mistake; she's taking a completely unnecessary and dangerous risk, coming to a practitioner cold-called out of the Yellow Pages. She has chosen this particular chiropractor because the office is en route to school — she can continue to the office simply by boarding the same bus as before — and because the chiropractor is female. She reasoned that if she was to be touched, if she was to be helped in this physical way, it would be easier with another woman. But now she thinks she has been foolish to put herself so recklessly in harm's way, allowing a total stranger to manipulate her vertebrae; all at once she gets a clear mental picture of her backbone entwined with its bundles of nerves leading to the brain, and she imagines a future of quack-induced paralysis and no one left to take care of Harry.

More second-guessing, the voice says. One foot in front of the other.

Sarah rings a doorbell at the top of a flight of exterior stairs, and a tall strong-looking young woman greets her. The woman has long red hair, pulled into a ponytail, and wears sneakers and an all-black sweat suit, as if she has just come from a workout at the gym. Sarah notes that she has a kind face, a nice smile, a warm hand, a pleasant voice. In the carpeted reception room, there is a desk (but no receptionist), a few chairs, a table with magazines. In one corner, near a window, an enormous yucca juts three fretted trunks out from its washtub-sized pot. The chiropractor asks Sarah to take a seat, passes her a clipboard with a medical form to fill out, and moves toward an adjacent room. Before withdrawing into this other room, she tells Sarah to knock on the door when she has completed the form and they'll "get started."

The form is the usual roster of questions about disease history and health insurance and includes illustrations of the human body, front and back views, with instructions to circle any areas of pain. Sarah draws a circle at the appropriate spot between the shoulder blades and then resists an urge to draw two big circles around the entirety of both illustrations. One question on the form asks what drugs she is taking, and she writes "none," though she recalls, with an increasingly familiar shame, that she has fallen into a habit of taking Benadryl at bedtime to help her sleep. When at last Sarah moves to the door and knocks, the chiropractor — in a preoccupied, nearly inaudible voice — says, "Yes?"

Sarah is about to say that she's finished with the paperwork when the chiropractor calls out impatiently, "Well, come on in."

Inside the room, the woman is inspecting a pair of X rays clipped to a light box on one wall. As Sarah enters, the woman switches off the light box, smiles, reaches for Sarah's clipboard, and asks her to sit at the end of a treatment table. A rice-paper shade covers the single window in the room, and on the walls are several colorful posters of the human body — just what you would expect, the skeletal and muscular systems, but now, to Sarah, they seem like horrid, garish pictures of real people with their skins ripped off.

The chiropractor scans the form on the clipboard, front and back, then says, "Right between the old scapulae, huh? I get that myself sometimes. What kind of work do you do?"

"I teach and do research," Sarah answers.

"Really?" says the woman. "What field?"

"Chemical engineering," Sarah says, and the woman raises an eyebrow as if Sarah has said something mysteriously significant.

"So you spend long hours sitting at a desk," the woman says.

"Actually, no," says Sarah. "I stand up, mostly, both in the classroom and the lab."

"Any recent changes in your routine, doing anything different lately?"

"No," says Sarah, having anticipated this sort of question and having already decided to lie. Briefly, she feels good about her lack of hesitation here, but the prompt denial has called Malcolm into the room and turned his death into another secret. Now everything that follows will feel loaded, she thinks, colored by the influence of this hidden thing, a suspicion that is immediately confirmed with the chiropractor's next question.

"How long have you been in pain?"

"About three weeks," Sarah answers, and, to her dismay, feels herself fighting back tears.

The chiropractor bends forward to look directly into Sarah's eyes, a gesture that feels to Sarah aggressive, then makes a note on the clipboard. "Fighting back tears," Sarah imagines her writing. "Clearly hiding something."

"Can you describe the pain to me?" the woman says quietly, with sympathy.

"Sharp," Sarah says, hating the way everything feels now, as if they both know that the conversation is proceeding on symbolic terms, as if it's understood that all physical pain is a metaphor; this angers her, which seems, thankfully, to help her hold the tears at bay.

"All the time?" the woman asks.

"When I move," Sarah says. "When I breathe."

"In other words, all the time," the woman says, correcting Sarah. She places the clipboard on a nearby counter, as if now she means to get down to brass tacks. "Okay, Sarah," she says, moving around to the left side of the table. "Just tell me where it hurts the most."

With her thumb, the woman begins pressing, sometimes gently, sometimes deeply, into the area that Sarah has circled in the illustration, saying, "Does it hurt here? Here? And what about here?"

She has placed one hand on Sarah's shoulder as she continues to probe, and Sarah feels a horrible, bittersweet impulse to turn her face toward the woman's hand, to lay her cheek against it. Soon it seems that the woman already knows the answer to the questions before she asks them, and she no longer poses them as questions, as Sarah merely nods or shakes her head in response.

She says, "Here?"

(Yes.)

"But not here."

(No.)

"And a little sharper here."

(Yes.)

"But less sharp here."

(Yes.)

"And hardly at all here."

(No.)

She moves around so that she's standing directly in front of Sarah; she crosses Sarah's arms over Sarah's own chest. "Okay," she says, "when I say, I want you to take a deep breath and hold it till I tell you to let it out, okay?"

Sarah nods, and in the next moment the young woman says, "Breathe in deeply and hold it," bends forward, and takes Sarah in her arms with so much authority it causes Sarah to inhale even more deeply than she already has, to catch her breath when her lungs are already full. The woman begins rocking her forward and back, gradually clamping her tighter and tighter, then says, "Okay, Sarah, breathe out," and it seems to Sarah that everything goes brilliant-white for a second, and that the pressure between her shoulder blades ignites into a razorlike burning sensation.

"Okay," the woman says, standing back and looking down at her. "Now, Sarah, you're not relaxing for me. Let's try it again, and this time let me do all the work. Don't do anything. And don't resist me."

Sarah hears herself saying "okay," but in another part of her mind she knows the woman has just hurt her and is now also blaming her for it. She obeys when she is told to take another deep breath. The rocking begins again, and she again exhales on command, this time to even more excruciating results. The pain, which now has grown duller and hotter, is spreading up toward her neck and down toward the base of her spine.

The chiropractor releases her, stands with

her hands on her hips, and shakes her head with great disapproval. "Well," she says. "We are very, very tense. And very, very resistant. It's no wonder you're in pain, Sarah."

Sarah closes her eyes and breathes, combating an urge to hit the woman. When she opens her eyes again, the woman smiles at her.

"You see, Sarah," she says, "pain is a signal sent from your body to your mind, a kind of alarm. It's saying, 'Let go.' Now I want you to close your eyes for a minute and think about what it is that you need to let go of. And then we'll try one more time."

Sarah doesn't need to close her eyes and think; what she needs to let go of is the urge to hit the woman. "I don't want to try again," she says. "The pain is much worse now."

"Worse?" says the chiropractor, fear crossing her face. "Is there something you haven't told me?"

"I don't know what you mean."

"I mean is there some medical condition here that I should have been informed of before I attempted the adjustment?"

Sarah climbs down from the treatment table. She says, "Excuse me," to the young woman and steps around her.

"What are you doing?" she says. "Where are you going? Sarah, wait. I don't think it's a good idea for you to leave right now. If you're really in pain —"

Sarah is already through the treatment-room door, and halfway through the other room. She turns and says, "What do you mean, if I'm *really* in pain?"

"Well, I mean, if it's really feeling worse —"

"What do you mean, if it's *really* feeling worse?"

"Goodness. So much anger."

Sarah leaves, slamming the door behind her. Outside, on the landing, she's greeted by a sudden gust of warm air, and she pauses, grasping the rail with both hands. Down below, in the alleyway, a little whirlwind whips dust and a few scraps of paper in a perfect swirling wreath along one wall.

They had to take a bus to Smithy's Barber Shop, and about halfway there Deckard worried that he'd miscalculated the time factor and they would be late to the soccer game. He also recalled that he himself avoided Smithy's on Saturday mornings because there was always a wait. But he decided it was too late to turn back now.

As they walk the three blocks from the bus stop to Smithy's, Deckard imagines Sarah at home, lying in the bedroom with the shades pulled, weeping. Maybe she really intended to go into the office today, maybe she thought she was up to it, but when the moment arrived to brave the world on the world's terms, she lacked the courage or the simple willingness to try. When he and Harry get back home, she'll greet them at the door in the same bathrobe she was wearing at breakfast, with the same sunken eyes, the same gaunt irritability. One thing was definite: you couldn't make a woman, not Sarah, not Lucy, not any woman, do something before she was good and ready. Women had their own schedules, for everything from getting dressed to getting over hurt feelings to . . .

He's wandering off down a familiar path — women, and how incomprehensible they are — and he quickly tells himself to stop right there, immediately. He might just as well bash his head against the nearest brick wall. Besides, he thinks, doesn't Sarah have a right to her anger? He recalls that when he returned from Vietnam, friends kept wanting him to get over it, telling him to put it behind him, and he recalls how enraging that was. Nobody understood that you didn't simply "get over" something like Vietnam in a couple of weeks. And now here he is, him of all people, putting time limits on Sarah. She has a right to all the anger she wants. He could be the one friend in all the world who doesn't rush her. There's an important opportunity staring him in the face, a chance to make a real difference, and so far he has been totally blowing it.

Meanwhile, Harry, who maintains a lead of about fifteen feet on the sidewalk, appears normal in every way. The only thing abnormal about Harry, Deckard thinks, is that he's so normal.

Earlier in the day, Deckard thought he might try to draw the kid out. While Harry was occupied with the fishing, Deckard would get a conversation going, say, about water currents and how sailors can read the surface of the water, then he would segue onto the subject of people and how you can't always tell what people are thinking by looking at their face, and then maybe he would get Harry to say a few words about how he was feeling. But somehow he hadn't managed to bring it off — Harry was peaceful at the river, if a little bored, and messing that up felt wrong. Probably, being with Sarah every day, Harry could never escape the subject of his father's death entirely — it was there all the time in her mile-long face — and maybe what Harry needed most, what Deckard could give him most valuably, was simply a day off.

Harry looks back at him, making sure he's coming along, and Deckard waves. "Stop at the corner," he calls out. "Wait for me."

That's all anybody needs, for Harry to get hit by a car.

When Deckard arrives at the curb, a garbage truck rumbles by, close, dousing them with fumes of carbon monoxide and rot, and Harry reaches for Deckard's hand. Deckard rubs it between both his own, saying, "Your hand's cold, Harry."

"Yeah," he says, craning his neck, dutifully looking both ways, as if Deckard's some old man he's about to help across the street.

To step into Smithy's is to step into the past, into a previous era. On the AM radio station, they're singing, "I like bread and butter, I like toast and jam," and Walter Smith, the proprietor, greets every customer who comes through the door as if he's his long-lost friend. Walter's cohort, Benny, who was friend and partner to Walter's dad — Smithy himself, the original owner, now deceased — still cuts hair at the age of seventy-something, though his hands shake way too much for comfort. This morning, as expected, Benny and Walter each have a specimen in the chair, and three more are waiting on the bench that runs under the mirrors along the back wall. One of the men, an ancient white-haired broomstick, is sound asleep. The six men in the barber shop who are awake — none of them under sixty — turn and look as Deckard waits in the doorway for Harry, who has hung back a minute to see if he can get hypnotized by the slowly spinning barber pole outside.

"Deck!" cries Walter, as if he hasn't seen Deckard in ages. "How in the world are you?"

"I'm fine, Walter," says Deckard, ushering Harry on through the door. "How long's the wait, do you think? We got a soccer game to catch."

"Soccer?" says Benny, pulling a face. "All I can say about that is, Pleasant dreams." The remark is aimed at the appreciation of the old customer in his chair, and he leans forward to catch the guy's eye and share a giggle with him before switching on his clippers and going back to work.

"Oh, I'd say about forty-five minutes," Walter tells Deckard. "Who's this?"

"This is my friend Harry," Deckard tells him, moving forward a few steps.

Walter pauses in his work long enough to shake Harry's hand and say how-do-you-do, then goes back to work with his scissors and comb. Deckard notices that everybody's now looking at Harry — it could be the first time they've seen a white boy in Smithy's — and it's interesting the way Benny and the two men in the barber chairs are looking at Harry secondhand, using the big mirror behind the sinks. When Deckard was a kid and used to come to Smithy's for haircuts, he would get mesmerized by the long tunnels the mirrors made, facing each other on opposite sides of the room. As Walter cut Deckard's hair, he always directed his remarks not to Deckard directly but to the foremost of a hundred diminishing Deckards in the mirror. This memory is as concrete to Deckard now as the wonderful smells of the place — pomade and menthol and talcum — a place that smells good like no other.

"Been fishing, I see," Walter says to Harry. "Catch anything?"

"A couple," says Harry, never one to brag.

"Did you hear about the woman," Walter says to Harry, "who was supposed to meet a man named Harry in a train station? She's never met this man before, you see, so she walks up to the wrong man and says to him, 'Excuse me, sir, but are you Harry?' and the man looks at her and says, 'Not very.' "

Gales of laughter all round the room. You would've thought it was the funniest thing any of them had ever heard. Walter's eyes brim with tears of mirth as he holds his scissors over the customer's head, looks down at Harry, and says, "Get it?"

Harry's smiling, but sort of goofily. "Yeah, I get it," he says, and looks at Deckard. Either

192

he's fascinated or wondering what Deckard's got him into, Deckard can't tell which.

"Forty-five minutes, huh?" Deckard says. "I wanted to get Harry a trim this morning, but —"

"I tell you what," Walter says. "Mr. Mason over there's next, but as you can see Mr. Mason's not in any big hurry. If neither of these other gentlemen object, I can do Harry next, in Mr. Mason's place, and let Mr. Mason catch up on his zees. How would that be?"

The other gentlemen hurriedly say it's perfectly all right with them, and the man in Walter's chair even offers to get up and let Walter do Harry right that minute. Deckard has the distinct impression that hanging out at Smithy's on Saturday morning is what everybody's into, and nobody's especially eager to be done and have to leave. When he looks down at Harry, to say, "What about it?" he sees that Harry's got that same goofy smile on his face as before, and now Harry's fixated on Benny's serious case of the shakes.

Unnoticed by Deckard till this moment, the music on the radio has changed to Jerry Lee Lewis and "Whole Lotta Shakin' Goin' On," just the kind of thing that Harry *would* notice and that would amuse him.

Once again, Deckard experiences that

other weird feeling he has been getting a lot lately — of having forgotten something. He instinctively pats his pockets for his keys and his wallet, notes that he's wearing his waist pouch, and then looks at the big clock over the door to the street. "Well, what about it, Harry?" he says. "We might still be a little late to the game."

Harry seems to be listening to the music.

Deckard says again, "What do you think, Harry?"

Harry looks up at him, right dead into his eyes, and there's something very poignant about it, this little white boy standing there on the green linoleum floor among these kind old black men, this deep tragic thing about him, unknown by any of them, and that — nothing having escaped him here: the music, the sweet smells, the trick mirrors, the cranky good humor — he's able to give himself so freely, so soon, to the cheerfulness of the place and time. Why, Deckard asks himself, is this so heartbreaking?

"That's fine," Harry says to him, shrugging. "That'll be fine."

"What are those?" she asks, looking down at the two blue oblong pills in Fritz Durgin's palm.

"Butalbital," he says. "For my famous

194

headaches, but perfect for what you've got too. They won't make you fuzzy. They just make the pain go away."

"I'm glad they won't make me fuzzy," she says.

"Oh, what do I mean?" he says, embarrassed. "Foggy . . . groggy . . . you know."

She allows him to drop the pills into her hand.

"Take a pill," she says. "Why didn't I think of that? I could've saved myself a lot of trouble."

"Pills don't work for everything," Fritz says. "I'll get you some water."

He reaches for a blue coffee cup that's sitting on her desk.

"You better check that for tissue growth," she says.

Fritz pauses, gazes down into the cup as if he has taken her seriously, then steps into the hallway and turns toward the water cooler.

Fritz Durgin, head of the department, was the last person she expected to find in the building on a Saturday. A year ago, he'd acquired a new wife — the old one had died four years earlier, after a long siege of uterine cancer — and Sarah believed that the new wife, half Fritz's age, had made him take a pledge about preserving weekends exclusively for her. Once recently, when Sarah was think-

195

ing about the eventual inevitable return to work, she'd thought about Fritz and his having lost his wife. She'd wondered if he would want to commiserate, and she hadn't liked the feeling it gave her. She'd hoped he wouldn't draw comparisons, and then, in her own mind, she'd begun doing just that — or drawing contrasts, really: Betty Durgin had been in her sixties when she died; she'd been sick for a number of years; she and Fritz had raised two children and attended both their children's weddings. Altogether a different story.

Minutes earlier, when the jangle of Sarah's keys brought Fritz out of his own office, he greeted her with a kind of paternal affection that she hadn't known he possessed. They'd worked alongside each other for twelve years, and though she was fond of him, she was fond of him from a professional distance; she couldn't recall ever even having shaken his hand, though she supposed she must have, once or twice. In the hallway, she'd gotten the office door open and dropped her keys to the floor, and suddenly there was Fritz, retrieving the keys, speaking her name softly, and embracing her with a surprising lack of clumsiness. So unclumsy, in fact, so apparently genuine, that when he whispered, "I'm glad to see you," she'd begun to cry. And even her tears didn't seem to throw him. He held on for just a few seconds longer, then guided her into the office, put her in her desk chair, opened the office window a crack, and turned to face her. He appeared to take her in, at her desk, where evidently he thought she belonged. "There," he said, quite satisfied.

"Oh, Christ," she said, pulling open a drawer of the desk. "I think I have a box of tissues here somewhere."

She found them, blew her nose, said, "For my *students*," and began to cry all over again.

Fritz, tall and gray, wore a pair of comical-looking fur slippers, most likely a present from the new wife, something the new wife would have deemed professorial. He leaned against the windowsill and remained silent, smiling sadly. There were extreme roses in his cheeks, and for a moment Sarah thought he looked chiseled from wood, painted with tempera paints, and stood-up near the corner of the room in storage.

"I'm not even crying about Malcolm," she said at last, "or not exactly, anyway," and then she told him about the pain between her shoulder blades and the futile visit to the chiropractor.

Mostly, Fritz shook his head intermittently throughout. When Sarah reached the end of the tale, he dug into the pocket of his corduroys and produced the two blue pills.

Now he returns from the water cooler, passes her the cup of water, and says, "Swallow these and let me drive you home."

"Home?" she says. "I just got here."

He shrugs his shoulders and holds out his hands, palms upward. "You're in pain," he says. "It's not the best time to undertake — well, there's no reason you have to do all this today."

This is an odd response, Sarah thinks, after weeks of his wanting her to return to work, after weeks of disappointment that she wasn't returning sooner. And what does he mean, All this?

The pills are already in her mouth and it seems she must swallow them, but as she does she suddenly imagines that Fritz has drugged her; innocently, she has mistaken his warm welcome; innocently, she thought he was glad to see her returning to work at last, when clearly something else is behind his warmth. She manages to smile and say thank you, and then she's furious at herself for having cried, for having let him see her cry.

"I'm here now, Fritz," she says. "I want to make a start, at least."

He peers down at her from his considerable height, unmoving, obviously at a loss. Finally he says, "Well, why don't you come down to my office, then, and we can have a talk."

"I see you have something official to tell me," she says. "It's all right, Fritz. You can tell me here. Would you like to sit down? There's a chair."

"Sarah," he says wearily. "Please don't —"

He pulls a wooden chair away from the bookshelves and sits. Now he looks miserable, rather crumpled into the chair, a heap of odd angles, a cubist sculpture gone wrong.

"Don't what?" she asks.

"I don't know what I was going to say," he says. "It's just that you and I need to talk about what your expectations are now, and I didn't think this morning — right now — I didn't think it was the best time. Especially considering —"

"My expectations?" she says.

"We didn't know when you'd be coming back," he says. "You haven't exactly been clear on the subject."

"So you gave away my class," she says. "That's what you're trying to say."

"Of course," he says. "We had to. After two weeks I asked Barry to take it."

"That was nice of Barry," she says.

He looks at her as if to discern whether or not she's being ironic.

"No, Fritz, I mean it," she says quickly. "I myself didn't know when I would be coming back, which is why I couldn't be clear on the subject. You did the right thing. And anyway, I'm going to have my hands full getting everything started again in the lab."

"That's the thing I wanted to —" He stops himself, prompted most likely by some additional light of recognition in her eyes.

"What?" she says. "Tell me."

"I didn't know when you were coming *back*," he says, nearly pleading. "You know what kind of commodity lab space is. You know how many people — well, it's not like I can just hang up a sign and nobody will ask any questions. There's a dollar value to consider, too, Sarah, as cold as that may sound."

"Who've you put in there?" she asks.

"You don't know her," he says.

Sarah notes the bizarre tone the conversation has taken, an errant husband confessing an extramarital affair.

"She's from La Jolla," Fritz adds. "She's got a reaction going, she's established a relationship with your two grad students, and I can't very well —"

"She's growing cartilage," Sarah says. "She's doing my work, using my lab and my equipment."

"I didn't know when you would be back," he says again.

"Equipment bought with my grant money."

"You didn't seem to want to talk about it."

The venetian blind over the tall window blows a few inches into the room and rattles back into place. Sarah hears herself say, "I still don't want to talk about it, Fritz," and she's aware that she probably sounds indignant, while that's not at all how she feels. Maybe the pills are already kicking in, she thinks, for she notices that she's taking an odd mischievous pleasure in the anguish on Fritz's face. "I still don't want to talk about it," would be such a keen parting shot; she could leave him there with it in his student's chair, having taught him a good lesson. But that's not how she feels. She feels, of course, inevitably, like crying — tedious beyond words — but tears now would be macabre, misinterpreted, and nearly malicious under the circumstances. She smiles down at Fritz's feet. "I like your slippers," she says.

"Sarah," he says. "Let me drive you home. Let's get together on Monday and talk things over."

"I do think I'd like to go home," she says. "But I don't want you to drive me."

"Sarah," he says. "I'm sorry. Let me —"

"I'm not angry at you, Fritz," she says. "I'm just thinking that a walk along the river would be pleasant. I can walk a bit, then get a bus."

"Are you sure?" he asks, relief already creeping into his eyes.

Out her office window, she can actually see a small piece of the river and three or four Canada geese grazing on the nearer greening bank. She imagines herself strolling along the river, pausing for a moment to observe a scuffle among a flock of the geese. She sits for a moment gazing out the window and recalls reading somewhere that these flocks grow larger every year. A glance at Fritz's face tells her she should probably explain that her mind has wandered to Canada geese, but it feels like too great an effort. She decides to let Fritz think whatever he thinks, she'll let all people everywhere think whatever they think, and she says, aloud, "Do you know how we came to get all these Canada geese?"

"No, Sarah," Fritz says, standing as if to leave, but then hesitating in the doorway. "Tell me."

"Originally, these geese were migratory," she says. "But hunters began capturing some of them and keeping them to use as decoys. In the spring, they'd put the geese out on leashes, around lakes and ponds. When the wild migrating birds flew over, they would see the decoys and land, and the hunters would shoot them and sell them at market. Then, in the 1930s, when that practice was outlawed, the market hunters released all their decoys into the wild — these geese that had basically had the migratory urge bred out of them, you see. So that was the origin of this huge population of geese who stay here year-round. About sixty-five-thousand strong."

She can tell that Fritz really wants to be safely down the hall now, behind his own office door.

"I'll ask you one more time," he says. "You're sure you don't want me to drive you home?"

"I'm sure," she says. "Thank you."

"Call me on Monday," he says, but doesn't wait for her reply.

She listens to the sibilant, slippered sound of his footsteps receding in the empty corridor and thinks of how Malcolm frequently used to invent reasons to meet her at school. Apart from wanting to see her, he liked visiting the magnificent buildings. He would never agree to meet her anywhere outside, he always insisted on coming to the office, and as they walked together down one of the massive corridors he would invariably gaze up at the high ceilings, awed by the sheer scale of things. The top three or four feet of the corridors were now occupied by the exposed pipes of elaborate sprinkler systems, vast air-conditioning ducts, and the thousands of wires, laid into metal ramps, that conducted the mosaic communications of a scientific institute. Once, walking with her through one of these corridors and gazing upward, Malcolm had remarked with wonder, "Pathways within pathways," and then began to delineate the organization of wings like massive shafts within the larger architectural form, the long echoing corridors inside the wings, the suspended metal ramps that held the thousands of tubes and wires, the smaller bundles of copper and plastic filament within their various jackets, carrying electric charges and light. Sarah pulls open the desk drawer and replaces the box of tissues in its snug corner, thinking how very satisfying it would be to tell Malcolm of her encounter this morning with Fritz Durgin. Malcolm would have appreciated its nuances, the ironies within the anxieties brought to so small a turn inside such a huge event.

Deckard thought to say, Your mother's gonna kill me, but he caught himself in time. He says, instead, "What do you think your mother's gonna say?"

They are standing on the sidewalk outside a sub shop, a few blocks from Smithy's. The sky has begun to cloud up, which seems, to Deckard, to mirror the darkening progress of the day.

"I don't know," says Harry. "Do you think she'll be mad?"

"I hope not," he says. "Let's go inside."

"Wait," says Harry.

"What?"

"We're getting pizza, right?"

"Yeah," says Deckard. "It's vegetarian."

Harry nods and follows him inside the shop.

After they've got their slices and Cokes and found a booth by the plate-glass window next to the street, Harry looks at him and says, "Stop staring at me."

"Sorry," says Deckard. "I guess I'm just worried about your mom. I mean I think it looks good, but I'm worried about what she's gonna think."

"You're making me worried," says Harry.

"Sorry," says Deckard. "Anyway, what's done is done, right?"

"It's not like I got hurt or something. It's just my hair."

"That's right," says Deckard. "It'll grow."

"I don't want it to grow," says Harry. "I like it."

"Okay," says Deckard. "I'm glad you like it."

"It's cool," says Harry.

"That's right," Deckard says. "Very cool."

Deckard distinctly remembers telling Walter to give the boy a *trim*. He said, "Just give him a trim," then settled down with a *Field &*

Stream for about three minutes, and the next thing he knew Walter was spinning Harry around in the chair for Deckard's inspection and approval. The old fool had buzzed Harry's head practically down to the skin, grunt style; the white stick of a lollipop stuck out of one side of Harry's mouth, he was grinning ear to ear, and Deckard thought he looked like a young sci-fi humanoid, drunk on Earth's atmosphere.

As they eat in silence — Deckard scarfing down his slice, Harry pulling bits of melted cheese off and slipping them into his mouth experimentally — Deckard feels himself sliding into a funk about the wayward tack the day with Harry seems to have taken. The fishing was a bust — a partial bust, anyway — the spontaneous haircut, though sorely needed, was only going to get them both into hot water with Sarah, they were going to be late for the soccer game, and the sky was starting to look like rain. He supposes he'd imagined that Harry might actually enjoy himself, that maybe at least one item on the agenda might shake that good-little-soldier dutifulness out of him. He notices the irritating way Harry's picking at his pizza, and despite the earlier resolution to the contrary, he feels his anger at Sarah welling up again. It's clear to Deckard what's happening to Harry: Sarah's struggle is so big it fills the house, and there's no room for Harry to have a struggle of his own. Deckard, at first surprised by the readiness of this analysis, suddenly feels himself tugged in a direction he'd rather not go, down the dirt road that leads to the junkyard where his own father, the elder Mr. Jones, presides. He looks across the table at Harry, thinking of his own father — not as the Mr. Jones rotted in a casket in Sacred Heart Cemetery but as the living, breathing beast that raged from sunup to sundown and thereby commanded the devotion of everybody around him. He imagines himself saying to Harry, I know what it's like not to have any room in your own house, but he says, instead, "What's the matter, Harry, you don't like the pizza?"

"No," says Harry, "I do like it."

"Not much appetite?"

Harry shrugs, then looks at Deckard and squints, as if he's trying to read something written on his face.

"What?" says Deckard.

Harry looks down at the pizza on his plate, and Deckard notices how, with pieces of cheese pulled away, it appears to be a relief map, bumpy yellow continents, red seas.

Without any direct premeditation, Deckard says, "Harry, my man, are you feeling sad today?" And he waits, thinking maybe he's opened a door, and if he just leaves it open for a minute something might come through.

But after another few seconds Harry looks up at him, squints again, and says, "Do we really have to go to the game?"

"No," says Deckard. "Not if you don't want to."

"Did you already pay for the tickets?"

"No."

"So it wouldn't be bad if we skipped it?"

"No, Harry, it wouldn't be bad. What's the matter, though? Tell me what's on your mind."

Just then, untriggered by anything visible, Deckard's fishing rod, which is propped up against the back of the booth, slides out onto the floor. He bends to retrieve it, and when he's got it back in place and turns to face Harry again, the boy is staring out the plate-glass window at something in the street. Deckard follows his gaze but sees only the regular flow of traffic, a city bus, the usual assortment of people walking by on the sidewalk. A scruffy-looking teenager is busy locking his bike to a telephone pole outside the sub shop. Nothing special.

At last, he says, "What are you looking at?"

"Nothing," says Harry, facing forward.

"You want to go to a movie?"

"Do you?"

"Harry," says Deckard. "This is supposed to be your day. We do what you want."

"I kind of don't know what I want," says Harry.

Deckard pauses for a second to admire the directness of this statement of Harry's. It definitely conflicts with a military (and to some extent civilian) concept of masculinity, not knowing what you want, but Deckard now thinks there's something manly about saying you don't know, right out front. "Well, let me think," he says. "We fished. We barbered. We ate. It's clouding up, looks like it might rain. What about we go over to my place?"

"Okay," says Harry, "but what for?"

"I could show you all my cool stuff."

"Okay," he says again.

"Watch TV."

This time he just nods, wide-eyed, alien-like, making Deckard think, again, that Sarah's going to kill him when she sees Harry's haircut.

The alarm sounds on Deckard's wristwatch. He shuts it off, resets it, then digs into his waist pouch for his plastic medicine keeper. He gets it out, opens the little door marked s for Saturday, and shakes out three pills into his palm.

"What are those?" asks Harry.

"Pills," says Deckard.

"Duh," says Harry. "What are they for?"

Deckard opens his palm and points to each pill, one at a time. "Blood pressure. Arthritis. Indigestion."

"Oh," says Harry.

"Sad, ain't it," says Deckard.

With complete sincerity, Harry looks at him and nods.

Deckard knocks back the pills with a gulp from his Coke can, and after a pause, he says, "Now tell me the honest truth. What do you think the mother's gonna say when she sees the boy's haircut?"

The mother had fully intended to walk along the river for a while before catching a bus home, but despite Fritz Durgin's promise that the pills wouldn't make her fuzzy, foggy, or groggy, she'd begun to feel very sleepy — too sleepy to think, too sleepy to sort out the day so far, too sleepy to stay awake — so she got herself home as quickly as possible.

As she inserts the key into the lock, she notices that indeed the pain in her back has drifted to sea, barely visible now, a tiny boat bobbing on the horizon. Inside, she climbs the stairs to the bedroom, kicks off her shoes, and gets into the bed. Vaguely, she thinks she should get undressed, but happily the thought of doing it seems adequate enough. She burrows down under the covers, turning onto her stomach, and pushes aside the pillows, making herself very flat on the bed; she thinks that with a very little effort she could will herself two-dimensional, liquid, perhaps even pass through the weave of the sheet and permeate the cotton batting of the mattress. Who would she be then? The woman who lived inside the mattress, the lorn, crotchety spirit rusting the coils; the woman who felt so sad that she *actually* dissolved into tears. It occurs to her in a mildly unpleasant way that she's hiding now, both physically and mentally, and that hiding is a bad thing, and she resolves not to hide anymore after this final major episode. Slowly, one languishing sound wave at a time, the very quiet house grows even quieter.

The mother, the father, and the boy are walking along the beach near the beloved summer house. It is a splendid day, long, tranquil, and full of color. The mother is thinking about a tiny boat she can see bobbing on the horizon — it has some painful connection for her, but the connection refuses to develop. Suddenly, the father, in a burst of youthful energy, trots ahead, over the dune between the beach and the public parking lot. The mother can think of no reason why he would do this, since the house is only a three-minute walk from the beach and surely they've not brought the car. She reaches for the boy's hand, and they climb the dune together.

The parking lot comes into view, bewilderingly empty save one car, an old white Corvair. The mother recognizes it as a car her husband has told her about, a car he owned as a young man. The car is there, but the father, her husband, has disappeared.

A man, not the father, sits behind the steering wheel of the Corvair. Perhaps he is sleeping. Nearby, an enormous puddle of rainwater reflects the sky. The mother grips the boy's hand tighter as they approach the window of the car. She says to the man, "Excuse me, sir, but have you seen my husband?"

The man in the car turns, his face egg-shaped, neon white, no eyes, no nose — only a perfectly round hole for a mouth, from which a glossy pink tongue suddenly protrudes and clucks out an unbearably loud report of a pistol.

As always, she wakes with a start, but this time she goes immediately back to sleep.

And dreams again.

The streets are dark and shiny, quiet, cold in a silvery sheen left by a recent rain shower.

Harry's face changes from green to yellow to red. Malcolm, bright white in the headlights, has somehow lost his good hat. Slumped against the tire, holding his head in her lap, she struggles with the buttons to his overcoat, wanting to keep him warm. At last, help arrives, decidedly American, weirdly patriotic, a bizarre Fourth of July celebration, a flurry of whirling red, white, and blue lights. Malcolm is moved onto a spine board, slid into the back of an ambulance, and sped away.

In the back seat of a squad car, she faints on the way to the hospital, but during the few seconds of unconsciousness she is aware of everything — the squad car coming to a stop, the door opening, the young policeman guiding her head down to her knees, Harry pounding her with his fists and shouting for her to wake up. She wants to explain to Harry that fainting is involuntary, a short-circuiting of the system over which she has no control, but she fully understands his panic and knows that somewhere off in the future he will forgive her.

At the hospital, the automatic doors make a strange expiring sound as they slide open and shut. Forrest Sanders, a detective, a Catholic, a nonalcoholic, is very kind to Harry. A young Latino intern with gold earrings comforts

Harry in the hallway. Deckard arrives, and Sanders assures her that both he and Mr. Jones will help her. Soon Sanders escorts her to the room where the beautiful Dr. Ives greets her with a warm embrace. The doctor seems to have been through an ordeal, and after releasing Sarah she dabs sweat from her own brow with a sterile gauze pad and says something about a trick knee. Behind the doctor, on a counter, there is a red plastic box with the word SHARPS written on it.

Dr. Ives takes both the mother's hands, clasps them firmly, and tells her to listen carefully. The woman looks into her eyes and tells her that they've had a very close call but that the husband has pulled through the surgery and is going to be okay.

In the long white corridor, everyone is smiling — Sanders, Deckard, Harry, the young intern, and two identical nurses in green scrubs. Deckard, who holds Harry in his arms, now sets him down. She hears herself softly whispering, He didn't die he didn't die he didn't die, and as Harry runs toward her she stoops to catch him.

When, through Fritz Durgin, Sarah became involved in tissue engineering research, Malcolm began calling her — at home, usually in bed — Dr. Frankenstein. He pretended for a while that the idea of growing human organs in a lab was only gruesome. He had a regular field day with the fact that a whole acre of human skin could be grown from the discarded "by-product" of one circumcision. "How are things at the la*bor*atory?" became his standard greeting, moaned out in the gravelly bass tones of an ogre. But when he came to understand the chemical engineer's role in the research — to develop ultrapure biodegradable polymers suitable as scaffolds on which cells could grow — he began to propose what he called "spin-off industries." If these polymers could be molded into scaffolding beds in the shapes of the desired organs, and then the appropriate cells seeded onto the scaffolding, where they would grow and become the new organ, why couldn't you grow just about anything using the same methods? If you could grow your own skin and bones and heart valves and livers and pancreases, why couldn't you grow your own *house?* You simply fashion the frame of, say, a three-story Victorian, using lightweight degradable plastics, you seed the frame with, say, oak cells, give the thing the necessary nutrients, sit back, and watch it grow. No hammer, no nails, no hungover carpenters calling in sick.

Sarah explained that engineering tissue was about studying the human body, learning from the body how the body does what it does and then mimicking those processes under artificial conditions. Fundamentally, growing human tissue in a lab was about harvesting cells and then tricking them into thinking they're in vivo — still in the body. The cells were already coded by nature to do their appointed task; the scientists just trick them into doing it under different circumstances. As far as she knew, a three-story Victorian was not something found in nature. You could conceivably grow your own oak for lumber, but she believed that was called a forest.

It was a phone call from Fritz Durgin last Monday that prompted Sarah's memories of these past exchanges with Malcolm. Fritz had phoned to see if they might get together to "talk things over." She put him off as gently as possible, told him she believed he had made all the right decisions, reassigning her class and her lab; she understood that there were financial details to be sorted out but he shouldn't worry, she would cooperate fully. It was a relief, having the extra time; he should think of her as returning to full-time status in the fall. Fritz seemed surprised and said it wasn't necessary to wait that long, but she said she wanted the summer free with Harry.

When the conversation was over, she went upstairs and lay down on the bed, resisting an impulse to pull down the shades and darken the room. She had returned from taking Harry to school a few minutes earlier, and she was feeling overwhelmed. The usually knife-like pain between her shoulder blades had ripened into a kind of pulsating lump, the size and hardness of a golf ball, more hot than sharp. The house was silent with Harry gone, and she supposed she should have anticipated this and made a plan for herself the first day without him. She recalled Malcolm's comic routines about tissue engineering, his proposed homegrown Victorian house, his la*bor*atory greeting, and in this cold context — alone in the house, missing Malcolm deeply — she realized how relieved she was about returning to the lab later rather than sooner. Deckard and others had pushed the conventional wisdom about salvation in work, but she'd had some instinct to the contrary. She imagined it had to do with the Frankensteinian nature of the work itself. Not the old familiar danger of science overreaching what should be its natural bounds, the Gothic horror of creating life in a laboratory; not Prometheus punished for bringing fire to man; but in this version a sad, grieving, female Frankenstein piecing together a human, having lost one so dear. Soon she fell asleep and slept most of the morning away.

On Wednesday, Sarah decides that her trouble is in the house itself, in its architecture and in the wood and plaster that compose it. She recalls the way sunlight on the stairs recently affected her, the way it drew and repelled her at once, a moment that had centered on the interesting play of shadows the balusters cast over the treads and risers. She conceives that the whole house presents a parallel problem: She returns to it after every errand with a similar double-edged sickness of heart; it remains standing, and it remains her home (and Harry's), even though an essential element of what made it her home has been rooted out; it has become the place most comforting and most dejecting. She supposes this is true for anyone in a like situation, but surely for her the horns of the thing are sharpened by Malcolm's spirit residing so solidly in the lumber and stone of the place — his loves and choices dwell in the sweet-gum sills and baseboards he scrupulously stripped in the dining room, in the simplicity of the lintel over the front door, in the blue slate tiles of the hearth. What other grieving widow pulls into the driveway of her house thinking Second Empire? Thinking, as she passes between the columns of the porch, abacus, echinus, cincture, astragal, scotia, torus, and plinth? Malcolm, it seems, has left her a wide unorthodox vocabulary for mourning. And there's no solution in moving out of the house, for to move would be to abandon the refuge with the sorrow.

Stuck at the table in the kitchen, where she has sat in a kind of daze since returning home from driving Harry to school, she sees that this vein lends itself to generalization. Almost everything that could be said of the house — about confronting Malcolm's loves and choices in its various details — could be said equally of the world at large, but before she can pursue this grim course, the telephone rings, on the wall just inches from her left ear. Though she expects it to be her mother (phoning to see how she's doing), she decides that even a talk with Enid might rescue her from the bleak drift she's taking at the kitchen table.

Right away, only a few sentences into the conversation, it's as if Enid has been tracking Sarah's thoughts from afar, has smelled the punishing philosophy in them, and has phoned to drive a few points home. She rolls her cannon behind the usual rampart: She too has lost a husband. "This is what you've got to do, Sarah," she says, "and I tell you this from my own direct experience. You've got to get somebody *in*. You make a detailed, thorough list, you take Harry to school, then you go downtown and spend the whole day shopping. Buy yourself something absolutely new, unlike anything from the past. And when you come home at the end of the day, everything's all done."

Enid's recipe for "getting rid of Malcolm's things," a critical step in the journey back to happiness. Rid the house of reminders.

Because of what Sarah was thinking just before the phone rang — about Malcolm's spirit lingering in the lumber and stone — Enid's advice makes her imagine, comically, returning home from a whole day of shopping (also comical) to a house gutted and flayed to its frame and foundation. She laughs out loud, a kind of mistake she has made in every conversation with her mother since the beginning of time. "I'm not laughing at you," she says quickly. "I'm laughing at something you made me think."

"I'm sure I don't quite get the distinction," Enid says. "I've got a matinee today. I should have known better than to call you on a matinee day."

"What do you mean?"

"I mean that you've spoiled my mood, Sarah."

"Don't take it personally," Sarah says. "I have that effect on people."

"You certainly do not," says Enid. "You've always been a perfectly cheerful person — you were raised to be cheerful — and you will be cheerful again."

The idea of raising a child to be cheerful almost makes Sarah laugh again, but she manages to curb it. In Enid's peculiar way, she's trying to pay her a compliment. Sarah says, "Thank you, Mother."

Enid asks for the third or fourth time whether or not Sarah has made an appointment with a grief counselor. She urges her, again, to do so. She asks how Harry is enjoying the Virginia ham.

Sarah doesn't tell her about Harry's recent conversion to vegetarianism.

Soon they break off, more amicably than usual, and in a nearly surreal turn of climate, Sarah feels as if she stumbled into, and escaped without injury from, a scene in her mother's play. Somehow, "You were raised to be cheerful," even without any malapropisms, has the fatuous, aristocratic air of a dowager come down to take the medicinal waters at Bath. It was the duty of the governing class, after all, trained in cheerfulness, to be cheerful. Maybe Sarah's failure to "pull out of it," and to pull out of it *on time,* is a failure of breeding, and Enid takes it as another in a long line of affronts to her own mothering. And yet, oddly enough, Enid's phone call has cheered Sarah. She thinks she has understood something, she has moved forward in some way in her connection to her mother, and she feels some pride in having refused to engage in old battles already fought. No, Father's dying of heart disease at the ripe age of seventy-two doesn't compare with Malcolm's being gunned down in his prime (and in any case Enid wasn't exactly devastated by Father's departure). And no, missing Malcolm's funeral doesn't compare with Sarah's missing the opening of *The Rivals.* And no, getting past her grief won't be found in getting Malcolm's clothes to St. Vincent de Paul's. "You will be cheerful again," proclaimed by Enid with the skilled vocal projection of a veteran trouper, is what Sarah will take away from the conversation, temporarily convinced by the illusion of good theater.

It is only the third day in the house without Harry. She can confess now, if only to herself, that keeping Harry back from school was selfish. She hadn't been ready to let him go, it's that simple, but she thinks she hasn't done him any harm. She hopes she hasn't done him any harm.

Bernice, the queen-sized black woman who heads up the intake desk at the VA, calls Deckard over to her cubicle midmorning.

"Deckard," she says, gazing down through her reading glasses at a stack of pink forms, "did you ever know of any woman with the first name of Jasper?"

"Jasper?" Deckard says. "No, why?"

He's resting an elbow on one of the gray-carpeted partitions that form the entrance to the cubicle, something he suddenly remembers that Bernice doesn't like him to do — she says it loosens the aluminum feet on the partitions and makes them wiggly — so Deckard removes his elbow and stands up straight.

Bernice weighs easily two hundred pounds and wears a jade-and-silver ring on one thumb. Deckard has noticed in the past that she has a habit of bouncing the eraser end of a pencil against her chin when she's thinking. She does this now for about five seconds, then shifts the pink form to the bottom of the stack, jangling the dozen or more silver bracelets she's wearing on each wrist. She quickly peruses another pink form, shifts it to the bottom of the stack, and peruses a third. "What about a woman with the first name of Marcus?" she says at last.

"What is this?" Deckard asks, putting his elbow back where it was before.

Bernice sorts through the stack of pink forms again, pauses at one of them, and says, "What about a woman with the first name of Henry?"

"I repeat," says Deckard. "What is this?"

She looks at him for the first time. "That's three out of twelve from yesterday afternoon," she says. "You've put these clearly male patients down as females, Deckard. Now, have you got females on the brain or something? Do you just automatically make a check mark any time you see the word *female?* Is it like a reflex thing?"

"Let me see those," Deckard says, reaching for the stack of pink forms, which she passes to him. No doubt about it, these are Deckard's forms from yesterday afternoon. It so happened that he had all males yesterday afternoon, and yet he'd registered three of the men as females. He begins to laugh, but he's aware that there's something decidedly nervous about the sound of it.

Bernice gives him a sidelong, impatient look and says, "Go fix 'em, Deckard. This is just the kind of thing that can lead to unwanted confusion."

Deckard says he's sorry and slinks away back to his stool at the front counter. A minute later, there's somebody standing there — even though his NEXT WINDOW sign is still out — and before Deckard looks up he assumes it's a patient and says, "Wait till you're called, please." Then he sees that it's the young intern Dr. French, the tall Denzel look-alike everybody calls Frenchfry, though Deckard, an underling of sorts, does not call him Frenchfry to his face; Deckard would like to call him a lot worse, since the kid drops by the intake desk several times a week just to torment him. "I'm busy, Dr. French," Deckard says, shaking up a bottle of pink corrective fluid.

"So," says Frenchfry, "did you get the Jaguar yet? A roadster like that must be worth a lotta benjamins, no?"

Frenchfry seems to have followed the news accounts of Deckard's connection to Malcolm Vaughn's murder more closely than anyone else at the hospital. Or at least he seems to be the person at the hospital who is most obsessed with the story. During the thick of it, hardly a day went by without his asking Deckard some question about the case, almost as if he were conducting a little investigation of his own. "So, how long did you know this Malcolm person?" he would ask in line at the cafeteria. "So, is that detective still breathing down your neck?" he would ask in the men's room. And sometimes, if the two of them happened to be having lunch at the same time — Frenchfry sitting with other doctors, of course; there were important class lines to be observed — Deckard would look up and find the intern staring at him from thirty feet across the cafeteria.

Throughout, Deckard has made it clear that Frenchfry's questions irritate him, but the kid is apparently undaunted by any manner of cold shoulder. From time to time, Deckard has even thought that it's precisely his irritation that fuels Frenchfry's bizarre behavior, that he doesn't mind getting a rise out of Deckard because even getting a rise out of him is a form of attention. Deckard has therefore tried to play it cool, but the nature of the situation sometimes gets the best of him; though he has never given a direct answer to a single one of Frenchfry's questions, though he has never volunteered one iota of information, Frenchfry has been able to ask the most personal questions imaginable because of what he has read in the newspapers. "So, about how many guns you have altogether?" "Who was this girlfriend you broke up with, did I ever see her at the hospital?" "What kind of drugs were you into anyway?"

Once or twice, Deckard has thought he might hit the kid — and that would, of course, mean his job. And it isn't easy to lodge a complaint against a doctor in the hospital and come away much appreciated by anybody.

This morning, Frenchfry's use of "benjamins" deeply annoys Deckard, as if all black males, regardless of their generation, belong in spirit to the hip-hop culture: Frenchfry, who was born somewhere in the Midwest with a silver spoon in his mouth and had Harvard and every other advantage laid at his feet; Frenchfry, whose own car, though he's got absolutely *nowhere* to go, is well worth more than Malcolm's vintage Jaguar.

Deckard wonders what it would be like to strangle the young Dr. French with the young Dr. French's own stethoscope.

Also, Deckard's feeling a bit touchy on the subject of the Jaguar. After Sarah finally got around to finding the title for the car, Deckard was completely unprepared to take possession of it. First of all, he was nearly floored by the cost of insuring it, but the main problem has been finding a garage he can afford; it wouldn't last a night on the street in his neighborhood. So, though he has taken the roadster out for the occasional spin, Sarah's been kind enough to let him keep it in her garage — which isn't the same as having it to yourself. When you have to take a train to get your car out of somebody else's garage, it doesn't exactly feel like totally yours. More like borrowing.

None of this is any of Frenchfry's god-damned business, of course, and Deckard re-peats, "I'm busy," dabbing a dot of corrective fluid on one of the errant check marks.

"Seriously, though," says Frenchfry. "Any idea what it's worth? You think you could really get fifty thousand for it?"

Deckard stops what he's doing and looks at him. "*Doctor* French," he says. "I bet I'm the only staff person in this whole hospital that you ever have a word for. I'm not talking about nurses and orderlies. I'm talking about administrative. I bet I'm the only one you ever speak to. Now why is that, do you suppose?"

The intern shrugs his shoulders.

"Do you think it's because I'm black and you're black too?"

Frenchfry shrugs his shoulders again.

"You think it's because you have some kind of daddy problem back home in Indiana or wherever it is you come from and you need some African-American companionship or maybe an African-American father figure or some such thing as that?"

"No," says Frenchfry, incredulous but starting to look a bit green around the gills.

"Because," Deckard continues, "I got a hot piece of news for you. You're making a serious mistake here. You're barking up the wrong tree. If you think you can come sticking your big black nose into my personal business, asking me all kinds of questions you don't have a right to be asking, and I won't mind it because I'm a *brothah,* you got another think coming."

"Whoa," says Frenchfry, and suddenly it's clear that he's actually saying this to someone over Deckard's right shoulder.

Deckard turns and sees that Bernice is standing behind him. From the look on her face, she has apparently heard the better parts of his hot piece of news for Dr. French. She scowls at Deckard, as if he's some kind of mystery item she never quite encountered before, and hands him another pink form. "One more," she says, then raises her eyebrows at the intern across the counter and begins walking slowly back to her cubicle, shaking her head. When Deckard looks at Frenchfry, he's surprised to see that the young doctor is watching, with a kind of randy attentiveness, Bernice walk away — which makes Deckard turn back to see what's so intriguing. He sees that below the hem of a calf-length skirt Bernice has quite nicely shaped ankles, and the way she moves is dumbfoundingly graceful, despite her size. Deckard looks again at Frenchfry, who meets his eye for about two seconds, then moves away from the counter with a perplexed, hurt expression on his face. Deckard continues trying to repair the check marks on the pink forms, but his hand is shaking so badly he can't hold the little brush still enough to do the job. He finally shoves the corrective fluid bottle, along with the pink forms, into his drawer, grabs his jacket from underneath the counter, and heads for the vending machines in the employees' lounge. A big part of his problem, he thinks, is that he's just so goddamned thirsty.

Last Sunday, Sarah took Harry shopping in the square for something new to wear his first day back at school. He picked out a black T-shirt with a skull and crossbones on it, which was fated, Sarah thought, for misinterpretation. All she said was, "Are you sure?," then paid the store clerk, and let it go. The skull and crossbones wasn't, for Harry, about death. Like the completely insane haircut Deckard had bought Harry, which made him look like a death-camp survivor, the shirt was about toughness. She understood that. Don't mess with me. She even thought she might buy one for herself. Afterward, they went to the market and bought jams and cheeses and carrots and cereal bars, non-meat items for Harry's lunches.

The next day, Monday morning, she awoke to the alarm clock with no particular dread of anything and got dressed. When she went to Harry's room, she found him completely ready, sitting on his rug, tying his shoes. He'd straightened his room, put away his toys, made his bed, doing his best to make sure everything went according to plan. He looked up at her from the floor and said, "Good morning," his dark eyebrows — more prominent now, in the absence of any hair on his head — turning his greeting into a question: There was still the chance that she would renege, turn despondent, keep him home.

She smiled and thanked him for all he'd done. She was about to cry and moved away quickly; seeing her cry was the last thing Harry needed today. At an earlier time, she'd wanted Harry to understand that tears were natural, even good, and weren't to be feared. But clearly it *did* frighten him when she cried, and though she couldn't hide it from him always, she didn't want to feel, each time she cried, that she was giving him another lesson in the nature and goodness of tears. She thought she should take into account the real effect tears had on him, whether she thought it was the right effect or not. And she was sure that restricting herself to crying alone, not letting Harry actually see the tears, had paved the way to his improved attitude toward her.

In the beginning, in the days following Malcolm's funeral, it had seemed he might stay angry at her forever. That horrible day when he'd overheard her conversation with Deckard, her untimely criticisms of Malcolm, Harry had refused to speak to her afterward, which had been nearly unbearable. When everyone had finally gone home and she and Harry were alone, he'd withdrawn to his room, still without speaking, and closed the door. She'd gone to her own room, undressed, got into the shower, and wept — astonishing, impossible weeping at the end of a long day of weeping. Consciousness-altering weeping, like a drug. Later, in her bathrobe, she went to Harry's room and knocked on the door. When he made no sound, she opened it and found him lying, still wearing his new blue suit, facedown on the bed. She sat beside him and put her hand on his back.

"Sweetheart," she said. "Can't you please try to forgive me?"

Nothing.

"Harry," she said. "Will you please turn over and look at me?"

At first nothing, then he rolled over and looked at her, not pleased with what he saw.

"Sweetheart," she said. "We have to try to help each other now. I'm sorry if what I —"

He interrupted her. "Your breath is bad," he said.

She was sure Harry was right — her breath was bad — and his saying it hurt her so deeply she thought she had never felt so alone in all her life.

Tears welled up in her eyes, and he began to push her away, first with his hands, then with his feet, crying, "Don't . . . don't . . . don't. . . . Don't cry in here. Don't cry in my room!"

She checked her tears and left him. She returned to the bathroom and washed her face. She looked in the medicine chest mirror and thought no wonder Harry wanted her out of his room — she looked like something out of a horror movie, red swollen eyes, red blotches all over her face, bright red nose. Harry's father was dead, and his mother had turned into a disfigured monster who'd recently crawled out of a forest fire. These last few days, she'd not spared him anything, because sparing him was beyond her capacity, and he was furious at her for it. How could she blame him? She wouldn't cry in his room again. This was something — even within her limited capacities — that she could honor.

Down the line, she'd understood that her not crying in Harry's room was the reason he spent so much time there; it was the one really safe place in the house, where his mother's tears were banned. It wasn't a perfect arrangement between them, but it enabled him to stop hating her. He'd gotten things organized in his mind somehow. He needed *her* to be all right. She was aware of his monitoring her and knew his sweet helpfulness was aimed at making sure she was all right. As long as she was all right, he could be all right.

"Don't you think he spends a little too much time in his room?" Deckard would say whenever he came to visit. "Way too much time in there by himself?" And she would try to explain that this was what Harry needed to do — it was the place where he didn't have to think about *her*, the place where he could lose himself in his drawings or playing his solitary games. Deckard also worried about Harry's not watching enough TV, for Christ's sake, but Sarah knew it was virtually impossible, even in cartoons, not to encounter violence on TV, and violence, even the silly orchestrated variety, was now disturbing to Harry. Deckard worried about Harry's being so "good" all the time, but she knew it was all part of a scheme to help her be all right, because that's what Harry needed most. It wasn't a perfect arrangement, but it was what was getting him through. She was doing her best. When she cried, she cried in her room, with the door closed. Because she needed him in the house with her, and needed him not to shut her out entirely, she'd found a way to make herself avoidable.

On Monday, when he was to return to school for the first time and he looked at her from the floor of his room and said, "Good morning," an inquiry in his voice and eyebrows, he wanted assurance that they would get all the way to school, that she wouldn't end up in her room with the door closed, crying. When she thanked him for what he'd done — referring to his being dressed and the tidied room — she included in her own mind his sticking by her these last weeks, seeing her to this point, waiting, with a minimum of complaint, until she was ready.

In the kitchen, she got the breakfast, got the lunch. Maybe, she thought, she hadn't been wrong to wait this long: the old daily routine, the dogged continuation of things, which at first had seemed so brutal, so impossible, now offered some unexpected comfort. The air of earliness in the morning kitchen was reassuring, like the gentle pressure to be on time — after all, there was a bell that would ring at school, and if you had your child in his place in the classroom circle when the bell rang, you knew you'd met one of the world's expectations, and, however remotely, you might begin to think it was a world in which you still belonged.

Being alone in the house on a Wednesday morning is not familiar or welcome. She moves to the stove and puts on the kettle for another cup of tea. She stares at the gas flame, the fluid way it spreads beneath the kettle like the perpetual blooming of a great blue flower. Prompted by Enid's phone call, she thinks of Malcolm's clothes, the shut-tight drawers of his bureau upstairs, the shut-tight door of his closet (a secret passage to dangerous adventure), and she feels her spirits, lifted only moments ago, start to plummet. The pain in her back seems to be spreading outward from its epicenter, up into her shoulders and neck.

Again the phone rings, and she turns and stares at it on the wall. The gritty safari woman inside her head says, Answer it, you fool, and in the short distance from the stove to the telephone, Sarah, always more a follower than a leader, thinks she is leading herself, that a stronger part of her is leading a weaker part, and while this split probably isn't healthy, it's better than nothing. Then she imagines that she will lift the receiver and hear Malcolm's voice. She thinks he might tell her what to do with the rest of the day, how to proceed from this strange lost moment forward. But then, immediately, she thinks it won't be necessary for him to say anything practical; the mere sound of his voice will suffice.

People have been known to come back, she thinks — simply because they have to, if only briefly. It's not science, definitely not science, but she has heard of such things happening in stories.

Deckard lets the phone ring about five times, thinking, Pick up the phone, Sarah, I know you're there. He's using the pay phone in the employees' lounge in the basement of the hospital, where a half dozen people are sitting drinking coffee at little round tables near the vending machines. He's about to hang up when he hears Sarah's voice — which, incidentally, doesn't sound especially steady as she says hello. He asks her if she's doing okay, and though she says she's doing fine, her voice sounds even shakier, and it occurs to him to put aside what he's actually calling for and pretend he just wants to see how she's doing, but this makes him resentful that he could be manipulated by her tone of voice, so he proceeds with Plan A. "The reason I'm calling," he says, "is that I was just really mean to this guy upstairs, one of the doctors here, and right afterward I felt like I wanted a drink, which is always a bad sign, and I think maybe it has something to do with you."

"What on earth do you mean, Deck?" she says, her voice now gone very flat.

"I don't know what I mean," he says. "It's just that it feels like everybody's busting my balls so far today and it's not even lunchtime, and on my way down to the Coke machine, I realized I was wondering why you hadn't called me all week."

"You're saying you're angry at me because I haven't called you all week?"

"Yeah," he says, already starting to feel foolish and petty.

"It's only Wednesday, Deck," she says.

"I know it's only Wednesday," he says. "But I also know Harry went back to school on Monday. I kind of thought you might call to tell me how it went. How it's going."

"So you're angry because I haven't called you to tell you how Harry's doing back at school," she says, in this exaggeratedly bewildered tone.

"Yeah," he says, trying to keep his own voice very even. "Is that as stupid as you're making it sound?"

She starts to say she's sorry, she didn't mean to make it sound stupid, but then, out of the blue, she's crying. Now of course he has to say *he's* sorry for making her cry, and he thinks, Nothing like tears to turn things around — but despite this speck of irritation he realizes that he really is sorry.

"No, no," she says quickly. "It's not your fault, Deck. I think I'm just trying to get used to being here alone, without Harry, you know, without Malcolm, without Malcolm and without Harry."

"Well, still," he says, "I didn't mean to —"

"I got some silly notion in my mind," she says, "that I was going to answer the phone and it was going to be Malcolm."

"Oh, Jesus," he says.

"I *know*," she says. "*Me,* of all people, the scientist."

She starts to laugh, which makes Deckard cringe, fearing she's going to be hysterical. Then, just as abruptly, it seems she's okay, perfectly composed.

"Harry's doing really well at school," she says. "At least I think he's doing really well. It's hard to get anything definite out of him, you know."

"Look, Sarah," he says, "I didn't mean to upset you. You don't have to talk about Harry or anything else."

"You didn't upset me, Deck. I'm upset. Period. You know that. Nobody does it to me. It's just the way I am right now. I'm sorry it's the way I am. I don't want it to be the way I am, but I don't seem to be able to change it. It's not anybody's fault."

"What about that freak in the white Corvair?" Deckard says, without thinking. "I guess you could lay some blame at his door. I mean, if anybody knew where the fuckhead is."

There's only silence from the other end, and Deckard thinks he's said the worst possible thing he could have said. To his amazement, he realizes that this is the first time either of them has mentioned Malcolm's murderer in any conversation outside a police station.

"It's just so abstract, Deck," she says at last. "When I think of it, I can't *see* anything. It's just a silhouette in an old car at night. A kid with long hair. I see little round taillights moving away down a dark road. There's nothing to hold on to. It's like something in a dream, something that evaporated before you could even tell what it was. It's like I dreamt Malcolm was shot and killed, and when I woke up I was really standing in a cemetery. Do you know what I mean?"

At first he thinks he hasn't a clue what she means, but then the image of that kid from Johnson City suddenly crosses his mind, the kid in Nam who gutted his own skull with an M125 pop-up. He thinks he has been dreaming about that kid, all these years later, but he doesn't exactly remember the dreams, and now he can't think for sure whether he actually saw this kid off himself in the mud under his hooch or if he has only seen it in his mind, from having been told of the incident. "Abstract I understand," he says to Sarah. "Is there anything I can do?"

There's another considerable silence, but somehow he can tell that she's seriously contemplating his question. Finally, she says, "Yes, Deck, there is. You could come to dinner tonight. Maybe Harry will tell *you* how things are going at school."

"Don't cook," he says. "I'll pick up some Indian food."

Unfortunately, this makes her start to cry again, and he knows he needs to be able to let her cry — as if his letting her had anything to do with whether she did it or not — but he can't help himself. It drives him crazy. Through her tears, she describes a not-too-spicy vegetarian dish that Harry likes from the

241

Indian restaurant. They agree on a time for dinner, Deckard tells her somebody's waiting to use the pay phone, says a quick good-bye, and hangs up. He turns back toward the employees' lounge, feeling weirdly unsettled, vaguely ashamed of himself for being pissed at Sarah to begin with — more specifically, for letting her know he was pissed — and now there's even one more humiliation waiting right behind him: the beautiful young blonde who recently took over the day shift upstairs at the information booth is sitting at a nearby table, close to the telephone, and it's clear she heard Deckard say that somebody was waiting to use the pay phone when actually there wasn't. Deckard hasn't yet so much as learned this young woman's name — though he has admired her seemingly endless parade of lightweight sweaters in a variety of pastel shades with shiny white buttons down the front, and the way she sometimes plays with the gold cross on a chain around her neck when she's answering a question — and now she gives him the honey-flavored dismissive look of a girl who would never in her life ever tell a lie, but even if she did tell a little tiny one on very rare occasions, she certainly hopes she won't still be doing it when she's his age.

At around eleven-thirty, a short time after

her talk with Deckard, the front bell rings, and when Sarah opens the door she sees what at first appears to be an apparition: the sun is very bright in the yard, and against this blazing backdrop Detective Forrest Sanders stands on the porch next to Antonia, the Brazilian woman who has come to clean the house. Sarah has forgotten that Antonia was coming today, but because she's very fond of Antonia, it's pleasant to find her on the porch. Finding her with Sanders, however, is bizarre, confusing, weirdly alarming.

Sanders, in his naturally charming and helpful way, says, "We got here at the same time."

"Oh," says Sarah, and greets Antonia, who further dazes her with a huge hug in the doorway.

"I have missed you," says Antonia. "I have kept you here," she adds, touching her own heart with her index finger, "and in my prayers."

Sarah thanks Antonia, who moves into the house, and Sanders says, "I don't really need to come in. I was in the neighborhood, you see, and I just stopped by to — well, how are you doing?"

"Come in," says Sarah. "I'll give you some tea if you like."

"No, thanks, really."

"All right," Sarah says. "If you won't

come in, I'll come out."

As she moves toward the stoop, she notices that all the tulip and narcissus bulbs planted in the borders of the front sidewalk are pushing up through last year's mulch and the fir branches that Malcolm laid out in January. He sawed off the branches of the Christmas tree, as he did every year, and laid them flat over the beds, as protection against the hard freezes of winter. Sarah is aware of a painful edge to this observation, but mostly she's taken by the sudden warmth of the sun on the steps, the general brightness of the day, and the surprise in how pleased she is to see Sanders, a man for whom she has had such a jumble of feelings.

They sit side by side on the stoop, and Sarah recalls the throngs of news reporters that used to hang out in the yard, waiting for a glimpse, a word, a chance to snap a picture, and now the grotesque nature of Malcolm's death, the anonymity and senselessness of it, feels connected to the voracious hunger of the reporters. She can't say why exactly, but it seems all of a piece, a symbiosis, a kind of ugly cycle. Sanders has taken off his jacket, which he folds carefully over his lap, and, she sees now, he has put on a pair of dark sunglasses. In the sunlight, his very white shirt appears to be glowing from within.

"I'm all right," she says to him. "Harry went back to school Monday."

"Oh," says Sanders, clearly repressing a mild shock that Harry has returned to school only this recently, and adds, "That's good. Very good. He's a great kid, Harry."

Sarah can see her own reflection in Sanders's sunglasses, two Sarahs looking back at her, and the convexity of the lenses gives her face a severe pulled-back quality, like someone undergoing acceleration stress. She thinks this an apt metaphor — a person in free-fall, a person being blasted off the planet — but at this specific moment that's not at all how she feels. There's something about the outdoors, about the fresh air and sunlight, even about the sudden companionship, though it's with this man who has such a strange connection to her husband's death and for whom she has felt such ambivalence. It occurs to her to tell Sanders that she can see herself in his sunglasses; it occurs to her to tell him that last Saturday afternoon she had a dream in which he figured — the dream in which Malcolm had been shot but survived — and that when, in real life, Deckard brought Harry home and woke her from the dream, when she confronted, as if for the first time, the fact that Malcolm was really dead, she herself wanted to die. She imagines trying to explain to

Sanders what a complicated, inadmissible feeling it is for a mother to want to die when she has a young child who still needs her care; but all she does is to thank him for saying that Harry's a great kid.

Sanders clears his throat, preparing to say what he came to say. "There's going to be a little article in tomorrow's papers," he begins. "I wanted to let you know about it before-hand."

"Okay," she says, "but I don't see the local papers."

"Still," he says, "you might hear about it somehow, and I wanted you to hear about it from me first. Some kids found a gun over by the reservoir. It was buried in the mud in what used to be a ditch . . . or a kind of overflow trench at the reservoir. It's the gun that killed your husband." Sanders holds up his hand, as if to warn her not to take this information and run anywhere with it. "We traced it," he says. "It turns out to be a gun that was reported stolen over a year ago. Licensed originally to a policeman up in Wilmington."

"What kind of idiot steals a gun from a policeman?" Sarah asks.

"I don't know," Sanders says, "and that's sort of the point. So far it's a dead end. We have the weapon, and that's always good, but it basically tells us nothing new. Chances are there wouldn't have been much of anything to take off the gun anyway, after lying around in a ditch for all that time. But the boys who found it cleaned it up pretty thoroughly before they took it home and scared the living daylights out of their mom. Besides, we're already ninety-nine percent sure the prints we took out of the car belong to the perpetrator."

"The ones you haven't found a match for."

"That's right."

"So that's it," says Sarah. "You found the gun. It tells us nothing new."

"I'm afraid so," Sanders says. "Sorry."

"I thought we had microbiology," she says, "DNA, all kinds of new things."

"We do," says Sanders. "If we ever do have a suspect, the other stuff we took from the car will come in handy."

"What other stuff?"

"Hair, mostly. Some of it was dog hair. The original owner of the car had a — I forget — some kinda long-haired dog. But some of the samples were definitely human and didn't belong to the old man in Winchester. Right now we know from the lab that the person who killed your husband was a young Caucasian and most likely male."

"In other words, what Harry and I already told you."

"Right," says Sanders. "And you were right

about another thing. The hair analysis showed traces of PCP."

"PCP?" Sarah says. "Christ, I thought that was a sixties thing."

"It was," says Sanders, "but it's fairly easy to make. And cheap. It still turns up from time to time."

"But this guy — the kid in the car — he didn't seem agitated. He seemed the opposite of agitated. We thought he kept falling asleep behind the wheel."

Sanders shrugged his shoulders. "He could've been mixing it with an opiate," he says. "Or what appeared to be falling asleep to you, from where you were sitting, could've been him getting lost in his — I don't know — the dirt under his fingernails."

"Hallucinating," says Sarah, and, looking out at the cross-hatched patterns of the fir branches in the flower borders, she wonders what that kid conjured up outside his car when Malcolm knocked on the window. Not a thoughtful, compassionate man trying to be helpful, but a cop ready to bust him, his dead grandmother back from the grave, a ragged goat from hell with a plaid hat and burning coals for eyes.

"I'm glad you found the gun," she says. "It's — I don't know — *real*, I guess. Not just something Harry and I made up."

"Nobody ever thought you made it up," Sanders says.

"No, I know, that's not what I mean," she says. "I'm not talking about not being believed. I don't really know what I'm talking about. I'm just glad you found it. I'm glad you told me about it. There's always a chance it might get mentioned at school, so I'll tell Harry."

For the first time during this brief visit, Sanders shakes his head in the old "tough . . . tough" style.

"The case is still open, you know," he says. "These kinds of killings, we call them spontaneous murders, they have a high rate of clearance. Don't think we've closed the case, not by a long shot. We're looking into all the details about the original theft of the weapon, seeing if anything there leads anywhere. So far it hasn't. But try not to give up hope."

Sanders is giving her the only thing he has to offer, and there's no point in telling him what hope has become: a waxy smell in a room where candles have just been blown out.

"I wonder," she says. "Do you ever think the whole world has gone nuts?"

"Every single day," he says, "without exception. But then I think that's why I've got a job, in a way. People like me used to be called peace officers, you know. Keepers of the peace. There was this thing, you see, that really existed, called peace, and it was the job of the peace officer to just take care of it, make sure it didn't get broken. But it doesn't feel like that anymore. Now it's like there's this other thing, insanity or whatever you wanna call it, that you're just always fighting against. You know, holding it at bay. The wolf at the door."

"A minute ago," she says, "I was thinking about the reporters out here on the lawn. I can still see them so clearly. They reminded me of something that occurs in nature when there's a grass fire. Predators swarm around it to prey on the animals that get flushed out of hiding by the flames. I was thinking there's some connection between the hunger of the press and what the world's willing to serve up. That the hunger for scandal and horror is like a beast that must be fed. And the world accommodates it because it has a corresponding hunger for — I don't know what — attention, I guess, fame of any kind, the media shower. . . ."

"Media shower," Sanders says. "I like that. It's like meteor shower. A pun."

She catches herself smiling at him, squinting against the brightness of his dress shirt. "That was an accident," she says. "A slip of the tongue. I didn't mean to —"

"No," he says, "I really like it, the media shower, that's good."

"Are you sure you don't want some tea?" she asks.

"I'm sure," he says. "But I want to say one more thing before I shove off." He pauses, looking down at his knees, choosing his words, she supposes. "I like you," he says at last, and holds up his hands, haltingly, as he did before. "I mean, I like you. Doing my job, I feel like you and me went head to head on a couple of things. You're very smart, you don't need me to tell you that. I probably could've done a few things different — better. I've never worked a case I didn't think could've been worked better . . . you know, with hindsight. Anyway, I want to apologize for giving you any extra grief. Any unnecessary . . . you know, aggravation. It wasn't my intention."

He quickly stands to leave, meaning, she guesses, to flee from such a courageous display of feeling. He reaches for her hand, to shake it, but then, through some subtle exchange of physical data — ants touching antennae — he ends up helping her to her feet. She thanks him but doesn't try to say anything more, for she can feel tears brewing, and she imagines they affect Sanders the way they do Deckard and Harry. In different ways, tears frighten them. But as she stands on the porch and waves and watches Sanders drive away, she begins composing in her mind a note that would send him gratitude for a small concrete desire he gave her this morning on the front steps — that some day she might think back on this hateful journey and recall its being marked by occasional moments of kindness.

In the weeks immediately following Malcolm's death, Deckard missed only two days of work, the Monday right after the shooting and the day of the funeral. But now, following his talk with Sarah on the pay phone in the employees' lounge, he goes back upstairs, returns to Bernice's cubicle, and tells her he's feeling dizzy (which is metaphorically true) and that was probably why he made so many mistakes on the pink forms yesterday, and he thinks he'll take the rest of the day off, go home, get in bed.

"Lean down here and let me feel your head," she says.

Deckard bends forward so she can put her hand on his forehead.

"You don't feel feverish," she says. "You know, Deckard, you're pretty conveniently located for seeing a doctor. Why don't you —"

"No, no," he says, "I don't want to see a doctor. You know I'd just wait around all afternoon for somebody to see me, and after poking and prodding they'd tell me to go home and rest 'cause I might be coming down with something. Which is exactly what I already know."

"Okay," Bernice says. "But if I didn't know better, Deckard, I'd think you were a woman going through menopause."

"Very funny, Bernice," he says. "Do I look like a woman going through menopause to you? Tell me the truth."

She studies him from head to toe for a couple of seconds, over the top of her reading glasses. "Actually," she says, "you look like how a woman *feels* going through menopause."

"I don't know what that means," says Deckard.

"That's because you're not a woman," says Bernice.

"Okay, Bernice," Deckard says. "Can I go home?"

"I think you better," says Bernice. "I think you better."

Because it has turned into such a beautiful day, Deckard worries on the walk home that Bernice might suspect him of playing hooky.

But then, immediately, he thinks he couldn't care less what Bernice suspects or doesn't suspect. Besides, he isn't interested in the beautiful day. Though he doesn't have any real physical symptoms other than a persistent thirst (now happily mutated into an ordinary craving for liquid, not liquor), he feels very strange in his head — *thrown* is the word that comes to mind. Some days simply get off to a poor start, and it's a waste of energy trying to steer them back onto track. Better to change course. He has envisioned the bed in his bedroom, he has envisioned himself in it, and that's his goal.

In the vestibule of the apartment building, he can see through the little filigree grates in the mailboxes that the postman has already come by, so he finds the right key on his ring of keys and opens the box: two pieces of junk mail offering low introductory rates on new credit cards, something from the Southern Poverty Law Center in Alabama (a brave soul, that Morris Dees), a promotional coupon from a new health club, a gun catalog, and a second overdue notice from the public library — Deckard has forgotten, again, to return the book he checked out weeks and weeks ago on the subject of memory and forgetfulness.

Mrs. Rothschild is waiting for him on the top landing. Or, at first, that appears to be what she's doing — she's standing there, looking down the stairs in anticipation of whatever might come up. Right away, though, Deckard can see from her crestfallen face that he is not what she's hoping for. When he reaches the landing and pauses for a moment, towering over her, she gazes up at him and shakes her head, back and forth, hopelessly, without a word.

"What's the problem, Mrs. R.?" Deckard asks.

"No problem," she says, continuing to shake her head and then drifting away back toward her apartment door on a shoreless sea of resignation. "No problem," she repeats, as she closes the door.

Deckard has never seen her looking quite so forlorn, which is saying something, considering that Mrs. Rothschild wrote the book on Forlorn. He stands on the landing for another few seconds staring at her door, and a very odd thing happens in what has felt, from the beginning, to be a very odd day: Deckard's mind seems to do a flip. It's the equivalent, in the brain, of a heart skipping a beat; it's that fleeting and scary, like one instant of free-fall. He turns to his own door, gets it unlocked and open, goes inside the apartment, tossing the mail onto a table in the hallway, and stands looking into his bedroom.

The bed is there, but otherwise, nothing's the way he envisioned it minutes earlier at the hospital, when he decided to go home. For starters, the bed is a mess, unmade and cluttered with junk: a dictionary (though he can't think what word he might have been looking up), some clean but still unfolded laundry (mostly T-shirts, socks, and underwear), and the cardboard box where he keeps old letters and other memorabilia. He does recall a tiny masochistic slip that morning, before leaving for work, in which he brought out a couple of old birthday cards from Lucy, containing particularly tasty messages about everything he meant to her, both cards signed "All my love, always."

Maybe that was what had set the day on its ear. He should have known better. He *did* know better.

Still in the dim hallway, he removes his jacket and unbuckles his waist pouch, dropping both of these to the floor, right where he's standing. Malcolm and Harry smile and wave from their red tractor on the nearby wall. There's some kind of noise inside Deckard's head, a kind of static he has heard before but not for a while. He moves into the living room and collapses onto the couch. As he hunches over to unlace his shoes, the staticky noise clarifies and grows louder.

Ah, it's the angels applauding. They've been silent for a long time, and now here they are again, assembled along the picture moldings, flapping their wings, blowing the cobwebs, and arousing the dust. Deckard first heard them somewhere out in the boonies south of Con Thien. It was a night during monsoon season, and every krait and bamboo viper and all the other poisonous snakes in the whole stinking snake- and leech- and hornet-infested country were engaged in a futile search for a dry warm place. Deckard's company was to be rotated the next morning back into Khe Sanh — in other words, rotated out of hell into the hairy maggot-oozing asshole of hell. Maybe some other people, when they get quiet enough long enough — or when what's left of their mind becomes overloaded to the point of convulsion — hear the voice of God. But that night in the boonies south of Con Thien, squatting in the soggy elephant grass, Deckard signed on as a life member in the Church of What's Happening Now, a denomination that apparently just gets clapping angels.

Later, she'll chastise herself for failing to recognize all the obvious signals, for having brought it up in the car, for not waiting until they got home; she should have waited until she got them home, gave Harry a snack and something to drink, and allowed him to get settled, allowed him to "transition," as his teacher, Julia, was fond of saying. The book Sarah read, long ago, about raising boys, warned against trying to have official talks with them; when you have something to discuss with a boy, you should cloak the conversation as idle chat during another activity. (Girls on the other hand often love nothing more than being sat down for a serious talk.) As she brushes her teeth, preparing for another night of sleeping alone, another night of lying awake for hours unable to sleep, she'll see this minor error in judgment as symbolic of all the larger ones, as a mere emblem for a great collective failure having to do with a selfishness that blinds her to the simplest, most obvious insights.

Outside the school, there is an odd moment. Harry's teacher, Julia, a beautiful Italian woman in her late twenties who is engaged to be married, stands in the schoolyard, as usual, among the children waiting to be picked up. When Harry comes running and climbs into the Jeep, Sarah sees that Julia is watching him rather intently; Julia smiles and waves at Sarah, and then one of the other children grabs Julia's free hand — and her attention — and Julia doesn't see Sarah wave back. It's a small thing, but it leaves Sarah with a feeling that Julia might have come over and said something, had she not been waylaid by the other child.

Harry is out of breath and rosy-cheeked from playing chase. He asks Sarah if they can stop at Vinnie's Spa for a watermelon slush, but Sarah reminds him that there's never anywhere to park around Vinnie's right after school lets out; she says she'll make him a lemonade as soon as they get home. She has grown so accustomed to Harry's being agreeable about everything that it takes her aback when he kicks the dashboard with his sneaker and says he doesn't *like* her lemonade.

"Well, then we'll find something you do like," she says. "And please don't kick the car."

After some silence, during the short ride home, she asks the stupidest question imaginable: "How was school?"

"Good," he says, staring out the open window, not turning to face her.

"Anything special happen?"

"No."

"Do you remember Detective Sanders?" she asks, noting an abrupt edge to her voice but choosing to think the abruptness inherent to the question.

Harry says nothing, and when she looks over at him she sees that he has put a strap from his backpack into his mouth and is chewing on it.

"Harry," she says, "I asked you if you remembered Detective Sanders."

Harry changes modes, deciding, apparently, to deflect everything with silliness. He looks at her with widened eyes, the black strap hanging out of his mouth, and gives her an exaggerated nod.

Still, she goes on. "Well, he stopped by the house today to tell me something I think you should probably know about too. . . . Harry, please be serious so I know you're listening. This is important."

He repeats the wide-eyed nod with the strap in his mouth.

"He wanted us to know that in tomorrow's newspaper there's going to be an article about a gun that some kids found over by the reservoir."

Harry takes the strap out of his mouth and, like somebody imitating a baby's voice in a cartoon, says, "A *gun?* Oh, *my-y-y!*"

"It doesn't affect us in any way," she says. "It doesn't change anything. But the police ran some tests and determined that it's the gun that was used the night Daddy got shot."

"It *was?*" he says. "Oh, *my-y-y!*"

"I can see that you're not going to be serious," Sarah says. "I only wanted you to know about it in case somebody reads the newspaper tomorrow and happens to mention it at school. I didn't want you to be surprised."

"If somebody says somepin about it to me," he says, in the same imitation-baby voice, "I'll waff myself to pieces and den I'll cut my toe on one of da pieces and spurt bwood all over da cwasswoom."

She looks at him.

"Yeah," he adds, "yeah, I *will*."

Of course he has always known the kid's name: Mason Miller from Johnson City, Tennessee. He was the kid who made the joke that Sunday after church services about "Light green and dark green" that made even the major general laugh. That was when little Mason Miller's feet were still planted on American soil. Jokes were uncomplicated on American soil. Later, jokes — and there were plenty of them — became something else, something not quite uncomplicated, hard candy with a soft chewy center of shit, and Mason Miller, terrified from sunup to sundown, wasn't making any.

One morning during the rainy season, they'd been patrolling the boonies south of Con Thien. The boonies south of Con Thien were always nerve-wracking because you were so out in the open. Everybody was a bit

on edge anyway, and then they'd been informed they were to be rotated back into Khe
Sanh the next day. Deckard, along with most
everybody else, had had plenty of dreams of
helicopters gliding down from heaven to lift
them out. But being lifted back into Khe
Sanh was not part of the dream. They'd *done*
Khe Sanh already. They'd slept in the tunnels
with their faces covered so the rats wouldn't
bite their noses. They'd crawled outside on
their bellies and rolled onto their sides to pee
on the ground, because to stand up for any
reason meant being shot. Any time you were
lifted into Khe Sanh and the enemy fire got
going, what did you see? Arms and legs sticking up out of the trenches, good soldiers hoping to take a bullet and get medevacked out —
anything to get the hell out of Khe Sanh. Now
they were going back. Why *us?* Why *us?*

Nobody was exactly thrilled with the news,
but Mason Miller took it especially hard.
He'd learned to live with bamboo vipers,
which tended to like to slither into your
mummy bag for warmth, or drop down onto
your neck from trees, or curl up inside your
boots. They called it the three-step snake, because it bit you, you took three steps, and you
were dead. Like everybody else, Miller had
learned to shake out his boots before putting
them on, but he had a psychotic phobia of

rats, and the idea of returning to Khe Sanh pushed him over the edge.

Nothing was more unsettling than to look over at a buddy and see fear in his eyes; it was like being spit on. In the afternoon, some of the guys, seeing that Miller was over the edge, seeing the fear in his eyes, decided to play a little game of fuck-fuck with him. The big peckerwood they called Doc Sylvester — Doc because he was a navy corpsman, a medic, Sylvester because of a story he was fond of telling about how he once ate the family parakeet, feathers and all, to impress his girlfriend — walked over to Mason Miller and handed him an M26 grenade with the pin pulled out. That was fuck-fuck; you looked down at your hand and it was holding a live high-explosive grenade and nobody was telling you who had the pin. Fuck-fuck was chiefly about the pleasure of watching human personality disintegration. Trouble was, little Mason Miller had less personality left to disintegrate than anybody had imagined. By the time Doc Sylvester showed mercy and produced the pin, Miller was not only over the edge but well into his descent. The fear in his eyes had been replaced with something very private, unreadable.

Deckard hooched up with him that night, and they drank some Jim Beam as the rain pelted the ponchos over their heads. Mason produced a roach from an old fairly rare opiated joint, they smoked it, and Deckard soon nodded off. His having nodded off for a few minutes, under the influence, probably accounted for part of the dreamlike quality of the event he was about to witness. For some reason he woke up — it was as if the whole hooch were vibrating — opened his eyes, and looked over at Miller, who was sitting cross-legged on a rubber bitch, an inflatable mattress, a few feet away. Sweat was pouring off Miller's head, tears were running down his cheeks, and he had his lips wrapped around the open end of a pop-up, which was trembling a little in his hand. Miller looked something like a snake charmer, sitting the way he was with a flutelike instrument protruding from his mouth, and indeed he was gazing, trancelike, down the flare's long cylinder at something: a king cobra had coasted into the hooch and, surprised to find anyone home, had reared up at the base of Miller's mummy bag, his glorious hood spread out, and engaged Miller in a staring contest, which Miller was rapidly losing. Did Deckard say anything? Did he say, You oughtn't to be playing around with that pop-up in your mouth? Did he say, Watch out that snake doesn't spit in your eye? Not sure. Maybe there wasn't time enough to say anything.

What Deckard remembers — and now, nearly thirty years later, he's sure he remembers *seeing* it — is Mason Miller's feet and legs, suddenly stiff, straight out, joggling and jouncing at an inhuman tempo, a ball of green fire where his head was supposed to be. The spasm and the fireworks lasted for quite a long time, and then it was over. Deckard believes that when it was over he said, "Oh . . . wow . . ." and looked over to see if the king cobra had seen what *he'd* just seen. But the cobra had vanished, taking a tale back to the nest that none of the other snakes was going to believe.

Then there's a blank space. Other marines must have come running to the hooch. Stuff must have been done, questions asked. But the next recorded moment — or accessible moment, anyway — is a moment when he was alone, in the dark, in the rain, smoking a cigarette, and though it would have been a physical impossibility, it seems to Deckard that he had his back to Vietnam and everybody in it. That's when he heard the angels applauding for the first time. The sound was a lot like the hissing of the rain in the elephant grass, but very distinct, much more pointed. They weren't approving of him in any way, not praising any specific actions. They were simply giving encouragement to his general existence, the fact of it, attesting to the miracle of the present moment and to the refuge there was to be gleaned from What's Happening Now, as opposed to what just happened a minute ago or what might happen in the next. This was really all they had to say — well, all they had to imply. Don't look back, don't look ahead, it's the only way out of the jungle. Oh, and one more thing, in the category of tidings: that Deckard's adolescent mission in the war, his motive for enlisting — to kill and be killed — would remain only half clinched and he would someday be stateside again, intact, sort of.

It was the closest he'd ever come to anything like a spiritual awakening, and of course when he was again stateside — intact, sort of — he did everything he could to forget everything he could forget, including the applauding angels, their encouragement to his general existence, and whatever glimpse of a spiritual awakening they might have been offering. But when he thought about it, he did have a definite sense that they were usually around, not far away. Now and then he would hear, usually faintly, their sweet ocean-foam static. But today, this little visitation in the living room was vivid, a regular production number. Why do you suppose they were coming around now, hanging out on the picture moldings with such gusto? It was downright vulgar.

Bathed and shaved, dressed in fresh clean khakis and a polo shirt, Deckard pulls on a windbreaker and glances at his wristwatch. He has just enough time to get a train, stop at the Indian restaurant, and walk to Sarah's without being late.

Once again, he finds Mrs. Rothschild lingering on the landing. Once again, he asks her what the problem is. Once again, she shakes her head and says, "No problem, no problem," and drifts back toward her apartment door.

This time, before shutting the door, she says, "I was just hoping Mr. Rothschild would be home for dinner. He's awfully late. He works so hard, you know."

Deckard scratches his head. "Well, why don't you go on inside and wait?" he says. "You can wait inside just as well as you can out here, and in the meantime you could be comfortable."

"You know, Deckard dear, you're absolutely right," says Mrs. Rothschild. "I could be comfortable *while* I'm waiting."

"You got it," Deckard says.

"I could be comfortable," he hears her muttering, as she closes the door.

"Holy smokes," Deckard whispers, starting down the first flight of stairs.

★ ★ ★

Deckard's upstairs visiting with Harry while Harry takes his bath, and though Sarah, downstairs alone, is pleased about this, she feels vaguely disappointed about the evening in general. She is sure that over the course of dinner Deckard sensed a new tension between her and Harry — or maybe she herself sensed it so strongly that she only imagined it to be obvious. For the most part, Harry continued being silly throughout the evening — to which Deckard responded by teasing him and calling him Silly Harry and holding him upside down by the ankles, swinging him from side to side like the pendulum of a grandfather clock. When it came time for Harry's bath, Harry ran out of the living room and into the hall, then reappeared at the doorway, enticing Deckard to chase him. Sarah watched from the couch as Deckard feinted toward the door and sent Harry squealing up the stairs. When Deckard turned back to the room, he caught her frowning — or at least not smiling.

"What's wrong?" he said.

"Nothing," she said, mainly because she couldn't have said what, exactly, was bothering her. It wasn't only Harry, but also Deckard — they both seemed jumpy, distant, and happy at conspiring, through silliness, to stay that way.

Now, when Deckard comes back downstairs, he only pauses in the doorway to the living room and says, "*Hasta la vista.* Gotta go."

She moves to the hallway and finds him pulling on his jacket. She says, "Well?"

Deckard shrugs, shakes his head. "I couldn't really get anything out of him," he says. "School's fine, his teacher's fine, being back is fine. No matter how many specific questions I asked him, he just said everything's fine."

She watches Deckard for a moment as he snaps the buckles on his waist pouch. "Deck," she says, "are you seeing the newspapers these days?"

"Newspapers?" he says. "You mean that crap people use for housebreaking their dogs? That trash written by scumbag lowlifes pandering to the public's addiction for misery and sleaze? Yeah, I see 'em sometimes. Why do you ask?"

"Forrest Sanders stopped by today," she says. "He wanted to tell me that some kids found the gun over near the reservoir."

"The gun?" Deckard says. "Oh, *the* gun. Do they know who it belongs to?"

"No," she says. "It was stolen, of course. It doesn't tell us anything new. Sanders just wanted to let me know that it would be in to-morrow's papers."

"Oh-h-h," says Deckard, "and you must've told Harry. *That's* what that was all about."

"What what was about?" Sarah asks.

"In the bathtub. He was asking me a bunch of questions about guns. Why people have them. Where they get them. Stuff like that."

"I didn't do a very good job of telling him," Sarah says. "He clearly didn't want to hear about it, and I couldn't get him to focus."

"I guess it would be kind of a hard thing to focus on. I mean if you think about it."

"Yes," she says, and it occurs to her that she needs to defend herself, needs to explain that she was afraid somebody might bring it up at school tomorrow, and that she didn't want Harry to be surprised by it. But something about Deckard's face stops her: he appears vaguely troubled — not irritated, which would be more usual — but unhappy, maybe even a little frightened. For some reason, she thinks of an observation Malcolm once made about Deckard's lone-wolf propensities — that he seemed to have few if any close connections to other black people, that it was a particular and surely complicated way of being alone. At last Sarah says, "Are you all right, Deck?"

"What do you mean?" he says.

"I mean are you all right," she says. "Feeling okay."

"Come to think of it," he says, "I left the hospital early today because I was feeling a little dizzy. But I had a nap and felt better."

He looks as if he wants to say more, so she gives him time, but at last he heaves an enormous sigh and says, "Well. Tell Harry I said good-bye."

"No, wait," she says. "He'll want to say good-bye himself."

She calls up the stairs to tell Harry that Deck is leaving, and Harry comes down in his blue wizard's bathrobe with the golden moons and stars.

As she watches Deck stoop to receive Harry's hug and kiss, she thinks that Harry must have gotten something useful out of Deck during the bath, despite Deck's claim of having gotten nothing useful out of Harry.

After she closes the door and latches it, Harry stuns her by reaching for her hand, as if he means for her to come upstairs with him.

She kisses the top of his head.

"Sleepy?" she says.

"Yeah," he says, "but will you read to me?"

"I would love to," she says, and they go up together.

"Sophie," Sarah reads, "*who was also staring into the glass jar, cried out, 'I can see it! There's something in there!'*

" '*Of course there is something in there,' the BFG said. 'You is looking at a frightsome trogglehumper.'*

" '*But you told me dreams were invisible.'*

" '*They is always invisible until they is captured,' the BFG told her. 'After that they is losing a little of their invisibility. We is seeing this one very clearly.'*

"*Inside the jar Sophie could see the faint scarlet outline of something that looked like a mixture between a blob of gas and a bubble of jelly. It was moving violently, thrashing against the sides of the jar and forever changing shape.*

" '*It's wiggling all over the place!' Sophie cried. 'It's fighting to get out! It'll bash itself to bits!'*

" '*The nastier the dream, the angrier it is getting when it is in prison,' the BFG said. 'It is the same as with wild animals. If an animal is very fierce and you is putting it in a cage, it will make a tremendous rumpledumpus. . . .' "*

Sarah stops reading, for she can see that Harry has drifted to sleep. She switches off the lamp and kisses him again on the head.

In her bathroom, as she brushes her teeth, she thinks what a fool she was to have brought up Sanders's news about the gun. Maybe she shouldn't have mentioned it at all, but surely she shouldn't have hit him with it first thing like that, in the car. Sanders's visit, though she felt grateful for his kindness, had left Malcolm's unknown murderer knocking about in her head. She almost never thought of the unknown murderer, for she had discovered early on that there was no comfort to be found down that particular blind alley, only a leaping shadow, and what was the point? She'd been out of sorts when she picked Harry up at school. She'd already decided to tell him about the newspaper article, she knew it would be unpleasant, and she wanted only to get it over with. Selfish. Stupid. Bad mother.

The minute her head hits the pillow, the leaping shadow knocks about in her head again, a brown powdery moth in a jar. She reaches into the drawer of the night table and pops two Benadryl capsules from their little foil card, the last two remaining. It would be good to sleep, good to have the real rest that only sleep can give. It's only the third day with Harry back in school, the third day alone in the house. It's a new challenge for her, just as school must be a new challenge for Harry. Another change, though in both cases it's a return to a form of something that used to be.

More time is needed. More time. Everything is a form of something that used to be, even sleep. You could still call it sleep, for example, though, colored as it is by dreams and periods of wakefulness and semiwakefulness and the boggy wool blanket of Benadryl, it's definitely only a form of something that used to be. There's a certain blessing in turning off the lights and being exhausted at the end of the day by the drudgery of one's own mind. And if you want to see how tired you really are, focus on the labor of your heart, which in its persistence can set the whole bed twitching.

At two-eighteen precisely, she's startled awake by a scream. When she reaches Harry's room, when he sees her appear at the door, he throws himself back down onto the mattress and yanks the covers over his head. "Don't let it in," he cries. "Oh, Mommy, please don't let it in."

Her hand is on his back, but he's wrapped himself tightly in the covers and won't relent.

"It's only a dream, sweetheart," she says. "Harry, wake up, sweetie. It's a bad dream."

Slowly, he goes back to sleep — she can feel his grip loosen — and she's able to free him of the covers. She gets him situated, his head back on the pillow, the bedspread more comfortably across his chest. Then she lies beside him for a while, facing him, stroking the bristly brush that used to be his beautiful hair. She can hear rain slapping against the windows. She closes her eyes for a moment, and when she opens them again she sees that Harry's eyes are wide open; he's staring straight into her face.

"Harry, sweetie," she whispers. "Are you okay?"

He turns his eyes toward the windows and blinks.

"That's just rain, sweetheart," she whispers. "You had a bad dream. Do you remember?"

He closes his eyes again and says nothing, but she can tell that he remembers perfectly, and that he simply won't tell her.

Through the glass panels of the library doors, Deckard sees a beautiful young redhead behind the circulation desk. Friday mornings, he doesn't report to the hospital until noon, and he has come to the library on this Friday morning early in May to confess his truancy regarding the way-overdue book on memory loss — not only has he failed for all these many weeks to return the book but now he can't find it, though it's bound to be somewhere in the apartment. He's cheered to see that he'll be coming clean to so fine a confessor, and in the few seconds it takes to get through the doors and over to the desk, he imagines himself turning on the charm as he recounts his tale of woe, making her laugh at the irony of his having forgotten where he put the book on memory loss, ha-ha.

He judges her to be about thirty, and he notes the tragic little blue ink mark just above her left eyebrow. She looks up from her computer screen and greets him warmly enough but lets him unload only about half a sentence before interrupting. "Hold on a minute," she says. "I don't do lost books. Could you step down there to the end of the counter?"

As Deckard sidles to the spot where she has removed him with such stunning indifference, she goes to a nearby office door, says something to somebody inside, and returns to her previous station, not so much as giving Deckard another glance. There's something menacing now, and insectlike, about the clicking noise her red-painted fingernails make on her computer keyboard.

Soon a sloppy-looking middle-aged bearded guy appears in a striped shirt that looks as if it was made from a piece of circus tent. "Can I help you, sir?"

Not really, Deckard thinks, but does not say.

It turns out the bearded guy is wildly amused by the irony of the misplaced book on memory loss. He's interested and attentive, friendly and sympathetic, and even has a nice twinkle in his eyes: everything, in short, the young redhead isn't.

"I'm afraid I'm going to have to ask you for twelve ninety-five," the man says apologetically, "but I'm certainly not going to make you pay the overdue fines."

Deckard pays the bill in cash, and there's a small slip of paper to sign. When Deckard passes the man the slip with his signature, the man holds it at arm's length and says, "You have beautiful handwriting."

"Thanks," Deckard says, surprised at how this compliment delights him, then folds his hands over his heart prayerfully and says, "Now can I take out another book? Please."

"Of course," the man says. "But do you think you can remember where the stacks are?"

"Stacks?" Deckard says, putting one finger to his chin. "Now tell me again. What's a stack?"

They both laugh, like great bosom buddies, and Deckard moves off toward the oak swinging doors to the reference room. It takes him about three seconds and one quick glance back at the guy — who's frozen in his spot, still smiling, watching him go — to realize that he has just had a flirtation with a bearded middle-aged man in a garish shirt. This is what getting old is all about, Deckard thinks, as he pushes through the doors. You get *variations* of what you need. You go into the world thinking you still know what you want, and the world says, How about considering this instead?

About three weeks ago, when he took the Indian food over to Sarah's, he went upstairs and had a chat with Harry while Harry was in the bathtub. Sarah, who'd seemed out of sorts all evening, thought Deckard might be able to get something out of him.

Deckard poured an excess of bubble bath into the tub, while Harry occupied himself with an old empty shampoo bottle, which he would hold under the water till it gurgled itself full, screw on the cap, squirt water at the ceiling, and let it rain back down on himself. Deckard figured this probably wasn't too good for the paint on the ceiling over the bathtub, but he thought he would have a more productive chat with Harry if Harry was busy with something else. The trick was to have a talk without Harry's noticing that they were having a talk.

Deckard positioned himself, far enough from the tub to avoid getting wet, on the little plastic footstool that Harry normally used at the sink. In contrast to Sarah, Harry had been cheerful throughout the evening, and Deckard thought it probably had to do with his returning to school and getting out of the house, away from Sarah.

When Deckard began by asking him how things were going, Harry said, cheerfully, "Fie-een," turning the word into two syllables.

"How you like being back in school?"

"Fie-een."

"I guess there must've been some catching up to do, huh? How's that going?"

"Fie-een."

Deckard could see that "fie-een" was the only answer he would get if he didn't phrase his questions differently.

"What's your teacher's name?" he said.

"Julia."

"You like her?"

Harry nodded, leaning back to strafe the ceiling.

"Is it good to see all your friends again?"

Another nod.

"I never hear you talk about your friends," Deckard said. "Is there anybody you think of as a special friend . . . like a best buddy?"

Harry shrugged, dunking the shampoo bottle beneath the suds for a refill.

"You don't know?"

Another shrug.

"But you like being back at school?"

Another nod.

"And how are things going here at home?"

"Fie-een."

"You getting along with your mom okay?"

Deckard fully expected another nod, but instead, Harry froze, looked penetratingly at Deckard for about three seconds, then back down at the suds.

Deckard said, "What's up?"

Harry continued to stare into the suds and whispered, barely audibly, "She's crazy."

"She's what?" Deckard said, but he was just stalling — he'd heard the word clearly enough.

Harry wouldn't repeat it, so Deckard said, "Why do you say that?"

Silence.

"Is it because she's sad all the time?"

Harry looked at him and nodded, though it was plain that "sad" was only part of it and Harry was just glad to be let off the hook, glad not to have to elaborate. "Sad" could be their code word for the whole can of worms.

"Well," Deckard said, "she's sad for a reason, you know. Aren't you sad too?"

Harry looked away, nodded again, and went back to playing with the shampoo bottle. Evidently, he'd gone as deep into this woodsy battleground as he wanted to go.

"Look, Harry," Deckard said. "In my opinion, the best thing you could do for your mom would be to show her that you need her to be a mom."

"How?"

It was a purely scientific inquiry, unemotional. Harry's feelings, briefly deployed, had retreated back in their foxhole.

"How?" said Deckard. "I don't know how. You're the kid. You ought to know more about this than me. Be creative."

"Okay," Harry said vacantly.

Deckard said, "Do you ever get her to read to you at bedtime, for example?"

Harry shook his head, then sat stock-still again, staring into the suds. Somewhere in the back of his mind, Deckard seemed to recall that Malcolm had been the one who always read to Harry at bedtime.

"Well, why don't you ask her to read to you?" Deckard said.

"You mean tonight?" Harry asked.

"Yeah, why not tonight?"

Harry screwed the cap back on the shampoo bottle. He said, "I have a question."

"What?"

"Who invented guns?"

"What . . . you mean the very first gun? I don't really know. There's thousands of different kinds of guns, you see. Cannons and muskets and mortars and bazookas . . . rifles, shotguns, all kinds of handguns . . . pistols, revolvers. Down through the ages, different men have invented different kinds."

"Only men?" asked Harry.

"I'm not sure about that," said Deckard. "But if I had to guess, I'd say only men, yeah."

"Where do you get one?"

"A gun? Best place is at a gun store. But you

have to be over a certain age and you have to have a permit."

"Why do people *want* to buy them?"

"Different reasons," Deckard said. "Some people buy them for hunting, some people just like having them, and some people need them, like for protection."

"I have another question," Harry said.

"What?"

"When you were in Vietnam, did you ever see anybody get shot?"

"Lots of times," said Deckard.

"Anybody you knew?"

"Sure. Lots."

Harry reared back again, unscrewed the bottle cap and fired water straight ahead this time — at the faucets and spout and the overflow plate, causing them to ring. When the bottle was empty, he said, "I have another question."

"What?"

"Did you shoot people in Vietnam?"

"Yes, Harry," Deckard said. "I was a soldier, fighting in a war. That's what was expected of me."

"So you killed people?"

"Yes, I did."

"Other soldiers?"

Deckard only nodded, thinking he would give Harry the simplified version of the story, but immediately dense eruptions of dust billowed up in his own mind . . . the roar of a truck . . . naked, emaciated children running in a road, screaming. . . . He suspected it wasn't Harry but himself he was sparing.

He allowed a few seconds of silence to pass, then said, "Is that troubling to you? Me killing people during the war?"

Harry shrugged.

"Because what happened to your dad was totally different," Deckard said.

Harry looked at him with those half-squinted eyes of his, behind which you could almost see wheels turning. A dollop of soap-suds hung from his right earlobe. Deckard had crossed over onto posted land now, private property. He wasn't sure if Harry wanted him to proceed, but he didn't want to miss what looked distinctly like an opportunity.

"There wasn't any *reason* for your dad to get killed," he said. "When you're in a war, you're fighting for a reason."

"What reason?" Harry said.

"Well, that's complicated," said Deckard. "It's not just one thing, it's a lot of things, and it's different for every war."

"Mom says the man in the white car was probably taking drugs and was probably scared."

"I bet she's right."

"Is that the reason you shot people?" said Harry. "Because you were scared?"

"In a way, yeah," said Deckard. "I mean you're scared of getting killed yourself, that's for sure."

Harry had stopped playing with the shampoo bottle. He'd reached up to scratch his nose, which left a glob of suds on his face, and now, with each attempt to brush the suds away, he was making matters worse. Deckard said, "Hold still," used his thumb to scrape the glob away, and wiped the suds on the shower curtain.

Harry was squinting at him again. At last he said, very pensively, "I don't think I'm going to be one of those."

"One of what?"

"A soldier," he said, "a soldier fighting in a war. Is that okay?"

Deckard didn't think it was the right time to explain about conscription, so he just said, "Of course it's okay, Harry. Believe me, it's not for everybody. And besides, I thought you were going to be a famous artist."

Without any answer, and without any kind of warning, Harry stood up, shockingly skinny, slick, and mottled with soapsuds. Deckard held out a towel and said, "Will you remember what we said about your mom?"

Harry reached for the towel, draped it over

his head, and clutched it under his chin, madonnalike. Eyes shut tight, he nodded exaggeratedly, about five times.

A short while later, as Deckard was leaving the house, he told Sarah that he hadn't been able to get anything new out of Harry. He didn't think it would serve any real purpose to tell her Harry thought she was crazy. But Harry's bringing up the war, right after Deckard's strange afternoon — Mason Miller, the clapping angels, and all that — had left him a little shaken, and Sarah must have noticed something was off. At the door, she asked him pointedly if he was feeling all right. He wasn't sure what to say. He said he'd felt dizzy at work in the afternoon and had gone home early. Under the circumstances, how could he have explained that he thought he might be coming apart at the seams?

The stacks are located at the back of the reference room, attached to the main body of the library like a silo to a barn. Because Deckard has been coming to this branch off and on since he was a kid, more for the refuge of the building than for any refuge inside the books, the place fills him with a kind of no-name nostalgia, a vague desire pointed backward in time but lacking any specific object. He has always especially loved the funhouse quality of the stacks, a massive openwork skeleton with steel grates for floors and steel staircases connecting the two aboveground and three subterranean stories — a cool dark echoing maze where footsteps clang deep and gonglike, and where you can look up and see shadows passing on the floor above, or look down and see the tops of heads below, crouch in one aisle and see in the spaces between the metal shelves fragments of a person in the next aisle: a hand, a knee, part of a shoulder. During his year in prison, that year of grasping at straws, Deckard took a small grain of comfort from the fact that the lockup reminded him a little of these old library stacks.

Today he means to find another book on memory, though his interest in the topic has evolved; what began as a concern about the forgetfulness that comes with age — a struggle for proper nouns, a tendency to leave his apartment without the keys, the habit of arriving in a room clueless about what brought him there — now feels like a need to investigate a strange phenomenon: Since his friend Malcolm's death, a change has been under way in the old memory bank, as if some long-sealed night depository has been reopened and any number of things are now coming unbidden through the slot. He's wide awake the better part of most nights — that's nothing new — but now, when he does sleep, he tends to dream about the war, the *war* for Chrissakes, and somehow it's a less restful sleep with a firefight going on inside your head and some pasty-white waterlogged maniac screaming coordinates at the top of his lungs. Occasionally, he wakes up with blood pumping in his temples and the very sure sense that he has just been sitting in the bush for a month, day after day in silence, feeding on centipedes, wondering where the hell Charlie's hiding and when the hell he's going to show himself. It's leaving Deckard overtired and vulnerable. Lately, he doesn't know, rounding a corner, whether Mason Miller's fireball skull will be waiting for him, or the scent of Lucy's perfume, or the lashing pop of his old man's leather belt. *Childhood*, yet, that old dead horse.

And, sorry to say, that isn't quite all. The last two weeks, he has been stuffing his waist pouch again with the small artillery that Lucy was so fond of calling his Post-traumatic Stress Kit: the pepper spray, the metal retractable nightstick, and so forth. He hasn't yet sunk to packing a piece, but don't think it hasn't occurred to him (a 1911 .45-caliber ACP would be his first choice, large enough to talk turkey, small enough to conceal). The day after the Indian food over at Sarah's, he returned with a present for Harry (a used Nintendo machine he bought cheap off Bernice), a weird thing happened with Sarah, and they got into a — well, sort of a fight, and now apparently they aren't speaking to each other, and nobody has even called to thank him for the present. His relations in the workplace have deteriorated almost beyond recognition — he thinks maybe his job's in jeopardy, though that could just be a little branch off the paranoia tree — and he finds himself angry, not only at Sarah but at nearly everybody he can think of. Too-dead Malcolm and the anonymous scumbag who shot him, too-picky Bernice, the needling young Dr. French, the cold-blooded Lucy, the punishing Mr. Jones and his don't-bring-me-no-bad-news head-in-the-sand-morning-noon-and-night missus. This, of course, is only the A-list. There's also a B and a C, but why bother? The point is: He's ninety-nine percent living in the past, as if he has been running for about forty years and now, for no apparent reason, he has stopped, and everything that has been chasing him is suddenly slapping up against his rear. Deckard has concluded that his memory is the horse this shit's riding in on, and if he can maybe learn something about it, he might be able to lay on some proper reins.

Downstairs, on the especially dark serpentine second floor, he locates the 153.1s, where books on memory are kept. There doesn't seem to be another living soul around, though he thinks he can hear the medieval footsteps of somebody far away overhead. One of the fluorescent tubes in Deckard's aisle is radiating a low hum and a nervous flicker, which strikes him as a perfect analogy for how he himself is feeling: the short-circuiting light show that precedes total burnout. As he begins to scan the shelf, right away he spies the same small softcover he checked out weeks ago, the one he was in the middle of reading, the one he supposedly mislaid and just paid to replace. He tips the book from the shelf with his index finger, experiencing a mixture of joy at finding a lost friend and disbelief at having been swindled. Book in hand, he immediately heads for the exit and for the circulation desk, where he means to see what's what, but somehow he's got himself turned around; he winds up not back at the stairs but in an unlit cul-de-sac where the stairs ought to be and where now, instead, there's a metal door painted the same don't-notice-me go-anywhere brown color as the walls. He stares into the gloom, resisting an urge to scratch his head, and stringing together these four disquieting beads on a string: (1) he must have returned the book and yet has no memory of returning it; (2) the library reshelved the book without logging its return and thereby just took him for $12.95; (3) you stupid fool, it's just a second copy of the same book; and (4) what has happened to what's left of your pitiful brain? He lets out a kind of hopeless guffaw, and at that moment the mysterious brown door swings open, flooding him with light, causing him to shield his eyes with the paperback.

A white kid with long black hair stands frozen in the doorway for maybe five seconds, his hand still on the inner knob. In a large brilliantly lit room behind the kid, Deckard can see a half dozen white people sitting on stools at tall drafting tables, men and women, all in a state of suspension now, interrupted, looking up from their work and staring at him. He has stumbled on the covert heart of the library, where the *real* business happens, the secret enterprise the physical plant only fronts. The long-haired kid says, "Oops! I thought —" and quickly closes the door, leaving Deckard with darkness and a druggy afterimage of six white heads bobbing on spindly white necks in a room that may or may not really exist.

Later, when Deckard recalls this odd moment, he'll imagine pounding on the metal door and demanding to know what's going on in there, but now something prevents him. He's suddenly assailed by a muted chorus of laughter from behind the door, and his mind seems to execute a kind of swan dive. He plunges into a murky pool encrusted with lotus flowers and swarming with jungle vines, and when he comes up for air, actually struggling for breath, he's sitting partway down the narrow aisle on a little rolling footstool and holding his head in his hands. He looks up at the army-green bookshelf six inches from his face where a fat shiny silverfish scurries out to the lip and twitches its feelers at him — as if to say, You go away, and find your own shelf, Baldy, this here one's mine — then runs back into the books to eat some more glue. Yum. There's an echo of laughter in Deckard's ears and the echo equivalent in his nostrils of some terrible stink like human excrement. At first he thinks with considerable fright that he himself is the source of the stench, but as he regains a semblance of steady breathing, he understands that, like some laboratory dog, he just had a bona fide reflex response — he just took a little trip inside his increasingly fleet-footed noodle and returned to Southeast Asia, where he'd been assigned to shit duty again. Thirty years ago, a VA shrink would have called it a "flashback," but in Deckard's humble opinion a fancier word is needed for something that can reach across more than a quarter of a century as if it's the mere blink of an eye and put a man back on shit duty in South Vietnam, back to shoveling stinking I Corps dung and burning the latrine pit and wishing somebody would just fucking shoot him and put him out of his fucking misery, while enduring throughout, start to finish, the ceaseless yellow heehawing of the men at his back.

Two weeks ago, Sarah screwed up her courage and phoned her doctor. She felt vaguely ashamed of having to ask for drugs — her stalwart doppelgänger, the usually helpful outdoors woman with no time for wimps, looked down from her toehold on a flat rock precipice, smirking — but Sarah overruled her. Things were getting worse at home rather than better, and how could she be expected to turn anything around when she was in pain all the time and strung-out from a lack of sleep? She'd prepared an elaborate explanation for the doctor, a kind older man who'd been her and Malcolm's physician for nearly ten years, but none was necessary; he already knew about Malcolm, expressed his sympathy, and asked what he could do to help. Sarah told him she'd been having some stress-related back pain. The doctor said, "And difficulty sleeping, no doubt."

"Yes," Sarah said, and in about three minutes the doctor was phoning prescriptions in to Sarah's pharmacy for a muscle relaxer, carisoprodol, and a sleeping pill, temazepam. Easy as pie.

Unsolicited, the doctor also gave her the name of a psychopharmacologist and encouraged her to seek antidepressant medication.

"I'm not depressed," she said, "I just have the back pain and I can't sleep."

"Those are both symptoms of depression, Sarah," he said, and Sarah pretended to write down the name and thanked the doctor.

The carisoprodol seems to relax a good deal more than Sarah's muscles; it seems (while in effect) to relax her expectations of almost everything, improves her outlook on life, and makes her regular telephone conversations with Enid almost chummy. But it also makes her too groggy to drive the car and a little apprehensive in the kitchen, among sharp knives and open flames. The temazepam does an admirable job too, dispatching her quickly into oblivion, but as it wears off it promotes vivid dreaming (the last thing she needs) and leaves her with a mild hangover in the morning. She has experimented with varying the dosages and with timing the taking of the pills to fit the day's demands (no carisoprodol in the afternoon before picking up Harry at school), but the results, finally, are only a slim improvement.

Another side effect of the drugs — this one nonmedical — is that another item has been added to Sarah's growing list of secrets. She has kept the facts of the back pain and the insomnia very much to herself, and now she speaks to no one about the drugs she's taking.

Secrets, and more secrets.

Three times over the last month or so, she has awakened in the middle of the night, climbed out of bed (trancelike from the temazepam), glided down the hallway, and quietly closed Harry's door. Back in her room, she closes her own door, moves to Malcolm's dresser, and opens the top drawer; she gathers in her hands a basketball-size clump of his T-shirts and boxer shorts, which she lifts to her face, pressing the fabrics hard against her eyes and nose and mouth as if she means to obliterate her senses; after a few seconds of this, she moves to his closet, steps all the way inside, and closes the door behind her, where the darkness is absolute and she can smell him, mostly in a favorite parka, which she gropes for in the dark and then clutches in her arms, allowing herself to explore the depths of its emptiness. She knows precisely what she's after: she's after this exquisite pain that (at least for now, in the middle of the night, drugged) is the only way she has of being close to him. It works quickly, exquisitely; she sinks to the floor of the closet and — confident that she has put enough walls and closed doors between her and Harry, so that Harry can't hear her — she lets herself get really loud.

After an indeterminate amount of time has passed, she rises from the floor, leaves the closet, leaves the bedroom, and goes back down the hallway to open Harry's door. She returns to her bathroom, pees, gets into bed, soon falls asleep, and sometimes dreams that she's inside Malcolm's closet, huddled on the floor in the dark, clutching his old down parka and wailing.

In the middle of the night — now two and three times a week — she's awakened by Harry's screaming. He's having the nightmare again. Always the same. "Don't let it in, Mommy, don't let it in!" Some kind of monster's trying to get into the house — or has already gotten in — and she's responsible either for keeping it out or letting it in or both. Always the same. Harry never wakes up entirely. He hides under the covers. She comforts him, eventually gets him situated. If she asks him about the dream, he won't tell her about it. (The one time she has asked him about it during daylight hours, he went solemn and said he didn't remember any dream, clearly lying.) She rests next to him in bed for a few minutes and then, after a while, returns to her room. It has all begun to feel rather ho-hum to her, and she thinks this is chiefly because Harry's nightmare wrenches her from a medicated sleep; it's almost as if the *drug* is annoyed with Harry for interfering with its duties. What isn't ho-hum is that she's keeping another secret. She speaks to nobody about Harry's recurrent nightmare, and, with that one brief daylight exception, she and Harry don't talk about it either.

Two Wednesdays ago, when Antonia was coming to clean, Sarah was straightening the house in preparation. In Harry's room, as she passed near his bureau, she smelled something, a familiar unpleasant odor she associated with urban alleyways. She opened each drawer, starting at the top and working her way down to the bottom, and in the last deep drawer she discovered a wadded stockpile of soiled sheets and underwear, emanating a stench of stale urine that nearly stung her nose.

She moved to his bed and stripped off the sheet. The mattress was marked by half a dozen pale stains, their outer rings overlapping one another in a pattern that suggested a large blossom, a giant rose or camellia. Yes, she began to cry, but it was the kind of idle weeping that she has come to pay no mind, finally not that different from breathing except that it requires the occasional Kleenex.

When Antonia arrived, the two of them hauled the mattress down the stairs. Sarah thought Antonia's cheerfulness during this task was overblown, aimed at undoing Sarah's obvious distress. As she bore the brunt of the mattress's weight on the downside of the stairs, Antonia said, "This reminds me of when I was a child; I would dream I was sitting on the toilet in my grandmother's house," and she laughed and laughed as if she'd said something hilarious.

They carried the mattress into the backyard and left it there to air while Antonia did the housecleaning. Sarah stuffed the soiled things from Harry's bureau drawer into a nylon laundry bag, took all of it to the basement, and started a load of wash. Before Antonia left for the day, and before Sarah left to get Harry at school, they returned the mattress to Harry's room. Sarah found a vinyl shower curtain liner folded in the linen closet and tucked it around the mattress, then recovered the bed with a fresh set of sheets.

Harry was hiding the sheets and underwear out of shame, and Sarah reasoned that confronting him would only shame him more. Of course, after that Wednesday, he must have seen that the soiled things were missing from the bureau drawer, and of course he couldn't help noticing the crackly vinyl liner beneath the bedsheet. There was no need to put him through more humiliation than he must already feel, so Sarah has allowed him to continue using the drawer as a laundry hamper, only now she checks it daily. She knows the bed-wetting, which has been only sporadic, will pass without her further intervention, and she knows Harry well enough to know that the most helpful thing she can do for him is not to make a big deal of it.

So they have a tacit understanding, another arrangement between them, but they have also entered into another small conspiracy of silence. It doesn't entirely escape Sarah that the trouble at home has at least in part come down to hiding dirty laundry.

Deckard hasn't called or been over in nearly three weeks — apparently he isn't speaking to her — and though Harry must be wondering what's happened, Sarah hasn't attempted any explanation. When she thinks about it, she sees it would be a difficult thing to explain, which means, probably, that she doesn't understand it well enough herself.

Recently, picking at a bowl of cereal before school, Harry asked if Deck could come over sometime and give him some tips on the Nintendo he'd given him as a present.

"Sure, that's a great idea," Sarah said, but that's as far as she went. She hasn't even made Harry phone Deckard to thank him for the present, and that's the kind of thing that really gets Deckard steamed.

The last time she saw Deckard, they'd got into a stupid quarrel. He'd stopped over after work with the Nintendo machine, an expensive present and a thoughtful one. Though she and Malcolm had held off buying video games for Harry even after some of his friends already had them, Deckard reasoned, reasonably, that now it was a good alternative to TV. He'd brought two games with the machine — basketball and baseball, both nonviolent, and she was honestly touched by his attentiveness and generosity.

Harry wasn't at home when Deckard arrived. He was having his first play date since his return to school, with a classmate named Miles. Miles's mother, whom Sarah only vaguely knew, had taken the boys from school to the park and then back to Miles's house. They'd wanted Harry to stay for dinner, but Sarah, worried that it might be too long a visit, suggested Harry come home around five-thirty. Miles's mother said Miles *really* wanted Harry to stay for dinner and convinced Sarah to let him, saying she would bring Harry home herself, not a minute past seven.

But around five-thirty — only a few minutes after Deckard arrived — Miles's mother phoned to say that things were going "a bit bumpily" and she thought she would bring Harry home before dinner after all, if that was okay.

"What do you mean, 'bumpily'?" Sarah asked.

"I'm not sure," said the woman, too cheerfully. "Harry just got sort of . . . *quiet* all of a sudden. And now Miles says Harry doesn't want to *do* anything."

The woman went on to say she thought maybe they'd made the play date a little too long for "Harry's first time out."

Why did this remark affect Sarah the way it did? Certainly it was irritating, the woman's refusal to acknowledge Sarah's original opinion about the length of the visit. But something about "Harry's first time out" really rubbed her the wrong way. It felt intrusive, none of this woman's business.

"What have the boys been doing?" Sarah asked, glancing at Deckard, who was seated across from her at the kitchen table. He was all ears already, having noticed the tension in her voice.

"Well, they had a great time in the park," the woman said, "and when we came home, I gave them a snack and they watched a little TV."

"What were they watching?" Sarah asked.

Miles's mother laughed nervously and said, "Is there a problem, Sarah? I mean, is there some reason it's not okay for me to bring Harry home now instead of later?"

"There's no problem with Harry coming home," Sarah said. "If you recall, it's what I wanted in the first place. It's just that if Harry got 'quiet' all of a sudden, it's for a reason, and since they've been watching television, it probably had something to do with what they were watching. Could you put him on the phone for a minute?"

The woman sighed enormously, then sang, "O-kayyy."

In the short interval, Deckard asked, "What's up?"

Sarah said she didn't know yet, and then Harry was on the line.

"Is something wrong, Harry?" she asked.

"No," he said, "I just want to come home."

"That's fine, sweetheart," Sarah said. "Did you and Miles watch some TV?"

"Yes," said Harry. "But I got tired of it."

"What were you watching?"

"Cartoons," said Harry, "but Miles didn't like it, so he put in a movie."

"A movie? What movie?"

"I forget the name. Something about a policeman and stuff."

"Okay, sweetheart," Sarah said. "You just sit tight and I'll be over to get you in just a few minutes. Now, can you put Miles's mother back on?"

She must have been visibly upset, because Deckard raised his eyebrows at her and whispered, "Easy does it, Sarah."

Unfortunately, Deckard's admonition had a fuel-on-the-fire effect, and when she heard the woman's voice again, she spoke to her with more anger than she'd intended.

"Harry says they watched a movie," she said. "Do you know *what* movie?"

"Oh, for heaven's sake, Sarah," the woman said. "I didn't mean to make you . . . whatever you are. We thought we were doing a good deed, inviting Harry over, but it's clear now that we made a mistake. I'm —"

"A good *deed?*" said Sarah. "You mean like charity?"

"I'm sorry, okay?" the woman said. "That's

not what I meant at all. I didn't mean for — listen, Sarah, this hasn't turned out well. I'll bring Harry home right now."

"I don't want you bringing him home," Sarah said. "I'll come get him. I just want you to understand that if Harry's upset, he's upset for a reason. You parked him in front of a television without even knowing what he was watching. He's obviously seen something that upset —"

"Oh, please," the woman said. "They watched about ten minutes of *Kindergarten Cop*, a kids' movie. I don't see —"

"My God, what's wrong with you?" Sarah said. "Are you so stupid you don't realize that a movie like that has people shooting people in it? Are you so fucking self-absorbed that you don't even realize —"

That was as far as she got before Deckard reached across the table, grabbed her hand, and shook his head at her. "Just get off the phone," he whispered, "and let's go get Harry."

The woman took advantage of the pause to say that Sarah was being "abusive" and she thought they should discuss this another time, when Sarah wasn't quite so "distraught and combative."

Sarah opened her mouth, but Deckard squeezed her hand. She said, "I'll be there in fifteen minutes," and hung up.

"Christ, I just remembered," she said. "That woman's a fucking *shrink*. This is *my* fault. I should know better than to let Harry go over to a fucking shrink's house."

"Why don't you give me directions," Deckard said, pushing back his chair from the table. "I'll go get Harry, and you can stay here and try to calm down."

That was it, that was all Deckard said — and she was ready to admit that she might have been shouting a bit on the telephone — but it just flew all over her. She stood up without a word. It's possible that she turned on her heel. She left the kitchen and went immediately to the table in the entryway where she kept her keys in a straw basket, but of course the keys weren't there. Keys were by nature mischievous things and seized on such opportunities as this.

A moment later, Deckard found her at the coat closet, where she was engaged in searching jacket pockets and the various zipper pouches of her backpack.

"Sarah," he said from behind her, "maybe I'm wrong here. Maybe I'm completely wrong, but I think this kind of thing's inevitable. Now that Harry's back out in the world, people are going to make mistakes like this."

She was rooting through the bowels of an

old purse she didn't even use anymore. Deckard's "back out in the world" reminded her of his previous "back up on the horse," which had infuriated her.

"You think I need to calm down," she said, not turning to face him, "and I think what needs to happen is that that woman should be taken out and sh—"

He placed his hand on her shoulder as if he meant to spin her around and said, "Sarah, you're acting crazy."

She quickly dipped out from under his hand, jerked herself away, and said, "Don't . . . don't touch me right now, Deckard. Please."

"Jesus, Sarah," he said. "I'm on your side."

It was too dark in the hallway to read his face, but he was clearly shocked.

In a really calm voice, she said, "I believe that, Deck. I do. I just wish it *felt* more like it."

He turned his palms up, shrugged his shoulders.

"If you're looking for your keys," he said, "they're right there in that little basket."

True. They were. Visible from where she stood. Extraordinary, mischievous things, keys.

Now she wishes she'd invited Deckard to come with her in the car. Instead, she'd left him standing in the hallway, and when she returned home with Harry half an hour later, she was hoping they would find Deckard still there. But they found only the wonderful present he'd left. Harry was overjoyed and she felt horrible.

Harry loves the games and has been playing them for an hour (the limit she has set for him) every day after school. Sarah keeps meaning to phone Deckard, to patch things up, but every time she thinks about it, she hears him calling her crazy. Now and then, she has thought that maybe she remembers it wrongly: Deckard didn't say, Sarah, you're acting crazy, he said, Sarah, *this* is crazy. And besides, it seems absurd that the whole silly wrangle is based on Deckard's mere suggestion — in the kitchen, when she was obviously in a state — that she should calm down, a reasonable suggestion, coupled with a practical offer of help. If only she didn't feel judged by him. If only she hadn't felt judged by him from the beginning. If only, somehow, he could stop disapproving of her.

She needs somebody to not disapprove of her, and while this seems valid enough, it also feels like a petty need, a childish need. She feels afraid of Harry's finding out that she has chased Deckard away with her bad temper (with her pettiness and her childishness), chased away the one real friend they have, the one meaningful connection to Malcolm who could be a part of their daily lives. She knows she couldn't begin to explain it to Harry, so she has had to keep what happened a secret.

Fritz Durgin has phoned twice about her returning to the lab, and she has told him both times that she wants to wait until fall. She has told him she thinks it will be better for Harry if she has the rest of the spring and the summer free. But Fritz feels guilty about having given her lab space over to the woman from La Jolla, and now he wants Sarah to come back to work chiefly because it would soothe his conscience. The reassuring Sarah is obliged to do irritates her, but any sign of impatience in her voice makes matters worse, convincing Fritz that she's angry and is refusing to return to the lab simply to spite him.

"Well, come in and see me," he said, most recently. "At least we could talk it over."

"We've talked it over three or four times already," Sarah said, carefully controlling her voice. "What more can I say, Fritz? I'm not angry. I think things have actually worked out for the best this way. And I'm grateful to you for . . . for being so flexible."

Out of nothing but impatience and self-interest, Fritz Durgin gave away her lab space to a stranger from California — a stranger who's using an autoclave and an incubator purchased with Sarah's grant money, a stranger who's reaping the assistance of grad students trained by Sarah — and now he has become the forbearing employer, indulging the grieving widow who claims she needs to spend the summer with her newly fatherless child. Sarah wants so much to be rid of him that she's even willing to paint him the hero. That's okay. She doesn't mind. But while everything she has told Fritz is mostly true, there's another thing she's keeping secret. When she has actually thought of returning to the lab — when she thinks of guiding students through the steps of harvesting cartilage cells, when she thinks of a calf leg lying bloody on the lab bench, when she thinks of stripping the meat away from the bone and digging into the joint, when she thinks of the meticulous dicing of the cartilage under the Sterigard and pipetting it into the culture medium, when she thinks of the snapping of rubber gloves and the whirling of spinner flasks and students accidentally gouging their fingers with scalpels, contaminating things, and having to start again from the beginning — waves of nausea overtake her. The secret she's keeping from Fritz (and from everyone) is that she's not sure she'll ever return to the lab.

★ ★ ★

Twice in the middle of the night, aroused by a dream, unable to sleep, druggy from the waning bedtime pill, she has tried touching herself, at first mechanically, almost dutifully, without hope or inspiration, but then as the body started to kindle images and images to stoke the body, as this familiar wheel began to spin and weave and then began to rattle the memory of Malcolm's breath on her neck, his weight pressing against her, of Malcolm inside her, his arms beneath her pulling her to him, suddenly Forrest Sanders sat glowing in his white shirt and sunglasses on the stoop of the front porch, bringing charm, clutter, confusion, and as if to erase him forever, Malcolm returned with such naked actuality she was taken clear away from sex, ravished by a new, breathless, sweaty, physical grief.

On a Friday morning early in May, Sarah returns from taking Harry to school, goes to the kitchen, and swallows a carisoprodol tablet. She has discovered that the medication is more effective if she takes it first thing, before the back pain has a chance to get a firm hold; she has also discovered that the carisoprodol helps ease the hangover from the nightly sleeping pill. This is entirely reasonable, she thinks, standing at the kitchen range, mesmerized by the blue flame spreading beneath the teakettle, but she can't quite avoid a feeling that the enthusiasm with which she looks forward to the medication and the instant (though slight) relief she experiences before it has even had time to kick in are indications of something not so reasonable. She recalls one of Deckard's maxims for right living, derived from his checkered history — "You know you're in trouble when you start thinking of a drug as a friend" — and at first she dismisses it as an example of Deckard's always-be-on-the-lookout-for-trouble philosophy (derived, she imagines, from his tour of terror in Vietnam), but in the next moment, as the kettle begins to rumble, she recalls that occasionally, spying the two dark-amber prescription bottles on the windowsill in her bathroom, she does greet them with a kind of unusual warmth.

"What do you *do?*" Enid said to her yesterday on the telephone.

This is what Sarah didn't say, the truth: she drives Harry to school; she comes home; she takes her medication; she makes tea; she sits at the kitchen table, often cupping her hands around the teapot, leaving them there right up to the very edge of pain (it's the antique pot, cream-colored with a pattern of forget-me-nots, her oldest possession, which once belonged to her grandmother, and this warm connection comforts her); she sits and thinks, usually in circles of one kind or another, analyzing some aspect of her inner or outer life; she generally moves to the living room couch and dozes off for a while; and then, midmorning, she switches on the television and watches soap operas until it's time to go get Harry.

"I have a lot of writing to catch up on," Sarah said to her mother. "Labs to write up from the fall term. And there's always a lot of reading too."

As usual, Sarah was at the kitchen table, sipping her back-from-school cup of tea and welcoming the first consoling whispers of her back-from-school carisoprodol tablet. In the first weeks after Malcolm was killed, there were a lot of worldly demands: Sanders and the newspapers and all that, Fritz Durgin and school and all that, but also a mountain of niggling paperwork, lawyers to consult, accountants to consult, forms to sign, death benefits to claim (still, to date, unpaid), applications to be made for one thing and another — credit cards and bank accounts that were in Malcolm's name, an extension on filing tax returns — but now a great desert of silence had ensued. It wasn't an option to tell Enid about the soap operas (even though Enid had sought and captured small roles in one or two when she was younger), and it wasn't necessary to tell her, since Sarah could "hear" Enid's responses quite clearly: unhealthy . . . depressing . . . beneath a woman of her intelligence . . . and so on.

"Reading?" Enid said. "What reading?"

Sarah said, "Biotechnology, Mother, biotechnology."

"Well, what about it?" said Enid. "Tell me. I want to know."

Sarah had to think for about two seconds to piece together something that would put Enid in her place. "I've been reading about the influence of laminar flow on gene expression in some endothelial cells," she said. "It's fascinating . . . all about how flow in an endothelial cell and smooth muscle cell co-culture seems to stimulate the expression of platelet-derived growth-factor RNA."

A brief silence. Then, "And can you possibly say that in English?"

"That was English," Sarah said.

Enid said, "You could have fooled me!" and they had a nice chummy laugh together, but afterward Sarah was left sitting at the table with her own deceitfulness for company — which was, she concluded, unhealthy, depressing, and beneath a woman of her intelligence.

Now, as the tea brews in the pot, she resolves to be honest with Enid if Enid should phone again today. She thinks, Honest, whatever that means . . . and then allows her mind to drift for a while over the nature of lies — lies of omission, lies of commission, crazy lies and clever ones, lying's link to fear, its link to pride and the urge to protect the self. Yes, protect the self, but from what? Suddenly, amazed, she sees that she is thoroughly *ashamed* that Malcolm was murdered, as if such tremendous bad luck has somehow marked her socially, lowered her into the ranks of all the hapless hopeless people (not anything like herself) whom tragedy befalls, whose names and plights and photographs end up in the Metro Section of the newspaper. That's what she's ashamed of, she's ashamed to be one of *them*. There's definitely a trap here to be observed, embedded in some kind of perverse elitism, a certain wrong to be righted in her spirit, a yoke to be thrown off, and yet she can't quite make her brain formulate an escape. And that, she concludes, is the nature of the thing, after all, the hard core of the shaming mechanism — that it is, precisely, inescapable.

"I have you here, Sarah," Antonia repeated two days ago, at the little table outside on the patio, "in my heart."

On Wednesdays, when Antonia comes, Sarah doesn't watch the soaps (though she's sure Antonia wouldn't judge her for it). She makes an effort to appear industrious, domestic, in charge. Sometimes she says to Antonia that she has work to do and closes herself in her bedroom and naps.

Two days ago, Antonia arrived early and joined her for tea. Antonia suggested they move from the kitchen table to the patio, and Sarah could tell that Antonia meant to get her, Sarah, out of the house, if only as far as the patio. Antonia made a big show of what a beautiful day it was, breathing in the air exaggeratedly, looking up at the clear sky and the trees, smiling. Sarah felt a bit led-by-the-hand and noticed in herself a gingerly approach toward the things of nature in the backyard — the tall lilacs in full sun against the far fence, the great old horse chestnut tree just getting its candles going, the fragrant patch of narcissus by the gate — as if they had some hidden power to hurt her. It was the same with clouds and birds, even a certain mild breeze that stirred everything pleasantly and moved away. The lilacs made her think of the lilacs at the summer house, the summer house made her think of Malcolm's beloved red tractor in the garage, the red tractor made her think of her father, who'd left her the house in his will (driving another wedge between her and Enid, though Enid had never seemed to care two hoots for the house), her father made her think of her grandfather and grandmother, who'd bought the house from its original owners . . . and soon the idea of summer, so rooted in the past, became the idea of a future, the growing out of what-will-be from what-has-been and what-is, terrifying in its vastness.

Impossible to explain to Antonia, even if Sarah knew Portuguese.

At the little round table on the flagstones, Antonia touched her fingers to her own chest and said, "I have you here, Sarah. In my heart."

"Thank you, Antonia," said Sarah, too quickly, then smiled and looked into Antonia's face. She saw, of course, the woman's plain beauty, a lace of sunlight and shadow falling over her hair; but in her eyes she saw . . . what? Simple frankness, she supposed, or frank simplicity. She knew Antonia to be unmarried, very close to her family (which included a disabled wheelchair-bound brother) in Brazil, devoutly Catholic, and currently sacrificing her own career as a history teacher to clean houses in America and send every penny back home: the city of Governador Valadares, where the family lived on an island in the Rio Doce, which flooded every few years. Most of the money Antonia sent to Brazil had been used to add second-story rooms to their house; now, when the river flooded, they could move their furniture and possessions (not to mention themselves) to the upper rooms. Antonia's saying that she had Sarah in her heart meant, astonishingly, that she empathized with Sarah (a woman who paid her the going rate to clean her expensive home far away from any flooding river), that Antonia regularly thought about Sarah, contemplated her misery, even prayed for her.

Sarah thanked Antonia again, hoping to make amends for that first careless response.

"I'm not sure how to say this," Antonia said. "I think you are lost in the — what is the word? In the mountains . . . *garimpo* — where the men dig down for the diamonds?"

"Caves," said Sarah. "No . . . mines. Mines."

"Yes, of course," said Antonia, slapping her head with her hand. "*Minas*. Mines. You are lost in the mines." Antonia formed a small circle with her fingers and held it at the center of her own forehead. She said, "You have no light."

"Yes," said Sarah, smiling, "I have no light," and it felt immediately apt — she was groping in the dark, lost in some deep place, even in danger — but then her eyes fell to the gold crucifix on a chain around Antonia's neck and she feared that Antonia would next say something about Jesus, the Light of the World.

But Antonia didn't say anything about Jesus. Instead, she asked how Harry was doing, and Sarah repeated the practiced reply about how hard it was to get anything out of Harry.

Antonia nodded and said, "He is a little boy," as if that explained everything, as if that was the last word on the subject.

"I'm afraid it's my fault," Sarah said. "I'm afraid he sees me so sad and upset, he doesn't feel the freedom to be sad and upset himself."

Again Antonia said, "He is a little boy."

"I know," Sarah said. Then: "What do you mean?"

Antonia appeared perplexed by the question, but Sarah imagined it was the perplexity of translation. At last Antonia said, "I mean he must find a little boy's way. Do you see?"

"I think so," Sarah said, but even then, at that moment, she knew that, being lost in Antonia's diamond mines without a light, she surely saw inadequately, she saw everything inadequately.

At the kitchen table, Sarah feels the pressure of these two recent conversations, yesterday's with her mother ("What do you *do?*") and the one with Antonia two days ago ("You have no light"); the recollection of them seems to have filled her head with something dense and heavy, and she finds herself ridiculously slumped in her chair. Before her taskmastering other self can quite bark, "Sit up, Sarah!" the telephone rings, startling her into better posture. Though it's Enid's slot, it's not Enid calling. Harry's teacher is phoning to see if Sarah can stay for a few minutes today when she comes to get Harry at school.

"Yes," Sarah says. "But, Julia — is everything all right? Is anything wrong?"

"I just want to check in with you," says Julia, plainly soft-pedaling. "I want to show you some of Harry's work. It'll only take a few minutes, and Harry can hang out in the library till we're done."

Sarah agrees to meet with Julia at a quarter past three, and after hanging up, she lifts her grandmother's teapot with too slack a grip and drops it dead onto her cup, smashing both cup and pot. The spilt tea spreads across the tabletop and drips like a brown beaded curtain to the floor. The teapot, exploded, looks like something from a shipwreck, blurry domestic vestiges of lost relations. With a kind of terrible complaisance, Sarah guesses the muscles in her hand must be pretty darned relaxed; she moves, dazed, to the mudroom by the back door — to get a broom, she supposes — but once there, a pair of garden shears, weaponlike on their hook on the wall, snags her attention and she reaches for them and takes them down.

She goes out the door and heads for the fence and the lilacs, stalking through the resplendent day as if it's so much smoldering ash from a recent catastrophe. In the past, she has brought clusters of lilacs into the house at this time of year — large vases on the dining room table and in the hallway, smaller ones on the mantel in the living room and upstairs — and she means to do it again, now.

At the fence, the most ready clusters are swarming with bees, but she's not to be deterred and wields the shears recklessly — a little, she observes even while she's doing it, like a madwoman. Despite the medication, the schoolteacher's call has set a small motor humming inside Sarah's chest, something like the buzzing of the bees, and she throws bough after severed bough of *Syringa* fucking *vulgaris* onto the ground, seeing of course that cutting flowers isn't what she's about; she's denuding the lilacs and thinking all the while, I'm discovered . . . I'm found out. . . .

By the time Deckard's done with his exciting visit to the library, he has only an hour before he's due to report to work. He's managed to pull himself together enough to escape the sinister stacks, get back to the circulation desk, and check out the book on memory loss — a copy of the same book he'd been reading before — though it's no longer clear that *loss* of memory is exactly his problem. Freaky, unwanted memories, yes, filling in the gaps left by whatever he's forgetting. On the steps of the library, he thinks of memory as a drug — he has found there are very few things in life that can't be thought of as a drug — if memory were a drug, he thinks, what just happened in the bowels of the library was definitely an overdose, uncut.

Since the weather's putting on such a splendid show, he decides to use his free hour in the park. He can settle himself on a nice grassy slope by the pond, and there'll be girls to watch doing their warm-day stuff, jogging in sports bras, biking in Lycra shorts, walking and talking, reaching back behind their heads to engineer ponytails. It's a bit early in the day, but there might even be a few sunbathers. Last summer, when he was lounging by the pond on a Friday morning before work — about twenty-five feet from two bikini-clad college girls who were sunning on their stomachs with their tops untied — Deckard spotted a white man, an average Joe in an undershirt, baseball cap, and (as it turned out, handy) Air Jordans. The guy was standing a stone's throw from the girls, behind a maple tree, unzipped, and going at it to beat the band. The girls' blanket was between Deckard and the maple tree, and all Deckard had to do was to get to his feet and start in their direction for the guy to take off running. The girls never knew anything had happened, but because Deckard had stood up and moved closer, one girl said something to her companion, and the two of them gave him a fishy look and started tying up their bikini tops. Ironic, of course, and he would like to have gone over and explained the situation, but that wouldn't have worked. He left right away after that. He'd been reading a book and enjoying his proximity to the girls, sneaking unobtrusive peeks now and then, but the working-class wanker behind the maple tree had spoiled everything, subsumed him somehow into a worldwide bachelor herd of lechers preying on girls in public. As he left the park that day, he noticed that nearly every outpost of girls-on-a-blanket had its hovering lone male somewhere in the periphery.

Perkins Street takes him straight to the edge of the park; he crosses a stone footbridge and heads for the pond along a woodsy bicycle path. The fine weather has indeed brought out hordes of the physically fit, joggers, bikers, bladers, and even young mothers boogying toddlers along in expensive big-wheeled all-terrain sport-utility strollers. Admittedly, Deckard's having another in a line of strange days, and to some degree his take on things is colored by this trend, but he believes that even an objective observer would note the mondo-weirdo quality of all the various human samples whizzing past him at breakneck speed this morning. There's something futuristic about it, as if he's trapped in a never-aired bucolic episode of *The Jetsons*. He's clearly too old, too fat, and wearing way too many clothes — Rip Van Winkle waking up in a world to which he's become completely irrelevant, where who he is and what he has survived doesn't matter to anybody. As the pond comes into view, he thinks, A walk through the park ain't what it used to be, and though there is a young white girl reading on the grass in shorts and a tube top, there's also an old black woman sitting on a bench in the shade nearby and feeding pigeons, and Deckard chooses to sit near her instead. He circumnavigates her so as not to scare away any pigeons, and once he's settled on the ground beneath a fruit tree that's currently in bloom, the old lady glances up at him and smiles.

Stretched out beneath the tree, Deckard opens his book, thinking that even his ability to recognize the words on the page as symbols with specific meanings is a function of memory. According to what he's already read in the book — and *recalls* having read — all forgetting is a result of interference. And interference can be anything, including everything learned before the forgotten thing, and everything learned after the forgotten thing. What's vaguely disturbing to Deckard is that every memory is encoded in a particular context and in a particular setting, replete with an array of associations, conscious and unconscious, present at the time the thing is learned or experienced. So that means that all *other* contexts and settings, along with their associations, potentially interfere with recalling whatever it is you want to recall. A drunk, when he's sober, can't recall where he hid his bottles, but the next time he's sauced, no problem; he knows right where to go. If this interference was absolute, and if new experiences didn't link up with old ones through association, Deckard wouldn't know who Bernice and Frenchfry were outside the walls of the VA. He couldn't add two and two outside his first-grade classroom. He would have to return to his childhood home every time he needed to tie his shoes.

Right now, the buzzing of bees in the branches over Deckard's head is interfering with his ability to concentrate on this vaguely disturbing business from the book, and he wonders if the reason it feels vaguely disturbing is because there's something vaguely disturbing about the buzzing of the bees. He recalls that he's reading the book in the first place because he was concerned, weeks ago, about his failing memory, and he notes that he doesn't feel particularly concerned about his failing memory anymore — he feels concerned about something else, but he's not sure what — and in another minute he's no longer stretched out beneath the fruit tree in the park but transported to a lake on a long-dead uncle's farm in South Carolina.

He was seven or eight years old, about Harry's age, and he'd been splashing around in the waist-high water near a splintery wooden pier that jutted out into the lake. Now he wanted to join his uncle and his father, who were fishing at the end of the pier, where they had a cooler stocked with cans of Jax beer and one or two Coca-Colas. The heat and shapelessness of the summer day had made Deckard feel lazy, and rather than wade all the way back to shore, he decided to climb aboard the pier, using the creosote pilings and two-by-fours that supported it. Tied up nearby there was a little red-and-white rowboat he could use as a launchpad.

A short while earlier — on the way to the lake, in the uncle's truck — Deckard had asked his father to teach him how to fish today, but his father had said he didn't have time to be giving no fishing lessons. Deckard was sitting on the bouncy seat between his father and the uncle, who was driving the truck. It seemed to him that since they'd come down to South Carolina, supposedly on vacation, time was the one thing there'd been way too much of.

The uncle took the stub of a cigar out of his mouth and said, "For crying out loud, Jimmy, why don't you teach the boy to fish?"

"You teach him if you want him taught," his father had said. "I came down here to do some fishing myself, and if there's one thing I know about fishing, it's that you can't fish and be teaching a kid to fish at the same time. It's Rule Number One."

"Well, what am *I* gonna do?" Deckard had asked his father, and his father said, "Use your imagination, boy. Use your imagination."

Now, as Deckard crouched in the rowboat and steadied it with his hands on either side, he thought what he was doing was a good example of using his imagination. He stood up slowly, moving one hand onto the pier's closest two-by-four. On the warm dry wood, he left watery fingerprints that soaked in and faded like disappearing ink. The two-by-fours were nailed to the pilings at sharp angles, so as Deckard climbed, he placed his feet carefully in the vees where the timbers met, mindful not to get pinched or wedged.

The trickiest part came at the top, where the pier's deck overhung the pilings by about ten inches. A heavy rafter ran the length of the pier, between the pilings and the deck, and he thought maybe he could grasp the rafter from underneath, swing one foot up onto the pier, and roll aboard it sideways. As he was contemplating this possibility, his eyes were about even with the edge of the deck, and a single black-and-yellow wasp emerged silently in the crack between two planks, no more than five inches from his nose. Some hard cold steel thing seemed to clamp down on his heart, and the muscles in his arms and legs went limp. He was afraid he might fall, which would mean cracking his skull on the rowboat, stitches at the hospital, and a good shellacking from his old man. Already he could hear his father's voice — *What a goddamned fool thing to do, Deckard* — but another

327

voice inside his head was shouting *Hurry,* and as he rammed his free hand under the rafter, his thumb and all four fingers sank into something soft, papery, and alive with a kind of quivering electricity.

All at once, the rims of his ears and the skin on his chest and stomach were on fire. It seemed he was outside himself, watching himself fall from the pier in slow motion, raking his ribs on the red-and-white rowboat before hitting the water. He heard a kind of long high squeal, as if an animal were being peeled and turned inside out, and realized the sound was coming from his own throat. In the sky, the sun was dotted with thousands of black specks, and then somebody was slapping him all over, even his eyes and ears, yanking him up, shoving him back down, slapping him, yanking him, shoving him back down. Just before the sun went out, he saw that it was his uncle, apparently trying to drown him, yanking him around in the water and daubing him all over with his nasty wet cigar.

Deckard had cracked a rib on his left side, where a bright-red patch of raw skin stretched from his hipbone almost to his armpit. His right ear looked like something chewed up and spit out by the dog, and his right eye was swollen entirely shut. The doctor said it would open again in a couple of days, which it did. Deckard had been stung twenty-four times altogether. His uncle, who'd come to his rescue, had been stung eight times, and the doctor told everyone that the uncle's immediate application of tobacco to the stings had "helped a lot." Deckard's father had not been stung — he'd stayed on the pier and watched everything from above — and for this, Deckard was very grateful.

The old woman who was feeding pigeons stands gazing down at him, and when at last he notices her, she looks as if she's been standing there studying him for some time and has finally reached her conclusion about him, which she's about to share. Deckard can see now that she's not quite as old as he first thought — seventies instead of eighties — but she's skinny and wearing an old woman's straw hat and an old woman's long navy-blue dress: church clothes, he thinks. He can see also that there's something not quite right about one of her eyes; it's not centered properly and looks clouded over.

"I was wondering," she says, in a voice that's not scratchy, as you might expect, but clear as a bell. "Is that any good?"

She means the book that's lying open, face down on Deckard's stomach.

"I don't know," he says. "I keep forgetting what I've read."

It takes her a couple of seconds to get the joke; then she throws back her head and laughs, placing one hand flat on the top of her hat. It's the kind of overreaction that's meant to hide the fact that she was slow to catch on in the first place, and now she seems a touch embarrassed. With her other hand she's squeezing the balled-up paper sack that had held the pigeon food, and she glances quickly over at the trash can by the footpath; she was on her way to the trash can, she stopped to speak to him, maybe now wishes she hadn't, and she's unsure about how to continue.

So Deckard smiles and says, "I was a thousand miles away."

"Oh, that's all right," she says. "In a happy place, I hope."

"No, not exactly," says Deckard.

She looks as if what she has suspected all along has now been confirmed. She knits her brow, which makes the brim of her hat tilt downward.

"You don't mind me saying so," she says, a declaration, not a query, "but you look like you might've lost your best friend."

"As a matter of fact I did," says Deckard. "Not too long ago."

"I *am* sorry," the woman says. "Well, the

Lord giveth and the Lord taketh away."

Deckard nods, not wanting to be impolite, though he's not in the mood for biblical platitudes. He looks at his wristwatch.

"And taketh, and taketh, and taketh, and taketh, and taketh, and taketh, and taketh," the old woman adds, pulling a don't-you-know-just-what-I'm-talking-about kind of face. She rolls her eyes back in her head, the slow one not quite making it to the top.

"So it seems," Deckard says, "so it seems."

"So it seems," says the woman — not sadly, but as if she swallowed this particular pill a long time ago. "I sure never thought I'd end up a bird woman," she says. "I'm *supposed* to be lying in my deck chair on the *Queen Elizabeth Two*. That's the picture I had hung up in my dreams anyway, this time of life. And here I am, look at me. Park bench for a deck chair. Pigeons by the duck pond instead of rum-and-Cokes by the swimming pool. What are you gonna do? What in the world are you gonna do?"

"I don't know," says Deckard. "I honestly don't know." He looks at his wristwatch again. "I guess what I'm gonna do is go to work," he says.

"Go to work," says the woman, and she fixes her gaze on Deckard in a way that makes him feel curious and edgy at the same time.

He sits up straight and says, "What?"

She steps closer and then very slowly bends toward him until she can touch his face with her hand. She caresses his cheek twice and cups his chin for a couple of seconds, and Deckard feels strangely moved, like a child awed by some adult behavior he doesn't grasp. A breeze stirs the fruit tree and causes a few pink blossoms to glide down to the grass, dreamily.

. . . his mother has crept into the room to comfort him, too late, way after the fact. Way too little, way too late. He sits on the edge of the bed, wiping his nose with the hem of his T-shirt. She reaches out to touch his face and he jerks his head back as if her gnarled brown hand's a snake about to strike. . . .

"Do you mind telling me your name?" the woman says, withdrawing her hand slowly.

"Deckard," he says, "Deckard Jones," and as he speaks his name, tears spring from his eyes — wild, high-flying tears, like tears in a cartoon — and though he's rattled by it, it seems the exact inevitable climax to everything that has come before, from the minute he saw the old woman and chose to sit close to her.

She straightens her spine and looks at him askance, almost with suspicion. At last she says, "Well, Deckard Jones, you got a lot going on, don't you, son?"

"Yeah," Deckard says, wiping away the tears. "Yeah, I guess I do."

Here's the point of studying the effects of laminar flow on endothelial cells: The treatment for myocardial ischemia involves bypass surgery, which generally uses either a saphenous vein or a mammary artery, but sometimes a patient who needs bypass surgery doesn't have a suitable blood vessel to spare; if you want to engineer vascular substitutes in the lab, you need to find out everything you can about how the biological factors of the situation interact with the mechanical factors; you need to learn not only how the thing is made but also how it works. Blood flowing through a vessel exerts pressure — what's called "shear stress" — on the vessel walls, and endothelial cells, which make up the inner lining of the blood vessel, respond to this stress. They elongate themselves and align their major axes in the direction the blood is flowing. They respond also by secreting some interesting things, like the platelet-derived growth-factor-B chain molecules Sarah mentioned to Enid a couple of days ago on the telephone.

Sarah — who, in her midmorning lilac-maiming frenzy, sustained two bee stings (both on the palm of her right hand) — now sits on a bench high up on a bank of the river, observing the flow of the water and some of its erosive stress effects on the natural levee. Her mind wanders in and out of a crazy meandering daydream about laminar flow and how the epic emotional stress of Malcolm's death has stretched and pulled her and surely reorganized all her normal functions. A shaky analogy as it stands, but if she had her wits about her (which she doesn't, not entirely), she imagines she could turn it into something worthwhile.

Directly behind her, across the flow of four lanes of traffic, stands the monastery chapel where Malcolm's funeral was held. She already knows that soon she'll cross the road and go inside. The moment the chapel came into view, she knew that going inside was unavoidable, and now, on the riverbank, she's trying to get used to the idea. The last several weeks, she has carefully avoided the intersection where Malcolm was shot, sometimes driving many blocks out of her way, but she never thought to avoid the monastery, and though she didn't set out this afternoon for the chapel, it now seems the inevitable destination — as if she arrived here because she neglected to *avoid* arriving here.

Earlier, when she was stung by the bees, she

sat on the ground in the backyard and stared at the two tiny red dots on the palm of her hand — watched two small coronas redden around them, on either side of the lines in her palm that formed the deep perfect *M* she'd cherished as a girl growing up: *M* for Marriage. Stung, staring at her hand, which was starting to throb, she thought, *M* for Mental. Her frenzy, induced by the call from Harry's teacher, was over. With a little of nature's help (two quick shots of *apis* neurotoxin) she'd moved from panic to stupor: progress. She pulled herself up from the ground and went into the house, where she confronted her grandmother's smashed teapot, so crude a symbol of loss, forget-me-nots in splinters on the floor. She realized she wasn't panicked about being found out in any specific way — her midnight wailing in the closet, the soap operas, her and Harry's weight loss, Harry's nightmares and bed-wetting — these were incidental. Her real fear was general: Harry's teacher had somehow discovered that she, Sarah, had been refusing for more than two months to continue living and that poor Harry, having lost his beloved father, now had a zombie for a mother, dead in life, lifeless but still roaming the earth.

She swept up the shards of broken china, mopped the floor, and devised a plan. She would take steps, literally. She would bathe, wash her hair, and put on something nicer than the old jeans and sweatshirt that had become her uniform. She would wear lipstick and earrings, the gold hearts that Harry had given her for Christmas. She would make an effort to improve her posture. She would get out of the house, go for a walk in the sunshine, along the river. Afterward, she would walk to Harry's school for her appointment with Julia. And here was the bonus of the plan: since she would be walking instead of driving, she could take another muscle relaxer.

When she rounded a certain bend in the river and the monastery chapel came into view, of course she thought of Malcolm's funeral, but she thought also of his fondness for the place. He'd gone there several times a year for mass, now and then for prayer services, and sometimes in the middle of a day just for quiet and solitude. For Malcolm, church and religion had been subjective and maddeningly uncomplicated. Anytime she questioned him about his beliefs he shrugged his shoulders. "I've told you before," he would say, "I don't believe anything," refusing to be drawn into theological debate. She recalled his returning home one night after compline and joining her in bed where she was grading papers, her challenging him again in some tried-and-true way. What had she been after? She needed, she supposed, to revisit this curious thing, Malcolm's occasional churchgoing, simply because she found it so curious.

"Don't you see?" he'd said. "The whole *idea* of theology is egotistical and completely misses the point. The whole point of God is that God's inscrutable, the one thing in the universe we can't bunkumize with our feeble words and ideas."

"That sounds like a belief to me," she'd said.

"Not really," he said. "Because I might be wrong."

"That's a belief by definition," she said. "You accept something as true without certainty."

"There, you see?" he said, as if *he'd* scored a point. "This kind of talk always ends up as a debate about the meaning of words. Words, which are our inventions. It's like trying to make music with — I don't know — playing cards or . . . whole wheat flour. We simply don't have the right materials for the job."

"But what about the liturgy?" she asked. "That's words and ideas."

"Well, it's what we're used to on this side of the ocean," he said. "A big long meditative poem. To tell you the truth I don't pay much attention. I just let the sound of it wash over me."

She returned to the student paper she was reading, which was something like a big long meditative poem, indecipherable on the subject of seawater desalination.

"Malcolm," she said after a minute, "darling . . . what does 'bunkumize' mean?"

He turned to her and smiled. He burrowed down into the covers, nuzzled alongside her, and kissed her elbow. "Just what it sounds like," he said.

He was happy not knowing certain things, preferred not knowing, chose not to know — a concept that eluded her entirely.

She heard her grandmother's voice: "Oh, Sarah, child, why do you have to ask so many questions?"

And her young-soprano reply: "Because I want to *know*."

At least part of Malcolm's response to the chapel, as with any building, was physical; he wouldn't have been able to attend religious services in a sports arena or in some Californian crystal palace. The monastery, like Malcolm's theology (or antitheology), was uncomplicated, humble, and in a paradoxical way elegant: Gothic Revival with a pinch of Spanish mission, designed in the early twentieth century by a man named Ralph Adams

Cram, who advocated the Gothic Revival style as a remedy to the rise of technology. To Malcolm, the remedial concept in design was essential. Buildings were meant to help people, after all; they were forms of shelter. From time to time, Malcolm had encouraged her to come with him to services, just to savor the chapel's wonderful interior, and she'd always intended to go. Except for the occasion of Harry's baptism years ago, she'd never been back. Not until the funeral — which, for all she'd taken from it, might have occurred just about anywhere gloomy and gamy with frankincense. But today, when she saw the chapel's granite walls, the place did strike her as a kind of shelter. She knew immediately that she would go inside, and she needed to put her back to it for a while. She needed to get used to the idea of doing something when she didn't know exactly why she was doing it.

On the riverbank, she thinks about the endothelial cells — she has seen them in photomicrographs — elongated, their very cytoskeletal structures altered, in the direction of the laminar blood flow. She has seen a Northern blot analysis of the messenger RNA expressed by the endothelial cells, stimulated by flow. A world within a world within a world.

Meanwhile, in the sky, ballistic lines of

white clouds career in all directions, like the vapor trail to the Big Bang. The trees on the opposite bank, reflected, have turned the water a deep green. A beautiful young man — her own Harry in a few short years — singly pilots an impossibly long scull downriver, cutting a silver, vanishing double seam in the channel. She stands and turns to the road behind her. The towering limbs of the sycamores on either side meet high overhead, the vault of a great airy cathedral — the monastery chapel a side chapel to this natural one, while inside, it has side chapels of its own — an observation Malcolm would have liked, his pathways within pathways.

She waits for a break in the traffic so she can cross over.

It turns out that the very act of remembering stimulates the memory in general, keeps it turned on, and Deckard reasons that Malcolm's departure, preceded so closely by Lucy's, has prompted a lot of remembering, and since remembering begets remembering, what he's got going on is a snowball thing, as if some lobe in his brain has gotten a taste of what it's like to be the star and now won't yield back the stage. As he feeds quarters into the coffee machine downstairs in the employees' lounge, he imagines that a certain amount of anxiety is completely normal under the circumstances, like a simple fear of the unknown, but then the paper cup drops with a pop into its little stainless steel niche, ready to receive the boiling-hot coffee, and Deckard thinks, No, not fear of the unknown, fear of the forgotten.

Dr. French, slumming among the plebeians in the employees' lounge, sits at one of the small round tables with the beautiful blonde from the information booth. Deckard turns in time to see her looking his way. She's wearing a pale green sweater the exact color of the toothpaste Deckard uses, and she's holding her gold cross thoughtfully between her lips: Dr. French has just said something about the bald-headed brother over at the coffee machine, and she has rotated a hundred and eighty degrees to get a look. Deckard smiles and wiggles his fingers at the two of them, then pulls out a chair at the table farthest away from theirs and positions himself so they can get a perfect uninterrupted view of his back.

He leans back in his chair, tilting it onto two legs like his mama taught him not to, opens his book, and begins to read — one major self-sufficient scholar.

There are two other people inside the chapel, a woman with dark brown hair worn in a

341

long single braid and a man dressed in black monastic robes. The man and the woman are sitting next to each other, apparently in prayer. Sarah takes a seat in a pew far behind them and on the opposite side of the nave. The chapel's stone arches and pillars, the iron grille, the parquetry of the chancel, and especially the altar's canopy with its four supporting marble columns are all like things remembered from a dream, from long ago. She sits silently and waits, expecting to be overwhelmed by — what? more grief? more anger? despair? — but instead she finds herself thinking of Harry, of Harry as a baby. She recalls his baptism, a thing Malcolm had wanted and a thing to which she had no objection and about which she had no special feelings. But how splendid Harry had looked in his all-white christening gown! She thinks of it now, yellowing in a plastic bag somewhere in a bottom drawer of her dresser, forgotten until this moment. She recalls the torrential rainfall the day of the baptism, and the joke the priest made about how, with all this water, Harry was surely going to grow up to be a bishop. She thinks of Harry in the red robes and miter of a bishop and smiles. Her mind moves back further, to the time of his birth at the end of November, at the beginning of the holiday season, and now she recalls how at the time his arrival mingled with the spirit of the season, the side of Christmas that had to do with the birth of a baby, and how, in those first two or three weeks, she'd grown the closest she'd ever come to religious feeling.

Soon, inevitably, she's crying, quietly enough, she thinks, but she notices that the woman on the other side of the nave is now turning for the second time to look at her. The woman whispers something to the man she's with, and the man whispers something in return. A conversation ensues sotto voce in which it appears that the man is trying to persuade the woman to do something or not to do something. The woman turns a third time and, unfortunately, this time meets Sarah's eye. Sarah quickly bows her head and stands, moves into the aisle, and starts to leave. At the gate in the grille, there is a three-inch drop where the diamond-patterned marble floor changes to slate, and Sarah stumbles; her knees buckle, and it seems to her that she simply glides to the floor, legless, ending in a sitting position on the cold blue slate. She's aware that she has let out a comical kind of squeak, and she's aware of footsteps approaching from behind her, loud, like the resonant clunking of boots.

In another moment the woman who was

with the monk is stooping beside Sarah and grasping one of Sarah's arms.

"Oh, dear," the woman says. "Are you okay?"

A bit dazed, Sarah turns and is surprised to see that the woman, who's dressed in a beige tailored shirt, black dungarees, and cowboy boots, also wears a clerical collar. The man in the robes, about the same age as the woman, thirtyish, arrives and kneels next to them, a mild distress on his face.

"I'm fine," Sarah says, "I really am," and starts to get up.

The woman, who hasn't released Sarah's arm, tightens her grip and helps her into a standing position.

Now that they are all three standing, Sarah sees that the woman is quite tall, taller than herself, taller than the man.

The woman smiles at Sarah. Then, as if nothing out of the ordinary has preceded this moment — as if, now that they are all happily on their feet again, they can start over — she says, "Hi."

At this, the young man rolls his eyes. Apparently he means to be helpful where the woman has not been helpful, and from somewhere inside the folds of his robes he produces several Kleenexes, pressed together into a neat rectangle, like a doll's pillow. He passes these to Sarah; Sarah thanks him and begins wiping her cheeks. During this, she's aware that the woman in the collar is scrutinizing her, not unkindly, not sentimentally, but with a good deal of purpose.

At last the woman says, "Are you sure you're okay? Is there anything we can do?"

Sarah shakes her head. She hears herself say, "No, thank you . . . I'm just . . ." She hasn't any idea where this sentence is leading, so she takes a deep breath, tries to put her thoughts into a line, and, to her dismay, bursts into new tears. She continues shaking her head as she cries, and she's not sure exactly what this means. She thinks of Forrest Sanders, his recurrent head-shaking. She's feeling an awkward urge to run, so she lowers herself into a nearby cane-seated chair. From beneath her brow, she sees that the man and the woman are now looking at each other; the man's face seems to ask, What now?

Sarah takes another deep breath and manages to tell them that she recently lost her husband. "His funeral was held here," she says, "and . . ."

Once again, she hasn't any idea where the sentence is going. His funeral was held here, and what?

The woman says, "We've lost somebody too, somebody very dear to us."

"She doesn't mean 'lost' in the same way," the man says, but because he has aimed the remark right down at the floor, it's unclear which "she" he's referring to.

"I mean we've actually lost someone," the woman says, ignoring the man. "A good friend of ours has gone missing, and we're afraid some harm might've come to her."

Now composed, Sarah nods. It's all she can think to do.

The woman suddenly sits in an identical chair next to Sarah.

"Listen," she says. "I need to ask you: Do you want me to pretend that I don't know who you are?"

At this, the monk, still standing in the aisle, not only rolls his eyes but lets out an audible groan.

Sarah's taken aback by the question, but everything falls quickly into place — she understands what the woman's asking her and, most strangely, she's suddenly taken with how beautiful the woman is and with the calming effect of her voice.

"Yes," Sarah says, "yes, I think I do."

"Fine," the woman says, and smiles again. "I wonder. Do you want to come out into the garden for a few minutes? It's really peaceful." She turns to the man. "We can go into the garden for a few minutes, can't we?"

"No," he says, in a tone that suggests that the woman should know better.

Sarah quickly declines the invitation as the woman stares a steel dagger through the man.

Flustered, he says, "Oh, please, I'm sorry. I didn't mean to be unwelcoming. It's just that the garden is for members of the order only. But we could sit in the courtyard. It's peaceful there too. It's early yet . . . or late . . . I mean, a lot of the bulbs have already gone by, but the perennials aren't quite. . . . Oh, Christ, I really am sorry."

He laughs at himself, briefly, and closes his eyes. He keeps them shut as he says, "It's just that I'm afraid we're invading your privacy."

He opens his eyes and says, "I really do wish you would come and sit in the courtyard for a while. Please."

Sarah notices now that the woman is smiling at the man, warmly, as if they are old friends and he has just pleased her in some old reliable way.

A brick colonnade borders two sides of the courtyard. Immediately Sarah spots a tall rose of Sharon near one of the exterior walls; based solely on its foliage — and therefore based on very little — she thinks it's the same cultivar as the one that grows next to the screen porch at the summer house, the shrub her grandfather planted more than thirty years ago as a gift to her grandmother: Helene, her grandmother's name.

Once they are all three seated on a bench under the colonnade nearest the chapel, the woman says, "Charlie lives here. He can get you a drink of water or something from the kitchen. Do you want anything?"

"Actually, water sounds wonderful," Sarah says, not quite recognizing her own tone of voice. She does feel suddenly peaceful, almost transported. Who *are* these people, and how has she ended up with them here in this beautiful place? Somehow it feels loosely connected to that second carisoprodol tablet she took before leaving the house. All at once, she realizes that the fall in the chapel — its rubber-legged soft landing — was probably connected to the second carisoprodol tablet too. "If you're sure it's not too much trouble," she adds.

"Not at all," the man says, and hurries away down the colonnade.

Sarah watches him go, as he passes in and out of sun and shadow, and once he's beyond earshot, she says, "He doesn't look like a monk."

"Well, he's certainly dressed like one," the woman says. "What do you think monks look like?"

"I don't know," says Sarah. "I don't even know why I said that."

With a single practiced flick of her wrist, the woman removes her clerical collar and unbuttons the neck of her shirt.

"There," she says. "And I don't look like a priest."

The woman smiles, and — again surprisingly, but in a way so natural and confident that Sarah can't possibly object — she places her arm around Sarah's shoulders. She leaves it there only briefly, gives Sarah a hearty squeeze, and then removes it, returning her hands to her lap. She gazes out into the courtyard, which is filled with a good deal of sunlight, and says, "I want to tell you something," then pauses, as if she's carefully choosing her words.

"I've been very worried about our friend who's gone missing," she says, after a moment. "And I was praying about it. The usual stuff: a begrudging Thy will be done, but really thinking, You better not let anything bad happen to her. In other words, I wasn't getting anywhere. In my prayers, I mean. Then you appeared. You looked familiar to me, and when I saw that you were crying I realized where I'd seen you before. Suddenly I felt myself let go of this struggle I'd been having. I remembered the thing I always forget again and again. That my friend's fate is completely out of my hands. I can try to *find* her, but as long as I'm having this wrestling match with my own fear, I won't do a very good job of it. I hope this doesn't sound . . . I don't know . . . supernatural."

"No," says Sarah. "Did you know my husband?"

"I never met him," the woman says, "but I'd seen him a few times, here."

The woman has leaned forward a little, so that she can see Sarah's face. Sarah looks at her for a moment and says, "I'm not dealing with any of this very well." Tears are brimming up again, but she forces herself to continue. "I have a son . . . Harry . . . and I haven't been able to . . . I haven't been any help to him . . . I've been so angry and . . . I've failed miserably at . . . I've been so . . . ."

The woman waits for a few seconds, then says, "Okay. This is only my opinion, but I don't think it's your job to deal with it. This is something you've been dealt. It's dealing with you. I think it's your job to ask for help."

Sarah, who still holds the Kleenexes, begins idly shredding them in her lap. Without looking up, she says, "You don't understand. I don't have my husband's . . . faith. I don't have your faith."

"Why did you come to the chapel today?" the woman asks.

"I don't know," Sarah says. "I didn't plan to."

"Well, let me tell you why *I* came," the woman says. "It wasn't because I think this is where God lives. I come here because it's the place where I feel the most encouraged to be helpless. That's one of the ways it's most different from all other parts of my life. I love that about it."

The man has returned with a small bottle of Evian water, and he sits next to Sarah on the bench. He looks past Sarah, at the woman, and says, "Oh . . . you've defrocked."

Sarah thanks him for the water, uncaps the bottle, and drinks. She feels like a patient in a sanatorium, administered to and observed by two earnest young doctors.

The man, adding to the woman's last remarks, says, "This place also makes you feel sort of smaller. I mean in a good way. Like it's *okay* to be small."

"Yes," says the woman. "There must be some place like that in your —" Apparently she's seen a stricken look on Sarah's face. "What's wrong?" she asks.

What's wrong is that Sarah has noticed the sundial at the center of the courtyard, which has prompted her to consult her wristwatch:

It's five past three. She has never been late for dismissal at Harry's school before, and it will take her at least fifteen minutes to walk there from the monastery.

He has never been very good about writing things down, and often, when he does make a list of things he wants to remember, he'll forget where he put it or simply forget to take it with him. The memory book suggests creating a mental vignette that includes the items you want to remember, an especially handy technique if you're lying awake at night and don't want to be bothered getting out of bed to find a pen and paper. At his table in the lounge, Deckard gazes away from the book and thinks:

> make up with Sarah and make a plan
>   with Harry
> buy toothpaste and nasal spray at the
>   drugstore
> pick up dry cleaning
> put Frenchfry's lights out

Then he imagines Sarah and Harry brushing their teeth at the neighborhood dry cleaners, when Dr. French walks in with a bloody nose. Deckard admires the way the bloody nose includes putting Frenchfry's lights out *and* buying the nasal spray, but he neverthe-less doubts he'll remember all elements of the scene and what they stand for.

The book further suggests taking the first letters of each of the items on the list and con-structing a sentence with words that begin with these same letters. Deckard pulls a pencil from his shirt pocket and writes very lightly in the margin of the page:

> H [for Harry and Sarah both]
> T [for toothpaste]
> N [for nasal spray]
> C [for dry cleaning]
> F [for Frenchfry]

Then he thinks, *Hairy toes never catch fun-gus,* and smiles at his quick ingenuity. He wads up his empty coffee cup, tosses it into the wastebasket a good twelve feet away — two points! — and leaves the lounge, not looking back at the table where Dr. French and the beautiful young information girl are having their little tête-à-tête.

On his way up the stairs, he thinks, *Never fuck holy Caucasian tarts* and begins to chuckle just as Bernice rounds the bend on the first landing.

"What's so funny?" she says in her gravelly tough-customer voice.

"Too hard to explain," says Deckard. "Long story."

She grabs the book out of his hand, turns it right side up, and holds it at arm's length so she can see it. "Humph!" she says. "You think maybe this'll help you remember that coffee breaks are supposed to be fifteen minutes and not half an hour?"

After dispensing with Sarah's effusive apologies, Julia took her to the library to say a quick hello to Harry. Harry, who was reading in an easy chair, greeted Sarah with a kind of extreme neutrality. Sarah told him that she was sorry for being late, just as earlier, at the monastery, she'd been obliged to apologize for having to rush away so abruptly.

Julia and Sarah have now returned to the classroom and sit in tiny red chairs opposite each other at a round wooden table. Julia has given Sarah a glass of water — more water — and Sarah is needing to visit the girls' room but can't bring herself to delay their meeting any longer than she already has. The small chair she's sitting in makes her feel like a big sweaty giant, a giant with a giant's bladder. Sarah notices that there are several crayon drawings of wedding scenes thumbtacked to the walls of the classroom; she recalls that Julia is planning to be married in a few weeks, right after school's out.

A large manila envelope rests on the table in front of Julia, and she has placed both hands on top of it as if she means to keep its contents from erupting prematurely. Sarah can see KEEP OUT written in black crayon across the front of the envelope, and she's certain she recognizes Harry's pristine lettering.

"The reason I asked you to come by," Julia begins, "is that I thought we should compare notes at this point."

Sarah nods, but barely. She knows a euphemism when she hears one.

"How are things going at home?" Julia asks. "I imagine it's been really hard."

Now Sarah notices that Julia is folding and unfolding her fingers over the large envelope, a nervous gesture. On her left hand she wears a colossal diamond. Sarah glances again around the room and sees that in nearly every wedding scene the bride wears a similar ridiculously huge diamond ring. To her surprise, Sarah feels something like compassion for Julia: young, at the threshold of marriage, having to conduct this difficult meeting with an obviously unhinged widow.

"Yes," Sarah says, smiling. "It *has* been really hard. How's Harry doing here at school?"

So much for comparing notes.

Julia says, "I think he's doing remarkably

well. He's quieter than he used to be, but that's to be expected, I think."

"You wanted to show me some of his work?" Sarah asks.

"Yes," Julia says, clearly feeling rushed. "I don't generally inspect the kids' desks. I think of their desks as a place for them to keep their private stuff. The only rule is that they can't keep any kind of food in their desks. A couple of days ago I noticed a smell in the classroom, and I thought probably that's what had happened — one of the kids was keeping food in his desk and something had spoiled. So after school I searched through the desks, and sure enough I was right." Julia laughs now, but not quite convincingly. "A banana."

"Harry left a banana in his desk?" Sarah asks.

"Oh, no," says Julia. "It wasn't Harry. It's just that in the process of looking inside the kids' desks I came across these. . . . I thought you should see."

She slides the envelope across the table for Sarah to open and continues talking. "Of course they're wonderful," she says. "They're *Harry's*. But, well . . . it's not like they're *disturbing* exactly — I wouldn't make too much of this — it's just that . . . I think he's clearly expressing something — you know, with the repetition. And obviously he was keeping them hidden. Feeling a need to keep them hidden."

Sarah's aware of a horrible percolating sound, which turns out to be the water pump in an aquarium near the classroom windows. The aquarium walls are caked with bright green algae, and she suppresses an urge to tell Julia she should move it away from the windows. As she slowly removes the dozen or so pages inside the envelope, she asks, "Does Harry know you took these from his desk and that you're showing them to me?"

She didn't mean the question to seem quite so accusatory; for her, it's a point of information.

"Well . . . no," Julia says, cautiously. "I thought you and I should talk about that together."

She looks at the drawings one at a time, moving them from the top of the stack to the bottom, so only one drawing is visible at a given moment. That seems important. She works her way through the stack silently and slowly — or at least what she imagines to be slowly — so Julia will think she's pondering their full significance, absorbing the depth of what she's meant to absorb. But in truth she's having some trouble breathing, and an ugly prattle has started up inside her head, a rapid incantation of *I will not cry in school I will not cry in school I will not cry in school I will not cry in school. . . .*

They are crayon drawings, accomplished even for Harry, probably the best work he's ever done — though Sarah can't help noticing an obsessiveness in the way color covers every square inch of the pages, out to every edge, filling every corner — and they all take the same subject: a horse, usually black but sometimes dark violet, engulfed in flames, menacing in its enormity (half as tall as the house), its always-open mouth, and its profusion of yellow teeth. In one drawing the horse gallops in flames down a city street, its head reared back, a bright red tongue jutting toward the sky; in another, the horse is inside the house, its neck and head twisted down to accommodate the room's ceiling, while around its four hooves, the carpet is in flames; in a third, a monstrous eye with fire pouring from both corners fills a window frame; in a fourth, the hideous head, wreathed in flames, presses against the black window of a bedroom where, inside, a child lies partly hidden under the covers.

On Monday, Sarah begins her day as usual with the boiling of water for tea, and standing at the range, as she often does, mesmerized by the blue flame beneath the kettle, she tries sleepily to discern what physical shift has occurred inside her. She knows something important began on Friday when she sat in the small red chair in Harry's classroom and looked through the startling crayon drawings — a bitter confrontation with the towering monument of her selfishness if nothing else — but she expected, then, an aftermath of remorse and self-loathing. Instead, she appears to have gained some new ground by accident, without trying, almost in spite of herself. After she put Harry's drawings back into the large envelope marked KEEP OUT, she thanked Julia for showing them to her and said she thought it best to return the drawings to Harry's desk and say nothing for the moment; she wanted to think about what to do next. She walked Harry home from school, and on the shortcut through the playground he reached for her hand. She had to move him to her other side and explain about the bee stings she'd got on her palm earlier that day as she'd ravaged the lilac bushes in the backyard. On the short twenty-minute walk home, she supposed she'd been noticeably silent on the subject of what she and Julia had discussed, for though Harry couldn't quite bring himself to ask, he seemed to want some reassurance that no drastic change — no *additional* drastic change — was about to occur; he asked her questions like, Why didn't you bring the car today? Why are you so dressed up? What are we having for dinner tonight?

A while later, after a lackluster turn in the kitchen (pancakes and syrup on paper plates), she stalled before the mirror in the hallway, where, over the past many weeks, she'd often endured the terse harangues of her drill-sergeant self admonishing her to straighten her backbone and face the music. It was dark in the hallway, and the image looking back at her appeared dimmer and more apparitional even than usual. "Shape up, Sarah, shape up!" snapped the harsh contralto voice in her head, and quite spontaneously Sarah responded, aloud, "I think I'll just ship out instead."

As if these words were a long-lost enchantment, Sarah suddenly felt her fierce overseer in the mirror withdrawing, seemingly borne in the mirror withdrawing, seemingly borne away on the wings of a bright idea. At the moment, she didn't know the exact nature of the idea, but by bedtime the summer house had fully formed in her mind. She would take Harry and go to the country. Wasn't the old house near the bay, where she'd spent so much of her youth, the place where — in the words of the earnest monk at the monastery — she felt most small "in a good way"? For the first time since Malcolm's death, she possessed a really clear sense of purpose: She and Harry were prisoners of despair, and (as with actual prisoners) the best measure against despair was a devotion to *getting out*. So taken was she by this new cause, with its wistful promises of sea breezes and clear constellations, that she forgot to take her medication Friday night and slept six full hours without waking.

Over the weekend, spring's rosy weather paled to a more compassionate climate, not quite warm, not quite cold, a silver-gray overcast sky, full of light, comforting in its ambiguity, and throughout Saturday and Sunday she privately nursed her new idea, let it swell inside her as she imagined herself and Harry at the old house, at the seashore panning tide pools, exploring the wilder dunes and remote fire roads that tunneled through the forest to the ocean cliffs. Sunday morning, she phoned her mother — precipitously, before the matinee of *The Rivals* — to say she planned to take Harry to the country for a while. It felt like a necessary step in the procedure, to test the waters, to hear herself actually say it out loud; Enid did not answer the telephone, so Sarah was able to hear herself say it out loud to an answering machine, which seemed to receive it favorably. Enid didn't return the call that evening, which, like much of Enid's behavior, was difficult to interpret. Both Saturday and Sunday nights, Sarah slept soundly, without the aid of any sleeping pills. She entered no wee-hour walk-in closets in which to wail, and Harry didn't scream in the night from any terrible dream of horses on fire (what, after the drawings, she thought of as his "nightmare").

Now, as she stands at the kitchen range waiting for the tea water to boil and trying to discern the exact physical nature of this vague sense of having gained new ground, she thinks she's simply more rested than usual, not hungover from sleeping pills — and then all at once it hits her: the knife between her shoulder blades has been removed, its slow twisting ceased and desisted.

Harry, as if he has heard a noise caused by this happy discovery and come down to investigate, walks into the kitchen wearing only his boxer shorts and a curious expression. He moves beside her and wraps his arms around her, rests his head against her hip, and she quickly backs away from the range, away from the flame, dragging him stumbling to the middle of the room.

"I have an idea," she says to him.

He looks up at her, worried. Sunlight from the window behind the sink — the first sunlight since Friday — gilds his eyelashes with a ragged thread of gold.

Sarah imagines, rightly, how everyone — starting now, with Harry — will disapprove of her plan, but surprisingly, it doesn't seem to matter who approves or disapproves. She feels Malcolm on her side.

Harry simply refuses to go. He tells her that if she wants to go she can go by herself.

"But you couldn't stay here alone," she says.

They are at the kitchen table, where Harry studies — with no intention of actually partaking of its contents — the bowl of cereal she has put before him. Now and then he appears to search for his own reflection in the spoon that lies idle beside it.

"I'll go live with Deckard," he says.

Sarah watches him as he glances at her and

quickly averts his eyes — he's checking to see if his words have inflicted the hurt he means them to. It seems to Sarah that even yesterday this remark might have cut to the quick, but today she hears it for what it is, the reckless-ness of a frightened child.

She hasn't considered her next move, and without any particular strategy she hears her-self saying, "And what about the nightmares, Harry? Do you think if you go live with Deckard you'll stop dreaming about the horse?"

It's too big a thing to bring out suddenly like that at the kitchen table, ambushing him with it, bullying him — a power play — but there it is, out, and it certainly gets Harry's wheels turning. He looks at her for a moment, his eyes glassing over with tears, then stares down at the cereal bowl, putting together the pieces of the puzzle she has presented him. She waits, and although she can see only his profile, he appears to move fairly quickly from shock and wonder to tremendous relief, a kind of thawing of something rock hard inside him.

Finally he looks up from the table and says, "How long would we stay?"

"Until we decide to come back," she says.

"You mean until *you* decide," he says.

"Yes," she says, "that's right. Until I decide. You see, Harry, I'm the mother. I haven't been acting much like it lately, but I am."

This remark makes him look at her again, and again she waits silently; she suspects that with "I haven't been acting much like it lately" she has recognized something he has wanted recognized. Again he stares into the cereal bowl, as if decoding an encrypted message in the design of the soggy flakes floating on top of the milk. At last he says, "When would we go?"

"Soon," she says.

"I'm not done with school."

"Do you want to be done with school?"

"But what about second grade?" he asks. "I won't finish."

"I'm sure I can work something out with Julia," she says. "I'm sure that over the summer we can prepare you for third grade. I think you should go in today, if you want to, and I'll call the school and tell them our idea."

"Your idea," he says.

"Okay," she says. "My idea."

Now he turns fully around in his chair and bends forward to examine a spot on his knee, scratches it with his fingernail. Despite the certain grudging language of his putting his back to her, she observes the wonderful white-knobbed cable of his spine, how close to the skin, how thinly armored the nerves and bones are.

Very quietly he says, "Will I stop having the bad dreams?"

"I don't know, sweetheart," she says. "Maybe. I hope so."

"What will we do down there, all by ourselves?"

"We can bring your computer. You can bring your video games. Since you've become a vegetarian, I thought we could make a garden, grow vegetables. We could bring things back from our walks at the beach and put together a marine aquarium, study the plants and animals we find. And after it gets hot, we can do everything we always did with your dad: swim, take the canoe on the pond, go for hikes in the hills. We can play baseball."

He turns around to face her. "Baseball?" he says. "Who with?"

"Just the two of us."

"You don't know how."

"I know a little, and you can teach me the rest."

"No, I can't."

"Why not?"

After a brief additional silence, he lifts the spoon from the table and dangles it thoughtfully for a moment above the bowl. With his other hand, he slides the bowl a few inches away from her and angles his knees just slightly toward the door to the hall, also away from her. She's thinking he wants to take the first bite without risking eye contact, without jeopardizing his still-uncommitted status, but she's thinking too, I have him . . . I have him.

The long freezing-cold corridor that leads from the men's showers to the spa area (the sauna, the swimming pool, the Jacuzzi) is, like the rest of the place, completely tiled, both floors and walls, the ceilings made of some kind of burnished metal that looks like nickel. Deckard surmises that this is so it can be scooted down with a high-powered hose: altogether a cozy place that might double in off-hours for slaughtering animals.

A couple or three weeks ago, he received in the mail a promotional coupon (one free visit) for a newly opened health club near the hospital, and since, this morning, he was awake at the crack of dawn and saw no future in going back to sleep, he decided to cash it in. Despite the hour (around seven-thirty now) and the so-far-unpromising ambience of the place, he's hoping there might be some early-bird water nymphs to scope out in the Jacuzzi. A red-lettered sign in the locker room instructed him to shower before entering the spa area, and now he's paying the price for his obedience. Dripping wet, he shivers in his swim trunks, his flip-flops flip-flopping way too loud as he heads up the empty, echoing corridor.

The sauna, a glass box not much bigger than the one they put Adolf Eichmann in during his Jerusalem trial, is unoccupied. In the small rectangular swimming pool, a solitary, walrusy-looking white man is doing laps. The pool water casts seasickening fairy lights on the ceiling. The Jacuzzi, a turquoise octagonal tub in the floor, is located only a few feet from the pool, and in it a lone woman appears to be snoozing, with water surging and foaming up around her neck. Deckard, who's beginning to see why the place is giving away free tickets, sits on the rough lip of the Jacuzzi, opposite the woman, and swings his legs into the churning water. He notes that the woman is old, older even than himself, but beautiful in a faded-and-still-fading fashion, an Indian woman with a broad face, coal-black hair pulled into a bun at the back of her head, and a dark brown dot at the center of her third eye. The way the underwater lights light her from beneath, she looks something like a female deity; there's something about her head floating on the bright surface that suggests she herself might be the source of the water's extreme turbulence. She opens her eyes and watches as Deckard thrusts his hips forward and slowly lowers himself into the water. He arches his eyebrows and says, "Hot."

The woman, though she doesn't in the least alter the placid composure of her face, appears to take this remark in. Deckard imagines that she even evaluates it: a profound grasp of the obvious. Once he's settled on the bench beneath the water and, submerged up to his own neck, has achieved equal status with the woman — once their five eyes lie in approximately the same plane — he ventures an unmistakable smile. Without a moment's hesitation, the woman straightens the straps of her swimsuit, rises out of the water, monstrous-breasted, and trudges toward the Jacuzzi steps and the two chrome rails that bracket them. She strains up the steps, and Deckard sees that she's morbidly obese — her body seems to cascade down from her neck in ever-widening rolls of flesh scarcely contained by the stretched fabric of her swimsuit — and he quickly looks away as if he has seen something forbidden. Why does this upset him so? Across the way, the man who has been swimming laps yanks himself up a ladder out of the pool, peels off his cap and goggles, and disappears into the tiled corridor, and Deckard is suddenly and thoroughly alone in this strange subterranean room. The chlorine in the Jacuzzi begins to sting his nose; the hissing of the water seems to grow louder. He speculates that perhaps he never actually awakened early and left the apartment to cash in his coupon at the new health club. Maybe he's still back in bed, at home, asleep, and all this is but another of his famous misery-and-rejection-themed dreams.

The weekend was a blur, lousy, gray nondescript weather that made you want to stay indoors and work on your toenails. He did a bit of reading in the memory book, catnapped, watched TV, made spaghetti . . . and what else? It was a blur. He did manage to get to the dry cleaners on Saturday and to the drugstore, where he remembered to get toothpaste (he thought of the information-girl's green sweater) but then stood comatose in the cold-remedies aisle for about ten minutes trying to think what the second item was he'd wanted to buy; when he finally returned home, entered his apartment building, and started up the first flight of stairs, a mouse ran across the landing and Deckard thought, *Eeek . . . nasal spray!*

Explain that one. Nothing about that in the memory book.

This small event made him think of elephants — how he'd learned as a child that ele-phants supposedly had good memories and that they were also easily frightened by mice. He encountered Mrs. Rothschild at the top landing.

"Deckard, dear," she said cheerfully. "I'm so glad to see you."

The old woman, hanging on the landing for no apparent reason, the door to her apart-ment ajar, didn't elaborate.

After a pause, Deckard said, "I'm glad to see you too, Mrs. R.," and rattled his ring of keys at her like Captain Kangaroo.

Though it was near noon, she was dressed in a hot-pink housecoat and matching terry-cloth slippers. The housecoat had a wide shiny collar that stood up stiffly around her neck and caught on her earlobes whenever she turned her head. Deckard's rattling his keys at her prompted a girlish giggle, and then, as he began to unlock his apartment door, she said something amazing. "I can't for the life of me think what I came out here for. You know, Mr. Rothschild had a memory like an elephant. I so depended on him to remem-ber everything for me."

Deckard looked at her and she tilted her head to one side and smiled, evidently imag-ining that she had pleased him somehow — which, in an odd way, he supposed she had.

He said, "I was just thinking about elephants as I came up the stairs, not two seconds ago."

"Oh, isn't that interesting," she said. "I have an old photograph from our trip to India after the war. The two of us riding an elephant, the silliest thing you ever saw."

She turned back toward her apartment, and Deckard assumed she was going to fetch the photograph. But once she was inside, she closed and double-locked the door. He waited briefly, just in case, but she didn't return.

That was the big highlight of the weekend.

Then, this morning, before being struck by the bright idea of the new health club, Deckard woke at the crack of dawn. He thought of cartoons he'd seen in which dawn actually cracked, audibly, waking the sleeping character, usually a pig or a rabbit or a family of bears.

He put his hands behind his head, closed his eyes, and saw in his mind an empty room. Two doors, which opened. Through one, Sarah entered. Through the other, Harry. He heaved a sigh and felt a kind of dull heartache over how much he missed them, and a slightly sharper pang of guilt over not having got in touch yet to patch things up. What, exactly, was holding him back? Was he procrastinating in order to teach Sarah some kind of lesson? Wasn't it, at the end of the day, his own stupid pride at work? And what would Malcolm think? If Malcolm were looking down at him right now from some puffy cloud, what kind of points was he going to give his best buddy? Deckard resolved to take action today, no matter what. Enough was enough. He would drop his petty irritations and put a little compassion in his life. Take a backseat for a change. He would phone Sarah today, no ifs, ands, or buts.

When he sat up on the edge of the mattress, touched his toes to the floor, and opened his eyes, he noticed that a long vertical spear of sunlight, formed by a slit between the window shade and the side of the window, was piercing a stack of hunting and fishing magazines across the room on top of his bureau. The stack was about eight inches high and something thicker than a magazine was wedged right in the middle of it, causing its top portion to list to one side. He squinted at this curious irregularity in the stack of magazines and continued squinting as he stood and moved toward the bureau; it was the misplaced book on memory loss, for which he'd paid $12.95 to the public library. He pulled it from between the magazines, setting it free, and held it in his hands as he looked back across the room at its identical twin on the bedside table. He retrieved the other book and pressed them together, cover to cover, a surprisingly satisfying experience. Brothers, separated by fate, reunited.

A minute later, barefoot and in his underwear, he stood gazing hopelessly into the refrigerator and had the idea of redeeming the health-club coupon. He could go now, before work, a good way to start blue Monday. Who knew? There might be some overachieving, upwardly mobile businesswomen in the sauna at this hour getting a jump start on the workweek.

On his way out, after he has finished getting dressed in the desolate locker room, he passes a public telephone mounted on the wall next to the toilets. He fishes a quarter and a dime from his pocket, drops the coins into the slot, and punches in Lucy's number. He does this without any conscious act of recalling the actual numbers involved; his index finger (with a memory of its own?) is merely duplicating on the keypad a familiar dance step.

It's eight-thirty now. Lucy will be up, dressed for work.

One ring. What could he possibly be thinking? What's he hoping to accomplish? What is it, precisely, that he wants? Two rings. Now let's see, the Jacuzzi turned out to be spooky and lonely-making, so now he's phoning his ex-girlfriend, who has clearly demonstrated (let me count the ways) that she doesn't want to have anything to do with him. Is this the enduring effect of his old man's belt across his backside, that he should become such a glutton for punishment?

If he does phone Lucy, ever, he certainly doesn't want to do it now, here, in this surreal morgue setting with its disinfected view of washbasins and urinals. And not from a state of such weirded-out emotional need. He rams the receiver into its cradle. Once again, another day has taken a bizarre, confounding turn. He supposes he might as well get used to it.

"There's actually a term for this in therapeutic circles," Enid says on the telephone. "They call it a 'geographical cure.' It's an illusion, Sarah. It doesn't work. It never works."

Enid has phoned Sarah, later in the morning than usual, in response to yesterday's message on her answering machine. Sarah had left her disconcerting message while Enid was in the shower, and unfortunately Enid played it back before leaving for the theater. She'd given a rotten performance at the matinee, thank you, because she hadn't been able to put this cockeyed *idea* of Sarah's out of her mind. Taking Harry to the summer house, what is that supposed to mean?

"Maybe it is cockeyed," says Sarah, upstairs, at the telephone in the bedroom. "But I imagine it has a better chance of succeeding than going downtown to spend the whole day shopping."

"You've never missed an opportunity to belittle what I think," Enid says. "Why should this be an exception?"

Sarah says, "Mother, brace yourself for a shock: this isn't about you."

"We should talk another time," says Enid. "When you're less acerbic. How soon are you planning to go . . . that's assuming you don't come to your senses?"

"Right away," says Sarah. "Maybe tomorrow or the next day."

"Tomorrow? Good lord, Sarah, isn't that just a tad impulsive, by anyone's standards? Can you not think of Harry at least?"

"I *am* thinking of Harry," Sarah says.

"Well, what does his teacher say about it?"

"I don't know yet."

"You mean you haven't talked to her? You haven't consulted the school?"

"No."

"Good lord, Sarah, you were never one to do anything by committee."

"I wonder where I get that from."

"I'm sure I haven't any idea, but this conversation is making me very tired. I'm going back to bed. I should try to nap. I don't imagine I'll actually be able to get to sleep, not after that hideous matinee yesterday and the look Randy gave me last night in Joe Allen, but I should at least try."

"Who's Randy?"

"Oh, Sarah, really. He's only the *director*."

The principal at Harry's school describes Sarah's idea as "abrupt" and suggests that Sarah come by her office at dismissal "to sit down and discuss the issue."

Sarah has never much liked the principal of Harry's school, a starved-looking woman about her own age, unnecessarily thin, who prowls the hallways with a bewildering, grim smile on her lips.

"I'm not sure what there is to discuss," Sarah says, still at the telephone in the bedroom.

"I think there are quite a lot of issues," the principal says. "I would want to speak to Julia, to get her input, for example. It might be a good idea for the three of us to sit down. It might be a good idea to ask Harry to join us as well."

Sarah has called the principal simply to inform her of her decision to take Harry out of school before the end of the term, and now she has the distinct sense — something tight and wounded in the woman's tone of voice — that the principal feels left out of the process. What is this perverse need in people, to make everything be about themselves?

"I definitely wouldn't want Harry at any such meeting," Sarah says. "He needs to have confidence in my judgment here. I wouldn't want him subjected to any second-guessing by you or Julia."

Now the woman is defensive. "I only meant that it might be *appropriate* to include Harry in the decision. After all —"

"Excuse me," says Sarah, "but this is a family decision. It's up to me which family decisions Harry's included in and which ones he's not included in."

"It sounds to me like you've already made up your mind," the principal says.

"Yes," says Sarah. "That's what I called to tell you."

"Well, I still would want to talk with Julia first."

First, before what? Sarah thinks but does not say. Before bestowing your blessing? "I need to know if Harry can start third grade in the fall," she says, keeping her voice calm, "if we do whatever catching up we need to do over the summer."

As if the principal has recalled for the first

time what's behind this conversation — the fact that Harry's father was killed a few weeks ago — her tone suddenly shifts, softens. "I'll see Julia over the lunch break," she says quietly, "and call you back."

All my fault, Sarah thinks, all my fault, this friction. In an effort to sail right through, she had used with the principal some stupid phrase like "We need a change of scenery," as if Harry were simply bored with his present life.

"Thank you," she says now, and wants to say more, but what looms in her mind is a kind of blinding-white geyser of all the things she has been keeping secret. The impulse is to say something that would convince the woman of her good intentions, something that would explain in a sentence the important correction she's trying to make in the course of her and Harry's lives, something that would reveal the exact nature of their trouble, so that her bumbling, regardless of how self-confident a spin she puts on it, would be understandable. But everything that occurs to her to say feels far too private.

The morning at the intake desk passed without incident except for a sudden broadside from Bernice, who appeared from thin air (no mean feat), slapped her hand on the counter with a good deal of rattling silver, and said, "Hey, sleeping beauty, quit your day-dreaming!"

Startled, Deckard called out, "Next!" and Bernice strolled away, laughing and shaking her head, deeply pleased with herself.

No question, Deckard had been caught in the act; he'd been flycasting, in fancy new waders, somewhere in the Green Mountains. He'd turned and looked upstream, where Harry was stretched out on a big flat sunny rock. Harry had agreed to come camping with him to Vermont, with the understanding that there would be no compulsory fishing; Sarah had agreed to let Harry go, with the understanding that there would be no hunting, no guns of any kind. Later, Deckard and Harry would pitch camp at one of the sites in the nearby national park and play poker by fire-light, using kitchen matches for chips. Deckard was in the middle of explaining to Harry what to do in case a bear wandered into camp during the night, when Bernice slapped her hand on the counter.

Earlier, during the morning break, Deckard tried phoning Sarah, but her line was busy. He tried twice more during lunch, but both times found the line engaged. Now he plans to try a fourth time during the afternoon break, which, according to the big-faced clock on the far wall of Reception, should be coming up in about ten minutes. Off and on all day, whenever Deckard could free his mind for a few seconds, he's been fleshing out the details of how he intends to turn over a new leaf with Sarah. First of all, he's going to come right out and say he *wants* to turn over a new leaf, admit that he has been a lousy listener, admit that he has a thing about women crying; it makes him want to run from the room. He'll tell her some little something about what he himself has been going through since Malcolm's death, how it seems to have triggered a whole shitload of unwanted dreams and sensations from the past: Nam, childhood, all that. Maybe he'll bring up his idea of the camping trip with Harry if all goes well. The important thing is that he be humble and forbearing. Make his apologies, say how much he misses them, say how much it means to him having them just across the river, and how he wants to be more of a regular part of their lives. Then let Sarah steer the rest of the conversation. That is, if she ever gets off the telephone so he can get through to her.

Deckard has filled in the last patient's date of birth where today's date belongs and vice versa, and he's making the switch when he becomes aware of an impending presence across the counter: Frenchfry, come down to needle him. "How's it runnin'?" he asks Deckard, and it takes Deckard a couple of seconds to understand that the young doctor means to refer to the Jaguar, once Malcolm's, now Deckard's; at first he thinks "How's it runnin'?" is some new lingo for "How are you?"

"Just fine," says Deckard, "but right now I've got people waiting over there."

The doctor glances over his shoulder at the waiting area. "Okay, okay," he says, holding up both hands in a gesture of surrender. "I can see you're a very busy man."

"That's right," says Deckard.

"By the way," Dr. French says. "Do you happen to know what time it is?"

"What's the matter with you?" says Deckard. "Didn't they teach you how to read a clock in all those fancy schools you went to?"

The doctor smiles and nods. "Just a little experiment," he says.

"What are you talking about?" says Deckard, starting to heat up.

"I made a bet with somebody that you wouldn't give me the time of day," the doctor says. "That's all."

Deckard actually thinks this is funny, but before he can reply he's struck dumb by the sight of a woman walking toward the intake desk — and that strange fraction of a moment before you recognize someone you know and didn't expect to see: Sarah, out of the blue haze of a daydream.

Sarah has been downtown to Malcolm's lawyers' offices — there were papers that needed signing if she was going to leave town for a long period of time — and hoping to repair her frayed relations with Deckard, hoping to get support for her new plan, she stupidly surprised him at work. As she approached the intake desk, where he stood chatting with a young doctor, she saw the odd mongrel look on Deckard's face (the stunned smile saying one thing, the eyes another), and recalled that he didn't appreciate surprises of any kind. She immediately began to regret the surprise visit and even apologized for it, but Deckard managed to arrange a few minutes away from his desk, then hurried her downstairs to the dreary employees' lounge for a cardboard cup of tea. Worst of all, she has sprung her news on him, hardly giving him a chance to catch his breath and leaping over what might have been some mutual words of reconciliation.

Across the small round table (which wobbles each time she lifts her cup), Deckard's eyes have gone dead of any feeling. He takes an unpleasant lecturing tone she has heard before. "You can't just pull Harry out of the world, Sarah," he says. "You can't just make the world go away."

"Why is it that people say 'the world' when what they really mean is the world's garbage?" Sarah asks.

"I don't know what you're talking about," Deckard says. "I'm talking about school and other kids. I'm talking about normal life: sports, newspapers, TV, movies, the world."

"Just what I said," she says. "Garbage. What about the ocean and the sky? What about silence and stars at night? Birds and tides and making a garden? Why aren't these things 'the world'?"

"You know what I'm trying to say," Deckard says. "I like those things too, but in my opinion you're already too isolated, and now you're going to make yourselves even more isolated. I definitely don't think it's the right thing for Harry."

It's a more aggressive disapproval than Sarah anticipated, and she has noticed that since they sat down Deckard keeps glancing past her as they talk — he appears to be monitoring who enters and leaves the room — as if he and she were having some clandestine meeting and might be seen together by the wrong person. She reaches across the table for his hand in an attempt to make him focus, and though he doesn't refuse her exactly, she can tell he doesn't like it.

"Listen, Deck," she says. "It's just not working the way things are. I think you know that. Even if going to the country turns out to be a mistake, I've got to try a change."

He withdraws his hand.

"So you're really going to do this?" he asks, as if she's only floating the idea past him, as if it's the most outrageous thing he has ever heard.

"Well, yes," she says. "You don't have to approve, but won't you at least give me the benefit of the doubt?"

Now she watches in disbelief as Deckard suddenly stands, clears the plastic spoons and paper cups from the table, carries them to a nearby waste can, and returns with a crestfallen face as if *he* is the one crushed. He lifts her shoulder bag from the back of her chair where she has hung it and gives it to her; another time, this might seem a helpful gesture, but now it's shockingly like being handed one's hat.

He says, "I've got to get back to work."

They climb the stairs in silence, and once they're standing in the noisy hospital lobby, Deckard says dismally that he will call her tonight and find a time when he can come over and say good-bye to Harry.

"Deck, it's only a two-hour drive," she says. "It's not like I'm taking him to Alaska. And you've got wheels now."

Oddly, this remark feels to her like another misstep. Is her reference to Malcolm's roadster, bequeathed to Deckard, obscurely vindictive?

"I just wish there was something I could do to stop you," Deckard says, and walks away, leaving her astounded by the open door to the hospital's gift shop.

In the few seconds it takes her to cross to the middle of the lobby — where her bag slips from her shoulder onto the floor, spilling some of its contents — her astonishment turns to anger. She has no doubt about this, for as she stoops to collect the lipstick and keys that have fallen from the bag, she notices that her hands are trembling.

PART IV

Singing Boy

Nobody knew the exact age of the summer house and, throughout her growing-up, nobody but Sarah seemed to care. As a child, she'd been made to feel it was a tedious concern, or worse, like certain mysterious sexual matters, an improper concern for a child. All her grandfather would say was, "Old, Sarah. Very old."

"But how old?" she would say, trying to make him look at her.

As he craned his neck down into the well or tacked up a fallen shake on the privy, he would say, "Old as the hills and twice as dusty."

In the sapphire kitchen, her Grandmother Helene would shrug and say, "Old, Sarah, I've told you before. Old. Very old. Why do you keep asking me?"

"Because I want to know," she would say, her hand resting on the cool white porcelain leg of the sink. Briefly, observing the sudden bulge and gradual taper of the sink's leg, she wondered how it had been crafted, how something so clearly uncarvable could be made so shapely.

"Well, child," her grandmother would say, "it's plenty old enough."

Many years later, long after her grandparents were dead and buried and after her father had died, leaving her the house in his will, Sarah learned of the famous county registry fire of 1923; for any history before that time, she had to rely on the secondhand and unreliable recollections of her grandparents. Before they'd bought the house in the forties, it had apparently stayed in one family, some Garfields from New Jersey who claimed a kinship to the slain American president. In the forties, all that was left of the Garfield family were two unmarried sisters, schoolteachers in need of money, who struggled to maintain the place and who, over time, had sold off pieces of the original parcel, including an acre and a half abutting the town road and a strip at the top of the bluff that commanded a view of the bay. What remained, what her grandfather had purchased and Sarah had inherited, were three and a quarter acres accessible through an easement across the formerly sold-off land. Too bad about the lost water view, but brambles and beech forest had been allowed to grow up along the younger borders, and the estate was pleasantly contained and private.

Sarah's grandfather doubted the Garfield sisters' claim of kinship to the American president, a kinship, as he told it, based on neurotic female delusions. One of the sisters suffered a recurring nightmare in which she saw herself as a girl on a railway platform in Washington, D.C., trying in vain to wrestle a revolver from the assassin Charles Guiteau's grip. When the Garfields and Sarah's grandfather had passed papers in Barnstable, the woman had told him this dream of hers, told him in front of everyone, lawyers and clerks alike, and had openly wept. For Sarah — though she'd got the assassin's name wrong and thought for years it was Charles Guitar — the story of the Garfield sisters and the recurring dream was indelible on the first hearing, initially because of its intriguing elements and then later, after her own marriage and Harry's birth, because she saw in it the grief and shame of a woman who thought she'd failed to preserve the integrity of her family.

Nine years ago, when, according to her mother, Sarah had wrecked the authenticity of the house by having baseboard heating and storm windows installed, the man who did the work told her he thought the house might be older than two hundred years. Sarah could recall the midsummer day when he'd told her. She was five months pregnant with Harry. The man, an Eastham native, typical-looking with long hair, a full beard, sunburned cheeks, and a permanent squint, had spent a good deal of time walking around the outside of the house; every now and again he would pace back some distance and view it from one angle and then another. Curious, Sarah had moved from window to window inside the house, spying on the man from the edge of the window frame. What was he doing? He'd already toured the interior of the house and poked around the upstairs rooms. He'd visited the cellar. Sarah had already counted the windows and doors, measured them, and written it all down for him on a sheet of paper. What could the man be doing?

Soon she saw that he was simply admiring the place, and at an opportune moment she stepped out onto the stoop by the kitchen door.

He shook his head once and appeared to brush something out of his beard.

"Some place you got here," he said to her. "How old is it?"

She smiled, thinking of herself as a girl, standing by the well with her grandfather, standing by the sink with her grandmother.

"I wish I knew," she said. "Old. That shed over there used to be the privy. And that one there is what's left of a windmill. I guess the top two-thirds of it blew away in a storm and they just put a roof on what was left and called it a toolshed. We keep the gardening things in there."

He nodded at each of the sheds, then pointed with his chin toward the garage.

"That garage there's got a sag in the ridgepole," he said.

Sarah gazed at the sagging garage roof and sighed.

"Yes," she said. "It's been like that for about thirty years."

"Probably ought to get it fixed sometime in the next thirty," the man said.

He came to the base of the stoop where she stood, placed one foot on the nearby bulkhead to the cellar, and looked up at her gravely.

"You got some vertical lathing upstairs," he said, "behind the plaster in those little bedrooms. This part here, where we're standing, is newer. But that part, up by the parson's door, it might be better than two hundred years."

That night, in bed, she told Malcolm what the man had said.

Malcolm had driven down late from the city and was tired.

"Hmm," he said, kindly feigning interest. "So vertical lathing means —"

But then the baby kicked — Sarah had been still now for a few minutes — and Malcolm cupped his hands over her stomach and told the baby in a deep voice to settle down and let Mama sleep.

One Saturday afternoon in August, after she and Harry had been at the summer house for about three months, Sarah lay on a quilt in the grass near the great old rose of Sharon at the corner of the screen porch. Harry had been having his nap, upstairs in the attic, but now Sarah heard his footsteps on the back stairs; soon he stood silently behind the door to the porch, looking out at her through the screen. She pretended to be asleep and peeked at him through her eyelashes. His own eyes barely cleared the screen door's crossbar. She knew his first words would be about the Italian ice she'd promised him before his nap, and she didn't feel like getting up, getting in the car, and driving into town. She didn't feel like the whole ordeal of promises, kept, compromised, negotiated, broken, delayed, deferred. But she could sense his debating within himself about whether or not to wake her, and at last, out of sympathy, she said, "Guess what just happened to me."

He pushed open the door, walked across the grass to the edge of the quilt, and looked down at her, his face bloated with sleep and disapproval. He wore only the knee-length dark-blue swim trunks he'd napped in, slung low around his hips. All summer he'd kept the buzz cut Deckard had introduced back in the spring — it was easy to maintain out here in the wilds, far from barbers, with the electric clippers she'd bought at a drugstore; his canines were only half-descended; and most recently he'd applied to the center of his chest a temporary tribal tattoo, a blue-black geometric pattern of stylized flames. Sarah thought he resembled a trailer-park thug, but the fact that his handsomeness survived this (mostly self-inflicted) vandalism made his good looks more striking, added something, the lure of the underdog, and made you want to root for it. That it resided in his father's features and coloring, Malcolm's light brown hair and dark blue eyes, added poignancy. She'd sorted this out one sleepless night when she'd been needing an analysis for why she would sometimes come unglued just looking at Harry; among his several powers for getting his way with her, there was this one he didn't even know about, and she'd wanted to understand it in order not to be entirely ruled by it.

"Just tell me," he said, rubbing his eyes, impatient with guessing games.

"A hummingbird flew right up to my face," she said. "It tapped its beak three times on my sunglasses and flew away."

She thought he might disparage it ("Big deal") or doubt her word ("Oh, yeah, right") or simply blackball it entirely ("Can we go get the Italian ice now?"). But he surprised her by lying beside her on the quilt and snuggling up close as if he were cold. She stretched out her arm for his head, and in the glimpse she had of his face he appeared only thoughtful, nothing more.

Out at the bay's horizon, the sun had sunk low enough that some of its blood-orange light was beginning to slide between the trunks of the locusts and the scrubby beech forest.

"I think I know what happened," Harry said at last.

"What do you mean?" she said.

"I think he thought your sunglasses were a flower," he said. "Probably they looked bright and shiny to him. He made a mistake. Do you think that's right?"

"Yes," she said. "I think that's just what happened. It was a little scary."

He turned his head and looked at her. *Scary* was of course a deep quarry for them, a loaded word (like *loaded*), like *weather* for sailors, and she suspected, rightly, that he would want to refine her use of it.

"But like a roller-coaster kind of scary," he said.

"Exactly," she said. "Thrilling-scary."

"Are fruit bats called fruit bats because they eat fruit?" Harry asked.

(A typical Harry transition: no transition at all.)

She said, "I think so . . . but it's hard to imagine them sitting around a little table slicing apples and peeling bananas."

That made him laugh, and nothing seemed to please her quite as much these days as making him laugh.

"Did you ever look at an upside-down picture of a bat hanging upside down?"

"Wait a minute," she said. "The bat in the picture's upside down *and* the picture's upside down?"

He nodded.

"So in the picture the bat's already upside down, and you turn the picture upside down, making the bat look rightside up?"

He nodded again.

"No," she said. "I don't think I ever did that."

"It's really funny," he said.

"What does it look like?"

"Like he's dressed in some kind of funny jacket," he said, "and he's dancing."

"Where did you see a picture of a bat?" she asked.

"In the encyclopedia," he said, and she recalled her grandfather's moldy set of *Encyclopedia Americana* that occupied three shelves in the alcove off the living room, where books were kept. One autumn when she was a child, she'd cut out a photograph of the moon from the volume MENAGE–OTTAWA and caught hell for it; she'd needed the picture for a school report she was doing entitled "Earth's Nearest Neighbor." When she thought of it now, it seemed impossibly feebleminded. The idea of using scissors on an encyclopedia — what could she have been thinking? But at the time, the big smelly brown books had seemed neglected and forgotten by everyone. She couldn't have been more surprised by the hysterical commotion that had ensued; the experience had formed some small part of her, an exaggerated respect for books that prevented her, to this day, from making even a pencil mark in a margin.

"We could learn about bats this fall if you want to," she said to Harry.

"I already know about them," he said. "I read the encyclopedia."

"But you didn't know why fruit bats were called fruit bats," she said.

"I was pretty sure," he said. "I was just checking."

"Well, we could learn more about them," she said. "We could —"

"Whatever," he said, meaning he didn't want to pursue any talk having to do with the autumn and meaning also that she'd been let in far enough and now he would begin to push her out.

"Do you still want that Italian ice?" she asked, wishing she hadn't reminded him, and wishing her reminding him didn't feel so much like penance for some vague sin she hadn't committed.

"Whatever," he said again, sitting up, disengaged.

At that moment, looking at him, she saw that he wasn't in fact wearing the blue swim trunks he'd napped in but a pair of cotton shorts close to the same color, and this detail arrived for her at a bad moment — she was feeling irritated with herself and with him — and she said, "Harry, did you change into those shorts when you woke from your nap?"

He stood and began to walk away, toward the corner of the porch.

"Harry," she called. "I asked you a question."

He stopped and turned, looking as if he would annihilate her if only he could control the trembling of his lower lip and the tears welling in his eyes.

"It's okay, Harry," she said. "I only wanted to know —"

"I didn't wet the bed!" he shouted, obviously lying, and started to round the corner of the porch.

"Where are you going?" she called.

He stopped again, turned again, and looked at her.

"I'm going to the garage," he said, trying hard for defiance, and walked away.

Now she was up too, following him between the end of the house and the woodshed, down the narrow grass path, under the clothesline, toward the back door of the garage. She was barefoot and stubbed her toe on a foundation brick that had fallen out long ago and lodged in the ground.

"Harry, the garage is locked," she called.

He was already down the final little hill to the door and hidden by an encumbrance of beach roses that swelled along the south wall of the building. Above the roses she could see a bit of the garage wall, the tops of two windows, and, higher, the slight sag of the ridgepole. A robin flew out of the bushes and up to the weather vane.

She heard Harry's voice. "I've got the key," he said. "I know where you keep it."

He was at the narrow door, struggling with the key in the padlock. She watched the sharp rise and fall of his bare shoulder blades, like the nubbins of latent wings. She heard the click of the shackle, then a rattle as he tried to pull it from the hasp.

"Why are you doing this, Harry?" she said to his back.

"Because there's stuff in here I want to play with," he said. "You don't have to come in."

He threw open the door so that it banged against the outer wall. She closed her eyes and smelled the damp cold scent of oil and gasoline, mildew, rotting wood. When she opened her eyes, Harry was inside. Because of the beach roses on one side and the forest on the other, mostly covering the four windows, the garage was quite dark; the wide doors at the front were closed and latched, but she could see the three vertical lines of light that defined them. From where she stood, she could see also a basketball hoop mounted on the right-hand wall, the black metal handle of a wagon at a thirty-degree angle to the concrete floor, a stain — probably the gas-and-oil mixture for the chain saw — near the threshold; and she could see, rigid at the middle of a piece of old beige carpeting, which was itself in the middle of the garage floor, Harry. His profile was to her now, and he appeared to be looking at something in the far corner.

How could she not follow him in, seeing him there in the gloom, his hands jammed, brave and Malcolmlike, into his pockets? She stepped inside, felt a chill, purely physical, invade her arms and legs, and saw past Harry's shoulders the red tractor in the corner, on the seat two straw hats, one bigger than the other.

She started to say Harry's name — an impulse to call him back from some danger — but then he turned and looked at her so purposefully it silenced her. For three months they'd avoided the garage, Malcolm's domain, the place where he'd kept his tractor and power tools and, in a corner by the brightest window, a drafting table. Any time Harry had asked about the locked garage, she'd managed to detour him, but now he'd taken matters into his own hands and gotten more than he'd bargained for. He turned away from the tractor, shot her a hateful sneer — Oh, okay, it said, you were right again — and marched past her toward the open door, throwing the key onto the cold concrete with a *ping* at her feet.

Later, she found him in the garden, crouching between two rows of corn.

"Harry," she said. "Come out. It's starting to get dark."

She could see only his bare toes and the balls of his knees protruding from the base of the cornstalks. More than any other plant in the garden, the corn belonged to Harry; he'd

402

insisted on putting in three rows of it, for when they'd first overturned the soil, they'd discovered the crushed clam and oyster shells the Indians had used for fertilizer thousands of years before them, when this whole valley would have been blanketed with corn.

"Harry," she said. "Come in the house now. Aren't you getting hungry?"

After a few seconds, she heard his voice. "I want to go back home in the fall."

The garden was enclosed with three-foot-high chicken wire to keep out rabbits and deer. Along the base of the fence, they'd planted marigolds. She stooped to pinch off a few dead flowers, and said, "We can talk about that. We can talk about going home in the fall."

"I don't want to talk about it, I want to *do* it."

"I just want to make a plan," Sarah said. "Remember how we sat down with a pencil and paper and planned the garden? That's all I mean."

She heard a rustling in the corn, and soon he was stepping into the dark honey-colored light and standing among the lower plants. Sarah noted the beautiful rosy brown of his skin and felt her heart skip a beat. She could not say, "Your skin is so beautiful," because he'd grown tired of hearing her say things were beautiful. The sky, the light, the sand, the bay at low tide, the starfish and redbeard sponge in their aquarium, the deep purple basil in the garden, the doe and fawn that surprised them one afternoon by walking right out of the trees into the yard, not ten feet away, staring at them in the hammock.

"You say *everything* is beautiful," he'd said one day, when they'd taken a drive and come upon a small glacier pond in the woods.

"That's not true," she'd said. "What about those wild turkeys we saw? I didn't say those were beautiful."

"You thought it, though," he'd said, and it was true. She had thought the ugly turkeys beautiful, and she realized that Harry was right — she had been forcing the issue in that irritating way people sometimes adopt when they want to cheer you up. Since then, she'd been trying to restrain herself.

Now Harry said, "The frog was here again."

"He was?"

"Yes. In the corn."

"Are you sure it's the same one?" she asked.

"Yes," Harry said. "I recognized him."

"Okay," she said, tossing a handful of dead marigolds into the grass outside the plot. "Why don't you pick a couple of medium-sized tomatoes and bring them inside. I'm going to start our supper."

She stood and waited for him. When he'd carefully chosen the two tomatoes and pulled them from the wire cages, he climbed over the fence and handed them to her. She smelled each of them and thanked him, commending his selection.

He began to move up the hill toward the house, mentioning as he went that he was sorry about wetting the bed again.

"I've told you before," she said from behind him, "you don't have to apologize. I just want you to tell me so we can take care of the sheets."

"I already did," he said. "I put them in the washing machine."

"It's not a big deal," she said, for maybe the hundredth time. As she followed him up the hill, the broomstick quality of his arms and legs brought to mind the Latin names of the bones — *radius* and *ulna, tibia* and *fibula* — and for some reason she recalled Harry's last day at school, when she'd gone inside to speak briefly to his teacher. Julia had prepared a folder for them, outlining the work the class would be covering over the remainder of the term. As they were leaving the school that day, they passed two child-made posters on the doors to the gymnasium; one read "Always Try Your Best," and the other read

"Follow Your Dreams."

Harry pushed open the screen door to the porch, which, because it scraped the floor at the base, always stood open until someone shut it again. He went on inside without another word, and as she turned to close the door and saw a single star pierce through the orchid sky over the locust trees, she felt a plummeting of her spirits. The quilt was still on the grass where she'd fallen asleep earlier and where the hummingbird had astonished her with its close inspection of her sunglasses. Where was that strange burst of optimism now, that sense that she and Harry were going to be all right? Could she close her eyes and wish it back? Will it back? Reconstruct a set of conditions that would duplicate the experience and its happy result? Nothing she'd designed, nothing she'd willed or even imagined had produced it; it had come mysteriously, and now, as she stood at the screen door looking out at the end of another day, she was left with a once-reliable impulse, a once-serviceable need, the desire to penetrate what was essentially impenetrable: she was left with the old familiar desire to know *why?*

Around eleven o'clock at night, she climbed the stairs in her bathrobe and looked in on Harry. The windows in the gable end of the attic room faced away from the moon, but through them she could see the moonlit aspens behind the old privy, quaking in a breeze. The screens in the windows whispered as she bent near Harry's bed and kissed his forehead. The nightmares had stopped, and he'd spent the summer drawing pictures of the treasures they brought back from their walks at low tide: hermit crabs and fiddler crabs, grass shrimp and white anemones, periwinkles and moon snails, sea lettuce and green sponge weed. He rendered them entirely recognizable in their shapes but invented all new colors for them, so they looked like cousin species found on an Earthlike planet. Progress, she thought, and yet the bed-wetting continued, and continued to humiliate him.

She'd been wrong to leave him so motherless in her grieving; she'd been right to make a change and bring him here; she'd been wrong to think she could cure him all by herself. She'd carried him only so far and now, apparently, they'd reached a plateau. It was as if there was medicine Harry still needed to take, so he could get well, and she was still trying to figure out the proper dosage or the proper administration of it, what he would tolerate. Too much of the unspoken, too much of the unspeakable, still lay beneath the surface of their daily life, and she felt that another form of arrogance had prompted her to create their present situation; she'd gone from being Not-enough to being his Everything, each in its own way a self-centered path. In her head she could hear Harry's school principal; she could hear her mother, actressy on the telephone; she could hear Deckard, despondent and full of reproach — all saying I told you so.

Deckard had not phoned them the night before they left — the climax, for Sarah, to what had been a mounting sense of his betrayal. Down the road, she'd had to explain to Harry, as best she could, Deckard's long absence. It was about a month ago, on one of their walks, when Harry had asked, "Where's Deckard?" as if Deckard had actually disappeared. Sarah had the presence of mind to give a general even-sided picture of the situation — she'd gone on at some length about the vagaries and paradoxes of grown-up emotions, grown-ups' unintentional failures to help each other — which Harry endured with admirable patience. When she was done, he said, "Why don't you write him a letter?" She'd smiled and said she thought that was a good idea, but so far, though she often saw herself and Deckard in some kind of small-minded standoff, she'd written no letter.

Over the summer, Enid's phone calls had grown farther and farther apart and more and more meaningless. About a week ago, after a three-week silence, she phoned late one very hot afternoon after Sarah and Harry had returned from swimming at the pond. In tears, Enid said *The Rivals* was closing. This was what theater had come to, a slave to the almighty bottom line. Horace had suggested to Randy that they take the play on the road, but Randy had just given Horace one of his famous looks. Could Sarah imagine: Sheridan on the road? London, maybe. But not Boston, for heaven's sake. Not Minneapolis. It was probably a good thing that the play was closing. Enid had to admit she was growing stale in the role. It was a stale role, finally, the kind of role that goes stale early. Not the kind of play that can sustain a long run. And anyway, it *had* been a long run, hadn't it? Much longer than anyone would have imagined. Even Enid couldn't squeeze any more out of it.

Sarah had said, "You can always come out here and spend a few days with Harry and me."

"Thank you, darling," said Enid, "I would love that. But not in August. You know how I hate the heat. Margaret Ginsler has invited me to stay with her and Frank in Belvedere for a few weeks, which sounds heavenly. Nothing to do but sit on the terrace and watch the fog roll in. I think I can handle that."

Then, a few minutes afterward, Detective Sanders had phoned, saying that he was "passing through," which Sarah thought somehow unlikely. Sanders was considerate enough to say right away that he had no news, and she invited him to stop by.

As Sanders got out of his car and came up the brief incline toward the house, he waved to her and Harry, who'd come out onto the back stoop. "Look at you two!" Sanders shouted, apparently referring to their dark tans, perhaps to Sarah's still-wet hair. Sanders himself, out of his work clothes, more handsome than usual in shorts and a polo shirt, appeared to have grown a few years younger since Sarah last saw him.

Sarah had made fresh lemonade, and when she was done in the kitchen, she carried tumblers and a pitcher to the screen porch, where she expected to find Harry and Sanders, but they weren't there. She stepped to the porch door and saw the two of them down at the vegetable garden, inside the fence. Harry appeared to be explaining something to Sanders; he was opening his arms in a slow, broad arc that took in the bluff, the valley, and Tom's Hill behind them, and Sanders had stooped among the tomato plants to pull a few weeds, which he tossed over the wire fence. Seeing Sanders, and seeing him with Harry, stirred something in Sarah: an everyday ache, undissected, she'd named simply "Malcolm," a habitual sense of inadequacy having to do with Harry's needing more company than she'd provided him and a less familiar anxiety about Harry's growing up, her losing him. She decided to leave the two of them be, and she sat in the porch glider and waited.

When, a bit later, Harry had gone to the attic to play a video game and Sanders had joined her on the screen porch, Sanders said he thought Harry seemed "a lot better."

"Yes," Sarah said. "I think so."

"And what about you?" he asked.

Sanders had sat next to her in the glider, and now there was some distraction in the problem of how in-unison or not-in-unison their attempts were to make the glider move back and forth. Sarah said, "I'm better too," and yearned for a question on which she might not feel quite so laconic.

Sanders had removed his sunglasses and hooked them over the opening to his shirt; he gazed out at the black locusts, and Sarah noticed how his eyes filled with light. He shook his head slowly and said, "I thought we would

411

have a suspect for you by now, I really did."

"That's an interesting way to put it," said Sarah.

"What do you mean?"

"A suspect for me," she said. "As if a suspect were something I could use."

"Oh," said Sanders. "I see what you mean. Well, sometimes it can be tough on a family. An unsolved case."

"I imagine the solved ones are pretty tough too," Sarah said.

"Definitely," said Sanders. "It's just that business about closure, you know. It helps people."

"I don't think I understand that," Sarah said. "I thought the hugest imaginable closure occurred when Malcolm was killed. I don't see how anything else could compare. I suppose there might be some benefit to society — finding the person who fired the gun, trying him, sending him to prison — but I don't see how it would help me or Harry."

Sanders sat silent, pressing his foot against the floor to stop the movement of the glider, which apparently helped him to think. After a few seconds, he began slowly nodding his head. "I never looked at it that way before," he said, "but I see what you mean." He smiled warmly and added, "As usual, you have a unique take on things."

Sarah returned his smile and said, "Thank you, I think." She felt a very small and surprising disappointment; though Sanders had obviously tried, she thought he hadn't really understood what she meant or somehow he'd not wanted to pursue the question any further; she imagined the notion and promise of "closure" had been a reliable incentive in the past, and now, unpleasantly, she'd shaken it.

He heaved a great sigh and stood, walked over to the edge of the porch, and stared out through the screen in the direction of the garden. He put his hands in his pockets and kept his back to her. "I told you I had no news to report," he said at last. "Which is true enough. The case will stay open. And you never know. A kid gets brought in on possession of cocaine and turns out to be the perpetrator in a more serious case. It happens all the time. What I wanted you to know . . . the reason I called you . . . I've taken myself off the case."

He turned to face her, removed his hands from his pockets, and crossed his arms. Evidently he'd said something significant, which was escaping her. She said, "Yes?"

"I like you," he said. "As you know. I told you before. I was hoping maybe I could see you, you know, socially."

Immediately, Sarah looked for the wedding

band she'd noticed before, now gone. She said, "I thought you were married."

"Where'd you get that idea?"

"I'm sure I've seen you wearing a wedding band."

"Oh, that," he said, looking sheepish. "I often wear it when I'm working. It's not entirely honest, I admit, but it can help people to open up a little better. If people think I'm all squared away it takes a certain kind of tension out of the air, if you know what I mean. Makes me more trustworthy in people's eyes." He paused for only a second or two and added, "I guess this is the last thing you need, right?"

"No," she said. "Not the last thing I need, not at all. It's just —"

"It's just like that old commercial on TV," Sanders said. "Star Kist wants tunas that taste good, not tunas with good taste."

"No, no," Sarah said. "It's not like that at all. I'm sure you . . . taste . . . fine."

They both laughed at that and there was the thunder of Harry's bounding down the back stairs. In another moment, he stood at the inside door to the porch, hanging there for a second and looking from Sarah to Sanders and back again. She stretched out her arm to him and said, "It's okay, you can join us."

Harry moved to the glider, and she pulled

him onto her lap, wrapping her arms around his waist. She looked up at Sanders, who, in the failing light, was something like a little boy himself, standing on the sidelines of a playing field as his team loses the game. Over Harry's head, she said, "You see, Sanders, I'm so far away from anything like that. You have no idea how far away I am."

After kissing Harry good night, she moved in the moonlight to the upstairs hallway, re-tied her robe, and descended the stairs. On the way to the borning room, where she'd been sleeping — she liked its monk's-cell quality and its window downwind to the garden; she appreciated its not being the room where she and Malcolm had slept together — she stopped in the book alcove off the living room and pulled out the MENAGE–OTTAWA volume of the *Encyclopedia Americana*. She fanned the pages with her thumb and quickly came to the large hole on page 299. She flipped the page over and saw that her child-hood scissors had butchered into incoherence brief articles about James Mooney (an early ethnographer of American Indians whose most famous work was *The Siouan Tribes of . . . ?*), Tom Mooney (a union organizer who was convicted in 1916 of murder in connec-tion with a bombing, but who was later . . . ?), and the mooneye (a freshwater herring of the family . . . ? and which has sharp . . . ?). As she closed the volume and laid it aside, she saw a small book wedged tightly among others on a shelf at eye level. Something about its lime-green spine triggered in her a dim feeling of significance, even before she took it down and saw what it was: a native's local history written in the thirties, which she'd read as a young girl. The book's spine had faded to a paler green than its cloth covers; its corners were threadbare, its pages yellowed. When Sarah left the alcove, she took the small book with her, for she seemed to recall that it contained some stories about the local Indian tribes, and she thought these might be of interest to Harry.

The moon shone through the white curtain in the bathroom, and Sarah, who'd decided to take a long soak before bed, stood in the tub, dripping, to switch off the light. She lay back down in the water and watched the room gradually rebuild itself in moonlight. Steam rose from the bathwater and turned white above her head. Then something like a nerve cell — a kind of wispy eruption in the moonlight — was gliding toward her from the ceiling, a daddy longlegs slowly lowering itself in uneven jerks toward the water. Sarah lay very still and watched. The spider — family

Pholcidae, not an Opiliones, which has no silk — touched the water near the spigot end of the tub and then, repelled, shot hysterically back up its invisible thread. It reached the ceiling, paused, moved a foot and a half in a random direction, and began lowering itself again. Again it touched the water and shot back to the ceiling. It moved several inches to another new spot and again lowered itself, touched the water, and flew back to the ceiling in an impossibly straight line. It moved now to a spot very near the wall, then lowered itself again, very slowly this time, bumping the wall at intervals on the descent. Again it touched the water and was rapidly repelled to the ceiling, where it staggered on all eight legs to the nearest corner. Sarah thought, No memory, no learning, though the spider did seem to have given up and was settling in for a nap.

The last ten days had been so hot and humid that white people were leaving the city in droves. Practically the only white people left in town were the very old, like Mrs. Rothschild, who weren't mobile enough to get out, and the very sick, who were watching TV in air-conditioned hospital rooms. Deckard had two weeks of vacation coming up starting Monday, but he had no plans because he had no money. His best friend had been dead for close to six months, and his best friend's wife and child, whom he loved, had taken off for the country last spring without considering how that might make him feel, and though he'd mailed some things to the boy (baseball cards and rare comic books), they were generally estranged. Stupid: estranged at everybody's time of need. His dead best friend had left him a $50,000 car, and the insurance premium on it was so through-the-ceiling he not only couldn't afford to garage it anywhere in his own neighborhood, he couldn't afford to go anywhere on vacation. He guessed he would get in the

Jaguar and drive around for two weeks, call that a vacation. His girlfriend Lucy had ditched him a year ago, and if he'd known then what he knew now — that she'd been his *last chance for romance* — he might have tried a little harder to make her stay. In the wake of all this, he'd been having a relapse of all the things that had plagued him after his return from the war: mostly paranoia, nightmares, and vivid memories, with the occasional auditory hallucination thrown in for good measure. And when he wasn't dreaming or obsessing about the war, he was dreaming or obsessing about his good-for-nothing father — a tragic irony, since the only good thing you could say about the old man was that he was dead — and lately he'd been making a comeback as the vagabond zombie of Deckard's dreams and reveries. If Deckard's boss, Bernice, wasn't already convinced that Deckard was on the verge of some kind of nervous breakdown, he would have approached her and asked to defer his vacation; the last thing he wanted right now was more quiet time with himself. No doubt he needed a meaningful change, but so far the only change he'd brought off was to let his hair grow back in. He'd started it three weeks ago, and now his formerly bald pate was sheathed in beautiful fresh fuzz, black with the odd sprinkling of white, about an eighth of an inch deep.

On the Friday night before the vacation officially began, he was lying in bed with the shades pulled down and the AC unit going full blast, watching some late reruns of *Cops*. But he soon grew weary of fat white policemen handcuffing young black offenders facedown on some filthy floor or patch of asphalt and switched it off. Sometimes, watching TV, it was enough to turn you into one of those black folks who are always gazing pie-eyed across the ocean in the direction of Africa. To tell you the truth, the whole African-American thing had never much floated Deckard's boat — he considered himself a black American, a United States Marine, a veteran; he'd never been anywhere near Africa, he'd never met a real African, he couldn't tell you the names of more than three or four African countries (they were the kind of names that went in one ear and out the other); he'd been born and raised right here in the U.S.A., he was employed by a branch of the government, most of his small appliances were made in Japan, he sometimes ate at McDonald's, and calling himself African-American didn't make him feel connected to some tall barefoot warrior dudes who'd sat around a campfire on the Serengeti a thousand years ago. He wished it did, but it didn't. Every once in a while, however, he did entertain a fantasy of traveling to Africa, hiking out into a field among some friendly beasts, and spilling a few drops of his blood into the soil. If he could do that, he would probably start calling himself African-American when he got back home.

Once he'd switched off the TV, he lay on top of the bedcovers in the dark, imagining himself alone on a sprawling plain somewhere in Kenya; the sun would be just going down, and for miles around everything would be glowing orange and purple and coppery gold. Snowcapped Kilimanjaro rises up in the distance, and far below, in a grassy valley, a herd of zebras grazes. Deckard stands facing the last light of the sun and pricks the ball of his thumb with the blade of his hunting knife. He watches his blood, deep magenta, fall into the dust at his feet, as high overhead there's the plaintive cry of an eagle. . . .

The telephone rang, nearly startling him off the bed, and he snatched up the receiver from the bedside table as if he were snaring a wild animal before it could attack a second time.

The moment he heard her voice — all she said was "Deck, is that you?" — he could tell she was crying.

"Lucy," he said, with a kind of breathless

wonder in his voice, mostly the result of the double whammy: startling telephone, startling telephone caller.

He could hear what sounded like traffic noise in the background, and when she didn't say anything immediately, he said, "Where are you?"

When she still didn't answer, he said, "Come on, Luce. You called. Now talk to me."

"I'm sorry, Deck," she said. "I really shouldn't be calling you. I just couldn't think of anybody else."

He briefly felt the thorn of this last-resort status but said only, "Are you okay?"

"I've just been mugged," she said, with some amount of amazement in her voice. "I'm outside a movie theater in fucking Revere, of all places. This guy just grabbed my bag in the parking lot and ran away like some kind of lunatic. He's got my money, my ID, my charge cards, my car keys, everything."

"Did he hurt you?" asked Deckard. "I mean, you're okay, right?"

She was silent for a moment, which made him feel he'd somehow missed the point of what she'd told him.

"Well, I'm a little shook," she said at last, quietly, "but yeah, I'm okay."

"The first thing you should do is find a

cop," he said, forgetting her deep distrust of policemen.

"Oh, right," she said, as if it were the most outrageous suggestion she'd ever heard.

"Just dial nine-one-one," he said. "Tell them where you are and what happened. Or go back in the movie theater and get them to call the cops."

"There's nobody *in* the movie theater," she said. "They've closed already and locked the doors. I'm standing here in the rain, looking at this completely empty parking lot — empty except for my car, which I can't get into."

Deckard was curiously snagged by the information that it was raining out — it felt like news from another world, perhaps the *real* world, as if he'd fallen asleep last summer after Lucy declared her independence and only dreamed the whole year without her.

He said, "It's raining?"

"It's pouring," she said.

"Well, there must be something open around there," he said. "A 7-Eleven or something. Somewhere to get out of the rain at least."

"There's a bar down the road," she said, "but it looks kind of scary. It's probably where that lunatic went with my bag. He's probably in there right now buying beers for all his lunatic friends with my money. Yeah, okay, you're right. I'll just call nine-one-one. Thanks a lot. I shouldn't have called, not after this long. It isn't fair. I'll just —"

"Okay, Lucy," he said, for he could hear a wobbly hysteria edging into her voice. "Tell me exactly where you are."

He wrote down the details and then phoned for a taxi, thinking how ludicrous it was to be the owner of an XK120 Roadster and then to have to call a cab because the Jaguar was garaged a half hour's train ride away. He stopped in the bathroom to brush his teeth and then found his waist pouch with all the precautionary devices previously scorned by Lucy. How many times he'd urged her to carry something with her! He'd even bought things for her — a purse-size Mace aerosol, an elegant pocket alarm, a whistle necklace — but she'd only smiled and wagged her head at him: so cute, so dear that he was such a hopeless paranoiac.

As he descended the stairs, he thought there might be some small satisfaction at finding Lucy stranded and unprepared in an abandoned parking lot, but what he felt instead was a keen absence of any such thing. For a solid year he'd moped around, wanting a call from her, and now that the call had finally arrived there was practically nothing about it that pleased him.

Downstairs in the vestibule, as he pulled a poncho over his head, he had the distinct (and familiar) sensation of having forgotten something important. Through the windows in the street door, he could see that it wasn't *pouring*, it was only sprinkling a little, and somebody was apparently enjoying the summer shower, sitting on the stoop under an umbrella.

Outside, Deckard found Angela Abruzzi crouched beneath a black umbrella on a plastic place mat, wearing nothing but a pink tank top and a pair of plaid pajama bottoms. A white van was parked on the other side of the wide street, its windows glossy black with rain.

"Not again," Deckard said aloud, and Angela gazed at him from under the umbrella. She looked as if she'd been playing dress-up, trying with lipstick and rouge and eye shadow to appear older than her paltry ten or eleven years.

"It's almost midnight," he said to her.

She opened her mouth to speak, but Deckard held up his hand.

"Don't tell me," he said. "Your mama's over there in that van talking to your dad. She told you to wait here, and if she's not back in ten minutes you're to go inside and call nine-one-one."

Angela stared down at her bare feet and her bright-red painted toenails for a moment, then tilted the umbrella in such a way as to cut off any further communication between herself and Deckard. He squatted down next to her and peeked in under the umbrella.

"What is it this time, Angela?" he asked, but she wouldn't look at him.

Finally, still not looking at him, she said, almost inaudibly, "He wants me to come stay with him for a week. He wants to take me to some stupid lake or something with his stupid girlfriend."

Deckard said, "You're kidding, right?"

She looked at him and smiled, suddenly beautiful and unbroken, surprised at finding a ready ally, somebody who thought the idea as ridiculous as she did. But the smile faded quickly, replaced by worry.

She said, "He's going to pay her."

"Pay her?" said Deckard. "What do you mean, pay her?"

Angela stared down at her toes again, ashamed and most likely regretting what she'd already revealed, but Deckard didn't need to have it spelled out: Eddie Abruzzi, because he was such a hothead, probably didn't have any legal visitation rights with Angela; Rosa was always hard up for money; Eddie had offered to pay Rosa if she would let

Angela come with him on vacation — possibly he wanted to impress the girlfriend with what a warm fatherly type he was — and right now Rosa was in that white Ford Econoline negotiating a price.

"Déjà vu all over again," Deckard said, staring out across the street at the misty rain drifting down beneath a streetlamp.

"What?" said Angela.

"Nothing," he said. "Why don't you go inside out of the rain. I'll check on your mama."

"I don't think so," said Angela.

"What do you mean, you don't think so?" said Deckard. "Do what I told you."

She gave him a kind of serious who-do-you-think-you-are look and stood up, almost poking him with the umbrella. She lifted the place mat, moved down the stoop a couple of steps, and turned, so she could look Deckard straight in the eye.

"I don't care how much he pays her," she said softly, "I'm not going."

Deckard stood and tugged open the door, held it for her.

"Go on inside," he said. "I'll talk to Rosa."

Angela came up to the landing, took one final look across the street, then turned and went through the door.

Deckard adjusted the hood on his poncho and started down the stoop. He was about to step off the sidewalk into the street when the taxi pulled to the curb.

Just as he'd done the night Malcolm was killed, he asked the driver to wait a minute, but before he'd even got around the back of the cab, Rosa was out of the van and trotting across the street toward him. Tonight she was wearing gold sandals with little clicky heels, tight pedal pushers, and a red halter top, and as she ran across the street, she straightened the halter and tucked her hair behind both ears, sort of frantically, as if she were trying to pull herself together. By the time she reached Deckard behind the taxi, she was pressing both her hands over her mouth, and though all she did was shake her head at him quickly before she continued on, he could see blood trickling between her fingers.

What Deckard didn't see was that somebody else had also got out of the van and was at this moment sprinting toward them. Deckard called Rosa's name as she started dashing up the steps, but she didn't even pause. Next thing Deckard knew, Eddie Abruzzi, in a navy-blue security guard's uniform, was bounding up the steps three at a time to the top, grabbing Rosa by the wrist, and yanking her back so it looked as if she might go flying down the concrete stoop. Deckard would forever remember what

Eddie said to her: "Get your skinny ass back over to that fucking truck, you prickteasing little spick slut." (Apparently Eddie had proposed that Rosa sweeten the negotiations with some Ford Econoline sexual favors.) Deckard hadn't yelled more than, "Hey, wait a minute —" when the spineless cab driver, smelling trouble, sped away.

From Nam, Deckard knew something about the mind-altering drug adrenaline, how it could affect your judgment. Despite Eddie Abruzzi's security guard's uniform, it didn't immediately occur to Deckard to worry about a gun, and despite Eddie's unambiguous display of abusive racist anger and his history of violence, it didn't immediately occur to Deckard to worry about Eddie's *using* a gun. Deckard's intentions had been simply to do whatever was necessary to get Eddie Abruzzi's monkey claw off Rosa's wrist and to stop him from slinging her around the porch stoop. After all, somebody could get hurt.

In the next moment he found himself three-quarters of the way up the steps and hugging Eddie Abruzzi from behind with both arms, like a tackle trying to wrangle down a half-back. How the devil Eddie got turned around enough inside Deckard's grip to get a shot off he would never fully understand (except of course that Eddie was probably twenty years

429

younger). Magically, the revolver appeared, midnight blue in the mist, like an anatomically correct toy, like a sick joke, nudging Deckard's ribs and suddenly all wrapped up in this weird interlacing of human thumbs and fingers, half of them white and half brown.

Did Deckard deliberately force the revolver upward toward the sky or had that been only a lucky consequence of the struggle on the steps? Some things he'd never know for sure. But when the gun discharged, the angle was such that the bullet augered out a little trough through the *musculus temporalis* on the left side of Deckard's head, an inch and a half north of his ear.

An inscription, written in pencil inside the small green book, read "To Pop, with love, Christmas, 1940."

"Pop" would have been Sarah's grandfather, her father's father, Jack Williams, and since Sarah's father was an only child, the inscription would have been written by him. There was nothing familiar about her father's handwriting. Well, certainly he'd never written her any letters in longhand; what few he'd written, mostly during her college years, were typed on an old Royal typewriter and pockmarked with strikeovers. She didn't recall ever having noticed the inscription before, but after seeing it tonight she fell asleep thinking of her grandfather, the country doctor who had sewn up the neighbor man's mangled hand at the kitchen table as she spied through the keyhole. She recalled her grandmother shooing her away, but she recalled also the sound of her grandfather's voice through the door. The injured man had been crying, a shocking enough thing to a child, repeating over and over again, "How could I have been so stupid, Jack? . . . How could I have been so stupid? . . . Tell me how I could have been so stupid." And her grandfather would say, over and over, "These things happen to everybody, Chester. It was an accident. Nobody has accidents on purpose. Now hold still and try to breathe normally." Sarah's keyhole view of the kitchen revealed only her grandfather's back, the legs of the table, and the injured man's bare and bony knees — which kept opening and closing like a pair of hand bellows her grandfather kept by the hearth — but she could hear her grandfather's voice perfectly, and she noticed that it had a tone she'd never heard in it before. He was a grown man, speaking to another grown man, and yet his voice was full of what sounded like tenderness, a flavor of love. He was indeed a tender loving man, but even with his family his voice was not quite so wonderful, so soothing and transporting, as if he could banish all troubles and bring on a peaceful sleep with nothing more than the repetition of a few words. Five or six years later, as a teenager, Sarah recalled the event and understood that her grandfather's voice had been full of sympathy, and she thought the sound of his voice, expressing sympathy, had been so compelling it was almost enough to make her want to go out and hurt herself.

After she fell asleep, thinking of her grand-father and the hypnotic sway of his sympathy, she dreamed she wandered the tunnels of a dark coal mine, trying to find the way out, and from time to time she heard her grandfather's voice echoing from deep inside the darkness. "How's my dancing girl?" he called out, a kind of thing he used to say when she was a child: Finding her in the kitchen helping her grandmother with breakfast, he would say, "How's my cooking girl?"; discovering her curled up in the hammock with a book, "How's my reading girl today?" "How's my thinking girl?" "How's my puzzle-solving girl?" In the dream, water dripped from over-head, and as Sarah stumbled along trying to follow her grandfather's voice, the dripping water became heavier until it took on the dis-tinct sibilance of rainfall. Suddenly she was actually awakened by Harry, who stood in his boxer shorts by her bed, not touching her but only whispering, "Mom, wake up . . . wake up!"

"Harry!" she said, and just then his silhou-ette lit up bright white in a flash of lightning.

He shushed her and whispered again, "Wake up."

"I'm awake, Harry," she said softly, raising herself onto one elbow. "What's wrong?"

He stood staring down at her, silent, again

illuminated milky white by lightning, and this time Sarah noticed that he held a baseball bat in one hand. She sat all the way up in the bed and reached for him, but he stepped backward.

"What's wrong, Harry?" she said. "Did you have a bad dream?"

Thunder rumbled far away in the distance. Sarah noticed that both doors to the borning room were shut. "Harry," she said, "sweetheart, did you close my doors?"

He moved to the bed again and put his lips to her ear. He whispered, "There's a man in the living room."

A blast of wind blew mist through the window screen, and Sarah leapt from the bed and pushed down the window. "Okay, Harry," she said. "Get in my bed. I'll turn on some lights."

"The lights don't work," he said, not moving from his spot.

She tried the overhead switch. "The power must be out," she said. "You know how that happens sometimes in a storm, Harry."

"It woke me up," he said. "It was scary in the attic, so I came downstairs. I was walking down the hall and there was lightning and I saw a man. In the living room."

"Okay," she said. "You stay right here. I'm going to go see."

There was another flash of lightning, and this time the thunder followed quickly, louder.

"Take this," said Harry, passing her the baseball bat.

She accepted the bat, opened the door to the living room, and peered inside. "I don't see anyone, Harry," she said. "Do you want to come look for yourself?"

He shook his head.

"I'm going to light the candles on the mantel," she said, and went into the room, found matches on the mantel, and lit the three candles there. When she turned back to the borning room, Harry was standing in the doorway; he'd pulled the spread off her bed and draped it over his shoulders like a child in a Christmas pageant.

"There," she said. "You see? Nobody but me and you."

"There was a man," Harry said. "I saw him."

She took one of the candlesticks to him. "Here," she said. "You carry this. Do you remember how to cup your hand in front of the flame, to keep it from blowing out? We'll walk through the house and inspect it. And we can close windows as we go."

He let the bedspread fall to the floor and took the candlestick, apparently glad to have a mission.

They went from room to room, upstairs and down, Harry's candle causing Sarah's long shadow to precede them. They ended in the attic room, which, in candlelight, was more cavelike than ever. When the last of the windows was lowered against the blowing rain, the sky opened, as if on cue. Sarah had never heard such rain. The force of it on the wood-shingle roof, so near their heads, was frightful. "My God," she said. "Listen to that."

Harry stood in the dark, holding the candlestick in both hands now, and gazed up in awe at the dark beams and rafters and wide planks of the roof. After a moment, he said, "What's going to happen?"

Sarah shivered in her nightgown and told him not to worry, nothing was going to happen, but she thought the old house had never seemed so like an ark, so like refuge.

The storm passed over them in its definite shape (more clamorous in the middle) out into the Atlantic, taking the lightning with it, and when at last they were settled again in bed and the candles extinguished, the house was restored to a darkness that seemed absolute. Sarah had let Harry take her bed in the borning room, and situated herself on the living room couch; with the door open between the rooms, he could see her only a few feet away. When she'd gone to kiss him good night, he'd told her once again that he'd seen a man in the living room. She'd told him that lightning could play tricks on you, and he went pointedly silent, hurt at her not believing him. She'd sat for another moment next to him on the bed.

"It's an old house," she'd said to him. "Full of shadows. It's not that I don't believe you. It's just that I think you were mistaken about what you thought you saw. Do you see the difference?"

He waited for perhaps a full ten seconds and then said, "No."

She'd asked him if they could talk about it some more in the morning, and he'd rolled onto his side and said, "Sure," resigned in some horrible way to a horrible fate in which adults always, always, inevitably disappoint.

Now she lay awake thinking about the chimney, which rose like a wide red-brick column straight through the house; as she and Harry had left the attic a while earlier, she'd seen rainwater gleaming down the mortar paths in the candlelight. She would have to find someone to repair the flashing. The old house was damp enough without a leaky roof. She was wide awake. It was almost a relief when she heard Harry's voice. "Are you awake, Mom?"

"Yes, Harry," she said. "You can't sleep either?"

They relit all the candles and placed them on the windowsill in the borning room. She joined him in the bed and began to read to him from the old history book she'd found in the alcove the evening before. The borning-room window was open a few inches, and a cool after-storm breeze brought indoors the steady rasping of an agitated surf and the wonderful wet scent of the garden, tomatoes and rosemary. Very little of the story was needed to carry them into the past, for everything around them suggested it: the brief dimensions and powdery plaster walls of the borning room, the eternal sounds and scents coming through the window screen, the flickering candles. Of course, the house stood on land (or on land very nearby) on which the narrative had actually occurred. Sarah thought there was even something out of another time about the nearness of the sea and the absent father, as if the storm had called the menfolk away or prevented them from returning.

Most likely it was this last intimation that caused what happened next. Sarah read to Harry from the chapter concerning the

Wampanoags, because she knew these would be of most interest to him; she read about how Miles Standish and his compatriots helped themselves to the Indians' corn and plundered their graves for treasures and trinkets. It was not a pleasant story, but it evoked more outrage than any other emotion, and as she reached a passage about a little white boy who'd gone missing in the woods for several days, she was taken by surprise:

When Massasoit heard about it, he sent runners to surrounding tribes, asking that they search for the boy. It was learned that the child had wandered to an Indian plantation in Sandwich, where he had been fed and cared for. From there he had gone with young braves to Nauset. Tribesmen brought him home in a shallop, carrying him on their shoulders from the sea to dry land. He was hung with decorations and his arms were filled with presents.

The white men made a party of the occasion, and gifts were exchanged. Everybody seemed happy but one very old Indian woman, who wept and lamented and made a quite unseemly racket. When the Pilgrims asked who she was, they were told that she was a widow whose three sons had been captured by a white man and taken away on a ship. She had come to look at the white men and found herself unable to restrain her grief. The sachem hoped her tears were not upsetting.

Reading the passage, Sarah too found herself unable to restrain her grief. She began to cry and had to stop reading, which apparently infuriated Harry. He threw off the covers and left the room. She called after him — "Oh, Harry, come back" — but soon she heard him stomping up the stairs. She'd gotten only a glimpse of his face as he'd left, but there had been tears in his eyes too, and that, she thought, probably made him angrier than her own crying. What was she doing, reading him such a sorrowful story? How could she betray him so?

She didn't go after him immediately, partly because she thought she should compose herself first and partly because she felt hopeless about having to go after him.

When finally she climbed the stairs, she found him in the attic room, sitting on his mattress in the dark. She went and sat next to him, but he moved away down the mattress. She said she was sorry the story had upset him, and he said the story *hadn't* upset him.

Well, I'm sorry you left the room angry, she said, and he said he *wasn't* angry.

"Well, what are you?" she asked.

"I just want to go to sleep," he said.

"You want to sleep up here?"

He nodded.

She helped him get settled under the covers, kissed his forehead, and moved to the door. What was the point? It was very late (or early), and they were exhausted. She stopped at the doorway, turned, and told him she loved him. She waited for him to say he loved her too.

After a brief pause, he said, "What happened to the Indian woman's sons?"

"I imagine they were sold into slavery," she said.

"And what happened to the woman's husband?"

"I don't know," she said. "It doesn't say."

"What's a shallop?"

"I'm not sure exactly," she said. "Why don't we look it up in the dictionary in the morning?"

"It's already morning," he said. "Almost."

Through the windows at the gable end of the attic she could see a square of the sky, which had lightened to a dark gray, and beyond the trembling aspens a silver bank of fog had settled into the hollow.

"We need to sleep, Harry," she said. "Do you think you'll be able to now?"

Another pause, after which he said, "Why did the Indian woman come to the party and then cry so much?"

Sarah returned to the mattress and sat down again. There was enough light now that she could see his face, dimly, like a face in an old dark painting. She said, "I think she had heard about the little boy who had disappeared, and she was curious to see what the white people were like. She saw everybody being so happy at having found the little boy. It made her think of her own lost sons and she was inconsolable."

"That means she couldn't stop crying?"

"Yes," she said, "sort of. Inconsolable means that nothing seems to make your sadness go away."

"Is that why you cry?" he asked. "Because you're inconsolable?"

"Yes, Harry," she said. "I suppose I am inconsolable. I won't always be inconsolable, but I have been, and I still am, and I probably will be for a while longer."

"How long?" he asked.

"I don't know," she said.

Yet another pause — he was thinking, in that visible way he had — and she felt it important not to leave him now, but she also didn't know how much longer she could keep from crying again. He looked at her, clearly seeing the brimming tears, and there was something like surrender in his face, a suggestion that he wasn't at this moment wishing her away.

At last he said, "I thought you cried because you miss him."

"That's right," she said. "I cry because I miss him so very much."

"I miss him too," he said.

"I know you do," she said. "I know you do."

"Am I going to be inconsolable too?" he asked.

She offered him her hand, and he willingly took it — or, more precisely, he gave her his own.

"No, Harry," she said. "I don't think you're going to be inconsolable."

"I have some tissues over there," he said, pointing to a box on the floor at the foot of the mattress.

She reached for the box and pulled out two. She blew her nose and thanked him.

She said, "Thank you," thinking what a spectacular understatement it was.

"I really did see a man in the living room," he said.

This made her laugh for some reason,

through her tears, and she blew her nose a second time and said, "Well, tell me what he looked like."

"He didn't look like anybody," Harry said. "He was an old man with white hair, and he was standing by the fireplace. Do you believe me?"

She experienced an avalanche of pure feeling, attached most unexpectedly to the young drug addict who was Malcolm's killer, the vast icy plain of the unknowable he represented, and though she couldn't name what she felt, she felt it at least partly as a physical shift just below her heart, an easing of pressure there, creating a pocket of emptiness. Harry was looking at her hopefully, as if, having yielded something, having moved in her direction, she was now obliged to yield something in return. She said, "Yes, Harry, yes, I do."

There wasn't anything extraordinary in her saying it; after all, it was the kind thing to say. What was extraordinary was that she meant it.

At the VA emergency room — where Deckard went under his own steam, pressing his hand over his head — Frenchfry was on duty, as well as two nurses known to Deckard from the intake desk, so he had to endure a fair amount of teasing. Just can't get enough of this place, huh? Good thing that bullet caught you in the head, where it could do no harm, ha-ha. And so on. He had to endure also the tedious you're-one-lucky-bastard postulating. Two inches to the right, and it woulda gone straight through your eye socket, old man; half an inch lower, and we wouldn't be having this conversation. The modest scalp laceration, which looked, in miniature, like something a spaceship might have left behind in Farmer Murphy's barley field, was stitched up, dressed, and bandaged. The intern assigned to Deckard, a young white guy from Idaho, teased him about how the bandage didn't want to stick to Deckard's new hair. (Why did Deckard have the feeling that the intern's touching his hair, feeling the texture of genuine black-

American hair, was the fulfillment of a life-long secret desire?) Deckard had scraped both knees on the concrete steps outside his building as he'd struggled to prevent Eddie Abruzzi from killing him, and the intern from Idaho painted Deckard's knees with something orange and bandaged them too. He gave him an oxycodone to swallow and another one in his pocket to take home, always a treat.

A blond policewoman dropped by the ER to ask Deckard a few questions, told him Eddie Abruzzi was in custody, and would Deckard please come by the station tomorrow when he was feeling better? He was required to put his John Hancock on a thing or two. The policewoman, a dead ringer for Elizabeth Montgomery on the old *Bewitched* shows, said, "Why do I get the feeling this isn't your first gunshot wound?"

"ESP?" ventured Deckard. He was sitting up in a chair by now (rather than laid out on an examination table), but he still wore over his underwear the unflattering blue-and-white hospital gown. He lifted the hem of it to reveal the pit in his right side below his rib cage. "Got caught sleeping in Nam," he told her. "A little surprise from Victor Charlie. AK-forty-seven, but as you can see I survived."

She rolled the sleeve of her shirt clear up to the department patch and leaned her shoulder in close to his face. He had to squint to see what she meant to show him.

"Smallpox vaccination?" he said.

"That's funny," she said, like a person who has no sense of humor, but then she let out a girlish laugh that seemed entirely honest. "Right here we have a surprise from a sixteen-year-old speed freak," she said. "With my own service revolver yet. Talk about being caught sleeping."

She laughed again, but then stopped and said, "How old are you, Mr. Jones?"

This sudden reference to his age completely destroyed any rapport they might have been building. "Old enough," Deckard answered, and thankfully one of the nurses appeared at that moment to escort him behind a curtain where he could get dressed.

It was while he was pulling on his pants with the rips in both knees that he thought of Lucy standing in the rain in an abandoned parking lot somewhere in Revere. He went to the nearest telephone and started to dial her number but halfway through realized he couldn't remember the arrangement of the last four digits, and this time his finger-memory didn't seem to be working. He tried three different combinations, got two number-not-in-service recorded messages and one answering machine belonging to a Spanish-speaking man named Guillermo. He thought of directory assistance but then recalled that Lucy's number was unpublished. Why did she have an unpublished number? Because he'd pestered her into it a couple of years ago, on account of his deep belief that all women living alone should have unpublished numbers, the first line of defense against the Richard Specks of the world. Probably it was just as well. By now, whatever the hell time it was, Lucy would have gotten home somehow or other and would be asleep. He would only be waking her.

Afterward, the nurse made him sit in a wheelchair and rolled him down the hall to the exit doors. Despite all Deckard's protests, Frenchfry, who happened to be going off duty, met him outside in his silver 911 Carrera (zero to sixty in 4.6 seconds) to give him a lift home. As Deckard waved the nurse away — he was perfectly capable of getting out of the wheelchair and into Dr. French's fancy car unassisted, thank you — he bristled inwardly with resentment: the young doctor's trim handsomeness, his tennis trophies back home in his proud parents' glass cabinet, his Harvard education, med school laid at his feet.

"This really isn't necessary," Deckard said, closing the car door.

"I know that," said Frenchfry.

"I walked over here — bleeding from the head — and I could walk back."

"I know that too," said Frenchfry.

Deeply irritated by this know-it-all attitude behind the thousand-dollar carbon and leather steering wheel, Deckard looked out the window and noticed that the road and the sidewalks were shiny with rain. A few small tree branches were scattered about, and here and there a stray plastic trash barrel had been blown into the street.

A minute later, back at the scene of the crime, he thanked the good doctor for the ride. "Now, Deckard," said the doctor, "will you *please* be careful?"

What was it, the patronizing tone? The implication that somehow Deckard, rash and infantile, failing to have put away his cowboy pistols, had brought this little visit to the ER on himself? Why did it feel as if God's gift to the medical arts, having slummed on over to the projects on an errand of mercy, was chiding one of these idle nappy folks who were always shootin' and knifin' each other up? Probably, mostly, it was the 911 Carrera, the sport tiptronic chassis, the climate control, the digital sound system, the dual power seats.

Deckard got out of the car and leaned down to the window, tapped on the glass with his knuckle — a small and simple maneuver that felt suddenly like going over the top in a Ferris wheel (the medication). The automatic window descended with a pleasant hum.

"Let me ask you a question, Dr. French," he said, trying to keep bitterness out of his voice. "Is there anything in this life you ever wanted, I mean really wanted, but you couldn't have it no matter how hard you tried?"

A mild surprise crossed the young man's face; then his dark eyebrows moved closer together, as if they might meet in the middle. "Well," he said thoughtfully, "I have a little brother back in Chicago, named Danny, born with Down's syndrome. I always felt like no matter how hard I worked in medical school, no matter how good I got at doctoring, I wasn't ever going to be able to change that, you know? Danny will always have Down's. Why do you ask?"

Deckard thought, Shot in the head, Deckard Jones, you fool, you've been shot in the head.

He managed to say, but not with any feeling of dignity, "Oh . . . no special reason."

"It was that crack I made about being careful, wasn't it," said the doctor. "It came out wrong. I don't want to give you the wrong idea, or support a wrong idea you might already have. I'm really not looking for a father figure. But believe me, Deck, from where I'm sitting, you look like a hero. I just meant be careful, you know? Don't get hurt. A man like you. At this time of life. Having survived what you've already survived. It would be like coming through a war and then slipping on a banana peel, you know?"

Deckard reached through and shook his hand and, most confusingly, had a sudden urge to climb back inside and kiss him (the medication).

It had to be after two o'clock in the morning, but apparently Rosa was keeping a vigil at her street window because she was on him the minute he got through the front door. He allowed her to "help" him up the stairs and let her open the apartment door since it seemed to make her feel a lot better.

Hearing some noise, Mrs. Rothschild, who'd long ago resigned the tedious ritual of actually sleeping in a bed, came wandering out onto the landing. "Oh, Deckard, honey," she cried, "you're alive!"

"That seems to be the diagnosis," Deckard said, moving through the door held open now by Rosa.

Right away he saw the little red light blinking like a silent clucking tongue on the answering machine — Lucy — but before listening to what she had to say (not that he was especially eager), he needed to get rid of Rosa and Mrs. Rothschild. Both women had followed him into the apartment, down the short hallway, and even to the bedroom. Rosa took his bloodstained poncho and hung it in the closet, and as he sat on the edge of the bed it appeared she might kneel and start unlacing his boots. He intervened by standing up and heading for the kitchen.

Mrs. Rothschild lingered in the bedroom doorway, appearing in every possible way snagged. She backed out enough to let him through and took up where she'd left off the minute before; she said, almost as if she were scolding him, "Well, thank heaven, Deckard! Thank heaven you're alive!"

"Okay, Mrs. R.," he said, "thank heaven, thank heaven."

He poured himself a glass of spring water from the fridge, and while he was alone in the kitchen Rosa managed to return Mrs. Rothschild to her own apartment.

In the hallway, Rosa asked, "You're really okay?"

"You know I am, Rosa," he said. "They wouldn't have sent me home if there was the least thing to worry about. It's just a scratch."

She followed him into the bedroom, and as he sat again on the bed, she stood staring at him with her arms crossed. She was wearing some purple sweats now and a pair of cheap sneakers with no socks. Her bottom lip was busted and swollen, and there were bruises on both her wrists. "We had quite a storm," she said at last.

"Is that a fact," he said. "I didn't know, 'cause I was in the ER."

She looked as if she might cry. "Oh, Deckard," she said. "I'm so sorry."

"Rosa," he said. "Why do you do it?"

"I know I know I know," she said. "You don't have to tell me. First there's all the money I've never paid you back, and now this."

"I don't give a damn about the money," he said.

She idly touched her fingers to her swollen bottom lip, as if she were testing it for tenderness. "I guess he'll be going to jail," she said.

He looked at her. "Rosa, if that's even a particle of sadness I hear in your voice, I'm going to be really mad. I'm not the person to try that out on. Not here, not tonight."

She dropped both her arms to her sides, as if she were coming to attention, snapping to.

"No," she said. "But there *is* something I want to say."

"What, Rosa?"

"Angela said she told you about Eddie's little idea," she said. "About taking her on vacation with him. Well, I want you to know something. I wasn't *ever* going to let Angela go with him. I thought I might be able to shake him down for fifty or a hundred bucks, but I wasn't ever going to let her go. Not ever. I want you to know that."

"Well, I'm glad to hear it," said Deckard.

"I just wanted you to know," she said.

She stepped forward and gave him a squeeze, very carefully, as if she was afraid of hurting him.

"Now, I don't mean to be rude," he said. "I'm not kicking you out, but you should know that I'm about to take my clothes off."

She smiled, really warmly, and probably it was only all the excitement added to the oxycodone, but for a second she looked almost as if she wouldn't have minded sticking around for the floor show.

"It was a mistake," she said on the tape. "I shouldn't have called you, and besides you were right. All I had to do was call nine-one-one — which, when you never showed up, is what I did. But I'm sorry for calling you in the first place. It wasn't right. It was a wrong thing to do. I guess you got me back, Deck. I guess we're even now, okay?"

He was standing by the machine, naked except for the white bandages on his knees and head. He returned to the bedroom, found the other painkiller in the breast pocket of his shirt, swallowed it, and went to bed. He fell asleep right away, no problem.

Around 5 A.M., the air conditioner began to rattle and spooked him awake. He felt a strange pain at the side of his head, just above his left ear, and suddenly remembered that he'd been shot. He got out of bed, staggered into the bathroom, peed, staggered to the air conditioner and gave it a bang with his fist, and got back into bed. He fell asleep thinking of his mother, of how she'd always complained about the .22 and the Remington 870 shotgun his old man kept in the house. "Those things are *dangerous*, Jimmy," she would say. "I do not want those things in my house. One of these days somebody's gonna get shot!"

Hard to believe, but somebody was rapping on the door. As he rolled out of bed, pulled on a bathrobe, and went into the hallway, he felt as if he had little dreamy fish swimming around inside his head, flashing their brilliant scales behind his eyes.

On the landing stood Mrs. Rothschild, who'd brought him chicken soup in a Tupperware container.

"Good for what ails you," she said, and it sounded to Deckard, in his dream-bogged state, to apply generally — he'd forgotten again about his gunshot wound. He accepted the soup, thanked her, returned to bed, and fell asleep.

He dreamed he was riding in the back of a flatbed truck somewhere out in the boonies of Vietnam, jolted so violently it felt as if his internal organs were banging against one another. Thick clouds of dust rose up behind the truck. Deckard peered into the dust, trying to see what was inside it, and suddenly he heard a sickening thud, an impact within the dust cloud, and Harry, thrown into the air, transcribed an arc over the cab of the truck, out of Deckard's reach.

When he woke from the dream, somebody was stomping on a wa-wa pedal that had been installed, while he slept, inside a chamber above his left ear. He touched the spot with his fingers and discovered something like a sanitary pad taped to his hair. He could see that the room was bright with daylight, and it occurred to him to get up, get dressed, and go to work, but then he remembered it was Saturday, and he closed his eyes — each of his eyeballs a perfect little fishbowl, a single perfect little angelfish in each one, purling circles in the vitreous humor. He fell back to sleep, but he slept briefly, for whatever was going on inside the northwest quadrant of his skull was really too noisy, and when he opened his eyes again, it was as if the story of his life, a recipe basically, was written on the ceiling: Deckard Jones, a little bit of Pop (don't-get-close-to-nobody-'cause-they're-gonna-burn-you-in-the-end), a little bit of Mom (get-yourself-a-good-set-of-blinders-and-some-earplugs), but finally a pretty decent man, fucked-up in any number of ways.

It was half past one in the afternoon. After taking two Advil tablets, he dressed and heated some of Mrs. Rothschild's chicken soup, which, when he'd salted it enough, tasted good despite its having in it some beany-looking things he couldn't identify. Later, he went to the window over the air conditioner and surveyed the day; it appeared that the storm had ushered in more bearable weather, for hordes of Saturday strollers were on the sidewalks in their summer wear. Deckard gave the AC a love pat. "They can keep their fresh air," he said aloud. "I like *you*." Later still, he went to the telephone and dialed Lucy's number, which he'd looked up in his book. He figured she would be out on a sunny Saturday afternoon and seized the opportunity to speak into the neutrality of a machine. She'd changed her message — it used to be a man's voice, his voice, on the machine and now, against what she knew would be his better judgment, she was telling every Tom, Dick (Richard), and Harry that they'd reached Lucy but she wasn't home at the moment. Deckard gave to the tape a thumbnail sketch of what had happened the night before, keeping it very simple, and apologized for not getting there. He assured her he hadn't done it on purpose. He mentioned that when his own violent incident occurred, he'd already called a taxi and was virtually en route to Revere. He told her not to worry about him, he was fine. As he said good-bye, he knew she wouldn't be phoning him again, and this felt only inevitable, in a detached sort of way. The next moment, still standing in the hallway, he realized that his desire for her return — this huge longing, for a year his ready companion — had run away in the night, and even if he tried to get it back he simply couldn't.

That was a surprise, and a load off, of course, and somehow, very strangely — as if it wasn't plenty important enough all by itself — it seemed to stand for something more far-reaching: The curtain had begun to fall on the drama about whether or not women still looked at him. Who cared? Surely there were more important things. Like cars, for example. He thought of his very own Jaguar in Sarah's garage across the river. He saw himself in it, on a road, on a highway. He was alive! A knock came at the door.

Angela Abruzzi stood on the landing, holding a flat package of some kind, wrapped in brown paper. She held it out to him, supporting it from underneath with two hands. He immediately invited her in, but she declined, looking embarrassed, a little frayed around the edges, but also beautiful. After a couple of seconds, Deckard understood that she was waiting for him to unwrap the package, which had his name written on it. He tore off the brown paper to reveal an eight-by-ten crayon drawing in a cheap gold dime-store frame. The drawing was of a girl in a straw sun hat, looking out at a river. A solitary seagull flew over the long rectangle of blue water, which was bordered above and below by bars of pink sand. What Deckard liked immediately about the picture was that it didn't ask much of you, only that you see it, and if somebody asked you, What do you see? you'd say, pure and simple, A river, a girl, a bird. He stood in the doorway, at a loss for words, but he supposed

Angela could tell he was pleased by the look on his face. She appeared pleased too, in a self-conscious way, and told him she'd done the drawing "in art." She added that she was sorry her father had shot him in the head. Deckard told her not to worry, no big deal, and thanked her — he hoped, not too hurriedly. He had a familiar terrible feeling that he was going to fall apart, so he retreated into the hallway and on to the kitchen to find a hammer and nail.

Out the window of the book alcove, Sarah could see down the hill to the salt marsh, whose grasses were lime green in a cloud of mist and fog. Once, she looked up to see the cloud brighten, as if it were lit from within. Another time, it seemed to darken and re-constitute itself; blown by a sudden two-minute wind, it marched across the face of the marsh in vertical columns, faded into huge fainter panels of mist, faded further into a single mass, fainter still, and was gone. Had she actually seen it?

Dear Deckard,
    During this long stupid silence, I've thought (with shame) occasionally of how disappointed Malcolm would be to find us estranged. Malcolm hated estrangement of any kind. He always regretted the distance between me and my mother and would urge me to make overtures toward her I couldn't make. In all the years of our marriage, he never went to sleep angry at me, and I used to

think this another of his noble feats. Later I understood that he was simply biologically incapable of falling asleep angry. It was as if he knew there was some danger in being angry with those dear to you. That some murderous freak might seize the very moment of your anger to snuff out the lights of the person you loved most in the world. Or was it <u>me</u> who felt that kind of danger? Maybe I've blended our personalities here. Our history together, and now his absence, makes me tend to do that. In any case, he wouldn't have wanted you and me to be estranged and I don't want it either. It has taken me this long to think of your feelings. I simply didn't have the room in my heart before. Now I see that when I brought us down here, we were leaving you alone, and I'm sorry. I believe I was right to make the move, and there have been some good results, but I was wrong to think I could do it by myself and I was wrong not to consider your feelings. Harry and I both miss you and need you. You'll be happy to hear that we have been eating better. We've put in a vegetable garden and now have tomatoes and squash and cucumbers. Harry's growing corn, but I'm not sure it will be ready before we return to town. He wants to come back home after Labor Day. I don't want to, but I think I must. I had thought maybe we could stay down here indefinitely and I would home-school him and we would get slowly better over the next twenty years or so, but I now see I can't do this by myself. We've also assembled a marine aquarium, and Harry's done some amazing drawings of the sea creatures, moon snails and sponges and hermit crabs. Recently he asked me to bring in Malcolm's old drafting table from the garage, and he's been designing houses. Of course I can hardly bear to see him sitting at Malcolm's table, busy with his pencils and rulers, but I understand that it's one of Harry's "places" he goes, either for comfort or oblivion. It turns out he likes to pull weeds in the garden, and I think it's for the same reason. He gets lost in it. We've been swimming nearly every day at the pond and sometimes in the bay. (The ocean remains too cold and scary.) Also recently, Harry has given me permission to cry, i.e., he seems to have accepted the fact of my crying and no longer hates me for it. We've made some progress. Once or twice I've actually woken up in the morning, brushed my teeth, and gotten as far as making the tea before thinking of Malcolm, before feeling the presence of this task that was laid before me — to accept the unacceptable. Finally, there is no way to <u>think</u> about our recovering from this thing. None of my old habits of thinking seem to work anymore. Yesterday, I recalled that first night in the hospital, when Forrest Sanders asked me if there was anyone I would like to phone, and I thought first of Malcolm. Hardly a day goes by that I don't think how much easier it would be to accept Malcolm's death if he were here to help me do it. Isn't that strange? I didn't mean to say all this. I meant only to apologize to you, to make amends. Deckard, I hope you will come down here and see us before we have to go back home. If you have any vacation time, will you consider spending a few days with us?

Love,
Sarah

She folded the letter into an envelope and sealed it. She opened a drawer and found a postage stamp, then went to the borning room for her address book. She couldn't think when she had last written a letter — all its disparate components made it feel obsolete, belonging to a former era; she'd had to find pen and paper, a suitable place to write, an envelope, a stamp, her address book, and now she would need to walk down the long drive to the mailbox — and as she wrote out Deckard's address, she imagined herself spiritually bound to another woman (one of the schoolmarm Garfield sisters?) who might have sat on this small bed in the borning room preparing a letter of amends to a friend. The house did that to you, and there was a perspective to be had in it, though not one that could always be put to any good use.

Now that the letter was ready, she felt an apprehension perhaps typical to a person who seldom wrote: Had she said enough or too much? She'd had one false start, with a long-winded opening about the fickle month of August; this she'd tossed into the trash, resolving in the next draft not to mention the weather. Certainly there was plenty more she might have said. She hadn't tried to explain that, throughout her life, knowing the solutions to problems and how things worked had been a constant yearning, as well as the source of her confidence, and now she'd been given a problem (Malcolm's death) whose only solution (his not being dead) wasn't available; she'd been confronted by a thing (getting past his death) that appeared to work differently each time you looked at it, and against her will she'd had to dwell in a kind of wilderness of not-knowing. She didn't tell Deckard about Harry's nightmares ceasing shortly after they'd arrived at the summer house — didn't say she believed it had to do with the overwhelmingness of what came through the senses, the sky, the air, the light, and how nature's surprises seemed to push wreckage out of your consciousness — because Deckard didn't know about Harry's nightmares. Likewise, she didn't say that since the night of the storm, when they'd read the story about the Indian woman whose sons had been sold into slavery, Harry had not wet the bed again — for Deckard didn't know about the bedwetting either. She didn't say that since Harry had given her permission to cry, she hadn't felt so much like crying, that there was in the permission to cry a hidden ironical permission not to cry. She didn't try to explain in a letter that some shift had occurred that night in Harry's thinking (or feeling): Hearing about an Indian woman who, hundreds of years ago, had been unable to control her grief in a public setting had lent a legitimacy to Sarah's tears. Since that night, Harry had begun asking her questions phrased to elicit stories for answers. How did you and Daddy meet?

How did Daddy's father die? What was the scariest thing that ever happened to you when you were a kid? Why did Daddy like to design houses and buildings? How young was he when he first started?

Nor did Sarah tell Deckard in the letter that yesterday it occurred to her that she had not listened to any music since Malcolm died. She supposed she'd avoided music for the same obvious reason she'd avoided the intersection of Huron Avenue and the parkway — it would make her unhappy and she didn't need any encouragement there — but also she'd confronted the old enigma of music: Why does a certain set of tones in relationship to one another, arranged in patterns to occur in certain rhythms, accrue to a sound that can strike the human ear and stir emotion? She'd found a ray of hope in there somewhere, in the business of pooled elements producing effects larger than the sum of their parts. A thunderstorm, a bit of local history from an old book (white boy lost in the woods), a certain light in the salt marsh, an errant hummingbird, the smell of rain in the garden . . . who could say what powers resided in their random combinations?

She heard Harry's footsteps on the stairs. She would ask him to walk with her to the mailbox. The rusty squeak of the mailbox door would flush out redwing blackbirds in the salt marsh. They would fly straight up into the air and back down again into the grasses.

Harry stood at the door, leaning against the jamb. He was wearing his black T-shirt with the skull and crossbones, and he appeared almost as if he'd been asleep — a returning-to-the-natural-world look she'd seen sometimes on Malcolm's face after he'd been working in his study too long.

"I wrote a letter to Deckard," she said.

"Did you ask him to come see us?" Harry asked.

"Yes."

"Do you think he'll come?"

She thought for a moment, then said, "Yes, I do."

"Was Deckard Daddy's best friend?"

"Yes, he was."

"How long did they know each other?"

"Oh, a pretty long time," she said. "Close to fifteen years."

"How did they meet?"

"Why don't you walk with me down to the mailbox," she said, "and I'll tell you everything I know about it?"

As they stepped out the door into the fine mist, Sarah said, "Wait a minute . . . listen."

Harry paused on the steps and began to

smile. The old Beasleys were at it again.

High on the bluff, far away and hidden in the trees, was a small gray house with a flat roof and a wraparound sundeck, built in the fifties. An old couple from New Jersey owned it, and though they were rarely in residence, it was always apparent when they were there because of their constant squabbling. In the great bowl behind the bluff that was skirted on one side by the marsh and on the other by the rise of Tom's Hill, sound traveled with unexpected clarity. Morning, noon, and night, the Beasleys could be heard, mostly quarreling about what was at hand — somebody hadn't bought the charcoal briquettes, somebody wasn't watering the impatiens — but occasionally there was a sordid exchange about how one or the other of them had ruined one or other of the children's lives. Now the old man was shouting in an attempt to make himself heard over the old woman's shouting, and when this failed, he resorted to yammering — "Yadda yadda yadda yadda yadda yadda yadda" — as Mrs. Beasley went on about something he wasn't doing right. "You can't do it that way," she was saying. "I've told you a thousand times, you'll break it if you try to do it that way. That's the lazy man's way of doing it. That's the way your father would've done it. Probably where you learned it. I'm telling you that if you break it, we're not paying for another. Why, oh, why will you never listen to reason?"

"Yadda yadda yadda yadda," the old man yammered.

Sarah envisioned him with his fingers stuck in his ears.

"What do you think *it* is?" Harry asked Sarah.

"I don't know," she said.

Suddenly there was a loud crash, a splintering-of-wood sound, then silence. Even the birds were quiet.

Then, "Well, I hope you're happy now!"

"Oh, for the love of Pete, will you never shut up? If you were to shut up for one whole minute the sun would fall out of the sky."

Harry laughed, and as they started down the long drive, under the arching lilacs and beech trees, Sarah recalled a night when the Beasleys had been at it and Malcolm had asked her if she thought *they* would end up like that in thirty years, bickering on the screen porch, sniping in the garden. She'd said they were more given to cold silence, followed by endless discussion, followed by sweet making up. Still, she'd said, you never know how things will turn out, do you?

There were two wheel troughs in the dirt driveway, with a ridge of grass in the middle.

Sarah walked in one trough, Harry in the other.

"Tell me," he said.

"Okay," she said. "This is what I know. For a long time after Deckard came back home from fighting in the war, he was sick. A lot of men came back sick. And for many years he spent time in and out of hospitals."

"Do you mean detox?"

"Yes," she said. "I didn't know you knew that word."

"Deckard told me once," he said. "He was addicted to drugs and whiskey, and detox is where you go to go cold turkey."

"Cold turkey?" she said.

"That means no drugs and no whiskey," he said. "It's an expression."

"Yes," she said. "So Deckard was in the hospital, in a detox program, and it happened to be a hospital where your dad was maybe going to do some work. They were going to add a wing or something, and he'd been asked to bid on —"

"By the way," Harry interrupted. "I looked up *shallop* in the dictionary."

"You did?" she said. "What does it mean?"

"It means a small boat."

"That's what I thought."

"Go on."

"So," she said, "your dad was being taken

471

on a tour of the building, I guess, the hospital people were taking him around, showing him things, and they came out of an elevator on a certain floor, and there was Deckard."

They had reached the mailbox. She opened the metal door, which produced a loud squeak, and across the road, in the marsh, two redwing blackbirds flew straight up into the air, then back down, disappearing in the grasses. She placed the letter inside the box, shut the squeaky door, and the birds duplicated their maneuver. She lifted the red flag on the box, to let the mailman know there was a letter, and paused for a moment at the edge of the road. The glare of the mist over the marsh was so bright she had to shield her eyes.

"I think it might clear up after all," she said to Harry.

Harry had found a stick alongside the drive and now swung it like a sickle into some blackberry vines. "Can we go swimming if it does?" he said.

"Why not?"

They started back up the hill toward the house again.

"There was Deckard," Harry said.

"Harry," she said, "this part is really personal. I don't think Deckard would mind my telling you, but you need to know it's personal, the kind of thing we keep in the family."

"Okay," he said. "Who would I tell?"

"I don't know," she said. "But don't."

"Okay," he said again. "So the elevator opened and there was Deckard."

"Yes," she said. "There was Deckard. He was having a hard time. I guess he was sitting on the floor and crying when your dad saw him."

This caused Harry to stop swinging his stick and to look at her. He said nothing, but clearly the image of Deckard sitting on the floor crying had shocked him.

"There were two orderlies with Deckard, trying to get him into some kind of restraints. Straps of some kind, to go around his arms and legs, to try to control him. They needed to get him up off the floor, you see. He wasn't supposed to be there. Not in the hallway, not on the floor like that."

"What's an orderly?" asked Harry.

"It's a person who works in a hospital, a kind of helper, but not a nurse or a doctor."

"Man or woman?" Harry asked.

"Usually men, I think," she said. "These were men. And they were trying to get Deckard into the restraints and Deckard was crying, and for just a second he looked straight at your father. Their eyes met. Your father told me that Deckard was wearing a hospital gown, but over it he'd put on the jacket to his military uniform, you know, the one with all the medals. Your dad happened to notice one of Deckard's medals and said to him, 'Is that a silver star?' A silver star is for exceptional bravery in battle. And Deckard stopped crying and nodded. Yes, it was a silver star. Somehow that calmed Deckard down. Maybe it sort of brought him back to reality. I think he felt noticed in some important way. Some way that nobody else was noticing him. And that was how they met."

"But what happened next?" Harry said.

They had reached the top of the drive, and Sarah first noticed that the squabbling Beasleys had apparently taken their skirmish indoors. A hole opened in the sky, and for about ten seconds the sun shone through, turning the shakes of the house blindingly white.

Sarah was standing by the old well, holding on to one of its whitewashed canopy posts. "It *is* going to clear," she said to Harry. "Look over there."

In the eastern sky, a widening break of blue could be seen out over the Atlantic. Another, larger hole opened in the blanket of clouds, and a sun-inspired din of birds rose up from the beech forest. Harry banged his stick against the well and said, "What happened next?" and then there was another sound, a deeper, increasing sound from the direction of the driveway. A car was coming up the hill. Sarah turned toward the mouth of the drive and flattened her hand over her brow. The grille of Malcolm's red Jaguar appeared in the tunnel of trees, taking away her breath, buckling her knees, and she reached again for the well post and lowered herself to the ground.

At the bottom of the hill, the mailman had been blocking the entrance to the driveway, so Deckard had had to wait. Off the right shoulder of the little road that led to the beach and the public parking lot, there was a marsh and, far away across the marsh, a stand of black pines where great blue herons nested. While Deckard waited for the mailman to get out of the way, he counted eight herons in various ridiculous positions in the pine boughs. The mailbox door squeaked something fierce, and two redwing blackbirds flew straight up out of the marsh grass and back down again as if they were on invisible elastics. The mailman retrieved a letter from the box and shut the door, causing the birds to repeat their comic stunt. The mailman, a white-haired old gentleman with a bright red face, turned fully around in his car to give Deckard a long searching look — concluding, Deckard imagined, that the domestic help had taken to driving awfully fancy cars these days.

Deckard eased the Jaguar into the drive,

and suddenly, briefly, the sun poked through the clouds. On the way up the hill, through the woods, Deckard thought for some reason of the day he'd taken Harry fishing at the river and afterward to the barber. He recalled Harry's making him promise not to take any pictures of the fish, because it would be unpleasant for the fish, and he recalled how the smells of pomade and talcum in Smithy's barbershop had filled him with nostalgia. As he gained the crest of the hill, he saw Sarah in the distance, standing by the old well, and as he drew nearer, she appeared to kneel on the grass, as if her legs had given out from under her. He put his arm out the window of the roadster and waved like a maniac, but she didn't wave back, and then, in the tree-arched opening of the drive, Harry appeared, barefoot and brown. Another beacon of sun swept the scene, and Harry came running down the drive to greet him.

Deckard, who'd come in the first place to atone, blamed himself for the shock he'd given Sarah. How stupid! he said. He should've called ahead, given them warning. He just didn't think. But Sarah took responsibility herself, saying he'd caught her at a weak moment and he mustn't worry about it. She did seem genuinely happy to see him, if a bit giddy. Harry seemed strangely fascinated to see him, and Sarah explained that they'd just put a letter in the mailbox inviting Deckard to come for a visit.

"It's like instant gratification," she said, still standing by the well, her voice a little shrill, like someone whose heart is thumping. "Come inside, come inside, come inside."

The real reason Deckard hadn't phoned ahead was that he hadn't made up his mind about stopping. He told himself he was taking a drive in the country, and if the drive in the country happened to put him in the vicinity of Malcolm and Sarah's summer house, and if, once he was in the vicinity, the spirit moved him, he would stop in and say hello. If he stopped and said hello, he would make amends for his long silence, the long infantile sulk. Nothing like a bullet to the head to help you sort out your priorities. He figured he could either sit around in his room, feeling unloved and unremembered, or he could seek the company he happened to be already blessed with. (The breakthrough in this regard had come one evening when he'd fallen asleep with the air conditioner on HIGH COOL and awakened with a vision of himself as a side of beef in an abandoned meat locker.)

"What happened to your head?" Sarah asked, as soon as they were in the house.

"Oh," said Deckard, touching his fingers to the new, smaller bandage, "nothing serious. I took a little tumble on the stoop of my building."

Maybe this sort of omission wasn't exactly putting your best face forward, but Deckard had already decided it would be the kind thing to do. Maybe in a few more years he would tell her what really happened.

They had moved into the kitchen, where tomatoes squatted in a row on the windowsill, and where the mineral-rich drip of the faucet had left a bright turquoise stain the shape of a teardrop in the porcelain sink. Harry stood in the middle of the room staring at Deckard as if he were memorizing every square inch of him. Deckard sat in one of the chairs at the old wooden table and held out his arms to the boy, but Harry didn't move from his spot.

At last Harry said to Deckard, in a tone that had just the slightest hint of accusation in it, "You grew your hair."

"Very observant," said Deckard. "I don't get a hug?"

"Not yet," said Harry.

"Okay," Deckard said. "Let me know when you're ready."

Sarah said she wanted to go get Deckard's letter out of the mailbox, but Deckard told her it was too late.

"Was there anything in it I should know right away?" he asked.

She was pouring lemonade from a carton into three blue plastic glasses. She too was barefoot and brown, like Harry. She wore a sleeveless shirt, and Deckard noticed what a nice color her arms were. She appeared, as usual, pensive, but maybe not quite so bitter as before. Deckard tried not to focus on her face, for he'd resolved not to be caught looking at her for signs of progress. He knew she wouldn't like that.

"Yes," she said, "but I suppose I can say them to you just as well."

Harry came over now and sat in a chair next to Deckard. He slid one of the glasses of lemonade toward Deckard and pulled one toward himself. "I have a question," he said.

"What?" said Deckard.

"When you first met my father," he said, "in that hospital . . . and he helped you get up off the floor, what happened next?"

Deckard looked at Sarah.

"Harry wanted to know how you and Malcolm first met," she said. "I didn't think you would mind."

"I don't mind," said Deckard. "But Harry, what happened next is the story of the rest of our lives."

Harry said, "I mean what happened *immediately*."

"Well," said Deckard, stroking his chin. "Let me think."

The day did clear, and after lunch a plan was hatched to go to Great Island for the afternoon. But before that, Deckard went with Harry to the garden — Harry wanted to show him his nearly four-foot-high cornstalks — and Deckard told Harry the story of the day Malcolm helped him get up off the hospital floor.

Sarah could see them from the screen porch, where she sat in a rocker and began to piece together in her mind all she wanted to say to Deckard. But very soon, without her being conscious of it, her mind had wandered onto organizing the food and drink she wanted to take with them to the beach. She saw that Deckard and Harry had stepped outside the fence of the vegetable garden now, and Deckard had stretched out on the grass, flat on his back. Harry sat beside him, listening to whatever he was saying, and now and then Harry appeared to fan something away from the bandage on Deckard's head.

There was in fact a sweat bee possessed by a persistent interest in Deckard's bandage. Deckard had warned the insect that it was not long for this world if it kept this up, so Harry, out of concern for the sweat bee, kept shooing it away. Harry also wanted Deckard not to be distracted by the insect. He wanted Deckard to be able to concentrate on what he was saying.

Deckard was delighted to share his memories; it was the first time since Malcolm had died that Harry had asked this kind of question. But he'd told Harry that it was necessary to back up a bit, to the time right *before* the elevator doors opened and Malcolm appeared.

"I was very confused," he said to Harry. "I didn't know which end was up. I didn't know which way the wind was blowing. I didn't know my elbow from my ear."

"I get the picture," Harry said.

"Yeah," said Deckard. "There was this other guy in my group, you see. Like me, a vet; like me, a drunk; like me, a drug addict; but unlike me, a white guy. I don't know where he was from. I think he just materialized one day right there in the detox unit. After I left the hospital, he probably faded away into thin air. His whole purpose in life was to torment me. His name was Broadus. I called him Broad Ass, but I didn't start calling him that until he established himself as a white-supremacist freak. One of those lunatics who join militias."

"What's a militia?" Harry asked.

"It's a group of frustrated, insecure guys who get together and play with guns and make plans for saving the country from all the blacks and the gays and the Jews."

"Oh," said Harry. "Like the Ku Klux Klan."

"That's right," said Deckard, "it's just another kind of Halloween. Instead of wearing bedsheets, they wear military costumes, and they tend to have a lot more artillery. This freak Broadus was trying to get clean so he could rise up in the ranks of this racist paramilitary outfit he belonged to. His imperial wizard or royal dragonmaster or whatever had told him he either sobered up or he was out of the club. Some people get quiet when they're coming off drugs and booze, but Broadus was the kind who never shut up. And one day, the day I met your father, I'd just had all I could stomach about how blacks were polluting the white race, and I told Broadus to shut up or else, and of course he didn't shut up, so I went over to where he was sitting and helped him."

"What did you do?" said Harry, fanning away the bee again.

"I put one of my hands on the top of his head and one under his chin and just squeezed. That was all I did, but it was breaking a serious rule. We weren't allowed to get

483

physical. As I said, I was very confused. I really thought I was being helpful. But the white drug counselors didn't see it that way, and they decided to put me in restraints, and that made me crack. I tried to run away and these two burly orderlies wrestled me to the floor in front of the elevators and that's when your dad showed up. You see, I was feeling completely misunderstood. I knew I'd broken a rule, but I felt like nobody was looking at what *led up* to me breaking the rule. Nobody was taking into account how I was provoked. Nobody cared about me."

"That's why you were crying," Harry said.

"Exactly," said Deckard. "That's why I was crying."

"So my dad came out of the elevator."

"Right," said Deckard, "and he looked at me, and I looked right back at him. This made him look away, but his eyes happened to light on my silver star. He said, 'Is that a silver star?' Nobody else there had asked me about it. Nobody cared."

"What happened next?" Harry asked.

"Well, the men he was with were very embarrassed and hurried him away down the hall. The orderlies could see I'd relaxed and was no longer a threat, and they didn't put me in restraints. That was all that happened. Now, do you know the significance of this?"

"I think so," said Harry. "You got well."

"Bingo," Deckard said. "I got well. I'd tried before, lots of times, and failed, and I would've failed again, I'm sure of it. That single question of your dad's changed my life. Of course he had no way of knowing this, no way of knowing what an important thing he'd done. So when I got out of detox, I went all over the hospital asking questions until I found out your dad's name. I looked him up at his office one day and told him the story, *this* story, and as you know the rest is history."

A yellow Piper Cub was approaching from the north, and Harry leapt to his feet and started waving. Deckard was convinced that Harry's efforts were in vain, but Harry persisted, continuing to wave both his arms as the plane banked toward the bay, and just as it leveled out again, the starboard wing dipped twice in salute.

Harry looked down at Deckard, who was still lying on the ground. He placed one bare foot on Deckard's stomach, like a picture he'd once seen of David and Goliath. He said, "I have another question. Why do you think my father asked you about the silver star?"

"Ah," said Deckard. "*There's* an interesting question. This is what I think, this is the irony: I think your dad hated to see anybody suffering. It made him very uneasy, like it does most people. So when he came out of the elevator and saw this grown man sitting on the floor and bawling, and then the man looked at him, it made him feel nervous and he had to look away. He happened to see the silver star and he latched on to it, the way a drowning man will latch on to anything any-body throws him. You never know when you're going to change somebody's life. You don't necessarily have to be trying to do it."

From the porch, Sarah called out, "Did he wave? Did he wave?"

Harry understood immediately that she meant the pilot in the airplane, and he turned toward her and nodded.

After the Jeep was packed for the beach and the three of them had climbed in, Harry sud-denly remembered his kite upstairs in the attic room. Sarah told him to run inside and get it but to hurry up.

While they waited, Deckard said he thought Harry seemed better than before, and Sarah was about to begin to say some of the things she'd told Deckard in her letter, but Harry had already stepped out onto the back stoop. Sarah saw him first, and some-thing about the look on her face made Deckard turn and look too. Harry held the unassembled kite in one hand, but instead of continuing on to the Jeep he was standing stock-still on the stoop and appeared lost, as if he didn't know what to do next. Sarah called out to him, and that seemed to wake him from whatever reverie he'd fallen into. He moved slowly toward the Jeep and got in.

"Harry, what's wrong?" Sarah asked, but before he could answer, they all three heard gunshots from the direction of Tom's Hill.

Sarah was out of the Jeep in a flash. "Stay here with Harry," she told Deckard, but Deckard turned to Harry, said, "Harry, stay in the car," and jumped down too. Harry, with no one to boss around, told the kite to stay in the Jeep, hopped out, and followed Sarah and Deckard to the dirt road that climbed the hillside. In another second they were all three running up the road, Sarah in the lead. Harry heard another four rounds go off and could now see exactly where his mother was headed. On the side of the hill, which was covered in knee-deep grass but very few trees, two boys with rifles were firing at something on the ground. Harry tripped in the sandy road, and by the time he caught up to the others, his mother was shouting at the boys, who looked pale and afraid.

"What, are you *crazy?*" she shouted. "There are *houses* around here! There are people *living* here!"

Deckard could see that the boys had been shooting only at a couple of tin cans, and that they'd placed the cans so that they were firing directly into the hillside, but he didn't say a word. It was clear enough why Sarah was upset, and he had a feeling that his presence, even more than Sarah's shouting, was frightening the boys. (He still resembled a marine, albeit an old overweight one.) The boys were young, not more than twelve or thirteen, each packed a twenty-two, and one of them managed to mention quietly that they'd seen no posted signs anywhere around.

Sarah was having none of it and told them to take their guns and get off her property — though Deckard seemed to recall that the dirt road a few yards behind him marked the property line. As the boys sauntered off up the hill, Sarah called out, "Where are your *parents?*"

There were tears in her eyes, and after the boys had disappeared over the crest of the hill, she sat on the ground and rested her elbows on her knees; then she dropped her head and folded her hands at the nape of her neck. Harry walked to where she sat and asked if she was all right.

"Yes," she said, without lifting her head. "I'll be fine." She looked up at Deckard and said, "Can you imagine? How old do you think those boys were?"

Deckard did not say, About the age I was when I got my first twenty-two. He said, "Twelve or thirteen."

"Christ," she said.

And then Harry put his mouth to her ear, whispered something, and a brief exchange ensued between them that Deckard couldn't hear.

Harry said to Sarah, "Mom. When I went inside to get my kite, I saw the man in the living room again."

Sarah said, "Harry, this isn't the best moment. Can this wait five minutes?"

Harry said, "Yes. Do you want me to take Deckard back to the Jeep and wait for you there?"

Sarah said, "That would be perfect. Just give me five minutes. I promise I'll be right along."

When they were done, Harry came over to where Deckard was standing, reached for his hand, and began to lead him back toward the dirt road.

Deckard allowed himself to be led, but as soon as they were out of earshot he said, "Is she all right?"

They had turned into the road; after a few more steps down the hill, the house came into view. A gray rabbit scurried out in front of them, leaving smooth dents in the sand, then cut back into the high grasses of the hillside. Deckard repeated his question, and Harry, with a poignant amount of composure, explained that no, his mother was not all right, but that she would be all right again in about five minutes.

When Sarah reached the Jeep, Deckard and Harry were sitting in it, up front, Harry behind the steering wheel. She was thinking about the boys she'd chased off the hill. She didn't regret chasing them away, but she wished she could have done it less angrily. As soon as Harry and Deckard had walked back to the road, she'd imagined Deckard saying to her, "Sarah, try to calm down; these boys didn't kill Malcolm." But of course Deckard hadn't actually said any such thing, and how ironical was that — that in the absence of Deckard's judgment, she supplied it herself, in her imagination?

She paused at the window on the driver's side, and Harry, now shirtless, turned to her and said, "I saw him again. In the book alcove."

Deckard leaned forward, so he could see her, and added, "And this time he spoke to him."

"You're kidding," she said. "What did he say?"

"He didn't exactly say anything to me," Harry said. "He just called out to me as I ran through the living room."

"Well, what did he call out to you?"

"He called me singing boy," Harry said. "It was like he didn't know my name, so he just said, 'Hey, singing boy.' Like that."

Sarah opened the car door and told Harry to hop down. As Deckard looked on, puzzled, Sarah sat on the Jeep's running board and pulled Harry into her lap. All Deckard could see now were the backs of their heads, rising above the seat of the Jeep. Sarah said quietly, but with no small amount of wonder in her voice, "Well, Harry, that sounds like my grandfather, who used to live in this old house."

Harry said, "You mean his ghost."

"Well, I can't explain it," Sarah said. "I don't really believe in ghosts."

Deckard, wanting to be included, said, "Singing boy, huh?" but they both ignored him, they were so wrapped up in themselves.

"Harry," Sarah said, "why do you think he called you that? Were you singing?"

"I think I was singing on my way upstairs to get the kite," Harry said.

"You were?" Sarah said, clearly surprised. "What were you singing?"

"I think I was singing that old song about the banana slug."

Still ignored but not the least bit sore, Deckard said, "You know a song about a banana slug?"

From somewhere beyond the roof of the house, from the direction of the bluff that overlooked the dunes that overlooked the tidal basin, he heard two crotchety old voices, one male, one female, coming through the trees in hot pursuit.

"Come and take at look at this!"

"I'm busy."

"You, busy, that's a laugh!"

"Bring it over here and show me."

"If you want to see it so bad, get up and walk over here."

"I don't want to see it, you wanted to show it to me."

"I don't care if you see it or not. I thought you might be interested."

"Well, I'm not."

"Oh, you're not interested in anything anymore."

"Why should I be? Bring it over here and let me see it."

Harry had pulled away from his mother and moved to the front of the car, listening to the voices from the bluff. He turned back around and said something that made no sense to Deckard. He said, "It's a different *it*."

They did at last get to Great Island and the beach that day, though they made a stop in town at the pharmacy for Deckard to buy a toothbrush. He'd been convinced to stay a few days, assured that, wherever they went swimming, he'd be able to go in his boxer shorts. They drove as far as the road would take them, to the spot where the road simply disappeared into the rising sand. They parked the Jeep and hiked out over the dunes, using a trail that Malcolm had first discovered. It led them higher and higher toward the bay, to the edge of a cliff that dropped ninety feet to a secluded beach that curved gently away as far as the eye could see. Deckard and Sarah traversed the sandy cliff carefully, but Harry dashed straight down, digging his heels into the sand and dropping into a roll at the base.

The beach was narrow at high tide when they arrived, but before they left there were acres and acres of six-inch-deep water reflecting the sky. Four hundred yards from shore, three sandbars emerged. On the sandbars, gulls appeared. Deckard helped Harry assemble the kite, and they took it out to the most distant sandbar and launched it. Later, they reeled it in and went to skip stones on the idle water. They hunted in the wrack line for jellyfish and bodiless fish heads. They each felt the slow expansion of time and space that a few hours on a secluded beach can provide, and Sarah took a long walk alone, growing smaller and smaller to Harry and Deckard's eyes till she was only a pinpoint and then nothing at all. They knew she was probably going off, at least partly, to cry — the day was so beautiful — but they didn't mind. Deckard took the big white sheet Sarah had brought along and fashioned a tent; he anchored one side with a heavy log and fastened the remaining two corners on sticks driven into the sand. Harry crawled beneath it into the cool shade and lay on a towel. The sheet tent popped and flapped in the wind. An Irish setter came running down from the cliff and splashed into the water. Somebody whistled from far away, high over the top of the cliff; the dog cocked its head, tore back up the sand, and disappeared. Soon the water was precisely the color of the sky, and the line of the horizon disappeared. Two of the sandbars merged, forming one long boomerang-shaped ridge, a giant whalebone in the water. Harry asked Deckard to tell him where and when he'd got each of his seven tattoos, but Harry fell asleep before Deckard was half through.

Sometime later, Harry heard voices, and thought he opened his eyes and saw his mother and Deckard talking, thought he saw tears on Deckard's cheeks, but he suspected he was only dreaming. Probably he'd mixed a dream with the story about how Deckard first met his father, how Deckard had been found crying on the hospital floor.

But Harry did in fact open his eyes; Sarah had seen him do it. When she returned from her walk, she sat in the sand next to Deckard, and at last he did what he'd come to do. He said he was sorry for not having been a better listener; he said that if she was game, he'd like to try again, start fresh. He was ready.

Sarah said she was glad, because there was a lot she wanted to say.

And Deckard made a proposal: This is what he was wondering, he said. Maybe when there was something that had to be decided about Harry, something important, maybe they could talk it over. He understood that Harry was not his son, but he loved him, and he cared what happened to him. You see, he didn't have anybody else in his life now but her and Harry. He would like to say that he wanted to be in on Harry's growing up for Malcolm's sake, but that wasn't true. He would like to say he wanted it for Harry's sake, but that wasn't the case either. He wanted it for himself. He understood that someday she might meet somebody and get married again, and he would have to bow out.

He promised to bow out gracefully.

He said, I'm talking about in the meantime.

Sarah said some of what she'd written in the letter. She said she'd not had room in her heart for considering Deckard's feelings before, and she was truly sorry.

Deckard was aware that an apology had been returned in kind, and he knew he should be feeling grateful, but he felt some unnameable churning thing instead. He heard himself say, You don't understand.

Surprised, Sarah said, What do you mean, Deckard?

Also surprised, Deckard said, I don't know what I mean. It's just that I . . .

He hadn't known this would happen. He began telling her the story of the children who had run behind the truck, and when he realized this was the story he was telling, he forced himself to continue against all contrary impulses. He forced himself through any amount of tears to describe to Sarah — so that she would understand — what he'd never described to another human being: the convoys, the deuce-and-a-half flatbeds with ten or fifteen marines in back, and the psychopathic ofay corpsman they called Doc Sylvester, how he'd shot Vietnamese children for sport from the back of the truck, how the kids, because they were starving, because there was no food to be found in that scorched land, would come running behind the trucks, choking on dust, as Doc Sylvester held up a can of C rations, luring the kids into the road, knowing all the while that another deuce-and-a-half was bringing up the rear a few yards behind, knowing — as he tossed a can of ham and beans into the road and as many as twenty or thirty emaciated children rushed into the impenetrable cloud of dust — that in the next moment the marines would see children's bodies go flying past them, higher than the truck cab, so great was the impact, children thrown into the air and killed because they'd chased a can of beans, because they were hungry, and then the deafening roar of the engines and Doc Sylvester's laughter as he prepared to set up the next group a ways down the road, an amusement, a diversion.

Deckard said, In a few hours, you see, this fearless son-of-a-bitch was going to be the one to save my life. It was impossible to cross him. I couldn't do anything to stop him because it meant my life. It meant my life. It meant all our lives.

Harry stirred, looked at them, then rolled onto his side, facing the bay. Sarah saw this but Deckard didn't, because he was sitting silent with his eyes closed, which seemed to be what he wanted to do for a long while. Sarah hooked her arm inside his and allowed him all the silence he needed. The water in the bay ebbed ever so slowly away, leaving lacy lines on the sand where it had been the moment before, like the rings inside the trunk of a tree. Sarah wondered if extreme beauty couldn't sometimes do this kind of thing to you, reach down and yank out what was eating your soul, but it was too simple a notion. Deckard's progress, like hers and Harry's — like everyone's, she supposed — was founded on influences and accidents far too tangled to sort.

Because he was asleep, Harry didn't see the tide ebbing away, but a while later, when he opened his eyes and observed at ground level the new wide band of shiny rocks between him and the waterline, he felt this change had been a part of his sleep. He'd been napping somewhere warm, outdoors, close to his mother, close to Deckard. The sound of their voices had mixed with the purring of the wind and the thrumming of the white sheet above his head, and as he slept, the huge place around him had continued to grow more immense — a little scary, but also intriguing — as if the water were pushing the horizon farther and farther back to hold more and more time. He sat up and saw, past his mother, Deckard, asleep on his stomach in the sand, a big blue towel spread over his back and legs.

He asked his mother what day it was, and the question appeared to amuse her; she smiled the way she did whenever he brought out something she considered especially intelligent. Still Saturday, Harry, she said, still Saturday.

When they left the beach that day, after they'd climbed the cliff and stood at last in the light of a sun so dim and near the rim of the sea that you could stare straight into its eye, Harry shouted, *Look!* and all at once they were in the midst of an enormous swarm of tree swallows, a flock of thousands that had stalled at this spot to turn a few grand eddies over the beach. The mighty whirlwind of birds was most of the time a hundred feet from the ground, but the cliffside arc of the circle put them over the higher shelf of land, and Harry felt he could almost reach up and touch it.

For years and years the spectacle of the swallows would return in Harry's memory and sometimes in his dreams. Had it been beautiful or merely thrilling? Had it lasted only a few seconds or several minutes? Had they gone to Great Island the same day Deckard drove up unexpectedly in the old Jaguar and gave his mother such a scare? Was that the summer his mother chased the teenage boys off Tom's Hill because they were firing rifles? The same day his great-grandfather Jack Williams spoke to him from the book alcove? He wouldn't be able to say for certain, but these memories of his boyhood, wavering in their order, would endure alongside those of the rain-slicked street where he'd seen his father slain by a nameless assailant, an arm protruding from the window of a car, at the end of the arm, a hand, in the hand, a gun. It was the summer he'd learned the word "inconsolable," and what a deep deep well of a word it was.